CHESAPEAKE SONG

CHESAPEAKE SONG

A Novel

Brenda Lane Richardson

Amistad

NEW YORK, NEW YORK

1409 1423

(A)

Amistad Press, Inc.
1271 Avenue of the Americas
New York, NY 10020

Distributed by:
Penguin USA
375 Hudson Street
New York, NY 10014

Designed by Gilbert D. Fletcher
Produced by March Tenth, Inc.

1 2 3 4 5 6 7 8 9 10

First Edition
Manufactured in the United States

Library of Congress Cataloging-in-Publication Data

Richardson, Brenda Lane, 1948–
    Chesapeake song : a novel / Brenda Lane Richardson.
        p. cm.
    ISBN 1-56743-040-6 : $19.95
    1. Afro-Americans—Southern States—Fiction. 2. Marriage—Southern States—Fiction. I. Title.
    PS3568.I31726C44 1993   93-26412
    813'.54—dc20   CIP

This book is dedicated to the memory of Marquel LeNoir

Acknowledgments

This book was created with the unflagging support and encouragement of Charles F. Harris, my publisher.

I am equally indebted to Dr. W. Mark Richardson, my husband and best friend.

Thanks are also due to my editor, Judith Riven; my agent, Marie Dutton Brown; members of the "Summer of '90" writing group: Chris Anderegg, Susan Cole, Florrie Collins, Bob Fournier, Helen Harris, Jeralyn Thompson and Joseph Torchia; and writing teachers Donna Levin-Bernick, Adrienne McDonnell, and Clarence Major.

In researching this book, I relied upon the expertise of the following individuals:

Science: Dr. Robert J. Russell, Dr. Linda Milks, and Gary Steele;

Science and Theology: Dr. W. Mark Richardson;

Agriculture: Nancy Steele, Mr. and Mrs. C. M. and Elinor Wilson; and Roy Sharp;

Psychology: Dr. Brenda Wade;

Languages: Nancy Chacon, Martine Barker, Dr. Joseph Roccasalvo, and Lisa Davis

Nanticoke regional information: Ollie Nutter Ashburne, Michael Ashburne, Nellie Monroe, and Martha Nutter;

General research: Janice Albert, Dr. Beverly Baker Kelly, and Gwen Collins;

Ophthalmology: Robert A. Phost, O.D.;

Medicine: Betty Kasson;

French Culture: Dr. Tyler Stovall;

Period detail: Dr. and Mrs. William Richardson.

Thanks also to the following for years of encouragement: Sheila Stainback, Dr. Brenda Wade, Dr. Bonnie Guiton, Nancy Katsura, Linda Evans, Sara Kennedy, Patty Vigorita, T. J. Robinson, Bob and Nancy Maynard, Paul Delaney, Angela Dodson, Jeanne Kostic, Diane Saxon, Dolly Patterson, Jamie Jobb, Denise Holt, Susan Levitt, Gary and Nancy Steele, Julie Patnaude, Ralph and Frances Caro-Capolungo, Diana and Elaine Richardson, The Rev. Dr. Dan and Deener Matthews, Kathy Buckley, Diane Schlinkert, Jane Groom, Lucia Chatsky, Katie Clifford, Catherine Calvert, Vicky Hsu, Sanjeev Joshi, Syble Dummitt, and the staff of Wildwood Schoolmates.

I want to especially acknowledge the Piedmont Book Company for their generous support.

Thanks are also due for one-time advice from Rosemary Bray, who encouraged me to write with "emotional candor" and to "tell only those stories that you can tell."

I am grateful to the following institutions: The Oakland Public Library, Anne Arundel County Library, Lindsay Museum, Maryland Department of Agriculture, Wicomico County Library, and the Eastern Shore Regional Library.

Finally, to my children: H.P., Carolyn, and Mark, Jr.

When she was alone, it was always the past that occupied her. She couldn't get away from it, and she didn't any longer care to. During her long years of exile she had made her terms with it, had learned to accept the fact that it would always be there, huge, obstructing, encumbering, bigger and more dominant than anything the future could ever conjure up. And, at any rate, she was sure of it, she understood it, knew how to reckon with it; she had learned to screen and manage and protect it as one does an afflicted member of one's family.

from *Autres Temps* . . .
The Stories of
Edith Wharton

Contents

Contents

1

Tamra October 1990

ON HER BED a suitcase gapes eagerly on its spine. The interior, pink silk, like a petticoat, soft intimate space inside a box for travel. It has been used once only on her wedding night, then yielding gowns for sleep and loving, grunts and sighs. Today she strips a dress from a hanger, pulls cotton undies from a bureau, and, rushing toward the suitcase, tries to remember the fullness of that night. Instead she recalls the harshness of a life lived together: thoughtless acts, missed cues, words of discord from the jaws of an angry marriage.

She places a hand on her hip but not, as she has in the past, to steady herself. She is dead calm. Nor is it a gesture of obstinancy. After this final course he'd chosen, her sassiness has been replaced by the shame of not wanting to leave him, and the certainty that she must. The hand is more a mother's nudge to a reluctant child, urging her to take off, to escape Nanticoke.

Only minutes ago, she dropped their children off at her mother-in-law's, down the road. But even if Dalhia phoned him immediately, she may not find him for several hours. He is somewhere out there on their neatly packaged thousand acres, more farm land, she has always heard, than any other black family in these parts.

Perhaps his mother has the children in the car and searches for him at their cannery, the newly refurbished corporate offices, or the depot, built to house a fleet of gold-toned eighteen wheelers, four combines, nine tractors; situated beside a grain elevator, 950,000 bushels deep. Of course he could be out of Mother's reach, paused along a quiet road, talking to Pa, laughing, certain when he returns home his wife will be there.

Hoping for last-minute magic on his part, she pushes effortlessly against the bay windows. They swing open without a moment's hesitancy or sigh of complaint. From this view, two flights up, in this house built on the knoll, which had, like a plump Delilah, beguiled her lover, she looks out over harvested fields, picked clean of life and trampled by Caterpillar tires. Beyond the land, she sees a glint of the Nanticoke River.

The scene arouses no sense of ownership in her. Bordered by a window casing, it looks miles away, a landscape in a museum perhaps, on a wall, to be gawked at by strangers. Ignoring the whole of the scene, she searches the roads for the movement of a wheel, the speeding top of a car's roof, listens for the sound of hurried squealing brakes, any sign at all of a car or truck, a tractor, some machine conveying her husband to this house that she has made into a home. The road is silent.

Shutting the suitcase, she places it by the bedroom door. There had been a dull finality to their quarrel this morning, but then they'd always argued, even the day after their wedding, when she'd rushed from the hotel to a movie theater. Thoughts of him had pervaded every frame. Back outside, on the streets, white strangers rushing past her, she'd walked, head down, finally looking up to see: brown face, high cheekbones, tall frame, wide, squared shoulders clad in a green cardigan and brown trousers, like a beloved Chesapeake tree.

He'd said, "I waited across the street in that Chinese restaurant, at the bar, drinking Cokes for two hours." He'd told the story, laughing, her face between his hands. The owner, believing he'd come to rob him, had frantically dialed the phone, screeching in Mandarin. The proprietor's family had gathered, packed the bar, and there they'd sat, eyeing one another, waiting for her damn show to end. They'd left that argument there on the sidewalk.

A parting look across the bedroom, along the walls and mantle, at the paintings and photos of his ancestors, a gallery of who's who in Black history. Her eyes are drawn to a spot over the fireplace, an early photo, circa 1849, of his great-great-great-great-grandparents; snapped by a paparazzo who, according to family lore, arrived on a covered wagon with a darkroom.

He'd photographed President James Polk, and passing through the Chesapeake, heard of free black folks, an entire family, landholders. They'd sat for
him, and all these years later, they still sit, he in top hat, she bareheaded,
backs so erect the two seem mounted on sticks. And here they remain, some
dead, others forgotten, all imprisoned in silver frames.

Noon, the clock says. She has timed it well. Two hours for the drive to
the Baltimore airport, long minutes to write goodbye. But first, she must
phone her parents.

"Seth Wells speaking." It is her father, answering as if he were still
principal. "Hi, baby," he greets her.

She tries to sound casual, but what can she say? The idea of her leaving
Charles would send them into a panic. She's taking a short vacation, she
explains, to New York to see Wadine, her best friend. Of course, he sends
his love, and says her mother is not home. She's with sorority members, the
opening of a new hospice, black AIDS patients, people without family or
hope. Now these people, his words imply, they have real troubles. I'll send
a postcard, she says, and hangs up, wondering why she bothered. For what,
after all, could her father, Seth Wells, tell her about having what everyone
else seems to want, and it not being enough?

2

Seth and Virginia March 1951

IT WAS ONE question, that's all, but it rattled Seth as if he'd been asked to remember something hellish from yesterday instead of five years ago. Anyone else would have known, from the way he was dressed, that he hadn't driven the eighteen miles from Salisbury to Nanticoke to sit on his cousin's raggedy porch and discuss armed conflict with a boy.

He was dressed to kill on this Saturday, his day off as assistant vice-principal at Carver High. He sported a thin, new mustache, a twice-breasted suit, two-tone jumpback shoes, and hair in that mixing bowl style: the rage since '48 for discriminating Negro men. Why it was fashionable he didn't know. Mamas had been putting bowls on boys' heads and clipping hair around them for decades.

The question was from his young cousin, Tumor, whose mama thought she was dying when she carried him, and named the boy for what she thought she'd had. Tumor kept rocking and asked again; "What were it like durin' the war?"

Seth tipped his chair back, squeezed his lids shut, and ran a hand down his face, as if the war had been smeared on him and he wanted it off. He didn't want to talk about Germany. But this boy, showing a lack of home training, pressed on. "Please, I'll polish those shoes for you."

There was no answer at first, just the wet sound of Seth's gold-labeled Scotch being poured into a jar.

He swallowed hard and looked again at his blue-gray Chrysler Windsor, its snout so round and wide it seemed risen from the bay. He spoke softly, like a train slipping into a midnight station. "Ooo-ooh woo, you don't want to hear about Dachau or Buchenwald. Those white devils left behind mounds of skeletons as high as that tractor, just there."

Tumor turned toward the rusted machine in the side yard and back to Seth. "But what happened when the Allies come?"

Seth leaned foward, making sure he understood the question. "What? You think those white soldiers cared about those bones because they were the remains of other white folks? Shoot, no more than they'd have cared if a cow had been slaughtered in Rockingham. I saw a G.I. take a leak on what had been someone's foot."

Tumor's mouth hung open like he was a bit touched. His daddy, Snake Pit, walked up and told him, "Stop worryin' Seth and go tell your mama I'll be back pret' near bedtime."

Seth smoothed his trouser legs, preparing his mind for the night ahead. He'd left nine years ago, gone off to college and a war. At the least Virginia Q. Henry owed him a smile.

He and Snake started out, the hump-backed, moonlit sedan behind them, dark joining their shadows, welcoming Seth back into Mother Earth. He heard the sounds of her body: birds rustling bushes like dry skin, cricket heartbeats, a gurgle from a stream.

Nearing Ghost Light Hollow, Snake asked if he was scared. Sure, Seth said, and meant it, as they passed the site where a plantation owner had died pursuing slaves, and where he still haunted, a lantern swinging from his ghostly form. Seth knew the occasional lights were probably a convergence of fireflies. But he wouldn't swear by it. Two years before his parents had died at this spot. Run over. Dead. Drunk. Passing the area for the first time in years, even with his eyes averted, he was reminded of the meanness of that trick. He'd gone off to war but it was his folks who'd been buried.

Snake's voice interrupted his thoughts. "Man, it's gonna be hot to-morrow."

The silhouette of his cousin's finger pointed at the red ring around the moon.

"We'd better stock up on some cold lemonade," Snake said.

Seth cleared his throat theatrically. "Too bad you don't have the benefit of my education."

"Oh really, and why is that?"

" 'Cause then you'd know that circle around the moon stuff is nonsense. But you're right. It will be hot."

"How you know, Mr. College?"

Slapping his cousin's belly, Seth said, "'Cause the locusts are screaming, boy."

Snake pushed him toward the bushes. Such a hush on Face of the Moon, a thunking piano could be heard down the street from Lord Henry's. As they neared the white frame house Seth approached often in his dreams, he prepared himself for Virginia's resistance. He'd written many times, though she'd never answered. What was there about the Henry sisters—Virginia, Florida, Tennessee and Maryland? They all had short, choppy hair and skinny legs, but they'd been the stars of the neighborhood. Fist fights had broken out over who was prettiest.

Thousands of miles away he thought he had figured out the secret to their popularity. He'd been in a tent on a river bank, west of the Rhine, when he realized how their father's constant vigil had tricked all the boys. Seth had been hunched over when a commander shone a light on a map, and he'd seen, along the walls, the shadow of a large butterfly. Looking closely he'd found it was a moth searching its way out, its shadow intensified by the glare.

Lord Henry sat at the front of the parlor, his skin the color of a peeled grape, a patch on his eye, sipping tomato wine. It was a room filled with neighbor boys and three of the Henry daughters, all in their twenties, still unmarried. Not one reveler seemed to notice Seth, but Lord Henry nodded a gruff hello. Seth was stifled by disappointment. Virginia, with her suicide walk, her hot ice exterior, was nowhere to be seen.

Times had to be hard. The sisters were treating former childhood antagonizers like visiting gentry. Old Two Jacks was dressed in short sleeves, with a comb in his pocket, and when he smiled he showed large, chalky teeth, strangers to his mouth. Florida tipped toward him, birdlike, feet slowed by a narrow hem and chunky heels. She offered Two Jacks peppermint balls in a cut-glass dish, and when he whispered in her ear, she laughed, red lipsticked mouth wide, tongue resting, exhausted.

Florida yelled, "Is that you, Seth with the mustache? Hey everybody, look what Snake dragged in." As boyhood acquaintances gathered around, Seth was awed by his sense of distance and wondered whether it was college or the war that had most separated him. Engaging in pleasantries, his eyes searched for Virginia. He'd stepped into his past to claim her and wanted to waste no time.

There was a bottom half of a skinny-legged girl as she bent to align her seams, and he paused, mid-sentence, while she brought herself up. It was only Tennessee, the youngest and still most audacious of the brood. She'd poked dandelions behind her ear and held a swiveled cola bottle under her mouth like a microphone. Working at the defense plant must have toughened her. A rose-shaped bruise marked her cheek, and despite a smile her mouth was grim. A thin fellow in a green suit played the piano as she sang.

> Mama can I go out dancin'?
> Yes my darlin' daughter.
> Mama, can I try romancin'?
> Yes, my darlin' daughter.
> But Mama,
> What if there's a moon
> shinin' on the waaata?

Tennessee paused. He heard a yawn, then turned and saw Virginia on the arm of Mr. Henry's chair. Her suit, with its slim waist, was stylishly dramatic, highlighting her aura of superiority. Her presence set the picture in motion. Time advanced.

Trained in midwifery, she was the only Henry daughter with a higher education. Seth had heard town ladies insist only Virginia Q. Henry could birth their babies, and their needs had transformed her. Her soft guiding hands, her gentle voice and scent of carnations had become legend. Devoted customers talked her up until the stories grew wings and ascended into lives of their own. Someone said she delivered a dead baby, got on her knees and blew life into the child. He knew much of what was said was soft-edged lore; feats so mystical and impossible, scenes so brightly lit and shining, at some point, people chose to accept these fantastic images in favor of the skin bruising, scoured-with-tears reality of a colored girl's natural life.

He held his ground, studying her for signs of thaw, noted that with her dark head of marcelled waves, full pink lips, and big breasts, her man-tailored suit made her look awkward, like a ballerina in a soldier's helmet. Realizing he was staring, she glared at him as if he'd forced his way into her dressing room, and then turned away. He did not exist, her body said.

Seth walked nearer the piano and saw it had long gray scratches. Big Mama and Maryland, the nervous looking sister, pulled ashcakes from the fireplace and sparks escaped to the rug. Maryland and three of the men stepped back while Seth stomped the sparks. Big Mama shook her head at the others and said, "Some folks make things happen. Others watch what's happenin', and the rest don't know what the hell's happenin'."

With the men laughing, Big Mama rested the pan on a table and fanned the biscuits. Maryland grabbed one, spread it with butter and sorghum, and ate it from a square of brown paper. The bread still hot, she blew at her fingers and licked them.

Seth walked up to Mr. Henry and said he wanted to talk with Virginia. Her gaze lingered on the hat in his hand. Without looking up, she shooed him away. "Daddy and I are talking."

He strode quickly from the room. To hell with her. Sipping from his bottle, he started down the steps, but a voice called him back. It was Big Mama, her forehead still damp. Every Monday night, she told him, her girls caught rides to Hebron Corners, where they met up with Mr. William, the school bus driver, who earned spare change taking a crowd to juke joints in Salisbury.

He tried to figure Big Mama out. In all the years before he'd left Face of the Moon, she'd never spoken directly to him, but now she talked as if they were picking up on an old conversation. "When the cab lets them out for the bus, Virginia walks to the Wicomico Theater, sees the same old pictures. Twenty cents on Monday nights, and she walks home . . ." She paused, as if to see if he understood. Virginia was scared to death of the Hollow, she explained, and suggested he show up to offer her daughter a ride. He thanked her and tried to cut the conversation short. After all those drinks, he worried he'd talk with a slip-hitch on his tongue. Last thing he wanted was to sound like his mama or daddy.

"Oh," Big Mama added, "sorry about your folks."

He stood up straight, grateful for her condolence, and headed for his car, thinking of Virginia, the girl who braved the Hollow each week to see moving pictures of someone else's life. This time when he passed the bushes, he stared in boldly, as if he could turn the very darkness into light.

3

Tamra *October 11, 1990*

DEAREST CHARLES:

Okay, scratch the "dearest" part and let's get on with it. You must know that after all that has happened with Cassie and Cousin Johnny, I have no choice but to leave. I won't mention their names again. I can't. But I do want to share two thoughts uppermost in my mind: I love you and I'm leaving your rusty butt.

Maybe I'd sound less bitter if I approached this more like a scientific presentation. Ladies and gentlemen, it was a fragile experiment and unfortunately, it failed. Perhaps that has to do with the weakness of my theory that two people who love each other can remain happy in marriage. I should have realized my data was too soft and fuzzy and that the control conditions were inadequate. It's widely understood the complexities of love and human behavior can't be put in a test tube and, furthermore, that what constitutes the actual truth is so evasive, compared to hard scientific fact, any hopes I had for grappling with love should have been dashed early on.

There were mitigating factors. Considering a future without this man made my knees tremble. But our most recent trouble has forced me to reconsider. Go on, life, scare me. I've tested his capacity to change and find him unwilling.

Sorry, Charles, if I'm glib. It's a defensive posture. Everyone will consider my leaving you downright foolish. I feel like the naughty girl pointing at the emperor. People have an idealized vision of my life. But you and I know the truth, don't we?

Are you reading this, thinking, here she goes again, complaining about a life most women long for? Well, you know what? I'm not the first to tell the truth about marriage. Have you ever considered what a cruel irony it is that for centuries people fought for the right to marry for love, but that once the privilege was granted so many of us have had the same regrets and antipathies that surely plagued the marriage in Cana at Galilee.

What do I want? How about this for starters: admit the truth about our marriage. Right now you've created a fairytale. When you walk through the door, you spot the pile of shoes in the foyer, the artwork the children have hung in the hallway, you hear our voices, smell dinner, and you use those details to maintain the myth of a successful marriage. The reality must be too bitter for you to contemplate.

There's something else that I want: to keep you in my life, but not the life we've led so far. I hope that by putting some distance between us, I can more clearly understand this essential flaw in relationships: If two people love each other and have the best of intentions, why is marriage still so difficult?

She pauses before signing,

With all my love,
Tamra

$\mathcal{4}$

Seth and Virginia *March 1951*

THE NEGRO BALCONY was deserted on Monday, so he had no trouble finding the back of Virginia's small head against the big screen, where Groucho danced with a large and disdainful woman in a satin evening gown.

He sat so close he could smell the artificial cherry of her JuJubes and the syrup inside her wax war planes, but she didn't acknowledge his presence. He risked a whispered hello. "No!" she said briskly, staring intently at the dancing figures, mouth moving almost imperceptibly, as if chewing a stolen meal.

Moments passed. He continued watching, impressed by her unwavering reverie. How could she so completely ignore him? Then remembering her father, he realized this was a woman who had been watched all her life. She had learned to close herself off. He felt for the outline of her thin arm. An elbow jutted threateningly. They were only half a foot apart but it was as if she'd joined the actors and left him behind.

He spoke again. "Could we . . ."

She turned toward him. It was not what he'd hoped. "I been looking forward to this, so please, leave me be." Worse than anger. But he would not bolt like a chastened boy. He had become an authority on any number of foreign subjects: the planets, world history, philosophy, and had taught himself French and English grammar. He could master Virginia Q. Henry if he tried.

He sat quietly, studying her. Sometimes, instead of chewing, she mouthed the characters' lines. The longer he watched the more he understood. The close-cropped hair, the low bangs, the black-and-white striped dress, it all belonged to someone else; none of it was Virginia's.

And this was not the way to court her. He rose slowly and headed for the stairs. No wonder she'd ignored his letters. For her, the written word was not real. Outside in the soft rain he streaked across the road toward Chicken Little's. It too was deserted, now that the Monday night crowd lived it up in Salisbury. He'd expected to hear Billie Holiday on the jukebox and was not disappointed. It was his favorite: "Stormy Weather."

He released himself to the words, her mood, easing onto a stool, as Chicken, the proprietress, poured blended scotch into a glass before he'd caught his breath. He watched her over the lip of his glass and saw her smile. Chicken was tall and muscular and he wondered, if he saw her in the daylight, would he spot a tiny mustache?

Tossing back two more shots, he settled onto his stool. Tomorrow he'd start preparing for the first twelfth-grade class in Salisbury's colored school system. He couldn't afford another drink. Well, maybe one more would help him devise a plan to woo Virginia. Signaling for another, he rested his chin on a fist and thought with his eyes open. The drink was finished in two swallows and Chicken held the bottle's neck, poised to pour again. He glanced idly at the gardenia pinned to her gown. Maybe, he thought, Virginia and Chicken weren't so different. Both wanted more than they could touch. But what could he do with this information? Time was running out.

"Chicken," he began, "what would I have to say to get you to sell me that gardenia?"

She said with amusement, "Not a thing. Often as you be in here, you already own it." Once it was in his hands, he was disappointed. It was cloth. He didn't give it back, though. For the moment this and a sketchy plan was all he had.

By the time Virginia walked from the theater, he was parked out front, leaning against the damp car, extending the fake gardenia, which he hoped would look as real under the red illumination of the marquee as it had in Chicken Little's. Rain fell from his umbrella like strands of tinsel, and there was something different about him. His hat, tilted oh so slightly to the side, was no longer in his hand. Virginia slowed as he spoke.

"I heard a story in Paris about these flowers."

"So?" It was her voice, soft but rich.

"May I tell you about it during our ride home?"

She studied him. At last, he thought. Finally, she nodded a silent yes and slid in, her heels worn down. Proud that the upholstery still smelled new, he began his story in a lilting voice. "There was once a king with many mistresses. They were tall, short, fat, slim, cheery-eyed, and somber." He described them in detail, imbuing them with traits he most admired, and found that he too was drawn into the fantasy.

"As the King went through these women like so many pair of shoes, his noblemen worried. They'd heard the populace complaining. 'He'll never settle down,' they lamented. 'He should marry and produce heirs.' " Seth talked on in the wet night, maneuvering the Windsor around deep puddles, past sleeping town homes, back toward Face of the Moon.

"Oh," he paused, turning slightly to convince himself she hadn't vanished. "He treated these women kindly. Did I tell you that?" She didn't answer, but at least she was watching him. "Each affair was memorable, extravagant, filled with gifts and long nights of passion. This guy actually made love on beds spread with the petals of these flowers."

He proffered an empty hand. The fake gardenia was under the seat, just in case Virginia was inclined to reach for it. "But they never lasted a fortnight, the affairs, I mean. Until one day when the King announced he would marry, and presented the chosen woman to the court." They passed Head of the Creek Road, swiftly nearing Face of the Moon. Never had this journey seemed so brief, so perilous.

"His noblemen were astonished. Well, she was pretty enough, and clever, had a soft and melodious voice, like a lute. Best of all, she danced a mean boogie woogie . . ." She laughed here. He took no time to enjoy it. "But so had all the other women been lovely and talented. The people looked her over, wondering what quality made her different. The King did not explain." He slowed the car, elaborating on details of the wedding feast, hoping she wouldn't interrupt to complain about their slow pace.

"History proved him right. She became one of the most beloved queens of Europe. They lived happily together, had many children, and died in old age, one day apart. And you know what? One of their subjects learned the secret that had captured the King."

Virginia's voice filled the car, as sweet to him as the flower he'd been unable to offer. "What was it?"

"I was hoping you'd ask," Seth said, smiling. "This old woman, a servant to the King's court, told her great great grandchild, and decades later, that girl confided in me. She was a hat-check girl. Said when the King made love to all those women, he'd followed a gypsy's advice. Each time he'd taken his heart out, quietly laying it beneath the petals. None of the others, except this one woman, had complained. It seems she stopped him after the first kiss, brushed aside the petals, and held on to his heart."

"What'd she want with that thing?" Virginia asked, amused.

"I don't know," he replied, and stopping the car along Face of the Moon, added blithely, "it's up to you."

When she smiled she brought her teeth down over her bottom lip, perhaps to hide her amusement. For him this proved sufficient. If ever he was to feel the warmth of a homecoming, this was it. She laughed, tittered, actually. "Your story was as phony as Chicken Little's flower. But I liked it."

Some of it was true, he insisted. "A heart isn't something you just give away. It's your only real treasure. But first you must find someone in whom you have unshakable faith, trusting he will care for it as his very own."

Outside the windshield, his headlights shone into the bushes, lighting trickles of rain that dripped lazily, like nectar, from one fat leaf to another. He could have burst with the pleasure of it all. He had her talking now, and he asked many questions, shutting the engine off, settling down, relishing the chance to really know her. They conversed for hours, with him finally blurting, "Why didn't you write me, even once?"

He pulled the flask from beneath the seat and offered it to her. She declined, asking why should she have bothered writing?

"I could have died."

"Cut the small talk," she said, and then giggled. Could it be true, Virginia Henry, playful? But she soon grew solemn again. "I'da been happy to go to all those foreign capitals."

"Shows how much you know about war," he said, the liquor scorching his throat.

Rain thumped the roof as her voice filled the car. "I know peace ain't what it's cracked up to be. It kin be another kind of war, 'cept they don't give out medals when it's over." She grabbed the flask as he lifted it to his mouth and told him he needed to just put that stuff away. On second thought, she had a better idea, and opening the car door, she poured the Scotch on the ground, throwing the empty canister onto the backseat.

He pretended he wasn't in the least concerned by her action. In the same tone of bravado that had worked outside the theater, he offered to teach her the dance they'd seen in the movie. She said she'd think about it, and did he have any more of those stories up his sleeves?

Looking back, Seth often thought their four-week courtship was a lot like the tango they danced at their wedding. Guests rolled up the rug in the Henry parlor and watched as he and Virginia pressed their fronts together. He leaned foward and Virginia pulled back. When he feigned indifference, her interest seemed to spark. Round and round they turned. The tenor sang in a high-pitched Spanish that no one in the room, except Seth, claimed to understand. It was an old tune about conquest or love, maybe both. Seth grew exhausted, struggled for breath, but they danced until it seemed neither could pull away without taking the heart of the other.

Driving off with Virginia, he heard the question ringing in his ears which Snake had asked him earlier. Why would a man who hated even talking about war look through a line of beautiful women and choose as his bride the only one sure to be a warrior?

Years later they returned to Nanticoke, with their daughter, Tamra, just in time for Lord Henry's funeral. Virginia wore a fox shawl and a saucer-shaped hat with a fishnet. It was a cold day and Seth put his arm around his wife's shoulders. At graveside, Tamra leaned against them both, her thin legs long by then, clad in white stockings. They remained with the Henrys until the guests were gone, as was only proper, and then rushed off toward Salisbury, as if they could put Lord Henry so easily behind them.

5

Tamra and Charles *October 1990*

HIS CAR ASCENDS slowly up the driveway, gravel cracking beneath the tires. He has no intention of giving in to her rage and self-righteousness. As she closes the door to their house, he's certain she'll shake the handle to see if it's locked. Sure enough, she jiggles the knob, as if someone would break in all the way out here. You'd think after thirteen years she'd understand that so many of his hands pass this way, heading to fields that radiate from this high and visible central point, a stranger would be noticed immediately.

He's already irritated so it doesn't help when she sees him, grabs her suitcase, and runs to her car. He slaps the leather of his passenger seat. As if he poses a threat. Her love of drama is exhausting.

He removes his jacket. It's a conciliatory gesture or at least he hopes it is. Years before, the day after their wedding, she'd argued with him because he'd refused to wear a suit and tie to a movie theater. Now he's in a suit every day, but she seems to resent it. He doesn't know what he's supposed to say or do anymore. It's as if she has a secret script and he has to guess his part. What does she want him to be today: Dominating hero? Clever rake? Petulant manchild?

She drives aggressively toward him, but he doesn't step out of the way as she comes to a shrill halt. When he opens her door his annoyance cools. She's wearing her urbane look, as if she'd never lived down here, and has only dropped in to study Black Americana.

At least he has arrived in time to see her. She's wearing those black stockings he likes so much, and high-heeled suede shoes. The skirt is short, her legs, as always, long and curving, barely legal, and her arms naked. Everything about her is just right, even her hair, nappy and pulled back from the regal aloofness of her face, with its small flat nose, wet with tears.

Oh yeah, he loves her all right, and he wants to tell her but not while she's like this, ready to chop him up for sausage meat. Maybe he can stop her. But wait a minute, he *could* just let her go. Asking her not to leave could be interpreted as begging her to stay. Even worse, it could draw him into one of her made-for-television dialogs, and somehow, once she starts he always knows his lines. That's it. If they could just not talk. If he goes with his instincts.

He's large and strong, so he lifts her easily from the car and she puts her arms around his neck, bringing a diamond lobe close to his mouth, but he doesn't kiss her, even lightly. Seeing her like this with the threat of losing her gives him a sense of unappeasable longing, and he torments himself with her.

For the moment it's as if she is new, scooped from the bay, late sunlight glistening water drops cool on chestnut skin; her full-lipped mouth, a summer cave to get lost in, the entrance to her heart, if only they can just not talk.

A hurt look crosses her face, as if she suddenly remembers. He rushes toward the house, wishing she had not locked the door. But she breaks the spell, saying fiercely: "When the quarter runs out does this ox ride end?"

When she makes him feel ridiculous he wants to bully her, so he says, "I could stop you from leaving."

"You've stopped me all these years and you didn't have to use force. Come on now, put me down."

He'd have to anyway. He still hasn't figured out how to keep her in his arms and get the door open.

"Charles, you're staggering. Put me down. You'll drop me."

He laughs derisively. "I lift equipment that weighs twice as much as you."

"How romantic."

Demoralized, he sets her back on her feet and she asks: "Did you really expect to march me back inside to make love?"

"Why would I when I know you prefer war?"

"This place is like Gettysburg."

"No, there the hope was for a more perfect union."

"I meant the part about dead soldiers, which is what I am. Tamra Lane is long gone."

"Ah, so you're the understudy."

"More like a *Doppelganger.*"

"A ghostly twin? That's pretty dramatic, even for you. Stay awake all night dreaming that one up?"

Her eyes narrow. "I've been up, all right, waiting for your black ass." She steps up, viciously seductive, her palm on the zipper of his pants. "I've dubbed this the tomb of the unknown soldier."

"A mouth like yours coulda made Hannibal an M.I.A. Hell, it could melt a nuclear warhead."

She mumbles, "Talk about delusions of grandeur. Anyway, what gave you the idea a wife's supposed to hang around and lick her husband's wounds?"

He nods in agreement. "Silly me, expecting my most formidable enemies would be white folks and bad weather."

She reaches to open the car door, but he blocks her, flapping his arms, knowing she hates this brand of sarcasm, but he's desperate. "Can't a ghost fly to wherever she's going?"

She's suddenly apologetic. "Oh, I'm going to New York."

"Why there?"

"To breathe."

"You're going to New York to breathe?"

"To see Wadine. She's the only real friend I have." She shrugs (as if to say, if that's all there is. If you aren't going to beg.) "Well, bye."

He touches her wrist. "I've got two requests."

She turns, smug and impatient, and he wants to tell her to go to the devil, so it hurts him to ask, "May I have a goodbye kiss?" As she busses him on the cheek he pulls her close. There are only seconds left but he knows this is not a woman excited by an ordinary embrace. She has erogenous points in the oddest places, like this spot, just below her brows, and he kisses her there, as well as her fingertips, each of them, lips never resting. He knows the points well. He could draw a map.

She closes her eyes as if she can't bear to see herself submit, but she does, and he works his way, with hesitation and small silent kisses up her bare arm. She leans into him, *ohhhing*, an ocean's sigh, his lips on her neck, her skin glossy and perfumed. She raises high on tiptoes; an eager, long-limbed dancer. But as if her body recollects the sadness, she twists away, keeping him from the dark, warm space.

He knows she doesn't really want to leave and he tells her that. But she insists, saying that if she doesn't go now she never will. She feels tyrannized by his dreams.

He'll never give her another reason to leave, he promises. He wants to make everything up to her, and faltering, adds, "even Cassie."

She holds his mouth, instructing, "Say that name again."

It's bitter on his heart. "Baby."

She climbs back into the car, slamming the door. "Just hearing you mention her name like you have a right to . . ."

She's crying again and he's thinking that even so, he'd had no choice, that he'd only done what he had to. He was continuing what had been started long before. But what he *says* is: "About that second request . . ."

"You just want me to miss my plane."

"I don't know when your damn plane leaves." He calms himself, and as she starts the engine, he says, "All I want is a prayer."

"That's all you've got."

He climbs into the car. With the sun roof closed his head pushes against the ceiling, but disregarding it, he begins. "Dear God, I know I'm the last person who should be praying. I mean, I need to, but I don't want to turn this into a soliloquy."

He looks up and sees her staring impudently at him. Reaching toward her closest eyelid, he slides it down like a shade and continues praying, asking the Lord to help him make peace with what has happened, and to take care of Tamra in New York. "She's lived a protected life," he says. She clears her throat.

He prays on behalf of their children. Their hopes for them are something they agree on. Her lids are closed, mascara beads on her lashes, and he knows she is praying with him, so he can't risk an amen yet. He has to give the brother upstairs some time to work on this one. "And Lord," he continues,

"I'd like to clear away some of this anger with a hymn."

He hasn't sung a solo in years, and only once this, to a gathering in a tent revival, when they'd been very young. He, pushed foward, stumbling; she, making faces in the front row. For years in this marriage, she has asked him to sing again, for her, and he has refused, saying, I am no longer that boy. But today, like the removal of his jacket, this is another signal: For her he will peel away layers, beyond the authority of the suit, beyond even the reasonings of his disciplined intellect, to this, an unadorned song of prayer.

"Precious Lord take my hand, lead me on, let me stand . . ."

His voice, cultivated as a child at the Saved By the Water Church, is clear and unselfconscious and he knows she will not interrupt.

"I am tired, I am weak, I am worn . . ."

To him, it's not a song but a heart's cry, learned along country roads, where he is home. Father and mother, son and daughter, passed it on. "Through the storm . . ."

Hopes numbed by trouble, suffering without comfort, only this— "through the night . . ."

Words to stir—"lead me on to the light . . ."

Offer peace, "take my hand precious Lord."

He is at heart a praying man, believes that what he asks for has already been received.

". . . take my hand precious Lord."

Finishing, he closes with "amen."

Her soft chuckle breaks the silence. He opens his eyes and watches her shake her head, sarcastic in her admiration. "That was really good," she says. She applauds. "If I'd been a stranger in that backseat I'da believed you for sure. Amen brooootha!"

He is up and out of the car slamming the door. "Go ahead," he shouts. "Leave!" His voice rises. "You're always talking about how you feel. Well, let me tell you, when I'm away I'm happy. At home, with you, I'm like a kid with one of those crackers working my daddy's land, talking about, 'Hey, boy. How ya doin', boy?' You're like a ghost all right, bringing back nothing but bad memories. And you know why?"

She looks off, as if bored, but he gets her attention by poking his head into her open window, a hand supporting his chin as he says slowly, "You're nothin' but a well-dressed mammy."

Her composure is glacial as she says, "I think I preferred you when you were still sloppin' pigs and you didn't share your feelings." The car backs up with a jolt. She shifts into gear and is gone.

He hates that he has come so close to begging, that he'd acted, he thinks, like some singing black fool. And because he also abhors the silence she has left behind, he shouts, telling her he's fed up with her, to never come back. Surely she cannot hear him. She has passed the old smokehouse, the hog confinement center, drives toward Head of the Creek's golden fields of hay.

The wind carries his shouts away from him, but only the insistent yelping of a small animal quiets him. Restlessly, he searches for the source of the noise, which comes from somewhere along the side of the house where a salesman has convinced him to test a new breed of golden raspberries, sweet honies they call them.

He discovers a baby fox squirrel that has foraged deep into the bush for the last berries, its paws now entangled in the net. It is so young the tail is straight, and its eyes are like coffee beans that watch him. He's in no mood for delicacy and tries to pull the trembling body free from the net. There is a nervous heart beat and blood on his finger. The squirrel has been wounded in its struggle.

The car phone rings but he doesn't stop. Gently he pulls away the mesh, untangling the tiny paws. Watching the squirrel limp off, fragile and disoriented, he thinks of his wife, realizes that he has not told her he loves her. And he wonders if he and this delinquent creature are marooned on high ground to learn a lesson about passion and it's closeness to pain.

Sweet honies they call the berries. Honey love, he thinks, ruefully nodding. It sticks to you, gets all over and through you, too much, too sweet, honey love. He says it aloud, tasting the sound of it as he climbs the steps. But he does not open the door.

6

Virginia and Big Mama June 1964

BIG MAMA AWOKE with a cold hand on her arm. "Oh Lord!" she cried and squinting in the dark, recognized the slender torso and long legs of her most foolish daughter. She listened carefully to the familiar voice. "I can't take another minute with him."

Even if she couldn't see the trunk of her body, she would have recognized that fancy way of speaking: all proper and breathless, as if she'd practiced talking with just the front of her mouth. "I left everything, except Tamra, of course."

Big Mama rubbed her eyes wondering why women always chose the middle of the night to leave good men. She watched the torso cross the room and bury a hand in a large lacquered handbag. A mouth could be heard making plans: "I'll send for her before fall . . . have to find the right school."

She assumed Virginia was planning on New York, a city with borders filled to bursting with runaway wives. The voice continued. "I put Tamra in my old bed. She fell right to sleep." Big Mama tried to make out Virginia's face but failing that, sat up halfway in bed. She looked so damn tall towering over her like this. Patting the mattress and employing a voice both impatient and commanding, Big Mama said, "Just sit down, okay?"

The face sank into view. Her hair had been pulled back tightly, fringe topping her forehead. Big Mama asked what she thought he'd done this time.

"It's not what I *think*."

The old woman sat all the way up, reaching for the lamp. The aluminum foil covering the bulb fell off and heightened her annoyance. "Just what was it?"

"Drinking again," Virginia explained, burying her face in her hands. A regular Sarah Bernhardt, Big Mama thought, wanting to shake her head. Oh, the problems people can think up when their lives are too good for them. Looking closely at Virginia she could see she hadn't been beaten. In fact, she was wearing that white suit with the droop collar, and her mock alligator coat was thrown across the bed. If she'd been fleeing for her life, would she have stopped to don her most fashionable clothes and rouge her lips? Well, she thought, Virginia might.

"What's new about him drinking? His whole family drank. The boy's mama was a drunk. At least Seth is a gentleman."

"Not tonight," Virginia said.

"How come?"

"He forced himself on me."

A smile played on Big Mama's face. "You mean he took him a little bit?"

She threatened to leave immediately if Big Mama joked about it. The old woman tried looking aghast and felt a wave of pity for her son-in-law. The man didn't even notice other women. Not that there weren't many noticing him, with his suits and ties and starched shirts. And that was just the way he and Virginia lived, like a gentleman and his lady. She considered telling her daughter outright that she'd had the hard luck of being born a fool but worried that might be the wrong approach.

Big Mama hoped another tactic would be more successful. Rounding out her mouth, she spoke in a kind of drone, in imitation of Virginia's imitation. She told her that sure, she had a right to be mad, but that didn't necessarily mean she had to leave him. Finally she had Virginia's attention, and she patted her hand. "Just teach him a lesson. You know, you can train 'em to do right. Little Joe Pritchard used to beat Hattie Bess, sure did. She was scared he'd kill her."

Big Mama lowered her voice as if sharing a treasured recipe. "Hattie waited 'til Joe was sleep, melted a candle and poured wax right down his ear."

Virginia frowned. "That could get you arrested."

"Better to be judged by twelve than carried out by six."

Virginia smiled. Could she talk her out of this foolishness? She pulled her daughter's head toward her large flat breasts and stroked her face, cooing. "I wish you two could get along, enjoy each other while you're young. Not much time. We come into this world going out."

Virginia spoke into her mother's chest, her face hidden but the voice lighter. "You said the same thing on our wedding day when we argued right in the church."

Big Mama added, "Where two or three are gathered in my name so shall there be fussing and fighting."

She felt her daughter's pout growing. "This time your jokes won't work." Virginia sat up. Her eyebrow pencil was smeared on Big Mama's nightgown. "Jokes won't make the truth go away."

"Since when does the truth have something to do with your life?"

"I know you think it's my fault we argue, but I've tried. I don't know where I went wrong."

Big Mama spoke cautiously. "You married the man you loved."

"And you?"

The old woman stared back aggressively. "I loved the man I married." She believed in her aging heart all marriages were trouble, but the covenant was only breakable by death. And surely, she thought, Seth wasn't dead, just as smart and handsome as they came, and he'd just been made principal of Carver. She reminded Virginia of that fact.

"What you see, Mama, is a principal. What I see is a man who———" She searched for words.

Big Mama interrupted: "You can't deny Seth works hard."

"That would be enough for you?"

"A man who works is a joy forever."

Virginia seemed determined to remain ill-humored. "I thought at least you would be sympathetic. You of all people should know a man can't be judged by his public image. It's what he's like when you're alone with him. He's more than numbers in a bank book. He's the sum of his secrets."

Oh Lord, who was this child quoting this time? Big Mama wondered how she'd raised a child to be so ignorant. Virginia would be the laughing-stock of Nanticoke. She pictured the Mouths unleashing a cyclone of gossip. Left that man? *Craaazy!*

They talked for hours but she was unable to persuade Virginia to stay. Big Mama warned Tamra might wake and have a crying fit. It didn't appear to move her daughter. She started for the door.

Big Mama mentioned female predators. Seth would be alone, lonely. Virginia left anyway, so sure of herself and her hold over that one good man. Virginia walked to the car, elbows jutting. Even the red taillights looked angry as they receded down the driveway and turned left at the tumble-down skeleton fence. Virginia headed for the Baltimore–Ohio Railroad.

$$Z$$

Tamra *October 1990*

SHE HAS SELDOM been away from her children, but any sadness is overridden by the excitement of seeing New York. Her eyes search LaGuardia for her friend. Is Wadine plump now? That question is answered as her friend sweeps in, thin and youthful, hair in a close-cropped Afro, dark, rich brown face still stunningly beautiful with its narrow nose and full lower lip gleaming, as if she has sipped from the Milky Way.

"Girl, girl, girl," Wadine says, clasping Tamra to her, adding that she's glad she has come to her.

Tamra shrugs. "No place else to go." Wadine assures her she hasn't changed and introduces Phillips, the pale-skinned Black man who has accompanied her and who insists on taking Tamra's bag. He walks behind them. He's their driver, Wadine explains, while Tamra wonders if she means *driver* as in a *chauffeur?*

A woman, obviously homeless, catches her eye. She has seen people like this on the streets of Baltimore and Delaware, but is unprepared for it at an airport. The woman is wide-hipped and dark-skinned, head wrapped in a burlap onion bag pulled tight like a turban and festooned with a rhinestone brooch. Draping from her shoulders, a second onion bag, and about her waist, a rhinestone belt that holds two more of the sacks, caftan-like on her hips, the words "Red Bermudas" in crimson letters across the rear. She hurries by with a shopping cart, stopping to genuflect before a United Airlines booth.

They search for a restroom. Each one has a line of women stretched outside the door. "Welcome to the Big Apple," Wadine says. Inside a stall, Tamra is childlike in response to the automatic toilet that flushes when she stands. She thinks of how Virginia, with her obsession for public hygiene, would love this, and she raises herself up and down, to determine how it works.

She finds Wadine waiting by a sink and watches as an elderly white woman approaches her friend, a concerned look on her face. "My toilet didn't flush."

Wadine's eyes grow wide. "What are you telling me for? Do I look like the washroom attendant?"

The woman backs off, stricken, and Tamra carefully suggests that Wadine may have overreacted. No, Wadine assures her. "You just don't know about New York. White folks are something else here. It's terrible."

Tamra longs to ask if all these offensive Caucasians include Wadine's husband but decides to drop the subject. Who knows how sensitive her friend may be on the subject?

A long limousine is parked out front, and Phillips passes bills to the attendant. She remembers traveling in a car like this for her wedding, and a funeral. The happiest day of her life, and the saddest.

It's a long way to Brooklyn Heights, Wadine advises, telling her to get comfortable. She presses Tamra for information on Charles. Tamra stalls. She has always been reticent about discussing her personal life, and so, coaxes Wadine to tell her why she has never mentioned this car. Does she take it everywhere?

"Just about. Have to," Wadine says, "especially when I go to work. I've moved my practice to the Bronx, where I work for free."

"When I picture the Bronx, I only see grisly images."

"Many of them are probably accurate," Wadine says. "But these days the Bronx, Queens, Manhattan, Brooklyn—they're all basically alike. The streets are dangerous and forget the subways."

But Tamra won't forget them. She feeds on the idea of danger. She has been playing it safe all her life, getting the right education, marrying the right man, being a good wife and mother. Where has any of it gotten her? Feeding on the sense of danger, she leads Wadine on. "I read there are fifty thousand convicted felons in this city."

Wadine smiles, obviously unimpressed. "Worry about the fifty thousand who haven't been convicted."

Phillips seems to have been waiting for a pause in the conversation, and as he speaks Tamra detects a Jamaican accent like the one Wadine had decades before, when she'd moved from the West Indies to Salisbury. He explains there's a problem with the traffic. "We got to do sumting. Boulevard, Mrs. Drake?"

Tamra has never heard Wadine's married name spoken before and she wonders if it now sounds refined because of this car.

Wadine is apologetic. Saturday traffic. They'll be forced to go through some pretty depressing neighborhoods. They pull off the freeway, Phillips expertly dodging a stalled car, as she evades Wadine's questions. Even without her natural reticence Tamra would have trouble answering. It's difficult not to stare at the streets. She has lived in a big city only once, in Paris, and even then, in the safety of a suburb. They travel through a neighborhood of small brick houses built closely together and she wonders aloud if they're in Brooklyn.

"Not yet."

"How can you tell one borough from another?"

Her hostess looks impatient with the subject. "There are few physical boundaries. In New York, a borough is more a . . . state of mind."

Two men push a timeworn white Volvo, smoke spewing from its hood. The car's bumper sticker reads: "Humpty Was Pushed."

On their left, a Corvette, driven by an elderly man in white Muslim headdress, passes, the car's rag top down. Here it feels like summertime. In the Chesapeake the late October weather had been unseasonably cool.

The limousine plunges into a commercial district where hundreds of pedestrians crowd the streets. She feels hot and claustrophobic in this car. They stop for a light and a woman crosses in front of them wearing thin braids, some bunched sassily atop her forehead. Her lipstick is bright red, matching the sweater that bares her shoulders, stretching over her bottom, down to her knees.

Just behind her, a nut-brown teenage girl with a Nubian face, lids heavily lined, stares toward the dark windows of the limo. She wears a white fishing hat, brim turned up, and pearl earrings dangling to her shoulders.

A man struts by in tight jeans, seams extending up his bowed legs like arrows to his rear. Tamra thinks that like her, he may have suddenly cut himself free. Intellectually she understands this freedom but envies what he seems to feel.

The limousine moves off and she rolls her window down. "I wouldn't do that if I were you," Wadine cautions. Tamra dismisses her with a wave of her hand, knowing she is being rude, but she resents being separate from the Black folks on the street and wonders why it doesn't bother Wadine.

They pass slowly enough through the honking traffic for her to read the hand-lettered sign in the window of a convenience store: ABSOLUTELY NO ONE IS ALLOWED TO ENTER WEARING A MASK.

Another sign taped to a wall: PLEASE DO NOT BLOCK THIS DRIVEWAY. Two ticketed cars are parked out front.

A burly man ambles by, dark face hidden by sunglasses and the brim of his flat leather cap. Beneath his leather vest is a tee-shirt that reads: "I'm Black."

At the next red light, she forces herself to turn back toward Wadine, who now looks alarmed. "Put your window up," she yells.

Tamra turns to see a thin, dirty, white hand poke through the window opening and hears a gruff voice demand: "Gimme five dollahs." Worried about hurting the owner of the hand, she doesn't want to press the "up" button.

Phillips gives the order, "Back, Miss," and with a broom handle whacks the intruder's palm. The hand is snatched back, its owner yelping. The car moves on as if nothing has occurred. She looks to Wadine for an explanation but her friend looks sedately aloof, saying she tried to warn her about New York.

Back pressed into the seat, Tamra's eyes are closed. New York has changed Wadine. From one side of her mouth she dispenses free advice to Black clients in the South Bronx. From the other side she is casually abusive to any white person who crosses her. Sure, that man had been wrong to stick his hand in the car, but had he deserved that treatment? And was coming here a mistake? She and Wadine have always had a contentious relationship, much like sisters, she'd always thought. But now she thinks she and her friend may have grown farther apart than she has from her husband.

As the car enters Brooklyn Heights she sees a change. Here, there are even more homeless people. One man in a tattered tweed jacket carries a paper plate of torn bread, kisses the pieces, and blesses the pigeons like a

Roman priest. Houses along the tree-lined walks are close together like those she'd seen in Queens. But the neighborhood is better tended, elegant, like a fashionable district in London. There are doors with polished brass and windows with flower boxes. Canopied apartment buildings have awnings with doormen standing beneath them. They round a corner where a massive crowd is gathered before a store. A voice calls through a bullhorn. Wadine says the Korean deli is being picketed, that the owner is racist.

Tamra dares to speak. "Maybe he's not the only one."

She's glad Wadine doesn't look insulted. *"Moi?"* She laughs. "Maybe I am. An interracial marriage may present the best opportunity for learning racism."

"How can you say that?"

"When you live in an all-Black world you think maybe life is different on the other side. From where I sit I see the small favors, the kindnesses, the way they trust each other. And I don't have to wonder if it's different on the other side, I know it is."

Tamra turns away, sucking her teeth and muttering. "This trip's gonna be a barrel of laughs."

The car turns onto a block where except for a few well dressed pedestrians, the sidewalks are deserted. "Norman Mailer lives over there," Wadine says, gesturing toward a stately brownstone. A few feet beyond, they glide to a stop before a building with a green and white striped canopy. A doorman in a coat with gold braid rushes to help them out. Wadine tells Phillips to call for them at nine, for dinner. Tamra thanks him for the ride.

The vestibule is narrow, art deco. Wadine insists they walk up and that she carry the bag. On the stairwell, dark and unlit, Wadine chatters about her neighbors. A clergyman who beats his wife lives on the second floor. Wadine went to him, she says, and threatened him with public disclosure. He offered her money, she says, laughing. "You'd think he'd just agree to stop beating her."

Tamra can only think of the wife's sadness and the shame of having neighbors know of her troubled home.

8

Big Mama June 1964

BIG MAMA WALKED into the room where Tamra slept and reached for the kerosene lamp that reminded her of Virginia's childhood. It had been plain and unadorned until Virginia painted clumsy orange tulips and blue birds on the bowls. She'd always wanted a prettier world. The match flared as Big Mama lit the wick.

This child sleeping beneath the rough army blanket looked like a young and fancied-up Virginia; a reminder of what Big Mama had not been able to provide for her daughter. Tamra was dressed in a red and white striped robe, its matching slippers lined up beside the bed. Look how she's grown, Big Mama marvelled, all twelve years of her. She thought of how Virginia would have loved having a robe like this. Tamra's hair was braided close and a soft, cylinder-shaped bang rested on her forehead. So this was who her foolish daughter had wanted to be.

She frowned remembering a lie Virginia had told almost thirty years before, long after they'd been forced out of their house and had to live in Hattie Bess's barn. They'd been there for two years, enough time for them to lose all earthly pride. But not Virginia. On the day of the lie Big Mama had been sitting behind the coop, having just wrung a chicken's neck. The bird was almost cut up for dinner when she heard children in the yard.

"You live in a barn like a cow!" they yelled.

Virginia's voice, most insistent of all, cried, "These aren't my folks. I'm visiting. My folks work at the White House but there ain't no schools up there for coloreds."

The children had known Virginia all their lives, making the lie especially outrageous. But she kept it going for several minutes, so convincingly, they had stopped teasing and run off.

It was then that Big Mama had walked from behind the coop, blood on her hands. Virginia tried to run but Big Mama'd caught her, saying, "If I was gonna beat ya, I'd have done it in front of those kids." When Virginia stopped struggling, Big Mama shoved her. "Go on. You'd best walk off and find your folks. You're right. You ain't ours."

She had thrown her arms around Big Mama's legs, begging forgiveness. "The kids were making me crazy. It was my only chance of stopping them."

"Try to stop someone with a lie," Big Mama warned, "and it kin turn around and bust you right in the face." It was one of the few times she'd seen Virginia cry. Her sisters had been using up all the family's tears.

Big Mama realized she'd been mumbling to herself again and shifted her huge body. Her breasts, without the support of a bra, were mere protuberances over her hips. No, Virginia hadn't even cried when old Doctor Percy said that for her wanderin' eye to strengthen she'd have to stay in the dark for two weeks. Big Mama frowned, rubbing her arms, remembering how Virginia had begged to be locked in the pantry.

All that time. She must have heard them coming and going but she hadn't called. She'd brought that child three meals a day, kept her pot empty, and always offered her a chance for freedom. She'd listened outside the door, hoping Virginia would cry. Had she listened hard enough? It had been so long ago. Oh Lord, she'd been so busy. But sure she had. Any mother would have listened. That child hadn't cried, not one tear, not that anybody saw.

Big Mama sat and rocked her body. Here she was, old now, with the rheumatism, sometimes rambling around an empty house, talking to Lord, hoping he'd hear her, wherever he was. And now she'd been given another Virginia, this one called Tamra, twelve years of uppitiness in a quilted robe, lying right smack in the middle of her past. She kept rocking.

She said in a whisper, "I won't have it." It had been too exhausting, this terrible burden of hurting for your children when you can't hurt for yourself. She'd find a way to make this visit a short one, give it a little time. Tempers would cool. She checked the scratched face of the old clock. Heavens, look at the hour. It would soon be daybreak. She shook her head. *Um, um, umh, umh.* She'd never understand why the good Lord had designed life so folks would start each day by getting out of bed, instead of the other way around. Blowing at the flame, she quietly placed the happy lamp back on its shelf.

9

Tamra October 1990

WADINE'S PENTHOUSE IS on the eighth floor but feels more like the sixteenth to Tamra, who is quietly gasping for air as her friend pulls the door open to reveal a hallway with a large oval mirror, antique wooden chest, and a basket of lush ferns.

Once they ring the bell, it takes only seconds for the door to be thrown open by Wadine's thirteen-year-old, Atunay, a tall, almost six-foot, tan-colored boy with dreds and an earring.

For the second time this day, Tamra finds it difficult to concentrate on social conventions. She barely greets him. The house is dazzling, from the formal dining room, which leads to an open space with a ceiling two floors high. There is a grand piano, tall ornate harp, baby trees, and a rooftop garden overlooking the mouth of the East River. Atunay points toward the Statue of Liberty.

Wadine's two other children race down a spiral staircase, and she introduces them. The youngest, at four years old, is Olu. He is extremely pale, lighter than most whites, and has straight blond hair and blue eyes. Shisheemay, the daughter, has a headful of silky ringlets and an olive complexion. She will be six in two weeks, she shyly tells Tamra. The youngsters hide behind their mother. She sees her friend is gentle and affectionate with them, as if she has checked her anger at the door.

Atunay carries her bag up to the guest room and is leaving when Wadine asks Tamra if she'll shop with her for cowboy boots.

The boy steps back into the room, frowning. "You wouldn't really wear those?"

Tamra's confused about what his objection to cowboy boots might be.

"I certainly will wear them," Wadine tells him.

"Please, Mom."

Wadine asks with irritation. "And why not?"

"Cause then everybody will know you've sold out."

"Like there weren't Black cowboys," she says, talking to Tamra as if he were not there. "You can't imagine what it's like living with the chief of the Black police."

Tamra smiles, aware that this is only an act of love they practice in front of newcomers. The closeness between them is obvious, as is Wadine's pride in her son. Tamra says, "You should be glad he doesn't want to be like everybody else around here."

"Awwright, Aunt Tamra. We'll get along just fine."

"Don't encourage him," Wadine says, smiling now. "He'll turn on you, too. Last week it was my entire Jazzercise class."

He says to Tamra in a confidential manner, "It was so bleached. Fifteen white women, and my mother doing the mashed potato to rap music."

"We were not." Wadine swats at him. He playfully grabs her wrists and while Atunay restrains her hands, she talks to Tamra. "I was the one who taught him cultural pride. He forgets I got up and drove him to Bedford Stuyvesant every Saturday for breakdancing classes."

He pleads his case to Tamra. "How could I forget? The instructor told her she'd better not bring me back like that. Dressed like a clown with an Afro and a sweater vest."

Tamra asks Wadine to interpret. "What's wrong with that?"

Her friend says with sarcasm, "Don't you know real Black boys don't wear sweaters?"

As he leaves, Atunay pulls a red wool ski cap over his head. His overalls, several times too large, drag over his heels and the crotch is close to his knees.

"Do your chores," Wadine calls as he closes the door.

They can hear him as he drags down the stairs. "Must think I'm Nigger Jim."

Tamra shakes her head, laughing. "I guess he's searching for an identity."

"Tell me about it," Wadine says, pulling the drapes back from the large picture window, which affords another spectacular view of the river. Tamra is unable to contain herself on the subject of Wadine's children.

"It would have to be confusing. Each of your kids was born progressively lighter. I wouldn't have even known that little blue-eyed, blonde-haired Olu was your child. He looks———"

"White." Wadine says resignedly. "The Lord musta heard me complaining about white folks and tried to get back at me."

Tamra giggles, feeling light-hearted at last. "One more kid and you'da had an albino."

Wadine grins and says, "I am so glad you're here." It's their first moment of closeness, and Tamra is thankful for it, realizing that Wadine is one of the few people in the world to whom she reveals her true self.

Still, although she knows her friend's two sons will be treated differently by the world, she does not say this. It seems too cruel a truth. She wonders if there will be many words between them that she'll have to swallow.

There's a knock on the door and a short, blond man enters. Bypassing Tamra's outstretched hand, Stephen opens his arms in welcome. It is the first time she has been this close to a white man, and the fact that Stephen holds onto her waist, forcing her to look down at him, adds to her discomfort. She hears Wadine snickering, and hugs him back. He holds on, his body seeming light and insubstantial. She's relieved when he turns to Wadine. The image of their embrace is startling, Wadine's lovely darkness in stark contrast to his ivory skin, like a chiaroscuro painting. They are so affectionate that even after they pull apart, Wadine holds his hand. Stephen apologizes for not being at the airport, he had to work.

He points to Wadine. "But this lady is so thrilled to see you. She's always talking about you." Tamra wonders if Wadine has told him that their marriage had strained the friendship. She thinks now that it should have been Wadine cautioning her about Charles.

Someone outside the door is blasting rap, and Atunay's voice can be heard leading the younger children through chants: "Ungawa, Black power!"

Stephen assures Tamra that once his son's door is shut, his room is soundproof. "I'll get them to quiet down some."

"They sound good to me," Tamra insists. But when Stephen opens the door, the noise from across the hall is amazingly loud. Tamra and Wadine wince and hold their ears as Stephen rushes out.

Alone again, Tamra is eager to avoid a discussion about Charles. "Wow, Stephen is——"

It works. Wadine is giggly. "How would the French say it? *Je ne sais quoi . . .'* "

Tamra places her hands on her hips. "Actually, the French never use that term, only Americans."

Wadine pokes out her tongue. "You haven't changed a bit."

"But I won't quibble," Tamra says. "That boy is fine."

"Yeah, he is," Wadine agrees. "He's an incredibly wonderful man." And she laughs when Tamra asks if they're as wealthy as they appear to be. "Not in the beginning," Wadine says. "His parents warned they'd cut him off if he married me. And they did, at first. They didn't see Atunay until he was two years old."

Tamra finds this disclosure romantic, his willingness to give up everything for love. Wadine is aghast. "It's not like we woulda starved to death." She checks her fingernails, long and manicured, like Virginia's.

"But now that I'm a mother, I understand his parents."

"What are you talking about?" Tamra asks.

"I realized how much I hate pigeons. They're all over this city, like flying rats. A whole family's nested under my air conditioning unit, with their horrible churning sounds."

Wadine speaks louder to keep Tamra from interrupting. "Last week, Shisheemay found a pigeon egg, and for three nights we kept it under a lamp, cushioned it in tissue and called a vet. She was hysterical. But as much as I love her, I was glad when it didn't hatch. Couldn't stand having one of those in my house."

"Do you hear yourself? Comparing yourself to a flying rat? Those people should be delighted with you."

Wadine assures her they're good in-laws now.

"They must be crazy about you."

"Not quite." Wadine says there had only been two brothers, and that after she and Stephen married, the other brother was designated heir to the family real estate business. "But he turned out to be a drag queen. They ran into him in the Village, roller skating in a tutu, with a sequined mask on a stick. Called himself Ballerina." She laughs at the memory. "Their parents had to decide which son's choice they hated most." She shrugs. "They couldn't. So they welcomed me and Kenneth's lover into the family, and both brothers run the company."

"So that's why you don't leave New York, because of his business?"

"Not at all," Wadine says. "You'll hear a lot of complaints about life here, but most folks aren't leaving. I love this city. Complaining about New York's a hobby. Besides, I could never leave my practice." She grows animated. Her techniques are nontraditional, improvisational, but they work, she says. Most of her new clients spend less money on their rent each month than her former clients paid her per visit.

"A lot of them were Stephen's friends," Wadine says. "You wouldn't believe it, limousines stacked up out there, waiting for me. . . . Oh, but it's good to be in the Bronx, finally doing something for my own people, working to keep our families together." She looks hard at Tamra, pausing. "Have you and Charles considered therapy?"

"Forget it," Tamra says. "Charles would never go for it." But she knows this is only an excuse. She couldn't possibly confide in anyone about her marriage. "I think he'd consider it a white folks kinda thing."

Wadine looks annoyed. "White how?"

"Just so . . ."

"Self-indulgent?"

Tamra says, "He'd say, 'Who's ever heard of Negro angst?' "

"Sounds like something Atunay would ask."

She hates this. It makes Charles seem so provincial, and she has always associated him with a moral purity that makes lying intolerable. But now she's not quite sure how to regard him. Oh God, if she allows herself to think about him she might tell Wadine the whole, ugly story, the part even Charles doesn't know—about Cousin Johnny. She rushes to open the window as her old friend continues talking.

"If what I give my clients is self-indulgent, then may the good Lord help us all."

_10_

Big Mama, Virginia, Seth, and Tamra _August 1964_

THE SUN WAS high when Big Mama reached into her mailbox and brought two envelopes close to her eyes. My, my, two more letters, two more money orders, one each from Virginia and Seth. If money kept coming like this she could afford to get the outhouse redug. Putting on her glasses, she opened the first letter, recognizing Virginia's handwriting. She tucked the ten dollar postal check back inside the envelope and read aloud slowly:

How did Tamra get those splotches on her face? Is she drinking enough milk? I'll be home Sunday.

Virginia.

As if she didn't know how to feed a child. Then she re-read the part about her returning. Today was Friday. Coming home in two days? What had happened? In the months since her departure, she'd only heard of the high life Virginia said she was living. Was she planning to stay in Nanticoke? Had she told Seth her plans?

She quickly tore open his letter, tucking his money order away without glancing at the sum. She scanned through his neat hand. Like the others he'd sent, it was written to Tamra. He told her he was attending summer school for principals, and answered her question about why spiders don't get stuck like flies when they walk on webs. He closed with: "I hope you're putting that microscope to good use. It's a lot better than your old one. See you soon."

How soon? Pulling her glasses off, Big Mama headed for the back of the house, where Tamra was peeling apples. They'd planned to fry them with bacon and heap it on biscuits. No time for that. Untying her apron, she called from the porch. "Child, bring my bag. We gotta catch us a ride to Western Union."

Tamra didn't look up when she heard the car in front of the house. Kneeling in the dirt, she glanced into the pails of muddy water. This might produce interesting results. The cab turned into the yard but she kept working, knowing Big Mama was in the doorway. "Thank you Lord," the old woman said, forcing Tamra to look up.

Even before the car stopped, a back door swung open and Virginia alighted, arms wide. "I missed my baby," she said. Tamra eyed her coldly. With her round hat and seven-eighths-length flap-pocketed coat, she looked as if she were dressed for a party on the moon. The driver placed her suitcases on the brown painted steps and Virginia could be heard taking bills from her purse. Tamra returned to her work, her arms and legs splashed with mud.

She listened as Big Mama explained that this activity with the buckets had to do with her wanting to be a scientist. "Anyway, kids need a little dirt to grow on."

"She's not a kid," Virginia said.

Big Mama wiped flour off her hands. She'd fixed Virginia's favorite supper, winter crest and white yams. "I want you to eat before you-know-what," she said in a code Tamra realized was designed to keep her from understanding. Pulling Tamra to her feet and pointing at Virginia, Big Mama scolded her for "cuttin' her eyes," warning if she didn't talk, she'd "slap her into Sunday." Her voice sounded angrier than her hands felt. "With your grown self, actin' this way."

Could she really be forced to talk to her own mother? If, in fact, that woman was actually her Mama.

"Why didn't you tell me you were going?" Tamra asked.

"I had to work," Virginia said.

"I coulda helped you."

Big Mama interrupted, pinching Tamra's arm, saying that was water under the bridge. They told her to wait outside while they talked, that they'd call her when they had a tub ready.

That's typical, she thought when she was alone again. They'd threatened to slap her for not talking; when she had, they'd rushed off. She continued filling her jars, wishing she could sneak in and overhear the real truth about what had happened, but she didn't dare. There was so little time remaining to complete her experiment. Reaching into the space behind the front stair, she retrieved the brown bag of specimens, spilling the half-dozen black egg-shaped spheres to the ground. It was dried owl vomit, in which she might find mouse skeletons. She knew she'd have to work fast. They'd soon order her inside.

In the bedroom of the cool, dark house, Tamra watched as Big Mama handed Virginia an orange rind. Her mother declined, saying she had lavender candies.

"Chew it anyway," Big Mama ordered, "nothing sweetens your breath better." Woodenly, Virginia did as she was told.

Big Mama coiled her braid into a bun, then reached hurriedly into a dresser, pulled out a girdle, and stepped into it.

Tamra, who sat on the floor, wondered if they were getting dressed for church. Why didn't they just tell her? Since she was accustomed to not being answered, she didn't ask. She rolled a stocking up her leg and leaned back, the wood floor cold on her spine. She held a nyloned leg in the air the way a model had posed in one of Mama's New York magazines. Virginia had told her she had long legs. That was good she guessed, surveying her hairy brown shank.

As Big Mama struggled to pull up her girdle, Tamra watched the layers of her grandmother's fat fight against the elastic. Tamra shook her head doubtfully. "I don't think you're going to get all that in there."

"Why don't you put those microscope eyes of yours to good use," the old woman snapped. "I think I just heard me a car."

Tamra jumped up, raced to the window, and saw her father step from his Mercury. He quickly turned his back to the house, and leaned against the fender as if he'd dropped by to take in the view. She rapped on the windowpane and Seth turned, waving for her to come out. Big Mama grabbed Tamra to stop her from racing out, and spoke sternly to Virginia. "Better greet your husband. God don't like ugly."

Virginia sat and crossed her legs. She wouldn't go until she was good and ready. The old woman released Tamra, who had only minutes before bathed in the tin tub. She could still feel water on her collarbone. Hurriedly lifting the hem of her slip, she pulled on the garter belt Virginia had brought her.

"Tamra, you've got to wear panties with that," Virginia chided. "No matter what else you have on, you must always wear panties." Tamra moaned impatiently, trying to get the snaps on the belt to work. Virgina walked slowly toward her, fixing the clips expertly into position and telling her to calm down. "You'd better learn not to run after a man, no matter who he is."

She tried slowing down as she pulled the hem of her mother–daughter shift over her head. When she'd carefully fastened her new shoes, she looked from face to unreadable face and ran from the room, slowing at the front of the house, quietly opening the screen door. Pursing her lips, she made the first bird call her father had taught her, the purple martin. Seth opened his arms and she ran to him. He lifted her up, swinging her, the new New York Cuban heeled shoes spinning like the seats of a carnival ride.

Virginia emerged from the house with two suitcases that she sat on the ground, and without a word of greeting, climbed into the front seat. Seth wore a half-smile as Big Mama winked at him. Having Mama and Daddy together felt good, like slipping into a rough and familiar sweater. But she was sad about leaving Big Mama.

At first, she'd thought she would hate being down there. In the country, drawers were lined with newspaper. Rough face towels burned her cheeks, and she was terrified of the bull, as well as of the snapping, roped-up dogs. And the girls were always chattering about boys and makeup. She and Wadine liked boys all right, but they also liked experimenting on bugs and pondering questions like whether birds sang to communicate or entertain.

She'd found no answers here. On quiet afternoons she and Big Mama had sat on the porch, hollering "hallo" at passing cars, and when they did walk along the road, Big Mama had a story about every house. She'd taught her about sticking a piece of bread down crayfish tunnels; and how to make medicines from barks and leaves, cures for boils, wandering men and child-less women. Through it all, slow days, long nights, after she'd confided her fears, they'd shared the big, soft bed where she'd listened to the old woman's heart and been comforted.

They climbed into the car and Big Mama handed Virginia a jar of pear preserves, crusted with ginger and white sugar, that she and Tamra had canned. She gave Tamra a paper-wrapped clump of blue violets, soil clinging to the roots. They'd grown en masse this year in Big Mama's yard. She seldom let her daughters leave without roots for their gardens. There were also letters Seth had written, now bound with string. As he started the car, Big Mama's face looked odd, as if it too needed string to hold it together.

"Sure you ain't got to go?" Big Mama called, reminding Tamra Virginia wouldn't stop at a public restroom. A new law had forced businesses to open bathrooms to Negroes, but Virginia refused to go where she wasn't wanted. Tamra twisted in her seat, saying she'd just gone, waving good-bye as they pulled off, wondering if she could talk her parents' silence away.

11

Seth, Virginia, Tamra August 1964

SHE WORKED AT keeping the drive from Nanticoke to Salisbury lively. "Daddy, do you like my new shoes? Mommy brought me these, some magazines, a dress and . . ." she giggled, "stockings and a heart-shaped radio. Did you get me a camera for my experiments?"

Seth said, "You're proof of the first rule of commerce: Human wants are insatiable." They sped past the entrance to Head of the Creek Road, where the Lanes, the wealthiest Negroes in Nanticoke farmed eight hundred acres. It was the home of Charles Lane, the smartest boy in Nanticoke. On they rode, past fields of crops, cannonball bursts of blackbirds, cows, rusted barns, and farmers defiantly breaking Sabbath; on toward the city, the car closing in on the bitterness.

She hummed to keep herself cheerful and soon could just make out the top of the forty-gallon hat on the cowboy statue puffing clouds of mechanical smoke. Seth spoke in the voice of a tour guide, "Welcome to Salisbury. Population formerly fifteen thousand, one hundred thirty-eight, now fifteen thousand one, four, zero."

The car turned right, past the New Hope Missionary Baptist Church, which occupied an entire block and marked the start of the city's Negro neighborhoods. A bulletin board offered the theme of last week's sermon:

"Jesus, The First Astronaut." She imagined the Lord on his cross, blasting into outer space.

Seth slowed, rolling the window down, signaling left and turning onto Suffolk Street. She looked for the children who usually played in front of the projects and darted from between the cars. Today the street was quiet, as if something had scared the children indoors.

They stopped for a light as one boy, sitting on a parked car, caught her eye. Fresh red welts crossed his cheek. When their eyes met, he ran his tongue slowly across his lips. She pulled back, burying herself between her parents.

The streets widened and the projects gave way to modest cottages and increasingly larger homes set further back from the sidewalks. As Seth turned down Rutland Road, she watched to see if Mama's face would change. It always did. Virginia waved to Mrs. Moore, the doctor's wife, who was watering her lawn, and she turned woodenly to Seth, still smiling, speaking to him for perhaps the first time in months. "What'd you tell folks?"

He also waved. "You took a vacation." Tamra was delighted. Even if it was only a few words, at least it was a start. Everything was going to be okay. She could just feel it and she sat up enthusiastically so Virginia wouldn't scold her for slumping. They passed a large brick house that belonged to the Motleys, owners of the Negro newspaper, the *Salisbury Defender*.

Wadine's house was next, and for a fleeting second she raised her hand in greeting to a girl on the sidewalk wearing a too-short pinafore and a checkerboard head of braids. But in a blink, the figure was gone. It had only been her imagination. Except for the screen door to the front porch banging open, Wadine's house was quiet. Probably the family was at prayer meeting. She would run over later and leave one of her coded notes. They couldn't meet tonight. Tamra had Seth and Virginia to tend to.

Next, the home of her favorite grownup neighbor, Mr. Barbour, and she nearly cried out in pleasure. His portly figure moved about the curtainless glassed-in deck of his upper story, adjusting a telescope. He'd be glad she was back. Since his wife had died in April, leaving a freezer filled with neatly labeled casseroles and desserts, he'd had her over often, for dinner and watching the stars.

He started every evening saying he admired her daddy, who'd rescued him from the obscurity of the post office, where he'd worked after earning his master's degree. For the decade in which he'd delivered mail, Seth had kept Mr. Barbour's spirits buoyed, leaving notes in the mailbox, promising when he was promoted to principal he'd hire him. And he'd made good on his word. Mr. Barbour taught science.

Before she knew it they were home. There was the plaster goose and quartet of goslings on the lawn, more chipped than she remembered. She admired the gleaming picture window of their brick house, the blooming snowball bush and bed of flowers, most grown from roots Big Mama and Virginia's sisters had given her mother. Next year there would be violets.

In the vestibule she paused beneath the portrait of Grandpa Lord, painted before he'd lost an eye to diabetes. The first piece of furniture that caught her eye was the liquor cabinet. It was empty and she wondered why. And there was something about their white living room and the bookshelf-lined den that seemed hastily tidied, not clean the way Mama liked it.

In her parent's continuing silence she talked for them both, commenting on how nice everything looked, how glad she was to be back. "Hello, chair. Hi, bannister." Virginia looked at her with scolding eyes, signaling her to hush. But like a junior scout Tamra kept her eye out for brush fires, eager to douse them.

Tamra was hungry, said she wished they'd eaten at Big Mama's. She offered to rake the leaves from the pond or plant the violets. She speculated about what Big Mama was doing. Oh, and she'd forgotten all her specimens. Maybe they could stop at her grandmother's next week when they attended that celebration for Charles Lane. She couldn't stop talking. Her urge to hold the moment so controlled her.

Virginia pulled out twists of clothes from the washing machine, dumping them into a laundry basket. Seth carried their suitcases upstairs, stopping first in Tamra's room, where the pink chenille spread was perfectly arranged, as was the crocheted pillow doll with its floppy hat, and her red stuffed dog. All back in place.

What was it, she wondered, that had frightened her mother off? There was something about that night at the back of her memory. She refused to let it through. "Are you hungry, Daddy? I'm starved. How about your special eggs?"

He stared at the wall separating her bedroom from theirs. She felt sure now that she'd heard something that night. Her parents had been arguing in muffled, angry voices. Daddy's had been different, less distinct, saying, "You're my wife."

Dragging herself from this memory, she asked if they could fish next weekend. He laughed at this, and held the frilly curtain away from the window as he looked into the yard where Virginia wiped the clothesline, the basket of laundry at her feet.

"I'll dig the worms," Tamra said, knowing he loved to fish with her, the two of them sitting quietly on the shore with him regaling her with bits of knowledge. She thought him so clever. Some kids had teachers for parents, her mother had once told her, but only six children in the whole town, white or colored, were important enough to go home with a principal. Fishing, she'd get him alone. He would quote to her in Latin and speak bits of several other languages. And he told the best stories, like how the moon had come to rule the ocean.

He was about to leave, but she stopped him. Her suitcase. She would need help. She wanted to surprise Mama, unpack all her clothes. He lifted the suitcase to her bed, opened it and left to join Virgina.

From her window Tamra watched him join her Mother. He stood motionless at first, then pinned a sheet to the line. Next he hung socks and shirts. Moving quickly behind him Virginia took each piece down, shook it, and began the rehanging. She liked them lined up, Tamara knew, socks with socks, sheets with sheets, all in a neat, orderly fashion. Seth stood back watching.

She didn't move, could not join them. She was remembering the night they'd left. Mama had said, "Don't! Let me go! Hush!" A prisoner's commands. She'd been crying: "She'll hear us." Tamra had heard springs, heavy, body-heaving squeaks, and had tucked her head beneath the pillow, finally sleeping. A dream, she told herself, and swallowed the truth. She was hungry and considered going down but couldn't face her parents, not yet.

Pushing her suitcase to the floor, she pulled back the covers, and without removing her shift, crawled into the bed and slept. When she awoke she was startled to find the room was dark. Padding to the top of the stairs, she listened, as always, for quarreling. There was only the familiar, hoarse voice of Rochester: "Okay, you the boss." Why hadn't they called her? They always watched "The Jack Benny Show" together at seven o'clock on Sundays.

She started down, making a mental list of all the questions she'd ask. Most had to do with the Lane farm back in Nanticoke. What should she wear to Charles's party? Should she bring a gift? She looked foward to seeing him. He was clever and not smug, better than any boy she'd known.

Last time they'd visited, he'd shown her a trick. Quickly scanning a page from a book she'd been reading, he'd handed it back and repeated everything, word for word, page after page. It was a book about beetles, and his brain had taken pictures. How had he done it? She would watch him closely at the party, study him like one of the insects she and Mr. Barbour discussed.

Tamra stepped into the den but quickly pulled back before peeking around the door frame. Her mother wore the apple-green dressing gown Daddy had given her for her thirty-fourth birthday. Made of a new wrinkle-free fabric, it was edged with white ruffles.

Virginia sat on the couch, Seth's head on her thighs, the gown open, exposing her breasts; dark, full, round, and tipped with fine raspberry nipples. He stroked one breast blindly and sucked at the other with a noiseless thirst. Tamra crept back up the stairs, the sound of her movements masked by canned laughter.

12

Charles *August 1964*

IT HAD TO be the last Friday of the month, Charles thought as he crossed the porch and dusted his feet on the worn mat. The scent of his sister's hair burning had hit him the moment he'd climbed from the Caterpillar. And sure enough, he found Vicky, who at fifteen was a year older than he, sitting in a chair, with Ma behind her, heating an iron comb at the stove. Vicky's hair, which had been washed and dried, was parted down the middle. Most of it was already slick and straight, like patent leather, but one patch remained a balloon of kinks.

Ma greeted him. "You got a letter from Pop Pop." She walked to a shelf to retrieve an envelope. With only a few seconds for a preemptive strike, he leaned toward Vicky whispering, "Help! it's the stalking broccoli."

She hissed her usual refrain, "Shut up and dig."

They were words grown increasingly harsh for him. While he knew his sister's concept of what he actually did was somewhat askew, the sentiment was not. He wondered how she had read his heart. Although they'd once been constant companions, they were no longer. Besides, his secret was new even to him, and from the start had seemed so dreadful he'd not allowed the thoughts to clearly form until now: that neither digging nor planting nor any farm chore could be enough for him, enough for his life. He wanted more. But how had she guessed?

He fell into an easy chair, admiring his stylish and elegant high-cheek-boned mother. There was no other farm wife like her in Nanticoke. He opened his letter. "Better take a bath," Ma said.

Slumping in the cushions and partially hidden in the semi-darkness of the den, he hoped Ma would forget he was there. The only sound was the clinking of Ma's charm bracelet. It had been a wedding gift from her father. Most folks down here, she often said, had never seen real gold, much less an armful of it.

He noticed Vicky watching from the corner of her eye. She could give him away at any moment, her diabolical smile said. "*Maaaaa*," she called. He pressed his fingers into a prayer position. She bleated louder, "*Maaaaa*."

Dalhia pushed her daughter's head down, directing the smoking comb toward the short hairs at the base of her neck. "I'm doing your kitchens," she warned Vicky, "so sit still. You're so tender-headed."

When the comb made contact, the grease sizzled like bacon in a hot pan and Vicky drew up her shoulders in pain. Dalhia sighed loudly, running her hands over the mass of kinks. "I just don't understand. Why would the Lord do this?"

Charles let loose a barking laugh and Dalhia turned, her face drawn with disapproval. "I asked you to bathe."

"Can I have a moment, Ma? I've been at it all day."

"That's *may* I. You should consider using proper language or you'll sound like the rest of these folks down here. Now bathe!"

He plodded upstairs, where he sat on the side of the claw-footed tub, the water running full force, as he read the letter from his paternal great-grandfather.

Hiya Son,

Your Pa said you were having trouble hitting curve balls. I know how angering it can be when a fellow can't get his body to do what his mind says he should. Take me. I want to be there for your land's day party but can't. My little sister's the trouble. She says if I go I won't return to Delaware. At eighty-two I guess it's time to start listening to somebody.

I don't want to talk about me. Bullah Mae, who says to say hi, is taking this down for me, but what with her rheumatism and all, her hands give out easy. So here's what I mean to say.

I been studying your problem and have some ideas. Where

CHESAPEAKE SONG / 51

you know a pitcher has a good curve ball, crowd the plate. Any ball you think you cannot reach will surely be a ball. Watch the ball when it starts to curve. Step into it. Have an easy, straight, relaxed swing. You don't have to swing hard to get hits, just try and meet the ball. You can get your share of home runs and not strike out too often. Frank Howard, the Dodger bonus boy, still has trouble with curve balls. He stands back from the plate and gets curved to death. I think he has struck out nearly one hundred times this season. I bet the Dodgers will get rid of him this winter. You can check this out with your coach and see if I ain't right.

I'm sending you something can't be mailed. It's a one-row cultivator for your tractor. Can handle forty- to fifty-inch rows while holding the sweep pitch constant. Cousin Johnny's promised to drive up for it next week, bring it back for you. You can break it in on that property you get tomorrow. That was the same piece of land your great-grandfather give to me when I was fourteen, how about that? Tell the others hello.

Pop Pop.

He wanted to just tear the letter right up. Not even Pop Pop understood. Ahh, his great-grandfather was all right. But just who had decided fourteen should be the starting point for manhood? He sure could have used a few extra years on the other side. Looking in the mirror, he checked for facial hair but couldn't find a sprout on the smooth, reddish-brown skin he'd inherited from his father, or anywhere near the high cheekbones, which were Dalhia's.

There was more than enough hair on his scalp, especially here, over the forehead, where it jutted out like a ski jump. Turning sideways, he sucked in his stomach and flexed his biceps. Now that Cindy Holland was back from Detroit, maybe he'd have a chance with her. Lowering his voice, he practiced talking to her. "Cindy, I've been keeping this cap for you. Will you wear it for me? I've kept it clean by licking it."

No, that sounded all wrong. He shook his head, embarrassed now that he'd even invited her tomorrow. She probably considered him a big doofus. With a hand in front of his mouth, he huffed and quickly inhaled. How had his breath smelled when he'd invited Cindy?

Maybe he'd carry Dentyne the way Cousin Johnny did. Look how well he did with girls. But he had to admit, Johnny's success had a lot to do with him being a good dancer and driving a fancy car. And now that he'd graduated from high school, he had a lot more time than Charles, who couldn't stop to brush his teeth after chores if he wanted to catch the school bus.

What he needed, he thought, was a life of leisure, like Vicky's. She didn't even have to study. Ma never complained about her grades. But if he earned anything less than an A, forget it, Ma would go wild. He sighed deeply.

Unbuttoning his shirt, he thought of the hundreds of guests tomorrow, who'd watch him get his first ten acres, which would be held in trust until his eighteenth birthday. At twenty-five he'd get another 290 acres, and by the time he was thirty, all of it would be his. Through the decades the land had been inherited by Lane sons, generation after generation, in varying amounts of acreage, passed on at a young age; encouragement to settle down and marry. The original twenty-five-acre section had been a wedding gift to Moses Lane in the 1800s when he'd married a descendant of an Indian chief.

Hooray for us, he thought bitterly, trying not to picture the scene that would unfold tomorrow: Reverend Noel presiding over the land blessing, dozens of family members telling him how lucky he was, that no other colored folks on the Chesapeake had ever built a farm like this. They'd pump his hand, slap his shoulders, give him gifts, then get into their trucks and cars, and in a rush to reconnect with their lives, speed past the family graveyard, leaving him in the dust of history. The way he saw it, the past was fine if it was something to read about. But when it came to a person's life, living with history meant a loss of the future.

He'd heard a truck drive up and that meant Pa would soon be in the kitchen eating. Ma wouldn't dare suggest he bathe first. The water burned as Charles sank into the tub. To heck with them all. Only he could know what he wanted to do. To underscore his point, he stood up, calf deep in water, thrusting his arms out. He wanted to be the world's best baseball pitcher, with the style of Juan Marichal.

When they did give him a minute to himself, he searched the paper for some mention of his hero. He could hear the Giants, visualize Marichal's dramatic posture as he threw, the crowd cheering him on, a roaring wave of encouragement.

Charles's thoughts returned to the smallness of his world. He sat, lathering his thighs, and thought about Cindy, wondered if what people said about her having been knocked up was true. It didn't matter. She was nice to him. He reached a hand between his thighs. Suddenly there was a loud banging on the door; probably his cornhead sister. "Get lost!" he shouted.

But it wasn't Vicky. "You hear me, boy?" It was Pa.

Charles jumped up splashing. "Sir?"

"Meet me up at the corncribs, right away. Got us some rats."

His father stomped down the stairs as Charles pulled his dirty work clothes back on.

Passing Vicky's door, he heard the smooth radio voice of Ernie, the "Night Train" announcer. Dalhia was in the kitchen, fussing over her new top-of-the-line stove, a Nash Kelvinator with a slow cooker built inside. Its low flames licking the sides of the heavy pot was tonight turning hens, with eggs still inside, into a specialty for tomorrow's feast. The counter top was covered with pots and pans of varying sizes, and he peeked hungrily at the starting lineup: tomato pudding, roasted potato salad with bits of bacon, string beans laced with sausage doodle, roast beef and peppers, carrot pies, and his favorite, gingerbread pudding. And tomorrow there would be baskets of oysters and crabs, and platters of fish that had been caught at dawn.

Ma smiled sympathetically, promising she'd leave a plate in the oven. He wanted something now, anything he could take with him. She wouldn't hear of it. It was so common the way folks down here walked around eating. What'd they think tables were for? But when he fell to his knees, she relented, laughing, and just to get him up, she said, "Only a few cornsticks . . . and use a napkin. The idea of a child of mine begging for food!"

The cornsticks were cold, but flavored with bits of wild onion and Smithfield ham, but he had little time to enjoy them. Pa had called ten minutes ago. Charles banged into the porch swing as he raced outside. His bicycle waited loyally against the spigot, but he passed it up, choosing to run instead. The bicycle's orange banners, domed bell, and high, wide seat seemed too boyish.

The evening breeze moved through a grove of young trees, lifting branches toward the sky. In the distance he saw the two grass-covered rises of their nearest neighbor's land. The Reardons owned them, the highest ground for miles around. Charles had always referred to them as mountains, until his godmother, his Aunt T.J., traveling in the Swiss Alps, sent him a picture postcard.

He'd conceded; Nanticoke had no mountains or even hills. Still, he refused to call these elevated land formations mounds. Cousin Johnny, who claimed he'd loved over a hundred women, referred to the area as Mother Nature's hips. Charles loved watching them on evenings like tonight, when they seemed wet, and in the moonlight, a glistening blue.

Stopping at the end of each twist and turn in the road, his chest heaved. He was not breathless, but hopeful. He'd heard a distant engine in the sky where tonight's moon was so large and close it seemed within reach, and so fragile and white it could have been cut from onionskin paper. The light plane, he had heard, crossed the luminescent face. The buzzing machine against the ancient scape seemed flimsy and modern, an audacious upstart in the endless sky.

It was one of those puzzles he loved considering. Was this plane something like his own life? A speck in time, a single breath in the universe? If two southern boys could build a machine that flies, why couldn't he climb on Mother Nature's hips, pull down the moon, and toss it, bubblelike, from hand to hand? He wanted to float upward, be transported anywhere beyond the flat spot where he'd been born. He checked his watch again. Heck. Pa was always after him about wasting time, dreaming. He ran on, his shadow buried in the night path.

When he heard the truck behind him, he kept going, refusing to look to his right or his left. Pa, with Cousin Johnny driving, pulled up beside him, pausing only long enough for him to jump onto the flatbed with Cat and Fish, their Chesapeake Bay retrievers. When they stopped again, he was first to leap out, worried about showing his fear.

Cousin Johnny shone his headlights on the grass. It was clear, the sweet mats they'd set out earlier, untouched. Cat and Fish barked wildly, tearing at the wooden door of the facility. Cousin Johnny shouted the obvious. "They still in there."

"Then they'll have to deal with us," Pa said and told Charles to search for rocks. Cousin Johnny locked the dogs up in the cab of the truck to keep them from getting in the poison and grabbed a lantern. Charles remembered that Cousin Johnny had tried convincing Pa to install electricity in the facility, where ceiling-high bins of corn were dried for replanting. He wondered if the two men thought of that now.

He loaded his pockets with rocks, heavy ones, working furiously, so fear wouldn't envelop him. Pockets full, he ran to the door and grasped the knob. "Ready, Pa?"

His father told him to hold on and the three men positioned themselves, shoulder to shoulder, until Cousin Johnny, who held the light and a pitchfork, pushed his way past. Inside the dark space, only silence. He prayed it would continue. Well, whatever Cousin Johnny had thought he'd seen, he'd been wrong. There was no sign of rats.

Cousin Johnny handed him the lantern, threw open the doors to the cribs, and poked at the piles of kernels that spilled to the floor, shifting into different patterns. Like a lookout, a single rat ran out. Cousin Johnny raised his knee and brought a heavy boot crashing down on the rat's back. Its small head protruded from beneath the boot, still alive.

A pack of rats exploded. They came first from one crib, then more of the creatures spilled out faster than he could count from another crib. With the lamp high in his hands, he saw their short black bodies pumping with quick and eager breaths, tails stiff, eyes tiny shining flames. He froze.

"Throw, boy, move!" It was Pa's voice. He turned and saw the men waving him out of the way. The rats' feet sounded like twigs against his boots. The stream of bodies against his legs felt like a thick, warm rope. Some of the rats ran for the walls, searching out hiding places. He felt a pinch, thought maybe he'd been bitten, and screamed, leaping on a cement block as he threw the lantern down.

The lantern cast a low slanted light on the floor. The rats seemed to pour from the glow. Two of them stood on hind legs, scrambling to climb on the block with him. Their faces, squeezed together beneath the eyes, were mean and angry looking, teeth bared. He wanted to kick them away, but he'd lost control of his body. His knees knocked, and his torso swayed like a quaked dwelling. He heard Pa calling to him to throw the rocks.

The coolness of fear washed over him as he reached into his pocket, clutched a rock, mechanically threw it, and then repeated the drill: pocket, grab, throw. Pocket, grab, throw. He heard their impact against flesh and the toylike squeals of pain. When the men had worked for a while, the numbers began finally to thin, but he continued throwing, watching as Cousin Johnny chased the remaining few rats from their hiding places. Charles, pockets empty, climbed down. In the slant of lamplight he could see the ground, wet with blood.

It didn't matter. He had turned off the fear. He heard the dogs barking in the truck. The rats were dead and he tried counting what he could see. There had been fewer than he'd imagined, less than a dozen.

Cousin Johnny opened the door to the facility. A crippled rat tried to crawl out and collapsed at the doorway. Charles counted in a whisper until he heard Pa's voice, kinder now, telling him to quit.

Charles's hands were balled into fists, as if still clutching rocks, and he relaxed them. Father and son stood alone in the facility. Johnny had freed the dogs to chase off any rats that had fled outdoors. Charles rubbed his palms together while Pa shoveled corn into piles and spoke haltingly. "We'll make you a good farmer yet."

He walked to where Pa stood and with the tip of his boot pushed a grain of corn around. He kept his head bent, thinking he might cry. "That pitching arm of yours came in handy," Pa said.

"Yes sir." He paused, not wanting any more battles, but went ahead anyway, letting go of each word as if tasting it first. "I don't want to farm. I want to play ball." He couldn't remember hearing himself cry before. His sobs grew into dry, seal-like honks, and his nose ran, wet and loose. He drew his sleeve across his face. Pa, he knew, would call it blubbering. For a long minute it seemed his father hadn't heard, but then he stopped jabbing at the corn and, nodding his head, gestured toward the door.

Charles was reluctant to leave the darkness of the facility, for he worried Cousin Johnny might see him crying. He picked his way slowly across the dirt floor, occasionally missing a bare spot and landing on a carcass. It was like trodding on wet sponges.

Outside, Charles admired the bend in Mother Nature's hips as he and Pa walked quietly. He didn't have to glance at his Pa, knew just how he looked: barrel chested, his face with its dark moles, like freckles across his nose. Pa spoke in a newly confiding manner. "Tell me something, did your ma put you up to this idea . . . about not farming?"

"No sir, not at all."

"It don't take a genius to know she doesn't think much of farmers." Charles didn't know what to say. He was embarrassed by this talk. Pa added, "I wanted to be a surgeon."

He looked up to catch the rest of the joke. Was this a tease? His father, the best farmer in Nanticoke? But he was not smiling. "I wanted to save lives," Pa said, shrugging as if his shoulders hurt. "But then there was this land and all . . ." Pa laughed grimly when Charles asked why he'd changed his mind. "Was changed for me. If it had been in the cards Cyrus wouldn'ta died."

He'd seen Pa's brother in photographs and knew only that he had been killed in the war that had ended so many lives and changed others, most especially Cousin Johnny's, now twenty, who would have been next in line to receive the land. But Cousin Johnny bragged to everyone that he hadn't wanted it, or college, either. Instead, he seemed happy with his cars and all the women in his life. And it had cost him. He'd gotten some girl in trouble. Charles had overheard his mother scolding Johnny about it. It had cost them all plenty.

Pa was still talking, said it had been hard for Dalhia to accept the change because she'd married him, thinking he'd be a doctor.

Charles straightened up. "I wouldn't have given in."

Pa sighed, saying, "Yeah, you would have. You will. You're my son." Charles shuddered. The words were haunting. He wondered if his grandfather had used the same words. Pa said, "Now I'm glad to be here."

"Yes sir."

"It's true. Farmers get to look over God's shoulders. Gives us an advantage. When you're up to your elbows in soil it's hard to think too much of yourself, like some folks I could mention."

He knew Pa meant Dalhia's family. Her father had been president of Holcomb State. Her sisters had married bigwigs and her brother, an attorney, had grown rich in D.C.

"Out here," his father continued, "we always know just who's in charge." Charles nodded. "Listen to me, son. I'm telling you right. Any fool can finish college. And any man can tell you how many ears will grow from a kernel. Only God can tell you how many kernels will grow on each ear."

"Know the biggest lie Negroes ever bought?" Pa continued. "It was that being a farmer meant peonage, that selling land and moving up North was progress. And just look what it got us."

Charles squinted in the dark. He could just make out the shapes of rusted farm machinery left dumped in a nearby field.

"It's what you don't see that hurts," Pa said. "When my daddy started working this land, at least half of all Negroes worked on farms. Now only about a tenth are run by us. We'll be lucky if there's even a handful of Negro farmers in the next century. Then you'll thank me."

Charles felt that he stood on top of his own grave. "I guess you're saying it's what you'd call inevitable, right, sir? I have to accept the land, don't I?" He was tearful again, but fought against it.

Pa stared longingly toward the hips. Charles wanted to hear another secret, anything to keep him talking the way they never had before. "Pa, back there at the corncribs. I was scared."

He put his arm around his son's shoulder. When had Charles last felt the weight of this, this safeness? "You were so busy dancing, you didn't see what I saw," Harlen said.

"What's that?"

"I was, too. Me and Johnny, both of us. Scared shitless. There are some things in life we have no control over."

Yeah, Charles thought, like this land. They worked on, burying carcasses and erecting a new binding the rats would find impenetrable. At dawn they chored the animals. There was much to do before the guests arrived.

13

Tamra and Charles *August 1964*

SHE LEANED INTO the V formed by Seth and Virginia's clasped hands and rested her knees on their fists. Daddy's Spandex watch was cold on her skin. Virginia told her to stand up.

She straightened her pillbox hat and smoothed her dress. This was so boring. Why was it so important to be here for this part of the ceremony, anyway? Daddy and Mr. Lane hardly saw each other except for their alumni meetings. And from way back here, she sure couldn't see anything. She'd like to be up front, so she could get a better look at the Lane's nearest neighbors, Art and Eve Reardon, the only whites in attendance. Tamra tried to peer over the high shoulders, toward the slender woman up front. Her long, blond, curly hair covered half her face, but even so, the half Tamra could see was spectacular. And she wore pants. How daring. The shoulder in front of Tamra shifted, putting Mrs. Reardon out of sight and reminding Tamra of her boredom.

She knew if she complained to her parents and annoyed them, she risked disturbing the delicate balance of their happiness. They looked so cute, holding hands like teenagers. She tried staring patiently into the turrets of heads, amusing herself by counting everyone in the vicinity.

Stopping at forty, she divided them into age categories. There were twenty-eight grownups, maybe. Did Cindy belong with the kids or adults? She was in the ninth grade, but folks said she'd gone to Detroit and had a baby. Did that make her a woman? She grudgingly admired the way Cindy filled out her baby doll blouse and simple, black skirt. It was easier to watch her in profile, when she wasn't so pretty. From this angle her chin spoiled her face. But yes, maybe especially from the side, with those big breasts, Cindy belonged with the grownups.

What about Cousin Johnny? He was another of those almost-adults, and look at him, so full of himself; the way he kept his hands in his pants pockets and shook his right leg. She could just make out his back, but wished she could see him from the front, with his drooping eye. There was something about him and the way he looked at girls, as if he knew something dirty about you. Her parents had been whispering that Johnny was the one who'd gotten Cindy pregnant, and that the Lanes had paid her parents off. But the Hollands were telling everyone they'd received a big insurance settlement, an accident in Detroit. She shook her head, an accident all right, just like it was an accident that Johnny's mama had run off and left him the night before his twelfth birthday. *Um hmm.* She knew a lot more than her parents thought she did.

She tried to continue her counting game of how many women wore dresses of this or that color, but losing count, she turned instead toward the sky, where there was one red sun.

If she liked swimming, it would have been a great day for the beach. But it was never a good day for standing around a big, flat field in your best clothes. This place didn't seem so special to her. The ears of corn looked like soldiers prepared to fire on the crowd. At least the last time she'd visited, she'd talked to Charles. Today she couldn't get near him. Everything had come to a halt. Driving in they'd passed an idle tractor, front lift poised in the air like a dinosaur frozen in time. All she could hear now was the preacher's voice and the infrequent traffic from the highway.

What was Charles thinking? When she'd seen him earlier he'd looked so uncomfortable in his black suit. They were probably sprinkling soil over his fingers by now. She giggled to herself. Maybe he was being buried alive. She tugged at Virginia's pocketbook, whispering loudly, "I have to pee."

Virginia's *"shhhh"* whipped at her like a blade. She'd warned Tamra not to use that word.

"May I please go?"

"Yes, but come right back."

"Yes ma'am," she said in imitation of the country kids. She knew Mama hated hearing her talk that way, but what could she do, yell at her for being polite?

As she hurried across the field, a flock of birds flew overhead, their wings flapping loudly, like Mama shaking out the sheets. The flock's shadow swept the ground. Tamra studied the formation, wondering how long the average bird lived, and how to tell the old from the young. Did feathers gray, bones grow frail? Questions always invaded her brain.

The crowd looked a world away. Could she find something interesting in the woods? No, Mama would kill her if she got her new shoes scratched. The heat was sweltering, her stockings were glued to her legs. She crossed the area cordoned off as a parking lot, crowded today with SceniCruiser buses that had brought guests from big cities, and paused at a tow truck, emblazoned with white hand-lettered words: "Caveman Towing."

The ceremony ended, the edges of the crowd softening as people left and streams of heat rose, giving the pastel-colored dresses an undulating effect, like floating lilies. She knew her parents would expect her to return immediately, but they'd have to wait. She had exploring to do.

Just off to her left was a new blacktop road, so smooth she wanted to skip along it, but she worried someone might spot her. She swung her pocketbook instead, the specimen jars rattling as she approached a graveyard of crumbling headstones, where one grave in particular caught her eye.

Without so much as glancing at the names etched into the stone, she used the tip of her shoe to nudge a log supporting a bunch of plastic flowers. It didn't budge. It had apparently been there too long for easy movement. A good sign.

Tamra glanced around to see if anyone might be passing. All she needed was to have Mama hear she'd been poking around in another graveyard. Pulling her hat off and discarding her patent leather purse, she fell to her knees and applied pressure to the log that now moved easily. Its soft roots tore free to reveal a treasure trove of worms and insects.

Was there something here for her collection? Tamra scanned the scurrying inhabitants and picked up a plump, stiff-haired, lobster-clawed beetle, bringing it close to her eyes for a better look. It had a leathery material on the underside and a wing sheath, coppery smooth. She pulled a bobby pin from her hair, feeling strands spring free from the confines of the French roll. With the tip of the bobby pin, Tamra lifted one of the beetle's largest wings, and found another soft crumpled pair beneath. They appeared useless, unable to assist the insect in flight. She chewed her bottom lip as she tried to understand the mystery.

Had these tiny wings once been the primary means of flight for this species? Why had the larger wings dwarfed what may have once been perfectly capable ones? While she considered these questions she reached down to pick up her purse, then held the strap in her teeth while she opened the clasp.

Plowing through crumpled tissues and candy papers, she found her glasses and put them on. Next a search for the specimen jar. Once found, she held the purse strap under her chin and unscrewed the jar so she could slip the beetle inside. Now this was something she was certain she and Mr. Barbour could discuss over dinner. Satisfied with herself, she started up the road. Everyone else was running to get back to the house to saddle up to the Lanes, eat their food, and talk about quite ordinary things, and here she was, investigating mysteries.

This area was closer to the water and further from the Lane house, but she convinced herself this had been part of her plan. She continued toward a sandless strip of land along the river, which had been built up with a dock and small shed. Tall reeds and cat-o'-nine-tails grew along the pier, and a row boat, tied by a thin rope, waited on the water. She hoped to find another beetle near here, something different from what she'd caught, and yet within the same family, for the purpose of comparison.

The shed took up most of the dock's floor, affording her only two alternatives. If she wanted to inspect the grassy, waterlogged shoreline, she'd either have to get into the boat, which she feared like death, or inch herself around the shed, flat on her belly, and reach from the safety of the dock.

Deciding to inch herself around the shed, she retrieved her second specimen jar and lowered herself to a crawl, so she could inspect the marshy land up close. It wasn't long before she heard voices. Fearful it might be her parents searching for her, she pressed herself down. Girlish laughter came from inside the shed.

She peeked through the corner of a broken window. It was Charles and that girl, Cindy. Listening to her talk, Tamra was struck by the girl's hillbilly accent. She'd never heard a Negro speak this way, and she listened in wonder. "Ah betta skedaddle," Cindy drawled. "Mah mama will kill me if she finds I'm with you."

Charles, who had his suit jacket off and a shirttail hanging out the back of his pants, pulled Cindy against his chest, leaning into her. But his eyes,

Tamra noticed, searched the shed for something. "We're both going to be in big trouble," he said. "But I don't care if I can be with you."

Cindy fiddled with Charles's tie, and puckering her mouth, brought her lips to his neck as if she'd found a spout. His eyes closed and his tongue snaked outside his mouth. Tamra panicked. How could she escape without being discovered? Seeing her parents last week had been embarrassing enough, but this was dangerous. Cindy's mouth was open and traveled along Charles's neck. She seemed as anxious for him as he was for her. He caught her face between his hands, groaning.

It disturbed Tamra. Her breasts tingled like they were going to burst. She tried gathering her senses, knowing this kind of eavesdropping was as shameful as the act. Reluctantly lowering her head, she began to crawl away but then stopped short. She'd dropped the jar.

Cindy's voice sailed through the window. "What was that?" Tamra pressed herself down. Charles spoke in reassuring tones.

"Relax, just the boat against the pier."

Cindy purred: "You git me so beaddled."

When they quieted, Tamra felt compelled to peek again. He had reached over Cindy's shoulder to a white feed cap. "I want you to wear my cap," he said, kissing her. "Know how I kept it clean for you? I licked it."

Uggh, Tamra thought. He pulled the brim over Cindy's face and their mouths came together again, sounding like wet rags landing. Charles brought his fingers up the side of Cindy's hip, stopping just beneath the hem of her blouse.

Tamra knew she shouldn't continue watching but felt trapped. If she crawled away, they might discover her on her knees and she hated to risk that kind of humiliation. Bringing her fingers to her head, she prodded herself to think up a plan. All she could remember, as she watched Charles's hand slip up Cindy's back, was that Cindy deathly feared her mother. Inside the shed, Charles had undone the clasp to Cindy's bra and freed the mounds of her breasts.

If only she could remember how Mrs. Holland sounded. Wouldn't the mother talk in as backwoods a way as her daughter? Could Tamra change her voice the way she did with bird calls? Could she scare Cindy and Charles away? Wetting her lips and shading her mouth like a yodeler, she called "C-an-dee."

Tamra actually heard Cindy gasp, and this success made her bolder. "C-an-deee," she shouted. Through the window, she saw Charles's shoulders in the doorway as he talked excitedly, pointing to the left and right of him. "C-an-deee." The girl's eyes were wide with panic. Tamra was certain that of the three of them, she herself was most frightened of all.

Looking desperately around, the girl bolted, taking off down the road. Tamra waited momentarily for the second phase of her plan to kick in: for Charles to run after Cindy. But he didn't. He stood there, looking furious. And as he started toward the back of the shed, his jaws and fists were clenched.

She ran in the other direction, away from Cindy, hoping Charles wouldn't recognize her from the back. But Tamra had only progressed a few feet when she heard running steps. She turned and saw him reach out, grabbing for her shoulder. He had her. Twisting away, she sped up her pace, fist throttling as she shot off. But his grip, viselike, stopped her again.

"Why would you do that?" he demanded.

Breathing too hard to speak, she shrugged, offering a conciliatory smile.

"Think it's funny?" he demanded, yanking her shoulder. "You're just mean and stupid." He pointed nervously down the road, hand trembling. "Gotta catch her . . . tell 'er what you did."

But there was no sign of Cindy, and even if Tamra had seen her, she had no intention of explaining anything to that—that baby machine. Meanwhile, he looked off longingly, like a man in a desert, watching his last sip of water evaporate. "Come on, please, there's still time."

Begging? This was too much. And he'd called *her* stupid. Tamra roared to her own defense. "I don't have to do anything."

She was shocked by his response. He threw a tantrum, pummeling the air with his fist, kicking dirt, running in place, screaming: "Why'd you do that?"

Tamra bent over with laughter. "You look like the Roadrunner."

Her taunting quieted him, and when he turned on her, his face in a furious knot, he grabbed both her arms.

"Let go of me, you crazy fool."

"Don't you know it's a sin to call someone a fool?"

"Only if it's a lie."

He dragged her along. At first, she laughed aloud. It wasn't until they had advanced several feet that she understood he was indeed powerful enough to move her anywhere he wanted. She reached up with her free hand, slapping at his cheeks. Charles didn't so much as flinch, a sure sign of a madman. She grabbed the collar of his shirt and tried to rip it, but he merely brushed her hand away. When she pulled back on her heels, to slow their progress, he jerked her along, and she began to trip and stumble. His iron grip kept her from falling as he continued dragging her down this road, which only minutes before she'd ambled up so peacefully.

The idea of him traipsing into that gathering with her in tow so enraged her that she opposed him all the more. It was no use. He was bigger and stronger than she'd imagined. Feeling that strength work against her took her breath away. She had to calm down and think. Her mind was her only ally.

Feigning exhaustion, Tamra walked peacefully before him, step by deceptive step. When she was a few inches in front and he'd loosened his grip, she made her move. She took a jump and came down hard, her sharp little Cuban heels grinding into his feet. Twisting around, she raised her knee and hit him sharply in his groin.

Charles flung her away, hollering. She was amazed at how much she'd hurt him. And she laughed loud and hard and thankfully. Though he pulled his fist back, she stood her ground, poking her chin out, shouting so loud her eyes watered: "Go ahead. I dare you."

He swung, his fist stopping just short of her nose. She thought she'd faint at the sight of it pushing toward her but instead thanked God she hadn't flinched, not a bit. She'd shown him. And she stood there, watching the anger drain from his face and waiting for an apology. He smiled contemptuously.

"I don't hit ladies . . . which you are not."

"And Cindy is?"

"You're a brat." He stepped back, as if she had bad breath.

"And you're disgusting," she said, closing her eyes, mocking him, "Ooh Cindy. I wants you to wear my hat. Let me lick it for you." He looked humiliated as she continued, calling forth every word she could from those movies Virginia loved watching. "Charles, you are appallingly loathsome. Just wait 'til Cindy's mother hears what she was doing." He blinked at this one and she knew she'd struck a nerve. But he retained his composure.

He said, "And are you going to tell your mama what you did?"

Now it was her turn to be frightened. "I . . . I was hunting for beetles."

A look of understanding crossed his face. "I get it. Beetles. Like that book you showed me last year."

She shook her head yes, glad he recalled that friendly time they'd spent together. But the memory didn't soften his tongue.

"Which beetle are you?" He grabbed her chin, considering her closely. "With that funny looking dress and those glasses, you must be one of those goliaths. Let's see your eight-inch wing span." He tried holding her arms out but she twisted angrily away.

Furious as she was, she couldn't help but be impressed by his powers of recall. He'd only scanned those pages. As if reading her mind, he continued, smug and childlike. "Or . . . are you one of those passalids with the small hooks on their heads?" He pointed to the crown of her head, where, she now realized, her hair was standing straight up, Mohawk-style.

He continued, comparing her to better-known as well as obscure varieties of the insect, and she watched his mouth, hoping to understand this trick. But as the reality of her appearance sank in, she couldn't tolerate another moment of his insolence. Her dress and stockings were torn and dirty, her shoes dusty. Now she'd have to face her mother.

Tamra turned, walking slowly in the opposite direction from Cindy, grasping at the flimsy hope that Charles would regain his senses, catch up to her, and apologize. But he was unrelenting, laughing, rambling from that now odious list of beetles.

"Maybe you're one of those giant burying beetles, or the black-tipped wood borer . . . European Searcher? No, no, how about the bronzed tumblebug . . . or the American Bombardier . . . that's it. She releases clouds of acid wherever she travels."

She tried striding lightly, as if on her toes, but she'd broken one of her Cuban heels and was forced to limp. Still, she refused to bend. Every few steps she pretended another book was being added to the imaginary pile balanced on her head. His voice had grown fainter but still she heard. He'd changed his approach. "Hey, wasn't Tamba Jungle Jim's sidekick? Tamba, your mama, she wants you, girl."

On she walked.

"Tam-ba . . . no . . . she don't even want you."

Here she imagined Virginia's voice, correcting his speech, saying in her front-of-the-mouth way, "No . . . not *don't*. You mean, your mama *does not* even want you." She tried grinning at this secret joke but could not. Straight-spined, she continued down the blacktop road.

14

Tamra October 1990

SHE PREFERS THIS stationary bike to the track. At least here she doesn't feel like the center of attention, and she can see Wadine zipping around while still keeping an eye on all the others in this gym. The bikes face the track, which runs around a basketball court, where on this weekday evening several men, dressed in gym shorts and turbans, are jostling for the ball.

Wadine jogs by, waving, inspiring Tamra to pedal faster. Thank goodness her friend doesn't look hurt or confused as she had earlier when she'd accused Tamra of being evasive about Charles. Wadine had been after her for the last week. But what was there to say? They just couldn't get along. As for the scandal involving Cassie and Cousin Johnny, she wasn't about to open that can of worms.

She'd tried responding to Wadine's questions as best she could. Yes. No. She didn't want to leave him for good. Well, maybe she did. She was staying for two weeks, a month. She didn't know. Was she in the way? Would Wadine prefer if she checked into a hotel? Sure she was touchy, but Wadine was asking too many questions. This girlfriend stuff was getting out of hand. Why wouldn't she be crying? She'd phoned Dalhia's house and no one had been home. Wasn't it normal to miss your kids?

She waves as Wadine passes. Yes sir, she'd turned into a regular brown Sherlock. She said it was concern, that she worried when Tamra stared into space. Well, she'd been staring all right, but not into space. In this city there's always something to see.

Maybe Wadine is too much of a New Yorker to understand. Only a native would fail to realize that this city is one big movie set, with characters walking about the streets, discussing in ordinary voices the particulars of their domestic mayhem, as if rehearsing their lines.

Tamra thinks it may be the presence of the homeless that gives the city its confessional air. Passing the sprawling figures, eyes averted, was like stepping through a stranger's bedroom; a foot poking from a blanket, toothbrush in a reclosable plastic bag.

Yesterday, she'd walked behind two self-absorbed pedestrians and had overheard one woman discussing her extra-marital affair. By the time the light had changed, the listener had absolved her companion of guilt, and they'd moved on, quickly, as if morally cleansed. Tamra was left behind, an involuntary confidant.

On her second night, Wadine and Stephen took her to a fundraiser on the city's westside, a bookstore some bibliophiles were determined to save. One of the guests was an ex-wife of Johnny Carson's, who'd arrived with a bag of cash. Painfully thin, she wore a leopard skin jumpsuit, huge sunglasses, and sipped from a gallon jug containing a vitamin shake. Later, Tamra heard the washroom attendant telling the janitor secrets Johnny's ex had shared.

Never. Wadine and Stephen would never lay in bed whispering about her marriage. It's true that as children she and Wadine had shared confidences, but the topics had been inane. Wadine jogs by again, and Tamra pedals all the harder, concentrating on her thighs. Charles had always thought them fabulous. Once he'd convinced her to put on a white shirt with a Peter Pan collar, high heels, and nothing else. He'd begged her to keep walking, and he'd grown hard, laughing less each time she'd passed. But here, the body standards were different. In fact, Wadine had raved about what great shape Johnny's skinny ex was in.

Tamra feels old and fat, particulary in these shiny black leotards, her thighs like two mother penguins. She looks elsewhere, taking in the scene, the first racially integrated spot she has seen in New York. Even here, whites are with other whites, blacks with blacks.

On the Stairmaster, two sisters with earphones dance in sync through a series of Temptation routines. A young Japanese man with bulging shoulder muscles perspires as he works a rowing machine. The manager of the gym, a slim Hispanic, whispers orders to his fitness trainers.

Wadine passes again, this time holding up a finger, indicating one more time around. Tamra pumps harder, picturing Charles's body. Her feet race, working the image away. Even worse, she remembers a scene from the family reunion, four years ago, when she happened on Cousin Johnny, his form bent over, as he removed his trousers, stripping down to black, slinky shorts, preparing for the three-legged races.

A short distance from the basketball players, a compact redhead in a yellow leotard and high ponytail performs an exhausting gymnastics workout. With a bounce, she flips head-over-heels, landing upright. Tamra wants to applaud and remembers clapping after Charles had sung that hymn. She'd been so venomous, she now thinks. But so had he. A well-dressed mammie, he'd called her. She shakes her head. Marriage.

Waiting by the water fountain she notices her friend is not out of breath when she runs by saying she has to cool down before they leave. The index cards on the bulletin board haven't been changed since she's been coming to the gym with Wadine. One advertises half a summer house in the Hamptons—$10,000 plus maintenance. She checks the zeros to ensure she has read correctly. Ten thousand dollars, plus, to rent half a house for three months? Why not? So much in New York seems different, including a skewed sense of time. Wadine and Stephen make dinner reservations for nine, while half the residents of the Chesapeake are preparing for bed. And in the packed restaurants, people crowd in line for the next seating.

En route to the gym, she and Wadine had stopped at a one-hour dry cleaner and laundromat, where each machine requires twelve quarters. She computes how much that would cost her family, but stops, telling herself she will only survive being away if she forgets what she'd once considered normal. This isn't her only rule of survival in New York. Whether in the house or on the street or in the car, she must never let her guard down. This, she figures, is a piece of cake. She has never learned to relax, anyway.

On the way over, Wadine told her about a break-in last month at the penthouse. Some fellow, escaping from another robbery, landed on her roof and pried open a window. She'd known he was in the house when her first alarm rang. The penthouse is divided into four security zones, and as he progressed zone by zone, individual alarms went off. She'd raced to get Olu, and halfway up had seen a man's legs. The robber had run off. But when the police arrived, they found his jacket flung over a flowering bush, a switch blade in the pocket.

Tamra had listened sympathetically to her friend. But to Tamra the most outrageous detail of the story was that someone she loved lived in a house divided into security zones.

"Ready," Wadine calls, and they are off to the locker room. This time, she will not be bullied into stripping publicly, like those other women. Wadine has always bullied her.

A woman in a baggy grey jogging suit sluggishly pushes a stroller with a red-eyed child. Tamra wonders why she looks familiar. Then she knows. It's the sprightly gymnast she'd seen minutes before.

Tamra wonders if she, herself, would appear as different to the Chesapeake neighbors who greet her and Charles and their children on Sunday mornings, if they were to see her now—alone and frightened in New York.

15

Charles *April 1967*

FEET SPREAD, FINGERS gripped close to the knob, he twisted his body and shifted to his rear foot, relaxing his hips and shoulders. In one deft sweeping motion, he stepped forward quickly, wrist snapping as he swung. He repeated the maneuver trying to raise a sweat, but it proved impossible. At sixteen, tall and full-shouldered, Charles possessed strength he could seldom exhaust, and today as he waited for a ride to his team's first practice of the season, he hoped he could put his strength to good use.

He would actually have preferred to quit swinging for a minute so he could peek down the road to look for the coach's truck. That he could not do, for although he'd tried many times, he had never overcome the land's hold on him, especially now. It was spring in the Chesapeake. The trees had leafed, the dogwood blossomed, and sun-pinked laurel crept along the gullies. Land lay about him like a belligerent temptress. Stripped bare through the harsh winter, it was now clothed in verdant robes and jewels of sudden wildflowers.

He devised a trick to help him ignore his surroundings, if only temporarily. But as he tried to concentrate on the front of the two-story house, he caught himself admiring a plum tree, its petals whirling down in the breeze like overfed snowflakes. This so exasperated him, he threw down his bat and reached for the ball. Spreading his fingers apart but keeping them parallel at the seams, he mock pitched a split-fingered fastball, trying to work the winter tightness from his arm. Ordinarily he was less aware of his attachment to the land. Today it consumed him with worry. Loving it didn't mean he wanted it. But the night before Pa had threatened to keep him from playing this season so Charles could concentrate more on agriculture and forget about anything, other than school, that interfered with his chores.

He'd asked Pa to give him this one last season, explaining that the team might make it to the state championships, and reminding him that last year a *Nanticoke Ledger* reporter had said that because of Charles the Cougars had played the "most exciting baseball in the league to date." His teammates depended on him. He would start college in the fall, and this was his last chance. Then there was all he hadn't said about his one small hope that a scout might recruit him away from the land.

Lifting his bat, he swung again, wishing he could remove this difference that stood between him and Pa like an unyielding stone. He heard an engine coming up the road and checked his watch. Maybe it was Ma. She and Vicky weren't home, and strangely enough, Ma had not left a note. He listened again. The engine's noise sounded closer. It could be the coach, but not much chance of that. This would be late for him. His heart fought in his chest as he moved onto the porch to a better lookout position. It was Pa on a tractor.

Returning to the lawn, he used the swinging motion of the bat to gather courage. High up in the seat, body arching as if he were riding an unruly horse, Pa drove into the yard. Charles kept swinging and watched him, wondering why he was driving their oldest machine. It had been in service since '50 and had finally been retired, after reaching the equivalent of 600,000 car miles.

Pa climbed down and Charles hung his head. He'd grown taller than his father and for this he felt apologetic. "Wanted to meet you at the bus," Pa said. "We never finished our talk."

"No sir, we didn't."

"You ain't playing ball. I told you last night. And just now, I told the coach."

"Why'd you speak for me?"

"Don't play the fool. You know I need you. There's a lot that needs your attention. Look around you."

He didn't have to. He knew Pa saw the land through different eyes. The early thaw had made the land's needs apparent. Grass grew where there once had been crops. The ground was crusted and tall weeds had shot up. The fields, he knew, required his hands. He was a reluctant groom unable to stall an arranged marriage. Watching Pa's face, Charles searched for signs of softening but could see his father had closed himself off to his claims.

Pa matched his son's angry stare. Charles had known this moment would occur but had hoped, when it did, he could be heroic. He was sure he could drop the old man with one swing and part of him wanted to, wanted to call him a son-of-a-bitch, grab him by the shoulders, and throw him down, clearing the way so his future could be his own. But that meant seeing Pa as evil. What he saw on this day, gently lit by spring, was that behind the meanness, Pa's eyes pleaded, "Don't shame me." Instead of a malevolent tilt to his head, Charles saw that Pa's jaw trembled. And Charles understood his father's fear of having raised a boy who would be first, among all these Lane sons, to break their blood oath. This man, who loved him as an only son, the man who Charles had never seen be cruel to any being. Fighting him, even for his own life, was too costly. And Charles lowered his head again.

"Change your clothes," Pa said, sounding gratified. Charles walked off to retrieve his bat and ball and Pa kept talking, telling him to look at Hammer's field and make a decision about what crop he'd raise there.

It was hard to speak but he tried. "Yes sir." He started off, then turned and said stiffly, "Do I have to change?" Pa looked guarded. "The clothes, I mean. May I just put on boots?"

Nodding, Pa offered a slight smile, a signal for reconciliation. All Charles need do was walk across to him, the smile said. Pa would forgive. He waited for a minute, then climbed back up onto the tractor. "Want a ride?"

"No," Charles said, leaving off the *sir*. "I'll drive myself."

In the pickup he felt his anger turn inward. All those years before, he'd thought he wanted the game, the cheering crowd, more than Pa's acceptance. When his fate had stood before him he'd been too cowardly to fight.

Hammer's field, close to the river, swept by heavy winds, was his, just as all the others would be. He walked across it slowly, bat in hand, over the stubble of last year's crop. A few dry and faded stalks remained upright, like monuments to his ancestors. He stood before a stalk, positioned his bat, and swung. The withered plant fell down with a crash. He kept swinging at stalk after stalk until they were all beaten to the ground.

The anger would not leave him, and the weight of what had occurred brought him to his knees. Why hadn't he fought, if only to say no; why hadn't he defied Pa this once, when it counted?

The soil was damp as he flung handfuls in the air. Much of it fell away from him, in clumps, while some rained down on him. He continued to sit for what seemed like a long time, listening quietly, waiting until he heard something, something from long ago.

When Charles first discovered it, in the summer of his childhood, it had seemed merely a breeze whistling through green stalks, cooling his skin. Today as he listened, on his first day of manhood, he heard it again, the haunting song of a deep and mournful wind that crossed the bay and its tributaries, a Chesapeake song.

Returning home, Charles found his mother's car still gone from the driveway. Parked there instead was a most elegant vehicle. Walking to the front of the beige car, he ran his hand along the gold-toned grill, then raced to the back to read the name. It was a Rolls Royce.

Inside the house, he heard a carefree chuckle, and he didn't wonder anymore about who was visiting. It was his godmother, Pa's sister, his Aunt Tommy Jean. He dashed up the stairs, hoping to get a bath, but calling out in her booming voice, she stopped him. "No hug for me, heh, heh?"

He saw, standing, at the foot of the stairs, his spectacular aunt. Six feet tall, Tommy Jean was dressed from knees to turban-wrapped head in lavender eyelet cotton. Her heart-shaped earrings jangled. Ignoring his own muddy clothing, Charles rushed to throw his arms around her. "What is this, heh, heh? Who's this man I'm hugging? Boy, you have grown." Her smile was wide and real, her clothes scented with ginger, the spice that had made her millions. Tommy Jean had left Nanticoke for college and married a man folks called the Black "mayor" of D.C. With her family money and his political connections, they'd built the Gingerbread Boy into one of the most successful restaurants in Washington.

"I'm here to take my godbaby for a ride," she said, her voice ringing through the hall, "but I see I don't have a baby anymore. You are a young man . . ." She held his arm, adding, ". . . who may have to drive me, heh?"

She led him toward the kitchen, to a basket filled with her famous jams and spices, containers of jambalaya topped with giant shrimp, and the enormous gingerbread cakes that had made her name popular in the corridors of the White House. "Like that car out there, heh?" Tommy Jean said, unwrapping a gingercake. "My sweet husband designed it for me. My name is written in gold in the glove compartment. Take a few of these with you and let's get outta here."

Her arms were strung with turquoise bangles and she wore several rings on each hand. Charles followed her to the car, puzzled over his mother's absence, but he climbed in behind the wheel without asking questions. The seats were pure leather, soft and fine, the same light color as the body of the car. A few crumbs fell from his mouth onto the seat. He hurriedly brushed them away, and glancing over at his favorite aunt, saw her watching him and smiling, her teeth small, perfect squares. "Go on, heh, heh."

He drove, jerkily at first, his foot anxious on the brake. The car felt as heavy as a tank. Tommy Jean pressed a button and the convertible top purred down. He wondered if she knew what had happened. She'd always taken his side.

After awhile, Tommy Jean said, "Looks like I drove up into a whole heap of your troubles, heh?" He pretended to be too busy concentrating on driving to respond. By now, the car seemed to steer itself, the ride so smooth, the road a carpet. "Do me a favor, little Charles."

"Ma'am?"

"Show me some of your land, heh?"

He sunk in his seat. "You mean my piece of it?"

"It's all your piece. Show me all of it."

As he turned up a familiar road, he hoped one of the boys from the team or school would pass and see him driving. It was late, though, dinner hour, and the roads were deserted. In a flat voice he said, "There's some, over there," and pointed at a field with green shoots.

"Now, if I kept driving down this road where would I have to turn so I could still see your land?"

Wondering what this was all about, Charles haltingly gave directions. She seemed to listen carefully, then said she wanted him to stop, that she'd like to drive and try an experiment. He walked around, and Tommy Jean slid over, rubbing her hands together. "You trust me, heh?"

He wasn't so sure, but he said yes anyway.

"Then I don't want any questions, okay?"

"About——"

"No questions."

What was she up to? And what did she mean by an experiment? But he finally agreed—no questions.

"Get up on the seat," she said.

He looked at her questioningly. "These dirty boots . . ."

"Doesn't matter," she assured him, so he raised himself up, slowly, watching her, first one boot, then the other. Far more of him was out of the car than in.

"You're fine," she called. "You can balance, heh?"

He nodded, too uncertain of himself to speak. Tommy Jean put her foot to the floor and the Rolls shot off as he crouched forward, grabbing the top of the windshield.

"No, up, up," Tommy Jean said, holding the steering wheel with one hand, indicating "up" with the other. He raised himself again but this time held his arms out like a scarecrow. She picked up speed. The tires squealed around a curve. He lost his balance, caught himself, and raised himself up again. They raced down another road. A chicken truck was headed toward them and the driver, a woman in a Sunday hat, waved and honked, motioning for them to slow down.

Charles was angry. What the hell was going on? Why did grownups give him so much crap? What was the point of being obedient if he was going to be killed? He started to sit but Tommy Jean grabbed the back of his legs. "You gave your word."

He held onto the windshield. He knew his parents didn't drink, didn't even allow liquor in the house, but maybe Aunt T.J. was a tippler. "This is dangerous," he shouted. She didn't look up. His arms ached but he had to hold on. He was in a semi-crouch now, but he was still standing. The tires screeched but Tommy Jean spoke calmly, as if out for a Sunday drive, even humming.

"Turn here, right? Oh, so much has been added on. Lovely. Harlen and I used to run in those fields. And just look." She pointed to an orchard of virgin trees. She'd lost her damn mind, that was it. How could he get away? Leap out? No, he'd slide down and grab the wheel. As he began his descent, Tommy Jean slowed the car, braking suddenly, tires shrieking in protest.

Charles held on with all his strength, trying to keep from flipping out. His hands hurt from the strain, but he didn't wait to open the door. When they'd come to a complete halt, he jumped out, then remembered to check on his aunt. He looked back only to find her studying the rings on her fingers.

"What the——"

Tommy Jean cut him off. "Now you know what it's like."

"What!"

"For a Black man in the lap of luxury."

He held onto the car. He needed strength. Just how far had she been willing to go to make a point, and where were they anyway? He saw they'd made it clear into Brazil territory and had stopped before a bulldozed field. Bands of darker earth criss-crossed the lighter soil in wide curves. Once he caught his breath, he'd walk back. He wasn't getting into that car again. And to think, he'd trusted her.

He saw her watching him, mildly amused.

Who cared if he sounded rude. "I don't get your point."

"Maybe not, but my brother does."

"What's he got to do with it?"

"He knows."

"Knows what!"

"Some folks are going to hate you for being Black, and the rest'll despise you for inheriting wealth. It's considered to be the easy way."

His voice cracked when he spoke. Usually he hated that but today he didn't care. "So what was that crazy ride about?"

"It was your life, darlin'."

Charles started to walk but stopped as she spoke to his back. "Whether you accept it or not, it's going to be sad and lonely. Your Pa doesn't know any other way to prepare you."

He turned and looked at her pleadingly. "I don't want it."

"Oh, honey. You could no more decide not to have it than you could choose not to have a heart."

He looked out, unjudgmentally, at the field he'd tried to shun. It lay before him, naked and raw, soil the very color of his skin. Spring rains and Pa's crew had left it pliant and moist, ready for seeding. He rested his arms on the car door, weary but still unyielding. "My mind's not cut out for farming."

Tommy Jean leaned across the seat. "Think my mind was cut out to cook? You don't have to be Old MacDonald. You can be one of the wealthiest black men in this country."

"I don't know."

She spread her arms. "Charles, Charles, a black man doesn't walk away from this. All those kin before us, they stood with their backs next to a high wall, put their children on their shoulders, and hoisted them over. Our values, our sense of self worth came down the line from them."

It didn't matter how much they hurt, she said, they just kept looking ahead, and that really took courage. She added breathlessly, "And honey baby, look at what you're starting with. All you've got to do," she snapped her fingers, "is add a pinch of dreams."

Wearily he climbed back into the car. They drove on, eventually heading toward the house. In the front yard, he saw his mother had returned. T.J. insisted she couldn't stay. Reluctant to leave his aunt, he asked where she would go when she left.

"Take time to enjoy this car, head over to Salisbury. I thought I'd stop to see Cousin Jasper." She shook her head as if saying, yes, that's right, ". . . he swore I'd never amount to much." She laughed, slapping the back of Charles's shoulders. "Well, we'll just show little Dr. Jasper, heh, heh."

Enjoying her joke, she unwrapped one of her cookies, and pointing it in an easterly direction, said some uppity colored folks in Salisbury had a sorority, and that early next year they would host a cotillion. "It's really something to see. I bet ol' Dalhia would let me introduce you to that crowd. Your daddy'll have a fit. But honey, those proper little girls . . ." She took a rough bite into the ginger cake. ". . . will eat you up. We'll see. You folks are too serious down here." She told him to let her do the talking, to just pack a suitcase, that she wouldn't go until she helped him escape. "And take a bath, baby. Put lots of bakin' soda in the water, heh, heh."

He looked down sadly, realizing he was still in uniform. His aunt shook her head. " 'Cause baby doll, you look like eight days 'til payday." She laughed loudly. Once inside, he took the stairs up to his room, two at a time.

$$\underline{16}$$

Tamra, Virginia, Seth *September 1967*

THIS ROOM WOULD tell the story. It was here that workmen lay the white, double-pile carpet that Virginia guarded like an ambitious sentry. She nagged some, insulted others. When Virginia requested all shoes be removed before entering the room, a few guests swore they'd never return, but she spoke with such authority that no one but Seth, who'd learned to ignore her, and Big Mama, who accused her of putting on airs, dared defy her.

Virginia vacuumed daily, her body leaning into the Electrolux, humming as she moved along the thirty-by-fifteen breadth of wool. Now in front of the sofa's feet, in between the piano legs, outward on an open stretch of white, round a love seat, a grand wing chair, and twin, squat, marble tables. Only the birth of Christ altered her course. Each December Seth carried in a tall tree, which she and Tamra decorated with strips of lace and plump, white lights. They stuffed sprays of baby's breath under the boughs and hung ornaments from thin wires. On schedule, the tree was denuded and carried out, Virginia's path once again unobstructed.

It seemed only a miracle could force Virginia from her stronghold. Instead it was a most ordinary occurrence: the approach of Tamra's sixteenth birthday. To her it meant a driver's license. To Virginia it was time to prepare

Tamra for Negro society. With the cotillion four months away, preparations had to begin immediately.

Virginia had been elected cochair of the Salisbury chapter of Sigma Delta Kappa, that most prestigious Negro sorority, sponsors of the winter ball. As such, she felt her daughter must outshine other debs. She could even create the gown. To this end, she would sacrifice the pristine space of the living room. Bolts of fabric could be unfurled, tissue-thin patterns cut along bold lines, and bits of white satin and lemon gossamar might be scattered about like the fragments of a torn chrysalis.

But as the struggle for civil rights raged about them, Tamra refused to be pulled into what she and Wadine called "Negro shenanigans." Still, Virginia used any and all opportunities for introducing the subject of the cotillion.

On this particular morning, she prepared Seth and Tamra's favorite breakfast, and while they ate at the kitchen counter, she mumbled. "So humiliating being a cochair and having a daughter who thinks she's too good to——"

Tamra stood abruptly, regretfully abandoning the last bite of canned salmon and melted butter over grits. The legs of the stool scraped the floor as Tamra repeated the party line. "Black people don't have societies to be presented to. Sororities are dated and bourgeois. May I *please* be excused?"

Seth, who'd been reading the *Defender*, covered her hand with his, wondering if she could catch a ride to school with Mr. Barbour. "I've got to stop at the doctor's."

Immediately concerned, Tamra tossed questions at him. Virginia plunged plates into dishwater. "You think she'd be just as concerned about her own mother."

With an air of self-righteousness, Tamra said, "Oh, Mama . . . forget it," and left the room.

Virginia swiped at the counter with a dishcloth. "I'm sick to death of that word." She pronounced it contemptuously. "*Bourgeois*. What does it mean, anyway?"

He didn't look up from his paper. "It has to do with the characteristics of private property owners."

"Think even she'd be glad for that."

". . . With views marked by a concern for material interests, respectability . . ."

"Sounds fine to me."

He raised his head ". . . and a tendency toward mediocrity."

She threw the rag down and poured a mug of coffee, which she tried to sip while shaking her head. "The way she pronounces it . . . *bushwa*." She stopped shaking her head, took a sip, then resumed the shaking. "Like it's some signal . . . (sip) . . . for that nappy-headed Rap Brown to jump from a bush . . . (sip) . . . and inspect this house . . . (sip) . . . see if it's Black enough."

Seth carried his plate to the sink and reached for his car keys. As she washed dishes, her voice brightened. "Maybe you could talk to her. You're so close. You owe me this. I do so . . ."

When the door closed, Virginia continued talking. ". . . wouldn't have to rush to the doctor's if he'd stopped drinking . . . and I'm supposed to just show up, explain about my daughter."

In her room, Tamra slammed drawers, racing to catch Mr. Barbour. She loved hearing his stories about Black scientists, hoped to be one herself, a biologist. As she rushed to straighten her bed, she bent to retrieve the red stuffed dog and pink cushion doll whose wide, tufted skirt and floppy brim Virginia had crocheted for Tamra's eighth birthday. She held the dog to her nose, taking in the familiar bedtime scent. It had been a faithful companion, but it was even uglier now than when first won, on the day Seth led the parade to open the fair. "First Negro to Lead," a county-wide newspaper had proclaimed, and a photographer from *Jet* had taken their picture.

Virginia had been at Seth's side, as was Tamra, marching to "Onward Christian Soldiers." The three of them had practiced together and marched that day in step, their heads erect but cautious. Seth had been warned some whites might make things ugly. None had. She, in her blue party dress, skirt buoyed by crinolines, had known the power of a ship's bow. Where the Wells led, two hundred followed.

At the fair they were placed first on every line, handed sweet, roasted corn on sticks, and at sunset, Seth had won this dog that she, now almost sixteen and battle-ready, kissed before tossing it onto the floor. She planned later to box it or perhaps throw it away.

She'd already covered the pink and white paper of one wall with a montage of Stokely Carmichael (mouth open), Malcom X (finger pointed), and three upraised, disjointed arms with fists in black power salutes. Another poster featured the Supremes in red sequins; eyes bullet-proofed with mascara. Above it all, a cover of *Vogue* featuring a model with carmel brown skin, like her own; full lips pouting and dark, as if colored with berries.

Grabbing her bag and books, she hurried from the room, knowing

Mama would be furious that she hadn't said goodbye.

It was her junior year at Carver. She'd looked forward to attending the school where Daddy was principal, but in the end, she felt being a student in his school had distanced them. He said, no, it wouldn't look right for her to work in his office. Nor was she allowed to stand with him at the end of the day, when he served as greeter and traffic monitor, waving the line of autos along the circular drive.

At first, when she'd passed him in the halls, Seth would give her a vee sign, a quiet reference to the imaginary devils' horns he planted behind her head in family photos. These days, though, upraised fingers could be politically misinterpreted. Winks had replaced the paternal joke. On this afternoon, as her father approached her in the hall, a wink was all she expected. But he stopped to talk, asking her to walk him to his office.

She protested. She'd be late for class. He said sternly, "I'll give you a note from the principal." His solemnity caused her to worry. Did this have something to do with this morning's medical appointment? She didn't have to wait long to find out.

"Your mother's upset," he began.

She sank into a chair. "*Et tu,* Daddy?"

His voice changed to a threatening tone. "Consider yourself on notice. I've heard enough fresh mouth." He stabbed an index finger at his desk. "It ends here."

Tamra couldn't meet his eyes. Instead she concentrated on a sleeve of his jacket, wondering why his suits never wrinkled. She considered him wrinkle-free also, a good Black man who'd been sidetracked by a nagging, henpecking wife. And she hated having him angry with her. When she apologized, he paced in his small office, telling her he was the one who'd convinced Virginia to try to join the Sigma Deltas in the first place, and that she'd taken quite a chance even approaching them about membership. She was one of the few sorors without a degree. "She took a chance on being turned down, just for us."

"Oh Daddy," Tamra said, "that cotillion is like a slave version of *Gone With The Wind.*"

He leaned across his desk, as if groping for patience. Tamra wondered if one of the drawers contained a bottle of Scotch and if he ever locked the door and drank in here, the one room where he could escape Virginia's nagging. She pictured Mama pounding on the door, begging to be admitted, and smiled to herself.

"So, you think this is a joke?"

"Why should I think the idea of some little colored ladies passing themselves off as the local *beaux mondes* is funny?"

He said Virginia would do everything. "All you have to do is waltz out when they call your name. And I'll be beside you."

"But you don't have to wear the gown. And it's more than that. Sororities are just one more example of our divisiveness. That's how the man has fed our slave mentality, teaching that some of us were better than others."

"Hello," Seth called, "you still there?" He rapped his knuckles against her forehead. "Before you go off on another tangent, you should read up on African history. What do you think tribes are all about? Think we had to wait for The Man to teach us divisiveness?"

Seating himself beside her, Seth suggested she really consider Virginia's request. "And stop tossing around empty slogans." His voice softened as he entreated her to go to the cotillion. "Before you enlist in the Black berets, or whatever it is, can't I have one night out with my two best girls? I want you to at least promise you'll think about it. I need some peace in that house."

When the conversation had ended, Tamra felt unsteady. Out in the hall she spotted Wadine on the mourner's bench. But this time her friend wasn't there waiting for a scolding from the vice-principal about her militant activities. She said she'd been waiting for Tamra, that it was so important she'd pretended she was ill so she could miss class. Wadine reminded her that they had to plan for Miss Emory's.

Tamra sank onto the bench dreading even the thought of their home economics class. For tomorrow's exam Miss Emory had asked the girls to prepare dishes and invite their boyfriends for a taste-in. It was the teacher's idea of fun. A boyfriend wasn't compulsory, relatives could attend. But anyone without a beau would be noticed. And they had to give Miss Emory the names of their guests today.

As the principal's daughter, and an honor student, she'd never been very popular and didn't have a boyfriend to ask. When they'd first heard of Miss Emory's plans, weeks before, Tamra had hoped if she learned to dance she'd soon have a steady boyfriend. Wadine had helped her with her dancing, but they hadn't been invited to any parties. There had been no chance to show off her new improved self in time for tomorrow's class.

Wadine wasn't much better off. She'd recently broken up with Beamer, a square-headed youth who, during the school bus outing, had touched Wadine's breasts and then shared the highlights of the act with the basketball team. As a rule, Wadine and Tamra didn't care about their lack of dates or cooking skills. After college, they planned to wear their hair in Afros, move to the motherland, and marry a man who wanted three wives. That way, their children would be sisters and brothers, and the third wife could cook.

At the start of school, they'd requested the masonry class, but their applications had been ignored as pranks. All girls had to take cooking and dressmaking. Tamra didn't even want to think about the fashion show they'd give next year or, for that matter, tomorrow's taste-in. Wadine suggested she invite her father.

"And you could invite Huff and Puff," Tamra said, needling Wadine about the fat twins who'd been pursuing her.

Wadine admitted that suddenly Beamer didn't seem so terrible, that at least he could wrap his cold lips around her FuFu.

Tamra pulled back frowning. "What's FuFu?"

"West African yam paste balls."

"*Ycch!* Beamer's the only one desperate enough to eat them."

They laughed, slapping each other on the back until Wadine pulled away and asked why she'd been with her father.

Tamra, knowing she was veering into dangerous territory, said she might have to do the cotillion.

"You wouldn't. It's against everything we believe in."

She was ashamed of having been weak. "You're right. I won't." Wadine made her swear, and they hooked pinkies, an action as worthy as an oath. When the class bell rang, they rushed to trigonometry, and at the door to the class, as final reassurance, shared Black power handshakes.

When Tamra returned from school, Virginia didn't answer her greeting. The stairs to the attic had been pulled down from the hall ceiling, but Tamra realized that even if her mother was working upstairs, she'd have heard her come in. Virginia knew Tamra hated a quiet house. Often when her parents argued, weeks of silence followed and she'd beg them to speak again. This time, determined to ignore the silence, she headed for the kitchen, for her after-school snack.

The table was clear, no plate of cookies, no glass of Ovaltine. It was a simple chore, she knew that, to stir powder in a glass of milk, lay three cookies on a dish, and fold a napkin into a triangle, a task she could easily perform herself. But it would not have been the same. Set against twelve years of constancy, Virginia's quiet snub caught her up as none of the pleas had.

She pulled three cookies from a ceramic kitty and climbed the stairs, morbidly wondering if animals often went to their deaths with the same sense of dread. In the attic, she found Virginia kneeled before a trunk. "Whatcha doin'?" she asked, crunching defiantly on a cookie.

"What are you doing?" Virginia corrected, never too angry, Tamra noticed, to ignore unenunciated English. Virginia folded a white uniform and said she was preparing a donation for her sorority's garage sale. She added the now-perfect square to a growing pile of uniforms.

Tamra kept crunching. "You don't think you'd like to go back and get a nursing degree? Big Mama says you were practically a miracle worker."

Virginia looked up. "These aren't what you think. I wore these that summer I was in New York . . . Long Island."

Ah, so here was the trap. Her mother never offered details about her past unless she was angry. Still Tamra was curious. The trap door, she knew, was about to slam shut. "Were you a waitress?"

"No."

"Nurse's aide?"

"A maid . . ."

Tamra smiled sarcastically, looked doubtful. Virginia said yes, she'd scrubbed floors for a living.

"You never told me about——"

". . . Or your father or grandmother, but I'm not ashamed of it."

She tried picturing her mother in a New York suburb, lined up waiting for a bus beside other maids in uniforms, like brown kewpie dolls on a lawn. "Somehow I can't picture you saying 'yes ma'am,' 'no ma'am' to some white woman."

"Because you don't really know me."

Tamra turned away. She knew the big lecture was about to be delivered, with the same old small-time ending. Virginia stood up and grabbed Tamra's elbow turning her gently around, pointing to the brown leather Villagers on her daughter's feet. "I learned to say what I had to to survive. I didn't have shoes like those at your age."

"I know, Mama," she said, talking in singsong. "You had to wait 'til the white woman Big Mama worked for gave you her daughter's old shoes. Then you broke the high heels off and walked to school in them, even when it snowed."

Virginia slapped her hard, across the face. They both froze. When Virginia did talk again, her speech was fast, as if to justify her reaction. She said she was tired of hearing that she'd forgotten what it's like to be Negro. "I couldn't forget if I wanted to."

Holding her cheek, Tamra stepped back. "Being Black isn't something you should want to forget. It has to do with how you feel."

"Huh? My attitude has nothing to do with it. You know what that white woman told me on my first day in her house?" She spoke in a mimicking voice: " 'We only have one bathroom, but that's all right, you can use it, too.' " Virginia laughed bitterly. "And she liked me," she added, snickering.

Tamra's head was bowed as she acknowledged that the experience must have been difficult. "I hate that you went through that. But I can't make it better for you by being someone else."

Virginia reached out a manicured thumb and ran it across Tamra's cheek. "I want you to be Tamra. She wasn't born in a ghetto or the projects or on some back road with no shoes. She has had music and ballet lessons——"

"Don't forget Miss Emma's Finishing School for Negro girls."

Virginia continued: "A fine home, a daddy who'd give her the world——"

Again Tamra interrupted, "And a mother who . . .?"

". . . Has only tasted joy in a dream." Virginia tucked the pile of uniforms under her arm and headed downstairs.

She sensed her mother had heard that line in one of her old movies and had saved it for a scene like this. But then, so what, she thought, she'd done the same many times. Maybe imitation ran in the family. She sat on the trunk Virginia had closed and ran her tongue over her teeth, telling herself it didn't matter if her mother was hurt, that any revolution was sure to leave people shaken by change.

She opened a smaller trunk of baby clothes but she didn't look in. She couldn't. Slamming it closed with her foot, she noticed her handsewn brown shoes and shrugged. They were nice but what did that matter? She pictured herself during the Depression, having a white woman fling a pair of homely high heels to her through an open door. Then she saw herself checking out the style and throwing them back. She smiled, scratching the back of her head. Miss Ann wouldn't have kept me on staff very long.

It no longer seemed amusing. When you get poor enough to have to take somebody's old shoes, do you have to be broken first? No, she quickly told herself. There was nothing broken about her mother.

She looked around the attic. It was filled with neatly boxed, carefully selected memories, and she felt small, like a Wonderland character. As if waking from a dream, she walked to the top step and called down to Virginia, knowing that wherever she was, even if she was running the vacuum cleaner, she'd hear her.

"Mama, I'll do it!" The vacuum cleaner stopped. And she whispered, "Damnit. I'll do it!"

And so she would.

17

Tamra and Virginia November 1967

THE DECISION MADE, the women of the Wells household began a rush of activity. Tamra had rehearsals to attend and spins and steps of the traditional cotillion dances to master. Partners were selected. Charles Lane, who she pretended to ignore, was appointed her escort. Whenever congratulated on her good fortune, she assured the envious deb she considered Charles nothing but a body in a suit. And with all the dance routines to learn, little chitchat took place.

Virginia spent every spare moment sewing. Six weeks before the affair, she'd finished Tamra's fully-lined, brocade, hooded cape, as well as her own outfit, and she'd started work on the ball gown. She would barely have time for Tamra's chiffon after-party dress. As for the rehearsal dinner suit, she insisted she'd make that, too, perhaps in black crepe.

Here, Tamra drew the line. Sure Virginia was a great seamstress, but department stores had not only reversed discriminatory policies, Blazer's, a downtown store, encouraged blacks to try on clothes. Virginia had been resisting, but this time Tamra won out: no mail order from the back pages of *Seventeen* or *Glamour*, no patterns or fabric, this time a genuine shopping trip.

"And it's not going to be black" Tamra said as she climbed into the Buick. "The idea of dark people not wearing loud colors is passé." She watched with annoyance as her mother laid her old Dale Evans lunchbox in the back seat. It was probably filled with tuna sandwiches and chocolate milk. She'd hoped they could eat at Blazer's lunch counter. But knowing her mother could only be pushed so far, she pressed her lips shut.

"Plum is popular. That would look pretty on you," Virginia said, easing into the plush seat and starting the car. "And it has nothing to do with your complexion. You're not dark. Wadine is what I'd call dark. You're medium brown with pecan highlights. If you'd use that cream it would bring out your tones."

"That cream is bleach," Tamra protested, but tried to rein in her exasperation. "Mama, the only place you'll find light on me is the soles of my feet."

Virginia concentrated on the traffic. A new signal had been installed on Bedford Avenue, but Tamra knew when it came to the subject of her complexion, it took more than a flashing red light to silence her mother. She'd once heard from a cousin that there had been a family argument over her coloring. Aunt Tennessee, the lightest of the sisters, had asked if she could hold Tamra, whose fair baby skin was the topic of conversation. Virginia was apparently insisting Tamra had Seth's fairer skin. But Tennessee had pulled back Tamra's ear lobe, announcing, "Just as I thought, dark. You can always tell what color they'll be by the backs of their ears." Virginia had flown into a state of denial from which she'd never emerged.

At Blazer's, Virginia looked around and complained everything was mini. Tamra heard music playing. It was "Natural Woman," one of her favorites. She sang along quietly and wondered if someone had put a radio next to the intercom. What a great idea this had been. Shopping was going to be fun. As she sang, she added a little movement, wagging her head along with the words and extending her palms.

"Stop that!" Virginia whispered, pinching Tamra's hand and warning that she was acting "just the way they expect us to." Defiantly, Tamra picked up a purple pantsuit, a navy and orange suede skirt, and a red and hot pink Banlon dress.

A smiling brunette asked if she'd like to try them on and ushered them toward a dressing room. It turned out to be one stall in a line of drab rooms, closed off with faded velvet curtains. Tamra was disappointed. She found it difficult to believe this was what whites had kept her from entering.

Virginia flashed a smile as the salesgirl left, then turned, whispering: "They'll probably mark down everything you try on. We should come back tomorrow for the sale."

She's determined to ruin this shopping trip, Tamra thought as she slipped off her pussycat bow blouse. Virginia said, "If you'd soaked that bra in vinegar it wouldn't be yellow."

"Mama!"

"I don't want to be here any more than they want me to be."

"That's what you said when they opened Meyer's bathroom."

"Hush! Lower your voice."

Tamra giggled and strutted, even though it was "Judy In Disguise," a song she hated, that was playing. But at least she could hear the music back here. This was too boss. She twisted in the suit. The pants were too tight, designed for a flat bottom. But the rust and navy suede skirt was more than okay. It was stiff and heavy but if she unsnapped it just above the knees, it would look great with the boots she'd received for her birthday. Could she soften Virginia sufficiently to talk her into buying this skirt, the dress and (yikes!) red shoes?

Her mother's voice interrupted her thoughts. "You'd think they'd play more refined music."

"Like some of your classical pieces?" Tamra asked sarcastically. "White folks probably hate that music as much as I do."

Virginia's eyes narrowed. "I've played that since you were an infant."

"I hated it then, too. I kept trying to tell you I'd never learn to dance if that was all I heard, but I didn't know how to talk. You probably thought I had gas."

Virginia frowned, disappointing Tamra. She'd hoped her jokes could improve her mother's mood. Getting these extra clothes wasn't going to be easy. "Mama, doesn't being here kinda—I mean kind of—remind you of when they opened Meyer's bathroom?" She slipped the red and pink mini-dress over her head.

"Why should I want to think about that?"

"Getting in was a religious experience."

"It was a pig sty, so just drop the subject."

"You put half a roll of toilet paper on the seat, then you wouldn't let me sit down. And when I washed my hands you gave me tissues to turn on the faucet." As the dress slid over her head, Tamra remembered the dryer and the burst of warm air rushing into her face.

"You even insisted on tissues to open the door. Daddy said if Old Man Meyers had known we weren't going to touch anything, he'd have stopped keeping separate bathrooms years before."

Her mama was smiling, but not, she realized, because of that story. She did look great in the red and pink mini. It was made of Banlon, and when she spun, it opened in a graceful circle before falling into soft flutes, high-lighting her long slender legs; her Mama's legs, Daddy always said. Against her skin, the colors were shocking. There now, she thought, this dress proves it. I am a woman, and Mama knows it.

Moving her thumbs like a hitchhiker, and ponying across the room, she swam through the air with her arms. She pulled Virginia toward the mirror, admiring her grey jersey dress and blue pearls. Mama had gained weight around the hips and it added to her look of solidity. Gently pushing Virginia in front, she placed her hands on her mother's shoulders, bobbing her head back and forth, from one side of Virginia to another.

This time her mama did laugh, adding. "You look right nice." She'd slipped into down home dialect, and Tamra knew she had her. But just then she didn't care about the clothes. She wanted to hold on to Virginia, and she did, for the first time in months, folding herself around the spicy, rich scent of Youth Dew.

"You may only have the dress, young lady," Virginia said softly. "But we'd better get out of here. They probably think we're trying to stick these things in our handbags."

Tamra smiled at the idea of anyone suspecting her mother of hoisting a dress.

18

Seth, Virginia, Tamra *January 1968*

AS ANXIOUS AS she was to run down to show Seth and Virginia how she looked, she was determined to walk slowly. She was still feigning coolness so they'd feel they owed her something for participating in this sham.

She'd tried the gown on before, through numerous fittings, but she knew her mother would be proud of the finished product: A white, diamond-patterned, A-line brocade with an empire waistline. The boatneck collar had been particularly worrisome, but Virginia had mastered it.

Pulling on her elbow-length gloves, Tamra admired her white satin pumps. She let her hair fall dramatically over her eyes. Yesterday, before final rehearsal and sorority dinner, she'd gotten her hair "did," as Seth jokingly said. Chemically straightened, her hair lay flat in a pageboy, close to her head and full at the neck. Tonight, when she moved, there was the added sparkle of tiny diamonds, Virginia's earrings, loaned with a dozen cautions.

It was surprising her parents weren't waiting at the foot of the stairs with their Polaroid. For the last fifteen minutes, they'd been fussing at her to come down, and she loved being the center of their happy attention. These months had been the most peaceful she could remember. Virginia had seemed too busy to notice the drinks Seth poured every evening.

But her stomach tightened. As she reached the stair landing, there was only silence. She moved toward the kitchen door, hearing their voices, low and angry. Pushing the door open, Tamra saw her mother empty a bottle of Johnnie Walker into the sink, heedless of splashing drops on her blue satin dress. Seth stood behind her at the sink, reaching around her. As Tamra entered, he pulled back.

Virginia left the bottle on its side and turned toward her, smiling. Seth used his Amos 'n' Andy voice, "Great guggala buugala, Kingfish. I don't know about this comin' out. You ought to be comin' *in!*" They laughed nervously.

They made it to the car without further disruption. But it was too quiet for Tamra's liking. She sat in the back, on the edge of her seat, watching them closely, gripping the backrest as Seth drove, and tried to make conversation. Her parents responded in monosyllables. She'd analyzed their blowups before, and knew if she could just get them to the hotel, this would boil over. They seldom argued in public.

Tonight, though, Virginia didn't seem willing to let the anger rest. She spoke to Seth through her teeth, the sarcasm charging the air. "Just do me one favor," she started, "don't accept any drinks when we get there."

Tamra interrupted, asking Seth if he'd remembered to bring Chiclets. He ignored her, and Virginia needled him, demanding to know how many drinks he'd had. Tamra begged her to stop.

"I don't blame the child," Seth said. "This is too much, Ginnie. How in the hell can I keep taking this? What's wrong with a few drinks before a party? Am I drunk? Is the car weaving?" Virginia tried to answer, but he cut her off. Tamra felt like a trainer caught between two prized animals determined to tear one another apart. She called out desperately for them to stop.

"Please! If you care about me, stop, now!"

Their anger had carried them beyond her voice. Pointing to a familiar brick building, Seth said he had folks to answer to all week, at the board of education. "I don't need another boss."

"That may be true, for some men."

"Just one more word and I'm getting out," he said, slowing the car. Tamra yelped.

Seth shouted at Virginia. "Your mother worried your daddy to the grave. I'm not going to follow him."

"You already have," Virginia said. "You're as good as dead and just don't know it."

He pulled to the side of the road and was out, the door slamming before a stunned Tamra could call him back. The two women sat, staring out into the twilight. Tamra's voice was laced with sarcasm when she thanked her mother for a perfect evening. "You begged me to do this."

"I don't beg anybody."

"Everything's ruined. I can't walk out there without Daddy."

Virginia insisted he'd be back, but Tamra didn't believe her. He'd walked quickly, away from Salisbury. She could no longer make out his form. Virginia said her only worry was that her sorors might see him. She slid behind the wheel, telling Tamra to get up front with her.

She did as she was told but she wasn't about to be quiet. "I have to say I'm on Daddy's side."

"Well there's a news bulletin," Virginia said, starting the car and looking in the rearview mirror.

"I just don't get it. I've never seen him drunk. He's a saint."

"It's nice you think highly of one of your parents."

"Why are you always on him?" There was a break in the traffic and Virginia pulled the car onto the road.

"That's not something I wish to discuss."

"You don't wish to discuss my life with me?"

Virginia looked away from the road as she responded, and Tamra worried they'd have an accident. Her mother watched her as she spoke about Seth. "Some men see a glass of liquor and can take it or leave it. Not your father. He pretends he can, but I see through him."

Right now, Tamra was thinking, I wish you'd see through the wind-shield. Her mother seemed to read the fear in her face, and considered the traffic. "I spend so many hours watching your daddy, sometimes I look in the mirror to see if I'm still there."

Her mother was always so dramatic, Tamra thought. She didn't want to get her any more worked up than she already was but she had something she had to say. "Papa Lord drank but Big Mama seemed all right about it."

"She suffered in grace." Virginia said, putting her hand to her forehead, a gesture that scared Tamra because it was one of the few times she'd seen her mother look distressed.

Virginia continued, saying Papa Lord's drinking started out just like Seth's. "But by the time my baby sister was born it was getting bad. I remember 'cause I was there. He said he'd always wanted a girl named Virginia. Mama told him, 'We already have a Virginia. There she is.' "

"But Papa Lord worked hard and left that house and a little something when he died."

Virginia turned the rearview mirror down and smoothed the corners of her eyes. "Honey, when a man's a drinker you can't just look at what he has accomplished. You got to ask what he might have done."

So what now? Tamra wondered. Virginia said they would walk into that Holiday Inn, just the way they would have if Seth had been there. Warning Tamra not to tell Big Mama what had happened, she smiled in the mirror, adjusting her face, Tamra knew, to fool the crowd.

At the hotel, they spotted Dr. Jasper Lane, just ahead, in his new Lincoln Continental. This was the first year the sorority had been permitted to host the event in a hotel. The doctor, beaming, seemed to get sheer enjoyment out of driving up and handing his keys to a white valet. She watched the short physician alight from his car, while a tall, muscular figure stepped from the passenger side. It was Charles Lane.

During the rehearsals, he'd ignored her silence, as well as the attentions the other girls showered on him. She was confused about how she felt. She'd never officially forgiven him for that day on the farm, but felt drawn to him.

She watched him now as he moved confidently toward their car, which was next in line. She reached for the door handle, but Virginia instructed her to wait, and a uniformed man swung the door open. A red carpet had been rolled out. "Wow!" Tamra said softly, filling with regret. It could have been kind of a lark, this night. It could have been fun.

As she approached Charles and Dr. Lane, they seemed to be discussing her. "Lovely as usual," Jasper Lane said, adding that he was glad she and Little Charles had become friends. She wondered what Charles had told his uncle.

Dr. Lane left to greet other guests, and Charles timidly smiled. She liked this shy side of him. It was as if he were unaware of how perfect he looked in his tuxedo, like he'd been ordered from one of her mama's Neiman Marcus catalogs.

"You do look real pretty," he said.

As soon as she spoke, she regretted her words: "Do you mean pretty good for a beetle?"

He smiled apologetically. "When this is over will you still dance with me, at one of the parties?"

She couldn't resist teasing: "Aren't you afraid my antennae will tickle you?"

This time he smiled wickedly. "I was hoping they would."

Before they could continue, her mother was at her side, and she was reminded of their dilemma when Dr. Lane inquired about Seth. Virginia tried out an excuse about Seth being delayed. Tamra was usually impressed by the smoothness of her mother's lies. Tonight she worried about whether or not Charles could see through them.

"So . . . uh . . ." he stammered. "Will you save me a dance?"

She barely nodded her head. Right now she had to figure out what to do.

In the lobby, Virginia was stopped by some of her sorors, who had pressing questions about the evening's schedule. Tamra waited off to the side, trying to keep the frown off her face.

Someone's hand plucked her elbow. It was Big Mama, on the lookout for trouble. She wanted to know what had really happened to Seth. Stalling for time, Tamra complimented her on her dress, which had a trail of sequins across the bodice. "I don't want to look out from the stage and see you flirting with somebody's grandfather."

"If I can find one with his hearing aid turned up, maybe I should flirt. You're going to need something in a pair of pants to escort you. Now, you'd better tell me where your daddy is, or honey, I'm going to shake you out of that gown."

She needed no more provocation, but forced herself not to wave her hands as she told of her mother's harsh treatment of Seth. Big Mama listened carefully and Tamra saw Virginia staring at them. Tamra tried to look as if she were making small talk, but she knew it was no use. Virginia would eat her alive for telling.

"We'll see about your daddy," Big Mama said, unfolding her arms. "He's not going to miss this." As she walked off, Tamra felt naked. She knew her mother was watching, even though she appeared to be concentrating on last-minute details. And she wished she could run after her grandmother who had disappeared through the front doors.

The ballroom was fabulous. The sorors had outdone themselves. The stage was decorated with large bouquets of red and white carnations, and a six-foot-high champagne glass, filled with red rose petals, stood midcenter. High above, a reflecting lamp rotated, casting varying hues over the many familiar faces. A platform had been built for the debs and their fathers.

What about her father? She brought her hand to her stomach. What would she do? Virginia headed her way, a frown on her face. An announcement from the mistress of ceremonies saved Tamra from a scolding. "All debutantes and their fathers, backstage, please."

Rushing toward the anonymity of the crowd, Tamra scurried around banquet tables and away from Virginia. Dozens of wide, floor-length, sweeping skirts slowed her pace, and she was surrounded by the smiling faces of Virginia's sorors and their husbands. Tamra wanted to stop someone with a trusting face and ask for rational advice. How could Mama expect her to pull this off by herself? She smiled at the greetings but was unable to speak as she pictured herself waltzing out alone before a stunned crowd.

"Dr. Livingston, I presume?" She looked up. It was Mr. Barbour with a new goatee that gave him a rakish look. "Save your nervousness for your Nobel Prize acceptance speech," he said. "In the scheme of your life, this ball is microscopic." She offered a weak smile. Should she explain her dilemma? Couldn't he escort her? Right, tell a neighbor about trouble in her house. Virgina would peel her skin off. She smiled broadly this time. "You're right," she said and moved on, saying she was needed backstage.

Tamra felt nauseated. Suppose she threw up? Maybe that would be best; then she'd have an excuse not to go through with the evening's events. She climbed the stairs, moving quickly behind the curtains. Backstage, a large photo had been pinned to the curtain with a handwritten sign that read: "Lest we forget." A contingent of Sigma Deltas dressed like flappers, circa 1925, were pictured marching down Pennsylvania Avenue, behind a parade of white, flag-waving suffragettes. She'd seen this photo before in the sorority's history book and remembered that after a heated debate, white feminists had voted to allow the Black sorors to participate in their march, but only if they brought up the rear.

The message and photo was the kind of reminder Wadine might have hung. Tamra missed her best friend terribly, and winced thinking of how angry Wadine had been when she'd learned about her participation in the cotillion. Everyone's angry with me, she thought, and I'm about to make a fool of myself.

Her anxious thoughts were interrupted by her mother's appearance. "Darling, I've found someone to take your daddy's place." Virginia stood with the infamous Beamer, Wadine's old boyfriend, who leered down the front of her mother's dress. She wanted to laugh and scream. Put an ugly man in a tuxedo, she thought, and it's like a giant Halloween surprise. She offered him the same frozen smile she'd been using all night. Better not to alienate him. But she inched away a few steps.

When he suggested they practice, she stared into his mouth. "Yes, you do that," Virginia said. "I'll be out front. It's so nice when a young man can waltz."

Tamra explained she just needed a minute to herself and stood by the curtain, fearful she might ruin her makeup if she cried. Out front, people rose for the national Negro anthem. She tried singing along: "*Lift every voice and sing . . .*" But her voice quivered terribly. She wanted her Daddy. No one would believe the story Mama had cooked up. She would look like a fool. Besides, he'd promised to be by her side. She reached into her tiny, satin handbag and pulled out a Hershey's Kiss. Virginia had stuffed one in there, along with a Kleenex. Well, she told herself, she had no intention of needing that.

Careful not to soil her gloves, she removed the silver foil from the candy and popped it into her mouth. When she noticed Beamer waiting obediently nearby, she felt more kindly toward him. But the glamour and gaiety of the evening sickened her. She glanced around at the other debs. From the start she'd felt separate from them, and she saw that Joanne Clark had also moved away from the others. She and Tamra were the only girls in the group who weren't high yellow. But all she felt she had in common with Joanne, soror Clark's niece from North Carolina, was her brown complexion. With her huge bust, tiny waist, and hair ribbons, Joanne looked like she was headed for a *Porgy and Bess* audition. The night before, at the rehearsal dinner, she had overheard Joanne ask her aunt to cut up her chicken breast. She'd been unable to cut with a knife and fork. Tamra had felt sure their white waitress had overheard them and her own face had grown hot with shame.

She'd known the other debutantes most of her life. Her mother was always dragging her to sorority picnics, Christmas parties, and fashion shows. Now she watched the girls as they preened, smoothing their skirts, fingers hovering over their heads, and practicing bows with their fathers. Everyone of these girls, except Tamra, would probably pledge when they were sophomores in college. She thought them snobs. Tonight, with their self-assurance and grandeur, they already looked like young Sigma Deltas.

The start of the event was heralded when the mistress of ceremonies announced Joanne's name. She'd been scheduled to sing "Ave Maria." Tamra listened to the first sad lines of the song. The girl offered clear, unwavering tones and a hush fell over the room as her voice soared. When Joanne returned backstage, the other debs crowded around, congratulating her. Now, Tamra felt entirely alone.

The debs and their fathers lined up to be presented, and as she watched, a tear ran along her nose. She looked enviously at the chattering girls, thinking none of them had parents like hers. Their fathers led them out, one by one. Audrey Lee, the Diahann Carroll look-alike, had conquered her thinness for tonight. In a bellshaped skirt, she looked womanly as she danced out. Paula Strong, the girl with the prettiest hair, thick and shiny and reaching to the middle of her back, had freed it from its pony tail so that it brushed along her bare shoulders. Paula and her balding father took careful steps. She'd limped since her automobile accident, but now her twisted leg was hidden by her lace skirt.

Jill Vincent, daughter of a long deceased jazz musician, was escorted out by her uncle, a lawyer for the Justice Department. Jill's gown looked dingy alongside the dazzling whites of others. But that was good. Everyone knew it had been her mother's, and this was a great honor. It had been worn twenty-five years before in a Sigma Delta cotillion.

She closed her eyes and prayed silently, apologizing to God for being disrespectful to her mother. She asked for the strength to get through this evening, and remained there, praying, for what seemed like several long minutes before she heard Beamer's voice.

"We're next, Tamra."

"Amen," she whispered, and opened her eyes. At least it was nice that Beamer was tall. She took his arm for a quick practice waltz. She heard the mistress of ceremonies begin to announce her entrance.

"Next, may I present the daughter of our esteemed cochair, Virginia Wells, and her husband, Seth Wells, principal of Carver High."

Beamer took her hand and she placed her left arm high up around him. They began to waltz. But they stopped as a man's hand reached up to tap Beamer's shoulder. And she heard a familiar voice. "May I cut in?"

She smiled deeply. It was Seth. Never had she been more thankful for him. Beamer stepped back and her father bowed. Thank you, God, she prayed, and this time she did cry, bringing her gloved hand to her mouth.

"Will you do me the honor?"

"Oh, Daddy," she said weakly.

The mistress of ceremonies repeated her name. "Miss Tamra Wells."

She and Seth moved through the curtained entrance, dancing up the platform and down again, accompanied by a burst of applause. He held her hand high as she curtsied to the audience, and they returned to a waltz position. The mistress of ceremonies encouraged the crowd, "Don't be stingy with your applause. Aren't they indeed a vision?" The clapping sustained her. She was weak in the knees, and as Seth smiled, she smelled Scotch.

They twirled and she saw the blur that was Virginia and Big Mama, on stage. Beside them, waiting for his cue, was Charles Lane. Seth waltzed her in their direction, positioned himself next to Virginia, and Tamra, as she had in so many rehearsals, curtsied before them. Lifting her eyes, she realized how much her mother resembled Big Mama. Seth took Tamra's hand. But they did not dance again. He joined hers with Charles Lane's, who bowed at her parents as she curtsied. Then away they danced, away from her family.

She tried looking at her parents over his high shoulders but could not see them. As for Charles, she thought he moved a bit woodenly. Was he actually counting their dance steps? The idea of someone else being nervous made her feel friendlier, and he seemed to sense the change in her mood. As the other couples joined them, dancing and twirling, he broke the silence between them. "I just wanted to say that I know, well, a few years ago when you came to my . . . you know, back there at the shed . . . I know I acted like a real jackass, I mean . . . I just wanted . . ."

She pulled her head back to get a better look at him. Smiling benevolently, she said, "Listen, I didn't behave so well myself, I was——"

He cut her off, saying, "A clown."

"No, I meant——"

He said: "Immature, idiotic, desperate, and jealous."

She scowled as he continued unmercifully.

"A pest, a busybody, no . . . a snob, a . . ."

She bristled while he laughed. He had the most annoying sense of humor. "Forget it," she said.

He said that he would and that he accepted her apology. Determined not to let him revel in her annoyance, she tried inventing a clever retort. Failing this, she asked about his plans for next year.

He said he'd attend Holcomb State. She was more than familiar with this local Black college. Everyone in these parts knew his maternal grandfather, who'd presided over the university for several decades, and was known nationally for having steered the institution to eminence as a leading center for research in marine biology. She hoped that she too would one day attend Holcomb.

She'd overheard Daddy say that Charles was resisting becoming a farmer. Who could blame him? Sentenced to life on a farm? She wondered if she could use this against him to make him feel as uncomfortable as he seemed to enjoy making her, but before she could manufacture something mean, he made a joke about it. "Tonight might be my last chance to party with you, unless you come to the farm in twenty years for a square dance."

Neither of them laughed. He closed his eyes for a few seconds, and although he worked at concealing his disappointment, it washed over them both. She thought, as they waltzed on, that it was as if his parents had opted to plant their only son in Lane soil.

"No one ever told me it was going to be this much fun," Tamra said to Joanne Clark. They'd been the last debutantes to break away from the adults and change into cocktail dresses. Tamra was exhilarated at the idea of the after-parties upstairs in the private suites. She'd heard that once the gowns were put away and the parents left behind that this was the best part of the evening.

Her chiffon mini brushed softly on her thighs as they rushed toward the elevator and stepped in, pushing the button for the penthouse. The mortician, Chester Higgins, had rented the place for his daughter's party. Tamra had never really liked Mona, but her face, with its chronic acne, was a familiar one, as it was to any Black family in Salisbury who'd lost a loved one. Mr. Higgins distributed fans to mourners which were updated each year with a new photograph of Mona. Seth loved poking fun at the inspirational quotes, such as "wither thou goest . . ." which also decorated the fans.

All the debs had been invited tonight. It was the biggest after-party. As the elevator doors closed she saw Charles rushing down the hall, signaling for someone to hold the elevator. It was too late, the doors closed. Good. He was so arrogant, as if he was sure she'd fall into his arms the minute he held them out. Well the other girls could just have him.

"He sure is a good looker," Joanne said. Tamra assured her they'd be perfect for each other. By the time the elevator reached the penthouse, it had emptied out and the girls were giggling. But as they rounded the corner Tamra found herself staring into Wadine's angry face. She gestured for Joanne to go on, and she and her former best friend studied one another wordlessly.

She did it, Tamra thought. Wadine's hair was styled in a natural that loomed wide and kinky around her oval face. She realized Virginia had been right. Wadine was darker. And never had she looked lovelier, a fleshed-out, breathing stroke of midnight.

Tamra managed a weak hello, but Wadine did not respond. They walked toward the door of the party, Wadine belligerently in front, wearing a one-shouldered maroon and yellow African print dress, wrapped around her like a sari. Her hoop earrings were as wide as saucers, and except for rings on her toes, she was barefoot.

Mona Higgins opened the door and stared at Wadine. Tamra was sure Wadine hadn't been invited, but that didn't seem to faze Wadine. Beamer grabbed Tamra's arm and pulled her onto the floor. The music was blaring "Expressway to Your Heart," but she had little energy. She was thinking instead of her lost friendship.

Beamer told her to pay attention to the beat and to put some soul into it. "This ain't 'American Bandstand.' " She couldn't respond. Her thoughts lingered on Africa and the end of her and Wadine's dream. The evening's magic had been broken.

When the music ended, Beamer rushed toward Wadine. Tamra leaned against a wall, staring out the picture window with its view of a parking lot and, further beyond, the lights of the town. She heard the doorbell ring, looked around, and realized Mona was backed up into a corner, whispering to Huff and Puff. Why did the twins always share a girl? When the bell rang again, she went to the door. It was Charles and he seemed relieved to see her. "Looks like I'm here just in time for a dance," he said.

As much as she wanted to dance with him, she was determined not to. He was so sure of himself. Anyway, who knew what her parents were up to. Wouldn't it be awful if Daddy had started drinking again. "No thanks," she said. Charles remained standing near her, his hand outstretched, looking about the room with exaggerated movements.

"It's not like anyone else is breaking his neck to get to you."

Before she could respond, he'd moved off, toward the crowd of revelers, and directly over to Joanne Clark. A match made in heaven, she told herself, disappointed that he hadn't insisted on claiming his dance.

She watched as several girls made excuses to wander over to where Charles and Joanne danced, hoping, she knew, that he would pick one of them when the record stopped. They're like lemmings, she thought, then smiled. No, more like white corpuscles responding to a wound.

Her first thought was that she could finally rush out to find her parents, but she didn't want Charles to think he'd ruined her evening. Mama and Daddy would just have to do without her a while longer. Defiantly, she plopped on a sofa and sat through Marvin and Tammy's "Your Precious Love" and the Temptations', "I Wish It Would Rain," working hard to keep her eyes off Charles and his partners.

When she felt she'd remained long enough to convince him he meant nothing to her, she stood, and prepared to thank Mona for inviting her. But Beamer grabbed her arm, insisting she dance with him. She declined, but he ignored her refusal and pulled her onto the dance floor. She'd either have to dance or make a scene. Lines were forming, boys on one side, girls on the other. Tamra stood across from Beamer.

"Come on, loosen up now, Miss Tamra," Beamer yelled. The girls madisoned across the floor, shuffling in one direction, boys in the other. As they danced, they sang along with Gladys Knight's, "I Heard it Through The Grapevine."

By the time the record had ended they'd all worked up a sweat and no one seemed prepared to stop. A chant went round: "Your house, your house, your house is on fire. Your house, your house . . ." She was soon lost in the chant, the stomping, the rhythmic clapping of the crowd. Her neck loosened. Her head bobbed as if beating drums. She was moving for sure now. Couples shifted up and danced down the middle of the line. When it was her turn to make her way between this stomping, soulful track, she jumped out, froze for a second, and slapping her thighs with a dramatic flair, sent her chiffon skirt flying. Someone called out: "Get down, principal's daughter."

It was Wadine, a long, skinny, sassy leg protuding through a slit, hoops catching the light. Elbowing her way over, she pounced beside Tamra. They didn't smile or greet one another, but just as they'd practiced so many nights together, they did the possee, taking mean steps, like bad dudes strutting into town, then quicker, like they were in pursuit. She saw Charles watching, a smile of approval on his lips.

Extending a hand to Wadine, they slapped five before moving on down between the throbbing lines, dancing again to music, pointing their index fingers and moving like the Temptations, swinging on one foot, then to the other, repeating the chant they'd practiced so many nights together: "To the bush, heeey! To the bush heeey! Ooh, Ahh. Ooh Ahh. To the bush!"

19

Tamra and Virginia *February 1972*

BY HER JUNIOR year at Holcomb State, Tamra could segue into the rhythms of black dialect without missing a beat. On this Sunday afternoon she sat in her unfamiliar bedroom in the Wells's new split-level house, shouting into the phone: "What chu talkin' 'bout, girl?"

"You heard me." It was her dormmate, Iona, delivering the news like a streetwise reporter. "He exposed you to the whole school and you betta own up to the shit."

"Not while I'm breathin' " Tamra said, her fierceness diminished by a volley of coughs. She and Iona, like many of their fellow students, were recuperating from the Siamese flu, which had swept the nation. She flipped through a text of *Mind and Brain*. She'd learned to reach for a book when Iona called.

"You'd better tell yo' folks," Iona demanded.

Studying a colored illustration of the brain, Tamra wondered where in her own convoluted mass she stored all the problems Iona tossed at her. She imagined the mental electricity this conversation aroused, a barrage of high-voltage, chaotic impulses dancing in her. Now, just where would they dance? Her finger scanned the illustration and stopped at the neo-cortex. Yes, she thought, right there. She wondered if each fold in her brain stored information on specifics, like the subject of cheating or angry boyfriends or news not to tell parents or, she wondered, were ideas organized by emotional content? And was it possible for too much bad news all at once to overload the system and render a person insane?

"Somebody'll tell your folks, better be you."

"Not on yo' life," Tamra said, working to erase rather than store that bit of information. But then she decided to let the idea settle in gently. Just how bad could it be? Their English professor had accused her of writing a report for Leon Houston, the young man she was dating. Professor Johnson had posted Leon's paper about Gerard Manly Hopkins on a bulletin board, with the words, "SOUNDS LIKE THE WORK OF MISS TAMRA WELLS," scrawled across the top in red, and graded 'F.'

Alongside this nightmare hung the paper she'd submitted in her own name, typeface identical, emblazoned with a matching 'F.' Professor Johnson, who was blind, was held in the highest esteem by both faculty and student body. And he'd always been so interested in her; so interested, it turned out, he'd probably caught on the minute his assistant began reading Leon's paper.

Squeezing her eyes shut, she pictured the entire campus discussing her, laughing. She'd hoped to be remembered as problem-free, a faultless scholar. Now this. But the truth was Professor Johnson couldn't prove anything. And that liar Leon wouldn't admit to his mother's name.

Wait a minute. She didn't know if her brain could handle the subject of Leon. Should he be packed into the same cerebral fold? This was, after all, classified information. She'd never actually told Leon what she'd done for him. She'd not only committed the crime but been her own accessory.

Leon had simply asked her to deliver his paper. She'd scrutinized his atrocious grammar, his unambitious theories, and redone the essay for him. She tried to stop thinking. When that didn't work she began to slowly take in Iona's blistering monologue.

". . . can't prove squat . . ."

And she tried to keep the subject of Leon distinct from the news about the term paper. Aha, so that's why Leon hadn't returned her calls. She probably should have consulted him on her editorial changes. Oh Lord, would he quit her in front of the whole school? She sifted through her memory, calling up the prayer she and Virginia had recited on their knees during her childhood.

Now I lay me down to sleep . . .

While Iona raged on, ". . . piecea crap . . ."

How had Leon learned about the paper? Could he have run into Professor Johnson?

Pray the Lord my soul to keep . . .

". . . and if your ass is finally ready for some advice . . ."

It wasn't like Leon was some prize or something, with his ex-wife and kids and graveyard shift at the shoe factory. He'd invited her to move into his mobile home with him. *Arrghh!* Mama would faint at the sight of her daughter in a trailer.

If I should die before I wake . . .

"And who the hell kin prove otherwise? . . ."

But spring's coming. Better to have Leon than no one.

"Are you with me? Tamra, have you heard one word I've said?"

"Right on! Peace, sister."

"Shalom aleichem," Iona hurled at her, and they hung up. She slammed the textbook down. I need Wadine, she thought. But her best friend had moved to New York to attend NYU. Wadine's mother thought Black colleges were fine as long as you got your degree from an "established" school. She hoped her friend would not hear about this debacle. Wadine always scolded Tamra about being too good to people who didn't appreciate her, although she'd never objected when Tamra had done her laundry.

She opened her bedroom door and listened for the electric bickering she'd grown accustomed to hearing between her parents. Silence. Recently, they seemed to be getting along. That was too strange. She'd once worried that with her away at college most of the year, unable to distract them, their rage would boil over. Instead, they'd become allies. But maybe they were fussing and she was too far away to hear them. The idea almost comforted her. In the hallway, she glanced back at her room, so elegant, so blue. She hated it.

Seth and Virginia had picked her up last week and driven to this neighborhood, which was all white, except for them. They'd wanted it to be a surprise, they'd said, and had led her to this room. She shuddered thinking about it. Moving men had walked through the interiors of her old room and touched her past.

In the den, she found Seth in an easy chair, a shot of Scotch in his hand; Virginia, on her knees, scraping debris from the metal runner of the glass sliding door, paused to frown at Tamra. Maybe she'd never grow accustomed to seeing Tamra in an African hairdo and clothing. But why shouldn't she? Her wardrobe was authentic, had belonged to a girl from Liberia who'd loved swapping her "original" clothes for Tamra's Shetland sweaters and A-line skirts.

Tamra rummaged through the refrigerator for a soda while listening to Virginia, who said she'd walked past her room while she was on the phone. "And young lady . . ." Tamra swallowed hard, wondering which detail she'd overheard. ". . . Do you mind telling me what language you were speaking?"

Breathing easier, she walked toward Virginia. "Does it really matter if the runner under that door is clean?"

"One day, when you're offered thirty-five or forty thousand dollars for this house, you'll be thankful I kept it up for you." She shook her head as she returned to her work. "You never appreciated how hard I worked keeping a clean house. No white folks are going to call us dirty niggers."

"I do appreciate your work, but not because it rates the white folks seal of approval. Why can't we———"

Virginia cut her off to ask Seth if he wanted a refill, and Tamra looked questioningly at her mother. Seth ignored them both. He was watching Cronkite's special on the war. "I don't get it," Virginia continued, returning to her most querulous voice. "Why did we pay for extra French lessons if you come home sounding like Pigmeat Markum?"

Tamra stood before Seth, mouthing her answer. "Maman, *ce n'est que d'argot.*"

Seth listened, smiling. "She says, it's only slang."

"*Je veux parler la langue de mon peuple,*" Tamra continued.

"She wants to speak the language of the people."

She laughed. "Right on, Daddy." Furthermore, she explained, she'd only learned French so she wouldn't make a fool of herself when she began her senior year as an exchange student at the Institute of Science in France. She'd won the Sigma Delta's Eslanda Goode Robeson Science Prize, named for the woman who had been one of the first Black analytical chemists and the wife of Paul Robeson. The award money would pay for three years of study, including her master's in microbiology. Tamra's picture had been in *Jet* and on the front page of the *Defender.*

"That reminds me," Virginia said, "we've got something for you." She walked toward the china cabinet, and Tamra perched on the arm of Seth's chair, surprised by the rolls of fat around her mother's waist.

Seth gestured toward the television screen where Vietnamese children screamed and ran for cover. "Your cousin Sherman should be saving those kids," he said. Aunt Florida's son had disgraced his family, running off to

Sweden to avoid the draft. Someone had told Virginia he'd taken up with a blonde.

She handed Tamra a bank book with several entries of tiny gray numbers on the first page. It was fifteen hundred dollars. A slip of paper inside read: "We're really proud of you."

Tamra jumped up. "This is fabulous! I can't believe it! Thank you. Thank you. Thank you. I can go around the world with this."

"Stop in and see Sherman," Seth said. "Don't lend him money."

"I wanna see Nigeria, Ghana, Ethiopia, Kenya and . . ."

"You've got the wardrobe," Seth muttered.

Noticing Virginia's annoyance, Tamra quickly added, "Venice, Japan, and India."

Seth lifted a finger, signaling that he had some wisdom to share. "Indians celebrate a holiday your mother would love."

Virginia, back at her work, asked why he thought so.

"It's called Diwali, the festival of lights. They welcome the gods, scrub everything, even the storm pipes and . . ." Virginia turned on the small battery-operated vacuum, drowning out Seth's words.

"This is *sooo* perfect." Tamra spun on one foot, waving the bank book in the air. She could take advantage of the student fares, fly to Luxembourg for $287. Seth rose unsteadily to get another drink. Tamra wondered if she should help, then decided offering assistance might humiliate him. He'd been diagnosed with diabetes last year, and sometimes it seemed the disease and the liquor were eating him up. "Who shall I call?" Tamra wondered.

"Whom," Virginia corrected.

It had to be a friend who'd appreciate how truly boss this gift was. Too bad Wadine wasn't around. "Call Iona," Virginia suggested, but Tamra couldn't do that. She'd just make fun. Iona seemed to believe the only way to be Black was to be poor and angry. She called Tamra a Black American Princess.

Maybe she'd tell someone in the dorm. She asked Seth if he planned to ride back with them. He was definitely in no shape to drive. "I wanted to see this show," he said. It was only a rerun but she understood. Seeing Black folks on television was fun, even if Moms Mabley *was* in a maid's uniform.

Daylight was fading as she walked down the hall, pausing at the doorway to her parents' room. She went in, hoping to find some answers, something about her father's job change. She thought their story about his promotion to office work at the board of education lacked credibility. Seth had loved being a principal. And what about their sudden move, from a neighborhood they'd loved, without ever mentioning it to her?

The room was as hushed as a tomb. She glanced at the top of the bureau where several official-looking envelopes were stacked. There wouldn't be anything interesting there. Mama always hid important papers. She turned instead to the walk-in closet, where each outfit was covered with clear plastic, the overhead bulb giving the clothing an ethereal glow. Here and there, sleeves hung like dead limbs.

An entire corner was filled with cartons. In one, a stash of Scotch, enough to last even Daddy for a year. She reached in, grabbing a bottle, tucking it under her arm, and her elbow hit against a pile of Virginia's shoeboxes. Dozens of candy bars scattered across the closet floor. She opened another shoebox, more candy. It was as if her mother was starting a business. No wonder she'd gained so much weight. Quickly she gathered the spillage and rushed from the room.

She hid the fifth of stolen Scotch in her suitcase. It would remain unopened. Few substances confused her more. As a scientist, she understood the world was full of mysteries, but most could be puzzled over, and in the end understood. When it came to liquor she had no scientifically-based evidence, no laws to prove her realities, only a scattering of anecdotal evidence. But of one thing she was certain. Liquor was key to her family, not just her father but to all the men her aunts had married.

They'd all been gentlemen who'd made something out of their lives, but it was as if this liquid ran through their veins. Her hope was that in France, once she'd finished her senior year and then earned her master's, she could become a member of a team researching a genetic link to alcoholism. Maybe one day she'd have some answers to her own life.

Back in the kitchen, Virginia pointed to a large paper bag. "I gave you all the leftover yak," she said. It was a name they'd made up years before, when Virginia had smothered spaghetti noodles with leftover rib meat, raw chopped onions, and soy sauce.

Tamra kissed her daddy good-bye and he offered to take her suitcase to the car, but she declined. "I'm a Mojumbee woman, built to carry baskets on my head, a baby on my shoulders." Seth settled into his seat. She glanced back at his figure, lit only by the glow of television.

On the front steps a black cat passed between her and Virginia with something struggling in it's mouth. Tamra bent closer. "It's a mouse. Must be his dinner."

Virginia turned toward Dr. Norley's dark house. "Maybe they forgot to feed him. They're out tonight." Virginia and Mrs. Norley, one of her white neighbors, had become fast friends. According to what she'd told Tamra, she'd even suggested to her sorors that this woman be invited to the weekly bridge games. The sorors had not responded kindly.

In the dark car, Tamra began to brood over the Leon term paper mess until she fell asleep, then awoke to find they were about twenty miles from campus, driving along a dark country road. She saw that the red fuel light was flashing as Virginia turned into a gas station. Seth had gone out earlier for fuel, but now Tamra guessed he'd probably spent the time in Chicken Little's. She knew one thing for sure. This station looked deserted. A dim light shone in the tiny office.

"Maybe I should call Seth," Virginia suggested.

"He'll be too far gone to find the keys, let alone the car." Tamra had ridden with him dozens of times while he'd been intoxicated, but she didn't feel right about it tonight. Perhaps it was seeing his instability when he'd risen from his seat. "How about someone from school?" she suggested. She told Virginia to wait in the car while she looked for a phone.

"Not by yourself," Virginia said, climbing out and catching up with Tamra.

She wondered how her mother would ever allow her to travel the world alone. They walked around to the side of the building and tried the door. Virginia warned, "Don't you dare go . . ." But Tamra had walked in. There was no phone, nothing. Great. Well, maybe it was. This way they could sleep in the car or camp out in these chairs for the night, and she could go directly to the lab in the morning, forestalling any of the ribbing she'd have to tolerate about the paper.

She convinced her mother to sit with her. There was probably less than a gallon of gas left. "It's better than being stranded on some dark road." They pushed the two chairs against the wall, but Virginia wanted to tie a handkerchief on the antenna. "Okay, in a minute," Tamra mumbled. She could fall back asleep easily. Virginia was determined to do it now. Someone might drive by and offer them help. She headed for the door and Tamra stood to join her. They stopped in their tracks. A pickup was cautiously backing up.

Two white men got out and inspected the empty Lincoln. Inside the office, Tamra and Virginia appraised them, the truck's headlights shining first on one man, dressed in an orange hunting vest and a cap, its flaps pulled over his ears, and then on a second man, short and stouter, wearing a T-shirt and pants that hung below his belly. The two walked around the car like shoppers at an automart, but when they looked up, the short, big-bellied one pointed at the women.

She heard a click. Virginia had turned the lock. One of the men laughed, as if he'd heard it, too. Now he knew they were afraid. For a minute, the two on the outside and the pair inside studied one another, then the men moved in, talking softly.

"Hi, gals," one called. She couldn't tell who was speaking. "Something wrong with your car?" They didn't answer.

The man in the hunter's vest rapped on the glass, but Virginia and Tamra had turned to a side window. "That old one look like Elsie the Cow, don't she, Mort?"

So, one of these animals had a name. What price would Mort exact from them?

The other man asked, "Don't you girls wanna take us for a ride?"

Mort spoke: "The car is dandy, but I like what's in here." He'd walked to where she and her mother stood and pressed his face to the glass, distorting his lips, his tongue darting in and out. Then he licked the pane.

The hunter spoke softly, as if experienced at luring scared animals. "Hey you, Smoke Meat." He's talking to me, she thought. Virginia moved her to another corner.

"Here moosie, moosie, come on out and play," the hunter said. "We just being friendly. That's what youse niggas want, ain't it?"

Mort had dashed to where they could see his lips, like suction cups on the glass, making white outlines of saliva and grease. She saw the large pores of his cheek. When the hunter pulled the handle of the door, Tamra jumped. Virginia pushed her down into a chair and spoke, barely moving her lips. "Keep your eyes on me, baby girl. Don't look."

"Hey, you, Elsie, I could mount you." It was Mort again, the hunter laughing wildly. "You want me to give it to you like a cow, Grandma?"

She tried keeping her eyes on Virginia, but Mort and the hunter shoved at the door. She flinched each time their bodies hit the glass. "Come on, open, you nigga dog face bitches."

Virginia crossed her legs. The chain handle of her green purse dangled from her wrist. She spoke as if Tamra had to read her lips. "Tell me what you'll study in Paris." Tamra's eyes drifted away. The hunter had unzipped his pants and was reaching in. Virginia grabbed her chin. "Look at me! Now!"

She forced herself to stare at her mother's mouth. "They will not get in here. They can have the car. Your daddy bought us that one, he'll buy us another." Her voice quivered slightly. "Now, I want you to tell me about your studies. At me! Now!"

"Uh, uh . . ."

"What kind of science is it?" Virginia asked.

"Genes. I, we isolate. Genes carry info———" She sucked her breath in. Mort and the hunter walked off, toward their truck.

"Keep talking," Virginia said.

"Ah, I'm going, ga, going to be looking into the . . ." The men had reached their truck but had not climbed in. They took something out and moved back toward the office. Oh God, she could see. Mort swung something, yelling like Tarzan. It was a crowbar. They were going to break the glass. They'd rape them. Kill them. Her mother, her fine, sweet mother. "Oh God, oh God, ah, ah, ah," Tamra panted.

"At me!" Virginia said. "Come on. Now that's right. Good girl. Just what I want you to do."

She couldn't. Not another word. She was breathing too hard. Crying. Virginia's hand reached up, shielded Tamra's face, jerked it backward, the movement sending her purse flying across the room as the crowbar struck the glass repeatedly, shattering it.

"Hey there!" It was another man's voice. Maybe someone powerful, maybe armed. Maybe Daddy. To rescue them. She peered into the dark. The men had stopped, were also looking. A small, thin, Black man in pajamas ran from behind the station. Damn! He had only one arm. He was shouting at Mort and the hunter. "What in the hell do y'all think you're doin'?"

Virginia and Tamra moved to the webbed glass to look out. The hunter was talking: "Now, Uncle Tommy. You don't wanna mess with us. Why don't you jes' go on back to bed." The men laughed.

"The hell I will," the man said. "I ain't goin' nowheres 'til you off this property." Mort rushed at him, grabbed him by the collar, and pushed him up against the shattered window, the stripes of his pajama top pressing into the glass.

"You want a ass-kicking, boy?"

"Well, you got three witnesses," the one-armed man said. "Or maybe you gonna kill all of us."

Tamra gasped. Virginia banged the clasp of her bag against the window. Following her lead, Tamra tapped the back of her hand against the pane, her high school ring clanking. Virginia raced to open a drawer, and crouching behind the desk said, "Hello, operator." She spoke loudly and in her most elegant English as she pretended to talk into a phone. "Get the police. Someone's trying to kill a white woman."

Mort had been slapping the one-armed man. He stopped, angrily pushing him to the ground.

Virginia continued. "I hear her baby crying."

"You nigga chickenshits," the hunter yelled.

They ran for their truck, climbed in, and roared off.

She and Virginia were outside before the one-armed man had picked himself up. "Are you hurt? Oh, thank God," Virginia said.

Tamra extended her own shaky hand. "Thanks, brother." He stared at her without responding.

"Can you get us to a phone?" Virginia asked. "I want to call my husband. They'll come back for you."

The man waved his hand. "They ain't comin' nowheres, not with all this mess. I know just who they is, too." He stepped over some glass fragments. "No ma'am, no phone, just got a little place in the back. What you ladies doin' here, anyway?"

When Virginia had explained, the man said there was no gas at this station. They'd stopped delivering weeks before. But he had a piece of hose and said he could siphon from his truck. It could get them to the next service station and a phone where they could call the sheriff for him. When he'd finished, Virginia gave him twenty dollars and she and Tamra drove off.

As the car moved back into the night, Tamra clenched her teeth. Suppose Mort and the hunter were waiting? The wide fields looked eerie in the dark. By the time they'd pulled into a gas station, she felt empty. She'd wanted her mother to comfort her, make her feel better. But Virginia sat quietly as the gas was pumped, and without a word, went to the phone.

Tamra tried smothering her sobs, knowing her mother did not respect weepers. Later, when they'd pulled up in front of the dorm, Virginia turned to her. "Just forget them. They don't exist," she said.

"I hate white people."

"Niggers come in all colors."

"It's the white ones I hate."

"Go ahead and fill yourself up with it, then you'll be equal with that sort.

Right now they're only up to your belt loops." Tamra kept crying, and when she looked up, saw Virginia watching her with compassion. "Sometimes I worry about you."

"Let me see if I've got this right. Some peckerwoods try to attack us, and you worry about me because I cry?"

"They were worse than some, but not all that different from the ordinary." She looked away, as if talking to the distant trees. "Some manager in a supermarket or a delivery boy or Mrs. Norley's sister . . ." She paused, as if trying to contain herself. "What I'm saying is, it'll just come at you from nowhere. Or you set your mind so you'll never be surprised. Accept life for what it is."

"And what's that, Mama?"

Virginia looked at her, as if debating whether she should tell her. Finally she said, "A series of indignities."

"I swear, if things don't change I'm never coming . . ."

Virginia shrugged. "France, the Soviet Union, the Chesapeake . . . won't make a difference. We're despised the world over. Know what? Bet even those Africans don't think too much of us." She nodded her head, agreeing with her own words. "The Jews say they're the chosen people. We're the unchosen. In the end there's only one thing to do: Make the times in between as sweet as can be. That's all, darlin'." Virginia now wore an ironic smile. "Wasn't it something? The two of us couldn't stop them, but an old man with one arm did."

They carried the bag through the silent dorm. Virginia insisted she couldn't stay the night, Seth would need her. This time, she promised, she'd stay on the highway, and she'd ring Tamra's phone twice, let her know she'd arrived safely.

After a sleepless night, Tamra went downstairs and found a tiny white box of candy in her mailbox. They were her favorites, pralines from the Candy Emporium. Virginia must have been saving them as a surprise. She'd written on the box in her neat, practiced hand, "For the times in between."

20

Tamra and Charles *February 1972*

SHE'D HAD TROUBLE sleeping, nightmares of the hunter stalking her and Virginia, and next week she had to appear before a disciplinary committee about the Hopkins papers. This required mental preparation, plus a phone call to Leon to see if he was finished with her. What would he say? She felt such deep shame about what she'd done that her body was weighed down by it. But for the moment, those concerns had to be placed on hold. No more excuses. She had to get to the lab, now. As a junior lab assistant she was expected to prepare bacterial cultures for the fifteen nursing students who, in three weeks, would begin a series of arduous exams. She'd procrastinated until finally the flu had interrupted her schedule. There wasn't a moment to spare. The process of isolating samples could take up to three weeks.

Outside the ivy-covered Coventry Hall, she couldn't resist smiling when she recognized Charles Lane's gray Mercedes truck. It had just the right touch of rustic elegance to describe who he was—wealthy, good-looking, self-assured—but in such an understated manner it was hard to hold it against him. Perhaps because of his modesty he never allowed himself to be the center of attention but was, instead, always on the sidelines, with that self-mocking smile. Tamra once said she could tell who the new women on campus were by their vacant, moony-eyed responses to Charles. Anyone who'd been around long knew he was as attainable as a Hollywood idol.

She wondered why he was in the science building at seven-thirty in the morning. As a senior Ag major, all his classes were in Krauss hall. Not that she kept up with his schedule. His reason for being there was his concern. She had work to do, and nothing, not even Charles Lane, must stop her. Rushing down the stairs, she entertained the hope that the binocular microscope was available. She'd need both lenses for her work.

From the hallway she could see into the bacteriology lab, where Charles worked at one of the slate tables, peering into the double lens of the very microscope she needed. Wishing she'd done a better job of picking out her Afro, she patted the back of her head as he turned to greet her.

Although she tried to restrain her smile, it didn't really matter. He'd quickly turned back to his work, writing carefully with a pencil. Gesturing toward the petri dish, he offered an explanation, without looking up. "The dean let me borrow his key. Some of my hogs stopped giving milk."

"So you're worried about mastitis," she said, signaling that she understood his concern about an infection capable of spreading quickly. She tried moving about silently, so as not to disturb him. Slowly unlocking her closet, she pulled out a lab coat. In the three years she'd been at Holcomb, Charles had rarely done more than wave at her. He seemed to hold it against her that she'd said no, all those years before, when he'd asked her to dance. She couldn't blame him. She held it against herself, also.

She found it difficult to concentrate on gathering her equipment with him in the same room, but she tried, unlocking a cabinet and removing a monocular microscope. Next, she gathered fresh slides, saline, and a Bunsen burner. Sliding a cabinet door open . . . she watched his broad back . . . and did a Gram stain . . . admired the nape of his neck. Had she ever seen one quite so perfect? She checked to see if she had a coccus, looking through her lens to observe cell structures . . . and up again, thinking he might be watching her. He was.

Her task this morning was to isolate *Staphylococcus aureus*, which looked like clusters of grapes, and *Neisseria gonorrhea*, shaped like kidney beans, generally a simple task. But instead she scolded herself anew for declining his long-ago invitation. When she'd read *War and Peace*, she'd sobbed as Natasha danced with the prince. How could she have said no?

Through the years, she'd watched Charles from a distance, making his way through life with his girlfriend, Claudine. Tamra could almost see her

through the microscope lens—as she rode on a float of white chrysan-
themums—her oval face surrounded by a wide shimmering Afro, the
school's first dark-skinned homecoming queen. Last term Claudine had self-
destructed. She'd been caught snorting coke in a public restroom. Tamra
looked over at him now, wondering if he still loved Claudine and liking the
idea that he might.

She adjusted her lens, noticing the long thin rods of . . . *Escherichia coli?*
She panicked. What were *they* doing there? She'd never get the plates ready.

He put his equipment away. Shouldn't she tell him she needed that
microscope? The words were hard to get out. He pulled off his wire-frame
glasses. "I just heard someone talking about you and I was fascinated by
what you did."

He had to mean the paper. The thought of people discussing her was
difficult to consider. "I'm glad you were so fascinated," she said, trying to
sound lighthearted, but it came out angry. The seaweed extract had solidified
and now looked like gelatin. She checked the temperature gauge to see
whether the incubator had stabilized at thirty-seven degrees. At least she
could do that right.

As he walked toward her, she was reminded that he was one of the few
men who actually towered over her. He stopped about a foot away from her
and stood watching. When he didn't speak, she shrugged and made another
trip to a cabinet, but she already had more equipment out than she'd ever
use.

His voice was a pleasure to hear, even when it probed too deeply. "Tell
me, Tamra Wells," he started. "We liked each other a lot once. Other than
some kid stuff, what happened? What about me makes you so angry?"

She walked away, concerned that her hands might shake and that he'd
hear the test tubes rattling. "What gave you that idea?"

"I can take criticism. Go ahead, tell me."

Sure he could. He, who was so accustomed to being loved by all. It
might actually be refreshing for him to hear an unflattering comment; not
that she had one. As she reached the counter, Tamra banged into the edge.
One of the test tubes fell from the holder and broke. They both stooped to
pick up the pieces.

"Oh heck," he said, bringing his index finger to his mouth.

Here was just the excuse she'd been waiting for. Tamra wanted to touch
him, and this time she wouldn't let the opportunity pass. "Let me see," she
said.

He insisted it was just a scratch, that he wasn't bleeding. But he held his finger out anyway. She assured him, "You're right. It's only a scratch." But she held onto him, fighting the urge to lick the tip, and he looked as if he fully expected her to. When they heard voices in the hall, they stood with a jerk. The voices passed, and he remained up close, his jacket open, the buttons of his overalls were only a few inches from her teeth. She could bite them off for him.

"Well, Tamra Wells, what if I asked you to dance?"

"Here?"

He laughed and she watched him, thinking, With a big man like this, this tall, with a voice so deep, you could probably feel him laughing all the way down to the small of his back. He said, "I read your paper."

Her face grew warm. That stupid paper. She turned to peer into her microscope, wanting to say, "hey, hold on brother man, you were saying something about a dance . . ." but she said instead, "What about my papers?" putting an emphasis on the plural.

"Everyone knows you're smart," he said, adding that it was no surprise to him that she could write two papers about the same crazy poet. "But what impressed me," he continued, "was that you cared so much about Leon, you were willing to cheat for him."

Offended by the word *cheat*, she asked, "Why should it surprise you that I could care about someone?"

"You're hard to read. A fellow would have to spend some time with you . . . to get to know you."

She had been right, he was flirting, and she wouldn't let him stall a minute longer. She had work to finish. She said an acquaintance was having a party on Friday.

"I'd love it," he answered immediately.

"Why don't you pick me up at eight?"

He had taken off the lab jacket but paused, appearing almost gleeful. "I knew if I ate my vegetables and said my prayers, one day you'd make time for me." Retrieving his notebook from the counter, he left.

She waited until his footsteps receded down the hall before rushing to the closet mirror to study her face. Too bad she'd looked. The sleep loss had left her with haggard circles beneath her eyes, and her lips were cracked and dry. But Charles Lane had actually asked her out. And he would pick her up at the dorm. Everybody would see them together. She wanted to jump and yell but worried he still might hear her.

Why couldn't she just have dropped that uptight professional demeanor long enough to show him the real Tamra? She pictured herself sweeping in wearing a pair of hip-hugging jeans, red high heels, a thin red tie falling between her breasts, and nothing else but an unbuttoned lab coat. Of course, her Afro would be picked out, lint-free, and her lips glossy and parted. Placing a hand on her hip and wagging her head, she spoke sassily as the reflection she had imagined.

"I don't know about war, Charles Lane," she said, pausing for effect, "but I sure could give you some peace."

21

Tamra and Charles February 1972

SHE'D DRESSED FOR riding in Charles's truck: jeans rather than the usual African, wraparound, floor-length skirt, and platform shoes, so she wouldn't strain her neck looking up all night. Not willing to sacrifice femininity, she'd worn a thin gold chain about her neck, and a cream-colored, soft, cotton, accordion-pleated blouse with a dipping neckline that accentuated her shoulders. She pulled on her warmest jacket. It was cold out there.

In the lobby, she saw him talking to the dorm counselor, Miss Slayden, who, Tamra noticed, was showing him all her gums. As Tamra approached, Charles looked up, admiration on his face. She knew then that she'd been in love with him all these years.

In the parking lot Charles pointed to a black Camaro, saying he'd borrowed it from Cousin Johnny for the night. To her, Johnny Lane represented the antithesis of all she believed in, with his constant womanizing, and his loud-mouthed swaggering. But tonight Tamra slid inside his car without protest, thinking only that its low-to-the-ground design was like its owner: low down, or *loooow* down, as in some unorthodox act performed with the shades drawn. When Charles started the engine, the car moved out like an animal led by the nose.

He turned toward her, a look of contentment on his face. "After all these years," he said, "we're finally together." She worried she could never live up to his expectations. In the few affairs she'd had, the boys had never committed to her. And Leon had summarily dumped her. He'd called at last, but all he'd said was they'd have to get their lies straight. They could deny she'd written his paper, say they'd ended their friendship months before when he'd returned to his wife. And, he'd explained, he had gone back to her. She sneaked an admiring look at Charles. Before Leon, one union had been so short-lived, she'd barely had time to pull her socks back on.

She read the directions aloud: down Market Street, past Lukie George's . . . The popular cafe was crowded, students lined up for twenty-five cent scoops of butter pecan ice cream, chilled Boone's Farm wine, and Lukie George's down and dirty dogs: fifty cents a wiener, piled high with canned chili, diced onions, and thick, runny slaw. A left at this next corner.

He asked what she was thinking, and she made small talk, measuring each phrase. Words seemed too risky without thinking them through. *Careful* was the watchword. Tamra was relieved when they finally pulled up to the row of student townhouses. The door to the apartment was open, revealing a living room shadowy in it's red lighting. A record player blasted "Papa Was a Rolling Stone," and a skinny marijuana plant grew near a wood-paneled wall on which hung a painting on velvet of a bare-breasted woman with a full Afro sitting in a wide-backed rattan chair.

She'd met the hostess, Joyce, in her accelerated French class and discovered that not only were they fellow science buffs, but they both longed to live in Africa. Tamra planned to visit Nigeria this summer, before starting her fellowship, and Joyce had suggested they meet for a weekend together on the Ivory Coast, where Joyce would be part of a student research team.

Joyce walked into the apartment, followed by two men carrying a folding table. She apologized to Tamra and Charles for not being there to greet them when they'd first walked in. She'd had to convince a neighbor to lend her his table, she explained. Tamra noticed a young woman in sunglasses, who'd come in behind Joyce, leaning shyly against a wall.

Pointing to an open box with plates and napkins, Joyce asked the others to set the table and suggested Tamra might be of help in the kitchen. For some reason Tamra couldn't fathom, Charles thought this suggestion terribly funny. One thing that hadn't changed about him, Tamra thought, was that he still enjoyed making fun of her.

She followed Joyce, her chubby form stuffed into flowered, gauzy pants and a midriff top, as she led Tamra into the tiny kitchen. The sink and counter were cluttered with dirty dishes, and a brown paper bag overflowed with garbage. Tamra watched a Chesapeake roach run for cover. "I didn't spend time doing a lot of cooking," Joyce said. She certainly hadn't used the time to clean, Tamra reflected, but she felt a measure of fondness for Joyce, who was unapologetic about hosting a dinner party despite the fact that she had to borrow a table and her kitchen was in shambles. Tamra wished she could be as relaxed.

Joyce lifted cartons of potatoes and greens from a white bag and pointed to the oven. "There's a roast in there you can slice. Why don't you get a knife from the drawer." Tamra was happy to pitch in but wasn't too sure about this first request. From what she could gauge, a simple act like opening a drawer could bring her face-to-face with a colony of roaches. She preferred her bugs outside, where they belonged.

"You get the knife yourself," she said in a commanding voice.

Tamra had expected a puzzled stare. Instead, Joyce smiled, as if to communicate that she understoood her guest's concerns, and sliding the drawer open, she selected a butcher knife for Tamra. Without missing a beat, Joyce chattered on about her family back in Chicago, while Tamra listened and kept an eyeout for the baby roaches, dashing about like mobile watermelon seeds. Joyce paused occasionally to crush one, then resumed their conversation. Her father, she explained, was a medical researcher, and as a child, she said she'd been banned from his laboratory because she cried about the rabbits he'd killed. "When he called this morning, he said he'd developed a terrible allergy to rabbit fur." She snorted. "Don't you think he deserves it? He'll probably come back in his next life as a big Easter bunny." She chuckled, and Tamra joined in, thinking that with that line of reasoning, Joyce would be the world's chubbiest cockroach.

In the living room, the two women found the table setting almost completed, with candles, cloth napkins, and china, but no utensils, an ommision not surprising to Joyce. She announced the party's only rule: "No silverware. We have to eat with our hands. It's a finger party." Her speech was followed by groans and laughter. Of all places, Tamra thought.

Once seated, Tamra recognized the young woman in sunglasses who now sat across from them. It was Claudine, thin and hollow-cheeked. But the sight of Charles's ex-girlfriend sitting directly across from them aroused no jealously in her. He remained attentive to Tamra.

To Tamra's right sat Eugene Sanders from "Action News." He'd appeared formidable on screen, but up close, he was puny and had sores on his hands. He lifted a slice of beef, and Tamra pictured the species of bacteria being passed around. She'd have preferred eating from one of her own petri dishes; at least then she'd know precisely what she was swallowing.

Charles worked hard at keeping a conversation going, but the music was deafening. He kept asking her what she was thinking. She couldn't tell him she was fantasizing about stripping his clothes off and dragging him into the next room, so she quickly tried to make something up. "Umm, that time you came to class with those hogs in the back of your truck and they escaped." He grimaced, but she couldn't stop herself. "It was funny watching you round them all up, all that squealing and hog feces."

How could she have said that during dinner?

He nervously tugged on one of his ears and said coolly, "So, you were one of those people standing around laughing while I made a fool of myself?"

She swallowed hard. "Uhhh . . . we were laughing *with* you."

His brow was deeply furrowed. "I wasn't laughing."

She bit her lip.

A broad smile grew on his face. Teasing again. But this time she figured she'd deserved it. Talking about him chasing after his hogs must have made him feel like a country bumpkin. At least, Tamra reflected, it was nice to know he wasn't as self-assured as he had a right to be. As she spread butter on bread with an index finger, she hoped she could relax, just a bit. She noticed Claudine, still in sunglasses, had not touched any of the food on her plate.

When Charles passed the meat to Tamra, she lifted a slice gingerly and thrust a crooked finger into the bowl of mashed potatoes. Her finger trembled as she brought it to her mouth. Charles caught her wrist. "This may be the perfect party for you. You either loosen up or starve."

Praying he didn't think her uptight, she promised herself she'd dig into the next bowl with gusto, even if there was hair on it. True to her promise, when the greens came round, she reached to the bottom, gathered a soppy handful, and stuffed it into her mouth, forcing herself not to gag.

Joyce poured Boone's Farm into an antique wine goblet from Nigeria. When it reached Eugene, he sipped, stuck in an index finger, and passed the wine to Tamra. How would Charles react to her not drinking? She'd sworn she would never touch a drop, and this was something she was absolutely unwilling to compromise on, no matter what the cost. She shook her head no and passed the cup to Charles. To her delight, he also declined, reaching past Claudine, who was studiously avoiding everyone, and gave it to Joyce. "Never touch the stuff," he said. "I'm hooked on pop." His grin was lopsided. Perfect, she thought, and, finally, relaxed.

All around her, hands dug into plates. Someone lit a round of reefer, and again, she and Charles begged off. Tamra put a finger tentatively into her potatoes. He munched away, a slice of meat between his hands. She thought of how Virginia would react to a meal like this. It might be one of the few experiences that could make her mother cry. The more she pictured Virginia sitting at this table, with Eugene passing her a bowl of contaminated greens, the harder she laughed.

"That's a lot better," Charles said between bites.

She felt intoxicated with the pleasure of him.

Suddenly, a thump and the clang of dinnerware as Claudine fell, face first into the potatoes. Charles rushed to her.

Eugene stood, pointing, holding his stomach, narrating into the goblet: "State homecoming queen smothers in greens. We're just approaching the scene of the accident."

Charles lifted Claudine and persuaded Joyce to stop laughing long enough to point him to her bedroom. Tamra followed, watching with envy as he lay Claudine on the bed and then sat beside her, tenderly wiping her face with his napkin. Tamra tried to sneak back out of the room, thinking she could ask someone to give her a ride home. But before she succeeded, Charles pulled the napkin from his shirt and asked her to soak it in cold water. To Tamra's surprise, the bathroom was clean and well-ordered. Strangely, though, the bathtub had been painted black. Joyce popped in to ask if she could help, and Tamra said that maybe a trip to an emergency room was called for. Charles assured them Claudine just needed sleep.

Tamra studied Claudine. A spot of potatoes clung to her frames. Tenderly Tamra took her shades off. Even like this, she was beautiful; flawless chocolate skin, lashes that seemed to reach to her cheeks, and dark, smooth eyebrows. And she was perfectly petite. Charles had lifted her quite easily.

She should go and just leave them together. Who could blame him for being tied to Claudine? If she and Charles were ever alone again, she wanted to ask if he still loved Claudine, but she feared his answer. Touching his shoulder, she said good-bye. He grabbed her hand, stopping her. "I know this is selfish," he said, "with Claudine lying here like this. But I haven't been able to eat all day, thinking about seeing you." Claudine groaned. Charles shook his head. "She deteriorated before my eyes."

"Did you try to stop her?"

He held up his hands. "If you mean following her around, or maybe tying her up, no, I didn't physically try to stop her. I already have a full-time job."

Tamra smiled, uncomfortable about defending her rival, but she felt the need to speak what was on her mind. "I don't understand your attitude. When you really care about someone who needs help, you have to make sure they get it. I'd never just cut someone off. If he——"

"Ho——, ho—— hold it! I've got a ten-year plan that needs your approval. How about if every time you start in on me, yapping about something that is ab-so-lutely none of your concern, if I just . . ." He made a screwing motion at his head, ". . . turn you off and focus us on something important, like how long and fine your legs are. I need your permission, so what'da ya say? Are you a generous woman?"

She looked meekly across to him. "You know, we've hardly eaten. . . ." He grabbed her hand, pulling her from the bedroom.

They sat outside at Lukie George's, on stone seats, munching one of the house specialties: a half-pound of breaded, deep fried beef on a bun, tomato and lettuce, smothered with mayo. The light from the cafe and the few late-night customers kept them entertained. Tamra had stopped muzzling herself and now talked easily between bites, asking him details about his business. "Why don't we get in the car and I'll drive you to the farm?"

It was cold, but that wasn't what made her shiver. The thought of driving on those dark roads made her fears surface. Although she'd not confided in anyone else, Tamra told Charles about the hunter and his sidekick.

"I wish I'd been there," he said fiercely. "I'da tried to kill them." Seeing the indignation in his face, she believed him.

They finished their burgers in silence. When Charles was through, he dusted his finger tips on his jeans, then pulled his heavy jacket off to wrap it around Tamra, although she already wore a coat. "You'll freeze out here," she said.

"I can't recall being more comfortable." And as if to prove his point, he stretched along the bench, resting his head in her lap. The muscles in her legs stiffened involuntarily. He lifted up for a minute as if to analyze her. "Loosen up some."

"It isn't easy for me to get comfortable fast the way you do," she said.

"You're not kidding about that. Rigamortis just struck." She tried shaking his head off her lap, but he resisted.

"Sit still. I give all my women this test."

"Your women?"

"Only the good-looking ones. The way I figure, anyone can look fine face forward. But from down here, I can count your nose hairs." Fighting a smile, she forced his head away. He said, "Now, don't go getting skunk eggs on me."

"Skunk eggs! Is that some country term for annoyed? What you should do with *your* women is give them a lexicon."

"You admit it then, about being my woman?"

"I admit nothing."

"I wonder why I like you so much, even though we have nothing in common."

She protested. "We have a lot in common."

"Oh yeah? How about that Hopkins paper? I could never have pulled that off. Not just cheating. You knew you'd get caught but you probably thought it was worth it so you could show off how smart you are."

She stood, saying it was cold and she needed to get back to the dorm. "I'm not going to sit in this freezing weather to be insulted."

"I insist on staying 'til we've talked this out."

"That's not an apology," Tamra said.

"What was your favorite television show when you were a kid?"

"I get it. This is step two in your agrarian courting ritual."

"I love the way you look when you're annoyed. Your nostrils flaring, your hair kinda standing on end."

"I am leaving." She started for the car.

He blocked her, dancing from one foot to the next. "So, what was your favorite show?"

"Oh, for goodness sakes! 'Davy Crockett'!"

"I knew it. I can picture you in a coonskin hat, riding a mountain lion, rasslin' bears. . . . Course you'd win."

She shoved him playfully. But when he pinned her arms to her sides, pressing into her body, she suddenly became quite angry and slammed her fist into his chest. "Don't hold me. Don't ever try to physically stop me."

Backing up, he lifted his hands to ward off her rage. "Sorry."

She'd embarrassed herself. "No, I'm sorry . . . I just hate that feeling, that's all." It was as close as she'd ever come to an out-of-body experience.

She had almost been able to see herself fighting him off, but it was hard to believe she'd reacted that way. She couldn't remember ever hitting someone before.

He pulled the collar of his jacket around her chin, quickly backing off, as if he'd forgotten he'd been ordered not to touch her. Then he whispered, "Those guys really scared you."

"I don't know what happened. I'm sorry."

"No, I am sorry. It was my clumsy way of saying I know what makes you tick."

"You can still say that, after my strange outburst?"

He shook his head yes. "Even *sotto voce*, in your softest tones, you shout. You've always known how to get exactly what you want. Like your career. You wanted to be a scientist, and here you are, off to France."

"I do not shout."

"I'm not talking decibels. I said it as a compliment." He timidly asked, "Ever been bit by one of those buffalo skeeters?"

She was still embarrassed by her earlier behavior. If only he would shut up and kiss her. Remembering his questions about the mosquitos, she said, "If this is another folk aphorism . . ."

"Come on, *you* know bugs. These look like the others 'cept you can't tell you've been bitten until the next day." Instead of red swellings, he explained, a buffalo skeeter left hard, achy rises. "That's like some folks. They look just like everyone else, but when you let them in close . . ." He moved two pinched fingers along her face and buzzed. She laughingly slapped him away.

". . . They turn out to be dangerous."

She wondered if he meant Claudine.

"You're different. You're out front with who you are and what you think . . ."

He had to be kidding.

"No matter what the cost. You do what you believe in." The conversation had shifted to a subject that made her uncomfortable.

"That day, when we were kids, outside the shed, with your hair looking like it belonged to Kareem Of Wheat . . ."

"Who?"

"Buckwheat—he got an African name." He laughed at his joke. "Really, I can still see you that day . . . your dress was torn, you were a pur-dee mess, but did you care?"

Damn straight, she was thinking.

"Only the pursuit of the truth mattered. I respect that."

She wanted to hear more of his perceptions, but the shift in the conversation made her uncomfortable. She wasn't crazy about even him knowing her too well. Besides, although she had both jackets on, the cold was blistering. As if reading her mind, he opened the car door and she climbed in. Once he got in Tamra turned to Charles and asked if he still felt tied to the land.

"About ten times a day," he said, adding that he had big plans. He hoped to turn the farm into a major agricultural concern. American farmers, he said, supplied corn to half the world. "If we didn't, millions would starve." He sounded excited just talking about it. "Can you believe corn is not only used for oil, sweeteners, and feeding livestock but also dozens of by-products?"

What she couldn't believe was that they were spending even a moment talking about corn, but she pretended to concentrate. He said he planned to take graduate classes in business administration. "Farmers aren't going to survive unless they know about business, veterinary science, plant research, as well as how far apart seeds should be planted."

"You also sound certain about what you believe in."

He was quiet for a minute. "You're one of the only people I'd share this with. I suppose because you're so honest yourself, but . . ."

He may be graduating *cum laude*, she thought, but if he thinks I'm open and easy to read, he couldn't survive one night with those man-hungry women in my dorm. He obviously assumed that people were as honest and forthright as he. She tried to concentrate on what Charles was explaining about the *Othello* libretto. He asked if she was familiar with it.

"I know a little something about Shakespeare."

"The opera's different. My godmother once sent me a copy with the section highlighted that was Iago's solo. In essence, it was his creed."

"Like in church?" she said, "This is who we are and what we believe in?"

"*Ummm hmmmm,* and in the opera, Iago admits he's not a very moral person. In fact, he says he's more like a devil. It's not easy for him to admit, but this frees him of any doubt about which direction he should move in, or how he should be dealt with."

Charles said that like Iago, he too had had to own up to who he was. "I work the land that was given me. I didn't have much choice. My vision of who I am and how I look at the world was shaped by my *sitzem leben.* Do you know that phrase?"

She teased him. "Is this an intelligence test?" But she answered yes, she did know. *"Sitzen sie* means sit, and *leben,* doesn't that mean life? Where you sit in life?"

"You've got it. You know, you're the smartest gal I've ever known."

She gasped. "I hope that's not as alarming as it sounds."

"Anyway, yes, it means my situation in life, in an historical–cultural context. Few Blacks have been born into a situation similar to mine, and the way things are going, there won't be many more. Sometimes, even when it hurts, I have to do what's right, because of who I am." He took her hand, adding, "Like those papers you wrote. You were brave to write them. And I hope you'll just go up there and tell the dean what you did, get it over with."

"I don't know. It could throw my fellowship, everything."

"Oh, heck, you're as good as in France. These folks are so proud of you winning that fellowship. The worst that could happen is they suspend you for a few days. So what? We'll hang out together."

He reached inside the glove compartment and pulled out a tiny bottle, spraying the inside of his mouth. The scent of spearmint filled the air.

She laughed noisily at this and said anyone who'd gargle right in front of someone else was completely lacking in artifice.

"I'm not gargling," he insisted. "But I know you've been thinking about kissing me. And after those raw onions, wouldn't you prefer spearmint to a lung wad?"

In the middle of her *"ycccch"* he kissed her, a long, not-at-all playful kiss, with his tongue moving across her bottom lip. She suddenly pulled away.

"What is it now?"

Her voice was soft. "Charles, speaking of the truth, there's something I have to tell you. But don't tease. It's important."

"What?"

"I've always, uh, been a bit in love with you." He looked away, embarrassed. Now she was sure she'd blown it.

When he did speak his voice was full of emotion. "I am so thankful."

She thought this quite romantic. "Thankful for what?"

And here, she saw his shoulders shaking in laughter. "That at last, you're admitting it. I've known for years."

What an exasperating man! She didn't know whether to hold him or scream at him. He reached for her hands, kissing the palms. "And I've always loved you, but not just a bit." This time, she kissed him. Tamra wanted to keep it up, to climb on his lap and ask him what they should give each other for their twentieth wedding anniversary. But once again, she pulled away.

He looked impatient, but she couldn't help herself. She'd made a habit of letting her heart dance while some brother was just learning to pronounce her name. She couldn't risk having Charles, for just a moment, and then losing him.

The lights went out in Lukie George's, and she said it was definitely time to get home. She had to be at the lab early tomorrow. He insisted she couldn't leave, they were just getting to know each other. "Besides, I don't have much time to court you before you leave."

She loved the old-fashioned flavor of it, a declaration of his intent to woo.

"How about this?" he said. "We have the weekend. Let's go to the lab and I'll help you. Then I'll take you to Nanticoke."

"Help me? How much do you know about science?"

"I know a catalyst makes a reaction happen faster."

"Then you should also know an absolute relationship is only attained by degrees."

"Okay, I get the message. I can take it slowly. We'll drive twenty miles an hour, and when we get to the farm *next* year, I'll gather oysters, shuck them, and let you watch those babies curl up in cream. I'll even feed you. Very slowly, of course."

"Do you do that for *all* your women?"

He carefully considered this question. "I've taken them to movies. I took Claudine to the skipjack races. But I haven't asked anyone to come home with me at dawn and watch the blue herons soar in wingtip-to-wingtip. They've got six foot spans . . . wait'll ya' see. . . . And know what? I haven't climbed Mother Nature's hips since I was a kid. I've been driving. We can walk up slowly, look down and see the beans, like an ocean of crops. There's so much to choose from . . . the river branches through the land . . . pick a creek, and I'll teach you to throw a rock so it touches down six times before it goes under. How's that sound?"

She sighed loudly, her chest heaving. "Very poetic . . . and I'd love sharing that with you. But we've been talking for hours. Aren't you tired of me?"

His voice sounded completely sincere. "I so love hearing you talk, I could eat the words that come from your mouth."

"I'm giving you a warning, Charles Lane." She wagged her finger mischievously. "I don't play when it comes to my work. If you so much as reach for that Binaca stuff, you're out of the lab." He laughed at this, and she warned. "It'll be a long night. You'll get tired of watching me."

He looked incredulous. "You're saying this to a man who has been watching you for seven years?"

"A man so unobservant," she said, as Johnny's car pulled out of the empty lot, "he didn't notice he was being watched back."

22

Tamra October 1990

SHE CAN BARELY keep up with Wadine, who explains, as they rush to the supermarket, that she needs glue and markers. She and Stephen and Shisheemay always make hand-lettered invitations for birthday parties. It's a family ritual. With the party only a week away, they have to get the invitations in the mail.

In the store, Wadine rushes off. The idea of the Drakes' ritual fills Tamra with jealousy. She wants to be with her own family and finds she cannot take her eyes off the Black couple just ahead, with their heavily loaded cart. From the look of their clothing, they live in the transient hotel across the street. But the man, who is carrying his son in his arms, seems proud about being able to fill the cart. Tamra hopes that's because he has just found work. When the wife says they need a bag of sugar, he hands the boy to her, insisting he will get it.

Tamra examines a jar of cocktail onions. She doesn't want them to know she's listening. The man returns with sugar cubes. "I didn't want that kind," the wife says.

"Same thing," he snaps. Tamra's thinking, Of course it's not the same thing. Suppose she wants to make a cake or sprinkle it on cereal. She turns to see if the wife looks annoyed but sees instead that she beams. "Okay, honey bunch."

As they move off, Tamra knows this woman has learned what she has not, what her grandmother tried to teach her, to be conciliatory about the little things, like sugar cubes or suits or chins held too close to dinner plates. What was it Big Mama had said about criticizing your mate? *What comes out of your mouth can be as dangerous as what goes into it.* If only. If only.

She looks around, but it's as if Wadine has disappeared. She sees a manager near the front of the store and assumes he can direct her to the stationery aisle. When he turns to respond to her question, she senses something hauntingly familiar about him and suddenly realizes it's the scent of stale Scotch on his breath. She walks off, confused.

In the produce section, she wonders if she is losing her mind. Her life feels like a puzzle, pieces of which have been scattered about. Out of habit, she pulls back the husk of an ear of corn, moving a kernel with her thumb. It's stiff and dry, picked when immature, and she thinks Charles would fire a field chief for sending out produce like this. On the Chesapeake, this could ruin a good name.

Though she tosses the ear back, she cannot walk away. Laying her face on her arms, she cries into the corn. Her head throbs from her secrets. When she looks up, she sees Wadine at a checkout stand with an armload of articles. Tamra hopes sunglasses will hide her tears.

"What's with the shades?" Wadine asks.

"I want to be a real New Yorker," Tamra responds, grabbing some of Wadine's items.

The wait may be a long one. Only this counter is open, and the cashiers work slowly, as if unaware of the impatient line of customers. One of the checkers, an exotic looking African-American with black and blond corn-rowed hair dotted with gold-toned studs, slowly tallies the groceries. She remarks to the packer: "Girl, I have to git me my earrings."

Tamra looks at the ones she's wearing. The size of half-grapefruits, they have a raised pattern. The packer, a young woman whose name tag says "LoShanna," asks in equally loud tones, "How much those cost?"

"Sixty-nine, but these imma get havva stone in 'em."

"Ooh girl," LoShanna says.

"He gonna give the others to me for seventy-five. I gotta pick 'em up tonight. They bigga."

Tamra wonders how she'll find the strength to lift them.

They leave the market and Tamra and Wadine now rush to the dry-cleaning shop only to learn Wadine's dress won't be ready for fifteen minutes. The owner offers to deliver it after he closes.

Tamra inquires about the white rings on his wooden counter and he seems eager to share his thoughts. "It's the yuppies, dey come from around the corner with the cups of cappuccino, plop 'em down. Do they care?" he asks rhetorically. "You should forgive the expression, Mrs. Drake and friend, but in New York, people don't give a fuck."

Tamra suggests that he scrub the surface with mayonnaise and a nylon pad. When he thanks her for this tip, she offers him another about using mildew shower spray as a stain remover on fabric. He too has tips to offer, and they continue the exchange for a few moments until Wadine pulls her outside, searching her face for clues. "You're really into this housekeeping stuff, aren't you?"

Tamra admits, yes, that it's really important to her to keep her house clean. "Everything in perfect order. It's a way to, you know, control things. 'Cause there's no way to control another person. If you're crying and you want to say, Don't get in that car and drive off, don't deliberately do what will hurt me, stay here, hold my face in your hands and kiss me, the way you used to. Don't make me ask. But even if you say it in the most tender way, you can't make someone do that . . . so you just don't say it, because you'll only be disappointed, or even if he does, he might hold you stiffly, because his mind is off someplace else, not really caring that you feel as if your insides have shattered into a million pieces over things you can't control, except the laundry or dirty floors. 'Cause those are the only things that instantly you can be sure of."

She knows Wadine knows she's crying behind her sunglasses, but Tamra pretends anyway, punctuating the end of her speech with something resembling a light-hearted giggle. "Who'da thunk it?"

"Want to talk?" Wadine asks.

Tamra shakes her head no. "Okay," Wadine says. "Not now, then." She puts her arms lovingly around Tamra's shoulder. "But you know, you can say that to me, Tam. I can hold you."

Tamra pulls away, insisting she's all right. As they walk, Wadine returns to the subject of Tamra's housework fetish. "The Twitch is going to love you."

Tamra pictures Mrs. Twitchell, Wadine's stern-faced housekeeper. Wadine continues, "Yesterday she told me that when I have my period she won't wash my panties."

"Girl," Tamra says, laughing while crying, like a sun shower, "I've heard of 'I don't do windows' . . ." She's unable to get the rest of her sentence out.

They chit like grass birds all the way up Clark Street.

23

Tamra and Charles *May 1977*

"I COULD SWEAR I saw someone go in there."

"You did."

She heard the impatience of the voices outside the door but, determined not to rush, she leaned against the stainless steel sink—her breath fogging against the mirror—as she pulled the skin beneath an eye taut, lined it with a pencil of charcoal, and wondered, as the plane gently rolled, if she were risking an eyeball for Charles Lane.

Lashes down, she edged the pencil along a lid, her other eye gaping nervously at the operation being performed on its mate. She'd developed a new-found respect for the complexities of this organ. Only yesterday, while still in Paris, she'd sliced the eyeballs of two dead cows.

Out of their sockets the bulging orbs had been slippery. She'd torn away the ciliary muscles, lifted the delicate curtains of irises, and after salvaging a bit of the clear jellylike substance, had pried the optic nerve away from the flesh.

Her thoughts were interrupted by familiar chimes and the voice of the flight attendant. "Ladies and gentlemen, we will soon be landing at Norfolk Airport . . . . The captain has turned on the seatbelt sign. . . ." She waited for the French version of this announcement, but that would not happen. After five years, she was back in America.

There was a tentative knock on the door. "Everything okay?"

Flight attendant? Passenger? She pictured a line of businessmen outside the door, their knees pinched together for the wait. She refused to answer. The first-class ticket Charles had sent gave her carte blanche to eccentricities. Face complete, she zipped the bag, tucked it into her purse, and opened the door a crack. The "mob" had moved on. Walk slowly, she reminded herself, and lifting her head, she stumbled toward her row. Her seatmate, who seemed to have been watching her closely since their first flight had departed from Paris, now stared up at her and asked, "Should I know you?"

Tamra smiled, pretending to concentrate on her seatbelt, and considered the question, as well as the sound of this woman's voice. It was at once amusing and threatening, surely the first "Southernese" she'd heard in years. So sweet and rich it could coat the tongue, make English edible. What she'd actually said was, "Shoood ah know you?"

Five years abroad had failed to dull the sensation of this Chesapeake sound. The voice was one of a rich, white girl, familiar with horses and high, round, black riding hats; who'd attended a college with a soft name, like Sweet Briar or Laurel.

She looked carefully at the face of the speaker, a dazzling blonde of uncertain age but surely no longer a girl. The woman's pale skin was lightly covered with a web of lines that didn't hold back her years so much as they embraced her fading youth. Seatbelt fastened, Tamra smiled again. "Pardon?"

"I was on the Concorde (Con-kud) with you from Paris," the woman explained. "I saw you transfer (traans-fa) at Kennedy. I thought you might be an entertainer (enta-tain-a) or married to a sports figure (figga). My nieces and nephews would kill me if I'd had the chance to ask but didn't (did-en)."

Tamra shook her head as if cold water was being sprinkled in her face. The plane bumped to the ground. She answered with the best French she could muster. *"Je ne comprends pas, et je ne parle pas Anglais."*

The woman's eyes widened before they narrowed, and as she gathered her belongings, she smiled uncertainly. Tamra glared back. She repeated the woman's words to herself: entertainer, sports figure. As if a Black woman couldn't afford first class any other way.

She took deep, relaxing breaths, forcing herself to unravel her frown. She didn't want to get off the plane looking angry. Charles had paid a fortune for her round-trip ticket, more than twice her monthly salary at the lab. But the money certainly seemed worth it. She'd left Orly only five hours ago.

Her flight companion pushed past Tamra, eager, it seemed, to disembark.

Tamra thought of Charles. He would be waiting outside. Anticipation slowed her breathing. Had he changed since Dubrovnik? It relaxed her to think of the vacation to Yugoslavia which they'd taken the year before. She'd traveled by train from Paris to Venice, sat watching the autumnal lights inside the churches, and at six that evening, just before the sun set, had boarded a near-empty ship that sailed the Adriatic. Her slow, foggy journey had primed her for love. And Charles had been waiting, his majestic shoulders wrapped in cableknit, holding a perfect nosegay. Arm-in-arm, they'd walked past crumbling castles, whispering when they spoke.

He'd visited her in Paris, also, but this time he'd insisted she come to Nanticoke. Maybe he was finally going to propose. Cheered by the idea, she smiled good-bye to the flight attendant and walked steadily toward the waiting room.

Although his head was bent down, she saw him at once, chewing a fingernail. She hated seeing him nervous, tried rushing around the crowd to comfort him, wishing she'd taken advantage of being at the front of the plane.

He looked up, smiling broadly. Could he really see her from there? She waved. Wait, what was happening? Her seatmate moved up to Charles and reached for his neck. Smiling uncertainly, he hugged the woman back with one arm, and snatching his head away, waved Tamra forward with a free hand.

Tamra bit her lip, tasted her ten-dollar lipstick. People were staring. He rushed at Tamra, bringing her up close to this woman who was repeating her question. "Charles, what are you doing here? I thought Art might have asked you to pick me up. . . . You obviously know this mysterious young lady."

She felt the heat of her deception rise to her face. "I sure do know her," he said, surveying her with pride. He introduced the woman as Eve Reardon, saying she and Art had been his neighbors "since I was a wee little . . ." Mrs. Reardon told him to hush, it hadn't been all *that* long. Tamra remembered her from long ago, but more as someone she'd heard about, the beautiful Eve Reardon. Charles introduced Tamra as an old friend. "I hope you'll see a lot of her."

She turned to Tamra with an eyebrow arched like a question mark. "Where are you from, honey?"

Refusing to continue the game, Tamra answered in King's English, saying she was from Paris by way of Salisbury.

"She's a biologist," Charles bragged, "a geneticist, and her folks still live right in Salisbury."

Mrs. Reardon stared piercingly. "I thought you were . . ."

Tamra insisted that she must check on her luggage and moved toward the escalator. She heard Charles urging Mrs. Reardon to walk with them. But she insisted on waiting in that very spot for Art. Of course Art would be disappointed at not seeing Charles, Mrs. Reardon said. Art did think so much of him, he was like family, she continued. I bet, Tamra thought. Why didn't Charles just come on? He was always so nice to everyone. She sped up her pace, realizing for the first time how the airport had changed. There appeared to be several levels.

She'd passed a stretch of brightly lit stores before Charles caught up. He said he was certain she would like Eve Reardon, that she and her husband were like a second set of parents, and he scolded her for not waiting for a proper hello. Pulling her into a bank of open telephone booths, he teased her about worrying over luggage. He sat down on a shelflike plastic seat that brought them eye to eye. "In fact," he added, "let's worry about everything else later."

Cupping her chin in his hand, he traced a finger along her forehead, like a priest administering ash. She both loved and hated being looked at so closely. Her eyes filled with tears.

"What's wrong, baby?"

"A year is a long time?"

"A minute can be an afternoon," he said, kissing the bridge of her nose. She worried at first that people might stare, but as his pecks gave way to slow, lingering kisses, to her cheeks, her chin, across her eyelids, she grew indifferent to passersby and argued only with herself.

She'd never leave him again. She couldn't stay . . . maybe for a while. She could taste him, like salt, an ocean. This moment would have to last another year. She could not wait. She saw herself on her red motorbike zipping toward the Champs Élysées, long legs in boots, knees propped high, proceeding from the Étoile to Place de la Concorde. His mouth brushed hers. Settled.

She was on a research team that hoped to pinpoint the genes controlling an individual's response to alcohol. They could move on without her. No. Her motorbike passed a row of cars along Rue de l' Université. At the Science Institute, the stairs at night were floodlighted and flocked with pigeons.

Laboratories were now in the former drawing rooms of this noble building, walls dressed in trompe l'oeil, windows draped in heavy satin; luxury and history, a backdrop for researchers with young and shining faces, probing the edge of life.

His tongue danced along her bottom lip. She brought his heavy hand to her mouth, kissed the palm. She was part of him. Something richer even than this passion held them, made them alike, made him intoxicating to her. He opened his mouth to her, and she tasted the danger. The need for him was always with her, skin close, keeping her tipsy. And that really was why she cried.

"Let's get out of here," he said. Hearing his voice, she opened her eyes and forced herself to see. She didn't want to see her folks or his, not yet. No, not home, he said, to his favorite place, where he wrote to her.

Their thoughts remained unspoken in the parking lot. The only noise was the car door opening and shutting, no squawking, no urban slams, just the muffled, neat sound of parts coming together. They drove on toward the lights and buildings of Norfolk, toward the piers. She stared straight ahead, the quiet hanging between them like an *amen* after a prayer. The evening air felt oppressively hot and moist, as if someone had covered her with a damp blanket. In the dark, she buried her left hand beneath his thigh. He pushed a tape cartridge in and sang along with Joe Cocker, telling her she was so beautiful.

Turning onto a residential street, he slowed for a speed bump, asking what she had called them as a kid. "Sleeping policemen," she said, and he nodded, seemed satisfied. They parked on a cul de sac silvered by a hint of moon. From the distance, as they walked toward the pier, she could see a ship had docked. It was a modern vessel, gray and lifeless, unmoved by either waves or wind, built to transport civilized treasures, aluminum ingots, animal hides, frozen vegetables and french fries, canned peaches, denim jeans, resins and ice cream, to Caracas and Bogota, in protective aluminum covers.

Charles broke their silence, speaking softly at first, then louder to compete with the longshoremen nearby. He said he thought about her a lot when he came here.

"Why here?"

"I started coming here a few years back. I'd been so cocky, investing everything in equipment for soybeans. The whole world wanted soybeans, right? Then the bottom just fell out of the market. I'd been working three days straight and I needed to get away."

"Some folks go to bars."

"I wouldn't have felt close to you in a bar."

"You could have phoned."

"I needed more than your voice. That night . . . Pa calling me a fool, bankers waiting to pounce on me, I needed your fighting spirit." He looked lovingly at her. "With you, a guy would feel anything's possible." But he said sometimes he just sat there and worried about their differences. "Even the basics . . . you prefer cities. I wonder if you could adapt to a farmer's life."

She understood. She'd had the same concerns. He pushed two crates together and they sat watching the shipworkers as they were led by a short, slender foreman with graceful movements. One gang worked the ground level, connecting a cable and hooks to a monster container loaded on the back of a rig. The foreman pointed to something above, shouting orders, and Tamra realized this was a woman. She wondered if she had children at home.

He took her hand. "I want to ask you something important."

Her thoughts raced. She had been sure he would propose and she wanted to remember every word. He began by saying that they seldom talked about her so he knew very little. "Especially how you feel about . . ." He seemed embarrassed.

She tried to help him out: "What is it, Charles?"

"Tamra, do you . . ." She held her breath in nervous excitement.

"Do you believe in God?"

She responded irritably. "What made you ask that?"

"It's important."

"Oh, I get it. Say the wrong words and I get bumped like . . ." She paused. She'd promised never to mention Claudine again, but, oh, to hell with promises. "Like you did Claudine?"

He sighed. "Whenever I ask questions you get angry."

"I'm sorry but you're always interrogating me."

"Now, that's a first-class apology." For the briefest moment she saw anger in his eyes, but just as suddenly he turned it back and looked toward the ship. The bright lights strung up by the workers accentuated his profile, bathing his neck in a surreal glow, making it appear otherworldly.

She watched the nape of his neck where the muscles above his collar seemed as forceful as the engine of a train. (She wondered if anyone else could hear his muscles working, as she could.) His skin was darker here, from bending in the sun, she guessed. This was also the spot where the hair on his head, though coarse and nappy everyplace else, gave way to fine, soft kinks, like a swatch of babyhood.

She'd traveled the world on student fares, worn out a pair of dancing boots at discos in Stockholm, been lost on a commuter train in downtown Tokyo, awakened in a hotel in Lagos to the prattle of voices from the marketplace below, all foreign and haggling, and as familiar as the New Hope Missionary Baptist Church. She'd had all that. Now what she wanted most was to inch herself over and brush her lips against the kinky-domed, sun-chosen, Karo-colored, muscle-chugging nape of this man's neck.

He turned and looked at her, any traces of anger vanished. "I wasn't asking for a loyalty oath."

"All this threw me," she said. "First you said we were going to go to where you think about me." She gestured toward a container of rotting fruit. "Then you bring me here. I would never have imagined this place, but I figured you'd say you look at this water and think about how it separates us, how much you miss me, or . . ."

He snapped back: "You want to write this script and star in it, too?"

She stood, saying maybe they'd better get to his mother's.

"Why do you always want to run off when we disagree? Come on, baby. I have so much to tell you. Some of it might surprise you, maybe not." He started to bite at a fingernail, then quickly took his hand away from his mouth. "I know a little about women." He put his hands in his pockets as if trying to keep them from his mouth. "But you? You're a mystery. You drive me crazy. You've got enough fuel in you to make twenty of the women I've known."

She leaned forward, thinking maybe he would finally get around to asking her. "And what does that mean for us?"

"How do you feel about kids?"

"I'm working on a way for the human species to self-pollinate."

He laughed. "You know, you're like one of my tomatoes."

"A hot tomato, eh? And I guess you're the big banana slug looking for a home."

He worked the back of his neck like a worry stone. "If you've tasted a hot-house tomato you know what I mean. They're bland, like wax. But then there are vine ripe tomatoes. Even the words *vine ripe* sound better. And they are. They have to be grown in the finest soil and when you pick one

. . . doesn't need salt . . . or dressing. Wipe it on your shirt. One bite and you taste everything good God can do."

Looking at his kind, dear face and stroking it, she realized she'd never answered his question. She asked if he'd assumed she was an atheist because of her work. He admitted he had.

"We really get a bum rap when it comes to religion. What do you think, I spend my days trying to prove God doesn't exist? Although it's unintentional, it's more the other way around. Science has given me a reverence for God's work. It's not just that I need to believe, and I do. There's so much in me I want to make better. I'm not good or pure, like you. For me, it doesn't come easily. There's a pettiness in me that God sees, but I know God loves me."

"I know he does, too," Charles said. "I bet he's delighted with you."

She couldn't be distracted. His question had triggered so many feelings. As a scientist, she'd always believed that evidence of God's genius was everywhere, and to make her point, she grabbed his hand. "Your body is so sophisticated, each cell in this beautiful hand carries more than a hundred thousand genes, and the information in those components is blocked or opened depending on the function of the body part. You think I believe this is the end result of two atoms smashing together? Not by a long shot." She kept rubbing his skin. "Your mama and daddy's genes made you this beautiful reddish-brown, but in your brain that same coding for pigmentation is dormant. Up there, it's the genes for intelligence, not color, that matter."

Charles shook his head like a chef who'd put the right ingredients together. "I see God's glory in his visible creations, while you see him in the microscopic mysteries." He slowed, as if expecting now to be disappointed. "But how does evolution fit in?"

"God's in the process, constantly creating more complex forms of life."

"Sounds more like you're talking about nature."

"And nature jumpstarted itself?"

"But if God's so powerful, what about human devastation?"

Her answer did not come quickly. "I certainly don't have all the answers. But I do know that if I were a parent, I wouldn't want my child's life predetermined. I'd want that child to know freedom. And the God I'm certain of wouldn't want to work our lives out for us so that everything, down to the last detail, can be accurately predicted. That means freedom of will, good and evil, and all the elements of surprise that make life life, from the indeterminacy of subatomic particles to the unpredictability of the evolutionary process."

"I'm interested in creation, too," he said. "When I plant a grain of wheat I have to believe it won't die, that it's gonna take on a whole new life."

"You're not just talking farming. You mean your life, don't you?"

"There's a lot you don't know about my way of life. Most of the families in my neighborhood have been around at least seventy years, and that makes for an ingrown, narrow way of seeing. I worry about how you'll fit in."

"Maybe I never will."

"Yeah, and maybe we're dumb enough to try anyway."

She lowered her head. "Yeah, maybe."

They strolled back to the car, a ceiling of stars overhead, the quiet water behind them. They would travel the Bay Bridge Tunnel, to Nanticoke, and the life he lived there.

24

Tamra and Charles *May 1977*

CHARLES PUT A peanut into her mouth and cracked the shell of another. Tamra glanced covertly at his family. With his parents watching them like this, she felt like a zoo animal at feeding time. Only his sister seemed to be ignoring them, as well as everyone else, as the Lane family "took in air on the extra porch."

"I want to make sure I understand the significance of your research," Charles's mother continued. "By studying someone's chromosomes, could you predict the future of his drinking behavior?"

This couldn't look very impressive with Charles feeding her like this, no matter how tenderly. "No more, thanks," she said, then locked eyes again with her inquisitor. "No ma'am. A good family history could probably tell us more. But we believe that a man's—I mean a person's—response to alcohol may be largely predisposed genetically."

She rested the small of her back against the cushioned chair and watched Dalhia's intelligent face, as she cooked up the next question. Dalhia crossed her legs and Tamra noticed her open-toed heels and the lavender toenail poking through, painted to match her silk dress. She must be the best-dressed farm wife in the state, Tamra thought, maybe in all of Western civilization.

"And what about women?" Dalhia continued. "Can they inherit the trait?"

Tamra licked her lips. "There are clear indications in men that alcoholism in a parent is the best predictor of alcoholism, but as for women . . ." She wondered if the Lanes had seen Seth recently and if he'd been drunk in public. She'd never discussed Seth's drinking with anyone outside her family. Was Charles waiting for her answer? She glanced at him. He whispered to his little cousin and the two stood and wandered off together. Don't leave me alone with this prosecuting attorney, Tamra thought. Before she could answer Dalhia's question, Harlen intervened.

"Why don't you give the child a chance to enjoy these peanuts, woman? Maybe she's tired of talking about her work. Go on, honey, help yourself, take a handful of 'em." He pushed the tray of fresh roasteds toward her. Charles's Cousin June Bug had brought sacks of them from Virginia and distributed them to friends and relatives throughout the neighborhood. The floor of the porch was covered with peanut shells, and the bushel basket that had held steamed crabs was now empty.

Dalhia stood abruptly, grabbed the swatter, and whacked at a mosquito, giving Tamra time to get a better look at the layout of the porch. Like all the rooms that had been added to the original farmhouse, this screened-in porch was shaped like a big shoebox. Driving in she had been struck by the jumble of the house. Rooms had apparently been tacked on as the family's prosperity had grown, without any obvious design. Everyone knew the Lanes had more than enough money to build a large and fashionable home. And Dalhia was obviously a woman who liked finery. But the frame of mind that had produced this multi-additioned house probably also accounted for the three rusted tractors sitting idly in the yard. The Lanes were unwilling to let go of the old and familiar.

Fortunately, from where Tamra sat she saw the crest of trees by the river. The four walls of screens that made "the extra porch" allowed circulation of air, which was of the utmost importance in a hot and humid climate. Unfortunately, the door to this porch was also an entryway for tough squadrons of mosquitos and iridescent green horse flies. Tamra watched Charles on his way back to the extra porch, hand-in-hand with his four-year-old cousin. They smiled conspiratorially.

"Close the door quickly," Dalhia said, swatting a mosquito.

"That must be the same one that got me," Tamra said, extending an arm scattered with fresh bites.

"Charles, run up to the house and mix a poultice of meat tenderizer and water for Tamra's arm," Dalhia said. "It'll draw the itch right out."

She hated the way his mother ordered him around. "I'll be fine, thank you, really," she insisted.

Dalhia said, "You've probably never heard of those old-fashioned cures, eh?"

"I've heard wild garlic onions lower blood pressure, and that sulphur's good for chickenpox."

Dalhia looked disappointed.

Strike one for Big Mama, Tamra thought.

Dalhia excused herself and stepped outside to choose flowers for the dinner table.

Charles and his cousin hovered near Tamra. "Carolyn has something for you." He looked down at the child. "Go ahead, give it to her." The girl placed a tomato in Tamra's palm which was still warm from the sun. She bit into its flesh. It tasted sweet and smelled of the earth.

As she chewed, she watched Dalhia, who was cutting stalks from a patch of brilliant red gladioli. Dalhia stooped to cut, her face trapped between spearlike petals. "The tomatoes weren't any good this year," she called sharply to the girl. "Carolyn Marie, why didn't you pick a munch-melon? They're sweet as pie."

Tamra turned to the girl. "I'll always remember that you gave this to me. Where I've been, you can't get Chesapeake tomatoes. It's perfect, like you."

Carolyn looked down shyly, all lashes, white hair bows, and brown cheeks. Tamra stroked her arm.

"You're good with kids," Charles said.

The screen door creaked open, this time for Mark, Vicky's five-year-old son. Charles's sister had been so quiet Tamra had forgotten she was there. "Look what we got us, Ma," Mark shouted, displaying a square shell. It seemed to Tamra that everyone shouted at Vicky, as if trying to rouse her.

Her shoulders slumped so that her chest was concave, and she seemed fearful of claiming more than a few inches of space. She sat with her legs tucked beneath her, shoulder-length hair and bangs covering her face. For the last hour, she'd been staring at the saucer of molasses and cake crumbs that had already trapped several flies. When she looked up to answer her son, she covered her mouth with a thin hand.

"Did he kill the turtle?" Vicky asked in disinterested tones. Could this possibly be the same high-spirited big sister Charles had bragged about? If it was, then someone had pulled a plug and let her joy leak out. Apparently,

Tamra wasn't the only one who'd noticed. The night before, when Tamra and Charles had arrived, Vicky had immediately made excuses to go to bed. Dalhia had watched her slow ascent up the stairs and whispered to Tamra, "She looks worse every time I see her."

Tamra had been startled by Dalhia's remark but admitted to herself that for a twenty-eight-year-old woman, Vicky did seem insubstantial. She knew that Vicky had married a banker and they lived in a sprawling house he had built in the city. Glancing back outside, Tamra concentrated on Dalhia, wondering what had defeated both these women. One had withered like grapes on a vine, the other was caustic, primed for attack.

Vicky rapped at the turtle shell. "Where'd you get it?"

"Cousin June Bug gave it to me," the boy said, explaining that his uncle-cousin had been driving down Big Road, wishing he had something good to fix for dinner. "And just like that, Mama, this box turtle crossed his path."

Charles chuckled. "June Bug gets one wish granted in his life, and he asks for supper."

Tamra wanted to know what Mark planned to do with the shell.

"Let it dry, paint it. I got a whole collection of 'em."

"They're more than just shells," Tamra said. "Terrapins are the only group of higher animals that carry their skeletons outside." She pointed to the ridges of the shell. "These shells are like houses. God built them to last because even though turtles are slow, they live longer than most folks. Did you know that?"

Mark stared wide-eyed and answered slowly. "No ma'am."

She suggested next time June Bug was hungry, he should buy a TV dinner. "Tell him turtles have been on earth about a hundred and seventy-five million years and that gives them more of a right to be here than us."

"Yes ma'am," the boy said, "I will . . ." Then he added softly. "Are, are you gonna stay down here?"

Charles bent to answer his nephew and smiled at Tamra. "She will if you show her all your shells. Then maybe you can see her collection of cow eyes. Ask her what the good Lord intended for those. Cows are her favorite animals. Aren't they, Tam?"

Inwardly she squirmed, remembering that Virginia had always warned her of her tendency to talk down to people.

Mark held a pop bottle up to his grandpa. "Will you open this?"

Dalhia practically tripped trying to grab it before her husband could.

But she missed, and Harlen stuck the bottle in his mouth, prying the top off with his teeth.

Dalhia pronounced this behavior "common" and folded her arms across her chest, her head jerking involuntarily to the side and back, as if the gesture could erase what she'd seen.

Harlen walked to the screen door cupping an ashy hand to his ear. "So you like cows, eh, Tamra? Those bullfrogs sound like they're mooing, don't they? Come on over here," he said. "Let me show you something."

He pointed to a spot a few yards away where the original barn had once been. "Hazel paid us a visit Easter Day, nineteen-fifty-four, blowing one hundred miles an hour. Took the whole dern thing with her. I ran out, couldn't find no walls, nothing. The cows were still chewing, though. Remind me of one of Dalhia's sisters."

Ignoring his joke, she asked if he'd lost livestock.

"Half my turkeys," he said, but added that the turkeys hadn't been destroyed by wind, that they'd drowned even before the hurricane. "Taught me to never underestimate stupidity."

"What do you mean?"

"Turkeys are so dumb, if you leave them out in the rain they'll drown themselves looking up."

He moved a few more steps away from the extra porch and pointed toward the Nanticoke River. When she walked near him he inclined his head and said in a whisper, "You and Little Charles better take a walk by yourselves. You didn't come this far just to sit around eating peanuts and let Dalhia talk you to death."

This proclivity he and Dalhia had of discussing family members in such demeaning terms troubled her. Virginia would never speak against her own family like this to outsiders. She felt a pang of guilt about not going directly to her parents' home and promised herself she would see them first thing tomorrow. But first, there was unfinished business to settle.

Dalhia walked up quietly, wanting to know what they had their heads together about. Harlen said, "Just telling her she should walk over to Hollerin Rock." He kept his eyes on Tamra. "There was a time when we could stand right on the beach and catch rockfish, cats, all the softshell crab you could eat."

Dalhia said, "The way I remember it, only thing you could catch was a jellyfish sting."

"That's right," he said, "all the good fish left when I married you."

Tamra felt caught between the sharp edges of their humor.

Dalhia said, "You told me that when you were a boy you dropped your bait in the water, reached in, and met a copperhead." She paused. "I thought that was why they named it Hollerin Rock. They could hear you hollering for twenty miles."

Sucking his teeth, he turned toward Tamra. "You do want to be careful if you wade in that water. Your daddy will shoot me if I let you get hurt."

He looked off into the distance. "Dalhia's family used to picnic down there every year. Shoot. Do you know her family? The most educated group of colored folks you ever want to meet."

Dalhia sniffed noisily. Tamra felt she was being used by the two of them, but she continued smiling politely.

Harlen continued, said that his sister, T.J., and he and Seth had been the first Negroes along their road to get a college education. "Course Seth went to the war. I couldn't. The farm, you know. Then your Daddy got his master's. But even Seth can't hold a candle to Dalhia's people. Let's put it this way. Her great-great-great-great-grandpappy probably taught King Solomon."

Tamra glanced at Dalhia, who had her arms folded across her breasts again, watching her husband humorlessly as he continued.

"One day, when I wasn't at the picnic with them . . . probably someplace gettin' my hands dirty . . . and they were sittin' around discussing their books and colleges and philosophers, you get the picture——"

Tamra nodded. Dalhia interrupted. "I thought you'd suggested that she take a walk."

"Let me finish," he said, and turned back toward Tamra. "All of a sudden they heard this child crying; one of the nieces. She'd wandered out too far in the water and was going down. They looked around for somebody who could go out there and save her. Wasn't a soul."

He paused, glancing at his wife as if he enjoyed punishing her. Her face looked pained by the memory. But Tamra couldn't resist asking: "What happened?"

"The child's daddy ran out there to get her. He couldn't swim a lick, either. By the time I got back it was all over. They both drowned. When they recovered the bodies, the child's legs were wrapped around her father. She'd held on for dear life."

"That's dreadful."

Harlen finished. "Three-fourths of this planet covered by water, and they'd cut themselves off with fear . . . all that education and fine clothes, wasn't one Negro out there who could save his own life."

She fiddled with an earring, ashamed to say she couldn't swim, either. Back then, her mama had always worried about ruining her freshly straightened hair.

Dalhia said, "If you and Little Charles are going, you'd better get some of my Skin-So-Soft off the dresser. It's only bath oil but it keeps the bugs away."

Tamra walked with her to the house, and then touched her elbow. "Maybe I'll help with dinner," she said. "I hear you're a great cook." Charles walked downstairs as they entered, his huge thighs exposed in shorts.

"I was just about to look for you," he said.

"I'm going to help your mother with dinner."

He grabbed hold of his throat, stumbling up the steps. "Ma, take pity on us. Miss Virginia hasn't given her a cooking lesson since Tamra was in the second grade."

Tamra watched Dalhia's face change from somber to amused. Who would have guessed this woman even knew how to giggle? Dalhia, who held her hands to her mouth as if trying to force back mirth, said between giggles, "Now, just stop it, Charles."

It was obvious he knew just how to make his mother laugh. "It's true, Mama. Tamra once invited me to dinner, and when I got to the dorm, she was pulling a roast out of her Easy Bake oven."

Tamra hit him across the head with her sweater. Dalhia playfully grabbed one of his arms, pretending she was about to whack his bottom. She told Tamra, "If he ever gets too big for his britches, remind him he has a mama who can still whup him."

Dalhia and Charles continued in this playful vein, but Tamra could only concentrate on his mother's countenance: girlish and without worry. How would Dalhia ever let him go?

In the same light-hearted voice, Dalhia thanked Tamra for offering to help with dinner. "I'd just love getting you alone so I can hear about French cuisine, but maybe another time. And I hope you'll explain more about that Japanese flower arranging." She reminded Tamra not to go out without stopping in the master bedroom for the insect repellent.

At the top of the stairs Tamra opened the first door to the right. She knew it wasn't Dalhia's room, or even the separate one where Harlen slept. Stepping inside a small room, she felt she'd traveled through a time tunnel.

It belonged to Charles, but he had definitely outgrown the place. It had a red and blue ceramic horse-head lamp, narrow twin bed with a blue and red cowboy bedspread, and matching curtains. She was about to leave when she spotted a photo of herself on Charles's nightstand. It was one of her favorites, taken during her first year in Paris.

She'd worn tight blue jeans, black high-heeled boots, and, back then, an Afro. It had been cut and shaped like a helmet, and with her head held jauntily to the side she looked like a triumphant soldier. But it was the sweater that captured the eye. Made of angora in hues of blue and yellow pastels, the wisps moving in the wind, appeared in the stillness of the photo to be powered by something inside her.

"What's taking so long?" Charles called, and she rushed out.

As they passed through a tangle of prickly bushes, she heard the call of a bird, more like a sigh for a missing lover, "Ah bob white, bob white." A plump, reddish-brown bird with gray tail feathers rushed by, and Charles held an arm out, barring Tamra's way. "Make way for another one," he whispered. One more of the birds scurried by. "Like women going to the bathroom," he said, "never alone."

On the beach, where they were welcomed by the cries of gulls, the wind tore at her hair and the hem of her gauze dress. Broken oyster shells, sand, and pebbles squeezed into her pumps and she pulled them off, running barefoot to the shore, marveling at the great salt water Nanticoke River that flowed from the Chesapeake Bay and enriched these farmlands. Steel gray, sunlit waves moved steadily, like glowing fish. Scrambling atop Hollerin Rock, she was momentarily blinded and turned back to look across the sweeping sand, toward the lush, undisciplined growth of weeds, marveling that one family had held on to this.

"Do you remember any of the Indians who were here?"

"I had a pal named Hawk. We'd dress up in tribal clothes and try to talk Indian." He told about the young archeologists who dug for arrowheads and pottery, sometimes interviewing the two boys about Indian life. "They'd scribble what we'd said into a notebook. Hawk and I'd see them coming, put our heads together and say: 'What lies should we tell them today?'"

She laughed. "I should arrest you for conspiring to thwart scientific inquiry. But what happened to your friend?"

He shrugged and threw pebbles into the water. "Got so busy around here I didn't have time to play. But his family was probably wiped out, like the others. I guess it was inevitable. Philosophically, Indians were the settlers' polar opposites."

"How's that?"

"Well, they looked to the earth and bodies of water for their gods. The settlers considered them heathens."

Tamra moved in closer; she could feel his breath on her face. "And must opposites always be in opposition?"

He said not necessarily, but that it was man's nature to battle. "We seldom teach one another the lessons we've learned."

A few feet away, on a massive rock, a nest of sticks was crowded with dozens of downy, young, blue herons, in near riot stage, pushing and squawking. They had spotted their mother descending like a parachutist into the mayhem, delivering a catch of frog skeletons and rotting fish.

She said, "It's so beautiful. Were there battles here?"

He said he'd heard his great-great-great-grandfather had been a mean s.o.b. "That's how he got the land as a wedding gift. Some Native Americans resented Blacks, because whites considered Native Americans and Blacks one and the same. Whites wanted this land too, but this old Indian chief knew the only way that land would stay in the family was to give it to Moses Lane." He showed Tamara the scorched land, where a wall of fire had been built. "I don't know if it was whites trying to run him off or not."

"Maybe he was trying to keep someone in," she said. "Think of it. Every first son followed through on the promise. Not one of you moved away, just added onto it."

Charles muttered, "Even when their wives didn't want it."

She realized he meant his mother and she pictured Dalhia with her fancy toenails, silk dress, and simmering anger. She understood Dalhia now. She was a victim of accidental poisoning. Her dreams had died inside her. Tamra shuddered.

His tone sounded more businesslike as he suggested they deal with the subject of their own misalignment.

"How do we start?" she asked. The moment had come. If he didn't introduce the subject of marriage, she would.

"Let's look at the obstacles between us."

She said there was only one.

"Your work," he said.

"I was thinking of your work," she said.

"Come on, look around you. I wanted you to see this place again, to understand why I can't just walk away from it."

"You're suggesting I can walk away from my work?" She'd imagined this conversation many times, though it had taken longer to occur than she'd expected. She'd pictured herself saying no, being a strong, passionless soldier, but the years had worn her down. "Charles, we were meant to be together."

"That was supposed to be my line."

"I know you can't leave the farm, but it's not just giving up my job. I'd find work in Baltimore or Annapolis. The research couldn't possibly be the same and I'd hate that, but I'd survive the loss if it meant losing you instead."

"Then what are you worried about?"

"Your attitude toward my work."

"What do you mean? I'm so proud of what you do."

"Yes, proud the way you'd be if your nephew won a baseball game. You don't take it very seriously."

He said solemnly, "I happen to take baseball very seriously."

She struggled with her annoyance. "That's just what I mean."

"Okay, I know I'm not saying this right, but I do understand science is part of who you are and I know how much you love it."

They had moved further down the beach, closer inland, where the branches of a tree offered shelter from the wind. Charles sat on a rock, held onto Tamra's hand, and looked up at her.

"Look, I've been practicing this for a week now, but you're going to have to translate for me, tell me if I'm getting it right." It took awhile, with the wind blowing, chopping off some of his words, for Tamra to realize he was speaking French. She was forced to lean forward and listen intently to the most abominable French she'd ever heard.

J'ai souvent essayé
    ("You have tried many times . . .")
de t'oublier;
    ("to forget me . . .)
oublier la forme de tes lèvres
    ("forget the shape of my mouth . . .")
après nos baisers
    ("when just kissed . . .")

et tu en voudrais plus encore;
  ("and I'm still greedy for more . . .")
ce que ton corps ressent
  ("The feel of my body . . .")
quand il me désire
  ("when it wants you . . .")
et après quand il est loin de moi.
  ("and afterwards when it's spent from you.")
Je fais tout ce que je peux pour ne pas penser à toi, ne pas te désirer, ne pas avoir envie de toi.
  ("You try hard not to miss me, need me, or want me . . .")
Mais il y a toujours la voix.
  ("But always there is the voice.")
Elle dit: Tamra, Tamra, Tamra.
  ("It says, Tamra, Tamra, Tamra.")
Je suis un homme simple . . .
  ("I am a simple man . . .")

Oh no you're not, Charles Lane.

Un fermier qui travaille de l'aurore au crépuscule . . ."
  ("A farmer who works sunup to sunset . . .")

He paused, his eyes smiling. "How am I doing?"
"*Parfait,*" Tamra said.
"What's that?"
She giggled, holding two fingers in a circle. "Ooh la, la, la, la."
"Then I'd better quit while I'm ahead. Tamra, if you'll be my wife I promise I'll take all that energy I wasted trying to forget you, and spend it making you happy ever after."
She stroked his face. "*Que je t'aime.*"
"I know that means you love me."
"You don't need a book to know that. But how did you learn all that French?"
"A teacher at Carver."
"Is she pretty?"
He shrugged. "It's a matter of opinion. Do you think women with whiskers are pretty? Hey, what about my proposal?"
"I want you to give your French teacher a message for me. Tell her that

from now on you won't need her help, that your bride can teach you French, from *amour* to *zephyr*."

He gave a triumphant yelp and they embraced. But as if he sensed that something troubled Tamra, Charles caught her face between his hands, trying to read her eyes and mouth.

Swiping at a tear, she pretended the wind had blown sand into her eye. Her sadness confused her. The man she had always loved had proposed sharing life with her. It was what she wanted, wasn't it? Oh, but surely she did. Needing time to think, she stood and turned to walk away.

Her loose dress swung sinuously about her calves. The belt, which was more like a rope of yarn twisted with bronze threads, had come undone, and he grabbed a loose end, holding fast. Unable to move forward, laughing with him, she descended backward as the wind made her white dress billow, tentlike, slow and soft over his knees.

They were together for a very long while, and later, when she recalled their time on the beach, it seemed that once he was inside her, it was as if a stake had been driven clear through to her heart, nailing her, she feared, to the earth forever.

25

Tamra and Big Mama *May 1977*

SHE SPED AROUND the turn. Big Mama lived only a few miles away and she felt a great need to talk with her. As her eyes wandered away from the two-lane highway, she realized how much she'd missed America.

France's Loire Valley had reminded her of America's agrarian communities—robust families and workers, noisy machinery, even the soil, mile after mile, zipped up with bursts of startling green. But now that she was back, she realized there was no other country as eager to communicate as America. The messages shouted at her. To her right, a hand-painted sign: ROADS MAYBE SLICK. Just ahead, a bumper sticker: MY EX-WIFE'S CAR IS A BROOM.

She slowed near Big Mama's church, where a bulletin board asked: WHAT WOULD JESUS DO IF HE HAD YOUR PROBLEMS?

Services had probably ended hours ago, but she scanned the area carefully for any signs of her grandmother and noticed how disproportionate the small-frame building was to the heavy, white steeple, which slumped forward like a weary acrobat taking a bow. The graveyard was heavily concentrated with headstones that abutted the walkway, porch, and stairs, as if the dead crowded out the living.

She drove past Luigi's Honey-chile Pizza, past Earl's Gun Club, and the Swedish Smorgette, on past The Meat Factory, and sighted Miss Auntie

Glover's gray house. It appeared to have new occupants. Sandy-haired children played in the yard, a Volkswagen bug was parked out front, and a sign in the dining room window urged: Vote Marvin Mandel Ex-Governor.

Murphy's gas station had closed down. Over the boarded-up restrooms, white-stenciled words, faded now, impossible for anyone except those who'd lived through it to read: WHITES ONLY . . . COLOREDS. Her hands gripped the steering wheel.

A few feet beyond she read: BINGO TONIGHT HOLY GHOST BASEMENT. She made a left turn on Face of the Moon and slowed in anticipation of the washboard road. Perhaps she'd hear a *"halloo,"* from a friendly neighbor. But there was little chance of that. She was disguised by Charles's fancy car.

Finally. Big Mama's hedges, her crooked driveway, the silent face of the white house with it's two doors and pink shutters. A pine that had been struck dead by lightning five years ago was still upright. Yellowed, it was a phantom giantess in lace.

She'd been certain the arrival of the unfamiliar car would pull Big Mama outside. But there was only a pair of barking mutts to trail her to the back steps. Crossing the kitchen, she inhaled the scent of cinnamon, lots of it, sprinkled on shelves and counter tops. Big Mama had been battling ants again. The green Formica table was chipped and had a rocking chair pulled to it.

Quietly, she called, worried she might startle her grandmother. She rushed through the living room. Where were the cut-glass candy dishes and peppermint balls? On she continued, to the back room, where white curtains fluttered ghostlike at an open window, and where she found Big Mama stretched out, mouth stiffly parted, white hair in frozen mounds.

Tamra gave a cry, tiptoed to the front of the metal bed, and lowered her nose to the old woman's mouth. She was at once comforted by an exhalation smelling of peanuts.

Big Mama's eyes opened. "Boo!" she said. When Tamra jerked up, her grandmother grinned like a naughty child. "June Bug told me you were here. Keep it up. Don't let us know your whereabouts and you'll walk in and find one of us dead."

Tamra howled with an open mouth. "That wasn't funny. Don't ever do that again!" She fell into a hug. "I thought something had happened to you out here by yourself." She could tell her grandmother was smiling wickedly. "It's true, if you got sick or died, who would have known how to reach me?"

Big Mama pulled herself free. "You ain't got nothin' to worry about. I'm gonna have a *looong*, slow, drawn-out death, give y'all plenty of time to gather 'round my bed and mourn me."

Tamra smiled despite the scare.

"*Um, um, um, um, uh.* You look just like your mama when you're miserable. . . . Seen her yet?"

"No ma'am," Tamra said. "I needed to talk to you first. Charles has asked me to marry him."

"I knew he would," Big Mama said. "You two were grown for each other."

"Oh, I love him so much. He keeps me from taking myself too seriously, and he makes me feel completely safe."

In the kitchen, Big Mama prepared iced tea. Tamra sat at the rickety table and lovingly watched her grandmother, who moved slowly, neck bent, like her church steeple. "You're one of the few people I talk to. You always tell the truth," Tamra said.

"Don't ever trust anyone who always tells the truth," Big Mama said. She pulled ginger cookies from a tin, spread them on a plate before Tamra, then sat.

Tamra took a bite. It was stale. She quickly washed it down with a swallow of tea. "He says he loves me because I'm a fighter. That's a great reason to marry someone, isn't it?" She forced herself to take another bite of cookie.

Big Mama shrugged her pillowed shoulders. "Some folks think of marriage as a way to comfort the afflicted." She paused to bite into a cookie, then threw it down disgustedly. "Looks like Charles thinks it's a way to afflict the comfortable."

Big Mama pried the cookie from Tamra's hand, dumped the rest in the garbage. "Aren't we polite? Eating cookies dry as dust."

"John the Baptist ate wild locusts in the desert."

"They ain't that bad."

Tamra pulled the rocking chair out from the table. "I'm not a bit hungry. Please sit."

Big Mama's forehead wrinkled with concern.

Tamra began tentatively. "Have you ever known anyone who was happily married?"

"Why you ask?"

"It seems people who are unhappy before they marry are worse off after they do."

Big Mama leaned back in her chair, rocked herself a bit.

"Did your mama tell you that I have this service that picks me up, drives me to town for groceries twice a week?"

"Yes ma'am."

"Well every time is the same, same route, same neighbors, same driver."

"Yes ma'am, but . . ."

Her grandmother held up a silencing hand. "Hush, baby. Then one day, the driver's different. Just as polite, same passengers, same route, but this driver has a new style: tilts her mirror, and wears a different color ribbon on her cap every day, and she's got fancy sunglasses. Then, instead of easing up to the houses, she speeds and screeches to a stop. Makes it kind of exciting. Get my point?"

"Not really."

"Folks can take the same old roads and the ride can be different every time. In this marriage, you and Charles gonna be the drivers."

"Oh, Big Mama."

"I know what's really worrying you, though, honey."

"Tell me, then."

"It's like a curse in our family, ain't it?" She had her elbows on the table, and their faces almost touched. Tamra felt she was looking at the raised map of her family's life.

"A curse?"

"You know what I mean."

"The drinking?"

"That's right. All the men. It's like my girls are married to ghosts, ain't it?"

"I don't believe in curses. Daddy wasn't cursed any more than Uncle Fitzgerald or Papa Lord or any of them."

"What was it, then?"

"It's a disease that came through their blood. They probably had parents or uncles or aunts who were drunks."

"What's it take in your book to qualify as a curse?"

Tamra sat pondering her past, wanting to put it behind her. As if reading her mind, Big Mama said, "Charles could bring it to an end. He doesn't drink, does he?"

"How'd you know?"

"Everybody knows. More than a century ago the Lanes led a colored temperance movement. To this day, they won't touch a spoonful, even in their cakes . . . nothing."

Her body glowed, as if someone had passed a cooling light over her. "You're right. Still, I hope to God I'm doing the right thing. I don't know if I can fit in here."

"Some kind of scared, ain't you?" Big Mama teased. Tamra admitted she truly was. Her grandmother chuckled. "Like that time when you went to Mr. Sandebaker's class early?"

Tamra laughed with her. "I was proud to be his assistant."

"I can still see that white man," Big Mama said, "great big Mormon with the—whatcha call it?—crew cut, and those white, short-sleeved shirts."

Tamra cut in. "He was so tough, if you even called out one word in class he'd say, 'Zero for the day.' "

Big Mama's mouth stopped laughing, but her eyes were playful. She'd heard the story dozens of times, but Tamra knew she wanted to hear it again.

Big Mama said, "You went to his class early that morning, didn't 'cha? What'd you do?"

Tamra stood, pretending to enter a classroom at dawn. "Got there real early to set up his lab, and I saw this crate next to his desk, so I pried it open . . ."

"And the next thing . . ."

"Frogs . . . all over the room, like escape from Alcatraz."

Big Mama slapped her thighs, making a hollow sound, as if she'd exhausted her quota of mirth.

"There I was on my knees, trying to get 'em back in the crate when Mr. Sandebaker showed up, yelling: 'Wells, that's a double zero!' "

"Umm hmmm. You thought you'd failed the class."

"Oh, Big Mama, I wanted so badly to be a scientist." A rush of sadness came over her.

"You can still be one, can't you?"

"I wanted to be one of the greatest." Sighing deeply, she stood, preparing to go. "I've missed you so much. There wasn't anyone like you in all of Paris."

At the door, they shared a last embrace. Walking toward the car, she turned, calling to her grandmother. "I'll be living close by, so we can take nice long walks, get some exercise."

"I don't have time for that foolishness. I'm too busy going to the funerals of my athletic friends."

As she closed the door it seemed the house had swallowed her grandmother right up.

26

Tamra, Virginia, Big Mama *July 1977*

SHE HELD HER arms high, giggling as Virginia and Big Mama stood on chairs lowering the four-foot-wide cone of lace and satin over her head. The lining of the dress brought a sudden chill to her arms, as if she'd dived into an ocean. She listened through the heavy fabric to their familiar voices, now sounding thick and bubbly, as if speaking underwater.

". . . Made my own wedding dress and———." Virginia said.

"Did not," Big Mama interrupted.

She held her breath, immersed in darkness, as they disputed this memory. The weight of the dress settled in one fell . . . swoop.

"There," Virginia pronounced, and Tamra gulped loudly as her mother's face came into view. Air at last.

Virginia helped herself and then her mother down from their chairs. They stared wordlessly at Tamra, their eyes shining. She matched their gazes, awestruck, unable to recall when she'd last heard them agree. *"Ahhh,"* Virginia said.

"Umm umh," Big Mama intoned.

Tara hesitated to speak, to move, so caught up was she in this moment of acquiescence and murmurs, a mothers' duet.

"Come see yourself," Virginia said, leading her toward an oval, full-length mirror. It was one of many pieces Charles's workers had lugged in to transform the gospel room of the Nanticoke Saved By the Water Church into a bridal chamber. She took exaggerated steps across the room, her mother tugging at her arm and Big Mama reaching for the dress' train. Waving her hand like a wand across Tamra's reflection, Virginia said, *"Voilà."*

Tamra looked at her new self. Her shoulders floated dark and bare above a sea of pearls and waves of satin. Adrift in well-being, she opened herself to it, let it seep into her pores. Her mother and grandmother, bulbuous figures in turquoise, hovered behind, their faces bobbing as they exchanged hopeful glances, hands plucking at the dress' train and zipper.

Tamra had always known them to be reluctant before full-length mirrors or cameras, devising ways to sequester their bodies, as if seeing the whole of themselves was disturbing. She stepped nimbly aside. As expected, they gracefully dodged behind her. She decided to stay put. No teasing, no tricks today. In one hour, she'd marry Charles. Pressing her mouth to the back of her hand, she pictured the long indentation that was his sleeping spine. She'd wake this part of him first each morning, blanket him with kisses.

She had even found a way to make leaving Paris feel better: a new job at an agricultural genetics firm. When she'd signed the contract she had promised herself she'd quit checking her watch for the time in France, wondering if her colleagues were any closer to identifying the segments of DNA they'd been searching for. Several times, in the last month, she'd found herself watching and listening for the signs of researchers hurriedly completing reports: the rapid clicks of typewriters, heavy cigarette smoke rising to the tops of lattice windows.

"Lean on me," Virginia said as Tamra stepped into one, then another lacy white shoe.

Her thoughts returned to her new job, back to the process of selling it to herself. It paid well and would put her in touch with Charles's work. During the day she'd produce strains of disease-and-heat-resistant produce. Evenings she would have Charles.

If only I could get rid of this weight, an interior voice nagged. Studying her form in the mirror, she searched for signs of her new ten pounds. Stop worrying, she told herself, you'll never be fat like Big Mama and Virginia. But she wondered.

At least this dress hid every serving of bernaise, croissant, ganache, creme brulée, Whoppers, fries, french dipped sandwiches, sweet potato pudding, she-crab salad, chocolate pecan pie, corn cakes, buttermilk chicken, and greens that she'd swallowed in the last month. She drew herself up to her full height, pearls shimmering. The gown her mother had insisted she choose was perfect.

Virginia sat her in a red leather bishop's chair that was minus an armrest. She propped her feet on a stool, feeling like the pope preparing to greet emissaries. Virginia said she would send Wadine in to do Tamra's hair and left with Big Mama. She listened to the descent of their bickering. Alone for a long stretch of minutes with her life-changing dress, she enjoyed the silence.

Wadine entered, her eyes averted toward the floor. "Hey, Dr. W.," Tamra said, chortling at the nickname she'd used since the completion of her friend's Ph.D. in psychology. Wadine smiled shyly, as if they hadn't howled together last night or shared, for a decade, every rib-and-bone section of their lives in monthly letters or whispered conversations.

Lifting the ivory comb from the table, Wadine began her work. Her tentative touch was annoying. Pulling away, Tamra looked up inquiringly. Wadine answered in a rush. "I have something to tell you."

"No kidding," Tamra said, wondering what could be so terrible, after all, from a best friend.

"I'm in love."

"So how come last night you said . . . okay, what's the big deal?"

Wadine ran a finger along the teeth of the comb and spoke softly. "He's . . . um, uh . . ."

"White," Tamra finished, and gently took the comb from Wadine running it through her own hair. She felt the teeth drag on her scalp. As she walked toward the full-length mirror teasing her curls, she wondered why in the hell Wadine had chosen this time to tell her.

"You're ruining it," Wadine said sharply, and reached for the comb. Tamra wouldn't let go. Wadine's hands fell to her sides as she spoke in a monotone. "Go on. Tell me I'm making a terrible mistake. You're obviously angry."

She wondered if this was the voice Wadine used with clients. If so, she thought, it didn't bode well for a promising career. She adjusted her bangs as Wadine continued. "You've been away for a long time. Things . . . are . . . different here." She realized Wadine had no way of knowing how much those words irritated her heart and she replayed them in her mind: *different here.*

She was determined to hold onto her mood and tried to drown out Wadine's words, but she could not.

". . . In the Village in New York," Wadine continued, "it's practically like a . . ." She seemed to be watching Tamra, waiting for reassurance. ". . . A little United Nations . . ." Her voice trailed off as Tamra sat back down, folded her hands at her waist, and bent forward. She wanted to look as if she were listening, but her stomach churned; a frequent occurrence when she tried to convince herself she wasn't troubled.

She'd always prided herself on her ability to swallow her blues. She'd hear about a dilemma, and poof, would simply shove any negative thoughts through a trap door. The only problem now was that it felt as if the lining of her stomach was being scraped with a scissor blade.

She wondered how these words had become so abhorrent? Was it because she'd been warned so often about Nanticoke? As if she couldn't see how different life would be here from Paris. In fact, she'd used those very words to herself, that things would be different here, a mantra, a soothing thought that here, with Charles, she could finally be happy.

It had been Paris where she'd heard these words, as if for the first time. But she didn't want to think about Jules and Philippe today. She'd have preferred covering her ears. Instead, she studied the furniture, sturdy, shining antiques. She'd have to ask where he'd found them.

Wadine's voice resurfaced. "Jung said only that which changes remains true. I consider . . ."

"You're misunderstanding me," Tamra said. "I'm not angry." How could she maneuver Wadine and her complications lovingly out of this room? How dare she bring this up today, of all days. Memories of Jules were dragging her down. Who would have imagined a Black American model, from Detroit of all places, would wind up with a French graduate student? Tamra had snickered when Jules told her. But she understood when she met Phillipe. He was convincing and sincere, and her warnings had died on her lips. Maybe *things could be different here. . . .*

"I thought if anyone would understand . . ." Wadine's voice trailed off, then she added hopefully, "weren't all those people you wrote me about at the lab white?"

Tamra relined her lips, noticing she'd drawn the shape too narrow, wiped it off, and started again. Virginia would be waiting in the hallway wondering what was taking so long. She'd be sure to knock any minute, rescue her.

"Deenie, I love you. I want you to be happy."

Jules and Philippe had been enormously happy in the four years before his eye surgery. Nothing serious, he'd said. But his parents insisted he move back to their suburban home, if only to recuperate, and he'd given in. His mother had one request: The Negress. She must not come, not to the house, not ever. His father, you know.

Weeks later, Tamra had accompanied Jules to meet him in the Jardin de Tuileries. Jules had worn an outfit borrowed from her designer, Givenchy, but Philippe did not see it. His eyes had been bandaged and he'd leaned on his mother, shuffling.

Struggling to surface, she rubbed her now aching stomach. Could she explain to Wadine her humiliation on that day? From the distance, she had seen what Jules could not: Phillipe was a boy being indulged by his mother with a lithe, haute couture mannequin of café au lait. To the French aristocracy, she was Juliette. And they rose to their feet when she pranced on a runway in a jersey slip of a gown with silver-sequined bodice and panels of point d' esprit. But on that day, Juliet, sacrificing dignity, sat in a public garden where there was no music and the flowers had been stripped bare by rain. She could not be greeted at Philippe's door, no maid to take her superior coat. The bench would have to do.

Grateful the ache had subsided, Tamra took a deep breath, deciding not to say a word of this to her friend. Tamra's silence made her no less certain, however. In their daily life, Wadine's love and, she must admit now, her own for Charles, would bring them face to face with conditions that had for centuries resisted deviation. Fashions would change. Even Tamra had changed her whole life for love. Juliet would grow old, and each spring the flowers would return to the Tuileries. Most aspects of life, in fact, would undergo change. Ah, but never this. Love, despite locale or strength of passion, seemed destined to disappoint.

C'ést la vie, she thought, smiling inwardly, realizing Wadine was right. Tamra had been angry, but not with her. It was a diffused, unfocused indignation, triggered by words that to lovers seem omnipotent but only for a while. Whispered, they misled; shrieked, they were tolling bells in a blitzed church; a hope-filled, winged, airbound prayer that things are different here.

She drummed a tube of lipstick against the glass table top and tried to listen to Wadine, who had veered off into reckless territory. "I know what

I said back then. We were in high school, for God's sake. If anyone has surrendered to conventional expectations . . ."

Wadine had to be stopped. Tamra reached up and brought Wadine's hand down over her shoulder. This act quieted her friend. "The news just threw me, that's all. But I want to hear about him. What's his name?" She stopped listening, stalled for time as she waited for Virginia to appear and end this madness on her wedding day. She forced a smile toward the yellow satin skirt of her dearest friend.

"It's just that after being away for so long I notice Black men everywhere," Tamra said. "You name it—Dairy Queen, elevators, the library. Yesterday a brother put gas in my car and tried to get the last drop in, talking out loud to the nozzle, 'Come on, baby, come on.' Just hearing him made me want to . . ."

"Want to what?"

"Come."

"Charles has got it made."

Tamra turned, animated, glad to see Wadine's face relaxed. "I'd always taken Black men for granted, but there really is no one quite like a brother who has it together, know what I mean?"

Wadine nodded as Tamra continued. "It's a certain style, and when a brother has it . . ." She paused, flicking her fingers out and bopping across the room, the dress dragging with her, her shoulders pulled up high, eyes rapturously half-closed. "Whether in a jumpsuit with the little shoulder bag, gym shorts, oh, and I go wild when I see one in a suit and tie."

Wadine laughed. At last, Tamra thought, hallelujah.

"Oh, I feel better," Wadine said. "My parents went berserk when I told them. Daddy gave me the standard colored-girl lecture: 'We didn't raise you to be with any . . .'" They hooted.

Tamra pulled back. "Don't you feel a little guilty?"

Wadine flapped a hand. "There's nothing like Black middle-class guilt." She grabbed her own face as if struggling with a monstrous gel. "But you got to scrape it off."

Tamra laughingly suggested she write a paper about it.

Wadine said only yesterday she had come up with a more original idea for an academic paper, "when I was in the supermarket with your mom."

"This ain't a 'yo mama' joke, is it? I don't play that."

"No, really," Wadine insisted. "I was watching her at a produce counter." She imitated Virginia's dainty walk. Tamra was embarrassed that her mother was so transparent. "She inched up to the watermelons. I could tell she really wanted one, but she was just too proper, you know, with her Pierre Cardin pantsuit, to let white folks see her buying this thing. So she passed it up for a nice safe, pale, hon-nee-dew."

Tamra frowned. She might have done the same thing had she been in her mother's place. "This is the basis for your study?"

"Yeah, girl, I'm gonna call it 'Fear of Buying Watermelon.' "

Their laughter was so loud and sustained they attracted Virginia, who rushed in, forcing them apart, asking if they realized how late it was.

Wadine checked her watch. "Is this wedding CPT or Kings's time?"

"You better get outta here," Tamra called after her retreating figure.

Virginia lifted the comb, tapping a few of Tamra's hairs and giggling. "Prince Charles has arrived."

"What's so funny?" Tamra asked. Her mother said he had a surprise waiting for her. She knew Virginia would tell her if she pressed. He'd sent many surprises since her return—a gold watch, a jeweled brooch in the shape of Africa, and flowers each day to brighten her room. None of it had actually been a surprise, thanks to her mother. This time she planned to divert her. "I can't believe you're so calm."

Virginia reached into the pocket of her coatdress, smiling. "Because of this." She waved a bank book and handed it to Tamra, who stared at the sum. A thousand dollars. "Wow," she said weakly, wondering how her parents could afford all the festivities, plus this.

"This is from me, just between us. Put it away somewhere and hope you never have to use it."

The conspiratorial tone worried her, as if she'd been offered an illegal bribe. "What's it for?"

Virginia bent, whispering. "In case you ever have to get away . . . quickly."

She stared back. "Why would I want to do that?" As she spoke, she thought of something from another lifetime, when she and her mother had fled into the night. She slapped the book on the table, cutting the memory off, and reached for the blusher. "Charles isn't like that," Tamra said, wanting to add "like Daddy."

Virginia's voice brightened. "You'll probably never need it, but tuck it away. Don't tell your husband everything."

Virginia lifted the headpiece from the box. Tamra thought it looked like a large, white spider being placed on her head. "I have some disappointing news," Virginia said.

Hoping to cut her off, Tamra made choppy movements with her hand. "I don't want to hear it, please, Mama."

Virginia insisted this was important. "It's your father . . ."

Pieces of ugly pictures fanned across her mind.

"I had to make him go home."

The scraping in her stomach started again, but she spoke calmly. "Did you two have an argument?"

Virginia said he might make the reception. "It's his little . . . problem." Tamra took another swallow of information. Her mother had stopped admitting the truth because it was too much for her to accept, like her image in the mirror.

"You mean he's drunk, right?"

Virginia pressed a finger to Tamra's lips. "Don't say that." "It's his medicine. He needs a new prescription." When she removed her finger, Tamra ran her tongue over her teeth, checking for stray lipstick.

"This has nothing to do with his diabetes anymore than it was diabetes that made him wet the bed the other night. Think about it, Mama. A diabetic drinking! He's killing himself!"

Virginia flinched. "Harlen will give you away."

Tamra shrugged, and her words poured out, glib, quick. "Maybe he'll show up just as I get to the door of the church. Remember at the cotillion?" She saw pity in her mother's face. Tamra straightened her back and smoothed the skirt of her dress. "It's okay. In fact, better than okay. I can see Daddy any time. . . . But what about the receiving line, if someone asks?"

"Let me do the talking."

"You mean I shouldn't even tell Charles? You know I've told him about Daddy's drinking and——"

Virginia interrupted. "That wasn't necessary. Every family has little . . . stories. Anyway, it's not their business."

"They're family now, too."

"Just don't expect them to share their little stories. I used to see families like theirs and wonder what the secret was to their happiness. Now I just wonder what their secret is." She noticed a flash of triumph in her mother's eyes.

She wanted to hug Virginia, smother her pettiness, but she knew what kept her at arm's length. She believed Virginia to be somehow culpable for Daddy's absence. The other day, at breakfast, Seth had been drinking even then. There was vodka or gin in his orange juice. She could tell from the way he'd held his glass with two hands.

She had tried to decipher their elaborate scheme: He hid liquor all about the house. Tamra had found it in tiny bottles, jelly jars, behind the hedges, in drawers, closets. And he returned from shopping trips without packages, but Virginia never asked for the mayonnaise or aspirin or for whatever it was he was supposed to have purchased.

On that particular morning, when he spoke, Virginia stood at the stove, the spatula in her hand as if prepared to use it as a weapon. He told Tamra about an article he had read about sharks, said they could smell a teaspoon of blood in fifty thousand gallons of water, and that he'd seen people who——

Mid-sentence, Virginia's voice had lashed out, sharply, telling him to just shut up, and strangely, he'd resumed eating and quieted down, the fighting streak in him apparently dampened. Tamra digested the harshness of their bargain: He accepted Virginia's invectives. She stood guard over his life.

"You've got to pull yourself together," Virginia said. Tamra assured her she was fine, and anyway, what was she doing that made her think otherwise? She looked into her mother's face. "Shouldn't I know whether or not I'm okay?"

"Don't be angry with Daddy. He couldn't love you more. The first night we had you home, you kept crying and crying and he held you all night, telling you stories."

She shrugged, thinking, This is supposed to make me feel better? The truth was she'd never really trusted him. For years, she had expected he would disappoint her.

Her thoughts were interrupted as Big Mama entered. Tamra brought her arms around their shoulders in an act of false gaiety. "This is as it should be, the three of us together minutes before my wedding."

Big Mama stared meaningfully at Virginia. "This ain't your wedding. It's your mama's. You just the star."

"I want you to know how much you both mean to me," she said, her eyes misty.

"Uh, oh, looks like I walked in the wrong time," Big Mama said, trying to pull away. "Call me when you're finished crying."

She wasn't crying, she insisted, and promised she would not. "I just love you two—and Daddy—a lot and I want to thank you for——"

"I'm leaving," Big Mama interrupted.

"No, I'm leaving," Virginia said. "If we don't get that photographer in here we'll miss all the best shots."

With Virginia gone, Tamra grinned at Big Mama and held her hands up menacingly like a Dracula character. "Vee ah alone and I can get as soupy and sentimental as I vant."

Big Mama met her with an uneasy look. "Listen, what happened about that job? You gonna take it?"

"Yes ma'am. Not the one with the university . . . but it'll be okay."

"Sure it will," said Big Mama, "Gotta work. Ain't got no kids or nothing. Even a broke clock gives the right time twice a day."

Her grandmother placed a gold-tone, heart-shaped compact on her palm. Tamra stared blankly as Big Mama said, "Open it. Won't bite."

It contained a sparkling, black powder, which Tamra quickly realized was coal dust. Big Mama said her mother had given her some on her wedding day, and that she wished she'd used it. "Put some on your lids, shade your eyes from your husband's faults."

Tamra sighed audibly. "Oh, Big Mama."

"You gonna find yourself harping on little things. Your grandpa picked his nose when he drove." She screwed up her face. "And he pushed food on his fork with his finger . . . um, um, um, um, uh."

Growing impatient with Big Mama's sermons, Tamra tried to lead her away from the subject. "Maybe that was God's way of teaching you tolerance."

Big Mama looked at her like she needed a strait-jacket. "How can you fix your mouth to say that? Why would God give your Grandpa a hundred faults to teach me somethin' I ain't never learned? The point is for you to see less harshly and criticize seldom."

When she opened her mouth to object, Big Mama continued, "What comes out of your mouth can be worse than what goes into it."

She nodded, dramatically clamping her lips shut.

"If you got somethin' nasty to say, call me, hear?"

"*Umm hmmm.*"

She pointed toward Tamra's eyes. "With those microscope eyes of yours I should have given you a twenty-year supply."

Tamra closed the compact, complaining that she was tired of waiting for the photographer to come back to the dressing room. The woman was one of Virginia's sorors.

Big Mama shook her head. "Better hope she doesn't have to give y'all any directions up there. That gal's voice is so high and squeaky only the church mice'll understand her."

"Hush! She might be right outside." Tamra realized that her grandmother and Charles loved seeing her come unglued.

"But what kind of photographer can she be? Her glasses are so thick . . . can't see . . ." She kept shaking her head. "And that tight dress . . . needs to be wearin' something more fittin' her age?"

"What would you suggest?"

"A cane and a seeing-eye dog would be a good start."

When she was alone at last, Tamra fished a lace hankie from her purse, placed the bankbook in the middle, then Big Mama's gift, and tied the corners together. Now for a hiding place.

She saw at the very rear of the closet hung with choir robes a dusty stack of hymnals, and pushed the package back there. It was a relief not to have to think about it for a while. The way she figured it, her grandmother had been telling her to play deaf and dumb, like those see-no-evil, hear-no-evil statuettes, and her mother's message was right in line with that. If she did see something she didn't like in Charles, she should get the hell out of there. She shook her head.

She loved her family and was glad to be back with them, even if her hometown was so backwards. When she had asked a waitress last week what the vegetable of the day was, the woman had said, "macaroni and cheese." At another restaurant, when she requested a bowl of fresh rather than canned fruit, the waiter had asked if she was from out of town. And then there was this summertime weather: so hot and humid. If she closed her eyes it was as if someone had left the shower running and opened the door to the furnace. Somehow, she was determined to make her coming home work, to fit herself in, but that didn't mean she planned to become one of them.

Where was that photographer? She was ready to move on. What was to stop her from doing without those dressing room photos? She rather liked the idea of heading straight for her new life, without artificial poses. In three long strides she was at the door and reached for the knob. Stepping quietly into the hallway, she closed the door on her antique-filled dressing room.

27

Tamra and Charles July 11, 1977

SHE WOULD ALWAYS remember the fluid movements of the heads, nearly three hundred of them, turning, mouths fishlike in *oohs*, as she and Harlen began their journey. The gospel choir, a capella, sang a wordless, soul-deep rendition of the wedding march. Each row of pews was festooned with garlands of wild grape blossoms, which grew white and lavender in raucous abandon along the roads and creeks of Nanticoke.

Even with her steps paced to the slow rhythm of the chants, she'd expected the faces along the way to be an unrecognizable blur. She was mistaken. They all greeted her, old men with new haircuts, elegant ladies in small hats and brightly colored silks, their half-smiles apologetic in their unfamiliarity; Virginia's sorors, she assumed. Here and there, youths, often as wide-eyed as the young women with sloping hats who sat beside them.

She brushed off the momentary sadness that threatened to seize her. It was Charles's father, and not her own, with whom she walked. Harlen took measured steps, his eyes downward, as if embarrassed by the elegance of his tuxedo. She wanted to thank him for stepping in, knowing he hated the spotlight, but finding speech impossible, she looked away from the gazes. An unhappy thought flitted through her mind, like a bird soaring over a silent stretch of water. Daddy would never see this, the same man who twenty-five years before had spun tales when she was new to the earth, offering his voice as balm, cheerful, happy endings.

She tried to picture him through an infant's eyes, his mustache like a strip of velvet. She'd known his voice since utero. When she could walk, they'd danced. Standing on his shoes she'd learned the tango. What had happened to that joy? What of that man, that father? Breathing deeply, she swallowed the sadness.

In a shaft of light a swarm of fruit flies twirled. As girls, she and Wadine had called this a wedding of flies. She blinked hello to Aunt Florida, who wore a shiny navy suit, her hair in rolled-up clumps, as if, after removing the curlers, she'd forgotten to comb it out. A row ahead and only knee-high, she saw the small, laughing face of a squirming boy, an unknown second cousin perhaps.

Her Daddy was alone and maybe her mother had been right about him being ill. She pictured him in a tuxedo, stretched out, and grew aware of a sudden pressure on her arm. Harlen had squeezed it to his chest. She smiled at him, saw the sprinkling of freckles across his cheeks.

Shifting the bouquet of white roses, she glanced frontward, her head tilted toward the high ceilings of carved mahogany and the double rows of balconies. The church had been designed in the early nineteenth century, for whites to sit in the nave, free Blacks, including, eventually, the Lanes, in the first balcony, and slaves in the uppermost reaches. Today this largely Black group was scattered with the faces of Charles's white business associates, and up front, seated with his family, Eve and Art Reardon.

She looked toward the draped, flowering altar, where Charles waited. The photographer's light, hidden somewhere behind, casting a hazy glow. He held his hands behind his back and was dressed as an African groom, in white brocade with threads of gold. He wore a skullcap with a pattern along the brow, a hip-length shirt with short, wide sleeves, pants that narrowed at the calf, and a long draping shawl hung from a shoulder.

Her attention was pulled away by the voices of older twin cousins, smiles of approval illuminating their round faces. They raised their heavy bodies on tiptoes. "Go on, girl," one called as she passed.

"You lookin' good, honey," another said.

"Allll right," they said together, their voices tingling her skin, as if tiny lights had been strung across her. She would not have cried. But the nearest twin reached out and touched her elbow, saying softly, as if they were alone, "You gonna be fine, you wait and see, ya hear?" Words of condolence, of seeing through, which tipped her tears beyond the veil, onto her chin and breasts.

Virginia and Big Mama seemed to be holding their breath, prepared to breathe for her. Her mother wore glasses, the lenses catching the light and masking her eyes as she held her chin up.

As Wadine laid her flowers in a wide basket, Charles reached under her veil, wiping a tear from her face, a public act of love, as if comforting a child. He smiled, whispering something.

She tried sniffing, but it came out as a sob.

"Think you can do this without making me look like a fool?"

"Piece of cake, my brother." She sniffed. "If you don't watch it I'm going to embarrass you for a change and kiss you before the ceremony starts."

He lifted her veil. "Go for it," he said, and moving quickly, she grabbed his shoulders, kissing him roughly on the mouth. There was a burst of startled laughter and applause. She held onto him, riding the cheers, her arms about his waist, holding on, so thankful for him. He'd pulled her to dry land.

Reverend Noel's voice interrupted the whistles and cheers, each of his words in deep timbre, like a separate song. "Dearly beloved: We have come together in the presence of God . . ."

She looked closely at the cleric, who had been educated at Princeton, and who, like her, had returned. Was he happy here? His bright blue and scarlet doctoral hood, which hung from around his neck and over his shoulders, added a festive splash to his black robe. ". . . If any of you can show just cause why they may not lawfully be married, speak now; or else forever hold your peace."

She heard tittering and turned to see Charles staring threateningly into the crowd, as if daring anyone to speak out.

When Harlen had finally given her away, they sat, the two of them, as Reverend Noel moved to his pulpit and took a long drink of water. "Some folks wonder why you'd even need a preacher at a wedding. Tamra and Charles already have our goodwill and prayers on this occasion; and from what I just saw, they certainly know what they want to do."

The congregation laughed heartily at this.

"I suppose they could simply exchange vows and we could get on with the party." There was a scattering of applause. "But I am here to remind you, for this one brief moment, about the importance of marriage." A man in back called, "Amen."

Reverend Noel continued. "A lot of you are just meeting Tamra for the

first time. She's a town girl, and in her young life has traveled extensively."
He said that while he hadn't traveled as much, he'd just returned from Kenya,
where he'd visited Machakos, Nairobi, and Lokitaung.

Charles whispered: "I think he picked up the wrong sermon. This sounds
like his travelog."

"On one of my favorite tours we visited a protected area filled with
giraffes. With the mists swirling about their long necks and legs and spotted
bodies, it was like watching a slow-motion ballet. But I learned something
important that day. When these animals drink from a river it is not an easy
task, for they are so tall, and it is unsafe. Low to the ground they can easily
be attacked by enemies. So when they drink, they go in pairs, like partners . . ."

"*Umm hmm*, now that's all right, Reverend," a voice called.

Charles whispered, "That's your uncle back there." Tamra pretended to
ignore him and covered her smile with the white Bible Dalhia had given her.
It had served at family weddings over a century.

The minister's voice rose. "While one drinks, the other stands guard."

The voice from the rear again. "Um hm, now put some salt and pepper
on it."

Charles poked his elbow into her side. "You didn't warn me about all
these countrified Negroes in your family." Now she fought laughter and
discovered Charles was a master at keeping a straight face.

The pastor continued, saying that Tamra and Charles represented a
marriage of science and nature, and that one should not be separated from
the other. "Like most scientists who have an exacting approach to viewing
the world," he said, "Tamra has discovered something about the relationship
people must have to nature. We can't be detached because we are immersed
in God's world. We are learning we can't get free from it, stand over it, or
manipulate it for our ends without extraordinary costs to ourselves and the
whole of creation. We are part of the very material and structure of the
universe itself."

Tamra found herself leaning toward Charles as she continued listening
to the preacher.

"In a very real way, they are influencing the course of creation. And
what we can expect from them is that they will do nothing less than change
the world."

The voice from the rear again: "Preach on in heaven."

"Tamra and Charles, you are saying to the world, 'We are better as two than as one.' It is a testament to enduring love . . . whether one is up or down . . . that God intends for human relationships."

The sermon ended, they stood to return to the altar, when a frail, elderly woman in a straw bonnet walked on stage with sheet music and a metal stand. Tamra wondered if there was something in the schedule she'd overlooked. Charles sat and urged Tamra to do the same.

The woman unfolded the legs of the stand and arranged sheet music. Backstage, someone could be heard fiddling with the audio system, placing a needle to a record.

The congregation rose. It was the national anthem. Tamra turned, narrow-eyed, toward Virginia, who stared defiantly back. It confirmed a nagging fear: This was the same soror Virginia had mentioned months before, who'd retired from half a century of teaching, and who'd taken up singing. When Virginia had first suggested this woman be allowed to perform at the wedding, Tamra had vetoed the idea. She saw now that she'd been overruled, and with "The Star-Spangled Banner," of all choices, for a wedding! The old gang of college militants who she'd invited would be sure she had lost her mind.

"O— say! Can you see . . ."

Oh, dear, she was off to a shaky start, an off-key, wavering, fake soprano. She turned toward Virginia and smiled with tiger teeth. Charles whispered loudly to the back of her head. "Loosen up, baby." She let her shoulders drop.

"Whose broad stripes and bright stars . . ."

As her voice rose Charles began to howl like a coon dog.

"O'er the ramparts we watch'd . . ."

"Owwwwwwwwwwwwwwww."

"And the rockets' red glare . . ."

"Yowwwwww . . ."

Tamra nudged his foot. When he persisted, she stepped on his toe, but he only howled louder. She looked around to see how their guests were reacting to his howling. Except for Virginia, who looked furious, a few others fought grins. Hoping to drown him out, she raised her own voice, singing along with the final chorus.

"Oh, say does that star-spangled . . ."

The congregation and choir joined in.

"O'er the land of the free . . . and the home of the brave."

Silence followed as the soloist gathered her music and left. Tamra looked smugly at Virginia. Finally she had someone who could handle her mother's manipulations.

Virginia nodded determinedly toward the altar. It was time to resume their position up front. Tamra grabbed Charles's hand and gave him a scolding look. He smiled like a saint. She'd been right about him all along, she'd never be able to stop him from doing anything he wanted.

At last, Reverend Noel asked the questions she'd waited for years to answer. "Will you have this man to be your husband; to live together in the covenant of marriage? Will you love him, comfort him, honor and keep him, in sickness and in health, and, forsaking all others, be faithful to him as long as you both shall live?

"Oh yes, I will," she answered, silently adding the words, *gladly, delightedly, assuredly, passionately,* as the pastor questioned Charles.

The ceremony concluded with: "Those whom God has joined together let no one put asunder," and she and Charles moved up the aisle greeted by a crashing round of applause that sent them spilling into the sunlight. They stood together, thanking their guests and posing for photos. Through the sumptuous buffet, she hardly knew what she ate or said. Cousin after cousin whispered in her ear, speaking of her good fortune, of the joyful life ahead, assuring her she'd found the perfect mate.

She rushed back to the dressing room to prepare for their three-day honeymoon. When she'd changed her clothes and was returning to the hall, she was startled to find Charles waiting behind the church with the surprise Virginia had tried to warn her about. He sat on a black charger that was decorated with pastel ribbons and tiny, pink roses. The scent of the flowers failed to mask the horsy smell, and the beast stamped its hooves threateningly as she approached. He then turned in circles, finally nudging her with his snout. She was awed by the animal's strength.

Charles said: "You're always calling me your prince."

Eyeing the saddle of brown, tooled leather, she wondered if she could actually fit up there with him. He told her to hurry and climb up, but she looked dubiously at the neighing horse. "You don't actually expect me to . . ."

"Did you know there was a war lord named Tamerlane?"

"You're making that up . . ."

"I swear, baby. Fourteenth century. Somewhere in Asia. Genghis Khan's great-nephew or something. Christopher Marlowe wrote a play about him."

"There's a point to this?"

"Well, I asked myself, what mode of transportation would be fit for his namesake, and on her wedding day?"

She backed off, protesting. "That thing's huge. I can't." The horse stamped, a large wet eye watching her.

"Come on, Tamerlane, give me your hand, hurry. Your suitcase, everything's in the car. Hurry."

"Can't wait to be alone with me, eh?" she taunted, while walking cautiously to the front of the horse, trying to work up the nerve to mount it. She decided to just get up and not think about the discomfort. Charles extended a hand as she struggled to figure out which foot to hook into the stirrup. He pointed to her right one. Her palm was clammy and slipped from his grasp as he pulled her up. The acetate travel dress clung to her skin. Before she could settle in, the horse reared up. "I don't think he's too crazy about all this."

"Skyrocket was thirty-one last week. He's tired, that's all."

No matter how much she twisted, comfort was impossible. It felt like she was sitting on the corners of two heavy boxes.

"What took you so long, anyway?" he asked, urging Skyrocket along.

"Had to call Daddy," she said, "but that's not important. I haven't had time to tell you what went on back there in my dressing room. First Wadine, then my mother and Big Mama gave me the strangest . . ."

"I want to hear about it, baby," he said, "but hold on. I've got to find a john."

She reached under his shirt, her fingers moving in circles. His belly was hard, flat, and the hairs on his chest so wiry they peppered her fingertips. She thought about it. They were really married. The wonder of it. Skyrocket picked up speed, and she said through giggles: "So this is the way you introduce me to the realities of farm life?"

"I didn't think we could fit on a hog."

Their laughter broke the silence of the road, and as Skyrocket moved beneath them, she was surprised at how fully she enjoyed the warmth and trembling of the horse's body through her stockings. On one side of the road, they passed a green field of young wheat, on the other, an idle plot gone to chickweed, wild garlic, and flowering dandelion. And she thought, as the horse began to trot, that she liked seeing the world from up high.

28

Tamra October 1990

IT IS DIFFICULT to see the hands on her watch. This guest room, although up high and so close to the water, is less sunny than other rooms in Wadine's home. She remembers a passage from the *Song of Zechariah:*

> Through the tender mercy of our God, whereby the dayspring
> from on high hath visited us;
> To give light to them that sit in darkness."

It's eight o'clock, the latest she has slept in years. But she's not surprised. In the eight days she has been here, her body clock has been reset. She wonders how this will affect her when she returns home. If she returns. She has expected some face-saving gesture from Charles, at least a phone call or a bouquet of flowers. Even better, his showing up on Wadine's doorstep. There has been nothing.

No time to dwell on this. She must try to reach at least one of the kids before they rush off to church. Dalhia answers and they exchange greetings; she says Joyce and H.P. are there, and Tamra's heart thumps as she waits. H.P. had seemed so grown-up when she'd left. Today he is an eight-year-old filled with questions she cannot answer. When is she coming home? Where's

Cassie? She hears "Sesame Street" playing. They haven't watched it for years. Her son needs soothing. And she can tell when her words begin to work on him. He teases his sister, an old joke. "Mom, I just finished a bowl of snow flakes."

Just as he'd known she would, Joyce snatches the telephone to correct him. "That's Frosted Flakes." When will she ever see through this ribbing?

She hears H.P. continue. "Don't have a cat."

Joyce scolds. "That's a cow."

"What's the difference?"

"If you don't know the———."

Tamra interrupts, laughing. They're like a Charles and Tamra act in miniature. Joyce whispers that her grandmother lets them watch violent shows and that they have Pop Tarts for breakfast.

Tamra says not to worry, she'll be back before their teeth or brains drop out. And then both of the children, one per phone extension, like valves to her heart, insist there's another reason she must rush: It's time for scarecrows. They need to raid her closet, so hurry, please.

Last year they had stuffed straw into plaid shirts, khaki pants, and even a pair of pink-striped OshKosh. They mounted the scarecrows on poles near the road, a family of straw creatures, as a signal to passersby: This is the home of a family.

Only a matter of days, she promises, she'll let them know. And oh, H.P. says in passing, Daddy's downstairs, he's taking us to church, he comes every day, sometimes twice. When he hangs up, she is left with Joyce, who appeals to her as one ten-year-old adult to another.

"You're going to divorce Daddy, aren't you?"

"Why would you ask that?"

"It's okay, I understand. A lot of kids in my class . . . their parents are divorced."

"Who? That's not true."

"Well, I know divorces. I got a book from the library."

"Oh, honey. You've probably been real sad."

"I'm fine and I don't want to talk about it. Daddy's waiting. He'll be looking so good . . ."

"Darling . . ."

Then a break in her voice. "You aren't going to, are you?"

"Oh, baby . . ."

"What does Cassie have to do with it?"

"It's not something I can explain right now. But remember, your daddy and I love you fiercely."

When they hang up, the loudness of the dial tone blares in the room. She remembers that the evening before she'd told her hosts she might accompany them to church. There's a new rector from Atlanta who makes them cry and think when he preaches, and Wadine wants Tamra to hear him. Fine, that's just what she needs, another good cry. She stands at the window. On the promenade, a few joggers dash by.

She makes her bed and straightens the area. When she emerges from her room, showered and dressed in a softly pleated skirt and a good pair of walking shoes, she waits at the top of the spiral stairway, listening. It is an old habit from childhood. Is it safe to go down? Do they need me? The spiraled, pine steps and white, metal rail give her the impression that she is looking into a massive conch shell.

Tiptoeing noiselessly down the steps, she discovers a breakfast table has been set up near the window looking out onto the garden. Along with muffins, strawberries, and orange juice, are a glass vase of white flowers, a royal blue bottle of water, and a thick Sunday paper.

A voice startles her. "Dey lef' just now. Der expectin' you'll come 'long." It is the uniformed, hairnetted housekeeper, Emma Twichell. Tamra sits uncomfortably, eating a few bites, as she listens to Mrs. Twitchell struggling in the kitchen with something. She pokes her head in the doorway. The woman is trying to twist the bowl off a Cuisinart. She glances up at Tamra and returns to her task. Tamra notices her reserve, her aloofness, the way, she is sure, Virginia must have been when she'd worked as a maid in New York.

"What happened there?" Tamra asks.

"One of de kids was grindin' granola bars," she says, annoyance in her voice. "De blade is stuck . . . can't be washed."

Tamra suggests she pour a teaspoon of Comet and half a cup of water in the bowl before turning the processor on. Mrs. Twitchell doesn't look any too confident but follows her advice. When she switches the machine off, she finds Tamra's method has worked. The bowl and blade are no longer jammed. Her frown softens. Tamra winks at her.

Speaking in a lilting accent, Mrs. Twichell explains the Drakes have attended both church services. "She left sum-ting," she says, reaching for a business card that has fallen between the muffins. It's the number for a neighborhood car service.

"Emma," Tamra begins, hoping she has found an ally. "I don't want to use a private cab. I've never visited New York before." The woman eyes her unsmilingly. "Do you think this church is something I could find if I take the subway?"

"Sure you kin," she says. "I take de subway each day." In fact, she suggests that Tamra might do even better if she has a subway map. "Dis is a secret just for we. I don' know a ting."

Tamra readily agrees. What's one more secret?

"I gon get de map." Leading Tamra back upstairs to the guest room, Mrs. Twichell's face brightens at the sight of the carefully made bed. And when they pass the doorway to the adjoining bathroom, where Tamra has scrubbed the glass shower stall and cleaned and dried the basin, Mrs. Twichell actually smiles.

She listens carefully to the directions. Getting there sounds simple enough until Mrs. Twichell cautions that the old men in the station will pose no danger, but to "Keep an eye on de teenage lads. If there's a gang, don get on de same train. Dey'd as soon dust you along the rails as to breathe."

She explains that it's a long ride between stops. "All de defenseless people. . . . The boys would be workin' dere way through, pillagin', lootin', and robbin'."

Tamra considers sneaking to a pay phone and calling the car service. But once she's walking up Montague, the peaceful street that just the night before had reminded her of streets in Paris, she finds it difficult to believe teenage muggers ride trains on Sunday mornings.

Finding the station easily enough, she pays the attendant and descends the long stairway. Mrs. Twichell has prepared her well for the scene that greets her. Several elderly men are on the platform, some in fetal positions on benches; others appear to sleep with their bodies propped against walls that are covered with intricate graffiti, like prehistoric cave scratchings.

Others also wait for the train. One teenage boy in a goose-down coat and fur-crested hood, heavy for the mild weather, wears his knit cap pulled only partially onto his head. He carries a radio on his shoulder with the volume up high.

Two Japanese tourists, cameras swinging from their necks, talk animatedly in their native language. Three well-dressed Black men, who she assumes from their conversations and stacks of literature are Jehovah's Witnesses, stand near the stairwell, while another woman, also by herself, appears dressed for business.

Tamra has been waiting ten minutes, but at least there is a theater, of sorts, for entertainment. A homeless man offers the woman a red rose, insisting she take it. She grudgingly accepts and flashes a guarded smile. The man bows and reaching under his jacket produces a white, styrofoam plate, stained from spaghetti sauce. "Donation, please," he says. The woman squeezes a quarter from her jacket pocket and drops it onto the plate. Tamra hardens her features and when the flower-giver turns toward her, and sees her withering stare, he passes.

The radio player nears again, along the edge, and she covers her ears. A homeless man is awakened by the volume. Very old with long white hair and lips so red and wet and swollen they look as if they've been soaked in formaldehyde, he moves about asking directions to Times Square. But everyone, including Tamra, who wears her angriest look, shuns him. Even the Jehovah's Witnesses, perhaps following Tamra's lead, give him unchristian scowls.

Only one of the Japanese tourists, who perhaps understands the confusion of being lost in a strange city, shows this man kindness. In fact, he pulls from his windbreaker the same sort of subway map Tamra has tucked in her pocket. She feels guilty about her rudeness, as the tourist patiently entertains questions from the white-haired man, who staggers as he listens.

When they've finished, the map tucked back inside the windbreaker, the white-haired man thanks the tourist profusely and catching him by the chin, delivers a sloppy kiss to the cheek. The tourist backs off, wiping his face with a hankie, and the others along the platform scatter. Tamra now finds herself closer to the edge as the train squeals into the station.

She watches, transfixed as her car plunges into a dark tunnel, passing another train, lights blinking. The trains slow, and through her window passengers float by. She searches their faces feeling she may spot herself.

Halfway down the car a woman, her tired face done up in garish makeup, nappy blond hair curled childishly, holds on to a shopping cart filled with styrofoam wigheads and stands quietly. But she soon begins to mutter. When her voice rises, Tamra understands her words: "You done dragged me bottom up and fucked me."

Her words are impossible to ignore. Several passengers, including the camera-laden tourists, leave through the sliding door. Still, the car is full of passengers, and the woman, although getting louder, does not appear to be dangerous. Tamra chooses to remain where she is. Signs warn of falling between cars and the sliding doors look treacherous.

When they reach the first stop, she's relieved when a policeman boards the train. He's freckle-faced and young, but with a live walkie-talkie hitched to his belt, he looks capable of handling any problems. And to Tamra's surprise, he is exceedingly polite to the bellowing woman, only warning her that she must stop shouting or get off at the next stop. With this, the woman raises an accusing finger toward the trio of Jehovah's Witnesses and repeats her charge, "He turned me bottom up and fucked me."

The officer stares coldy at the men and asks, "Which one?" Tamra watches the men cringe, and she can't help but think that pressed up against the wall, clad in raincoats, they do look like suspects in a police lineup.

Her attention shifts as they pull into the Wall Street station and she searches her pockets and purse for the handwritten directions. She's frantic. It is no longer there. Perhaps she has dropped it along Montague Street. But she comforts herself. After all, she does remember the name of Trinity Church. Wadine and Stephen have boasted that it is one of the most famous in the world.

The shrieking woman is behind her as she steps onto the platform, and Tamra rushes up and outside. To her relief, Trinity, with its proud steeple, stands just before her. She hurries into the foyer only to learn from an attendant that the sermon has already started. When Tamra resists going in, he suggests she wait in the graveyard. Captain Kidd is buried out there, he says. She smiles, thinking it fitting that Wall Street's largest church houses the remains of a pirate. Although she has always been fascinated by graveyards, she does not want to stay. Emboldened by her train ride, she prefers to walk the quiet Sunday streets.

29

Charles September 1982

HE CENTERED THE notebook on the table and reached inside his jacket for a pen. His eyes scanned the twelve restive faces of his managerial staff as he rolled his antique pen between his hands. He could look anywhere but over his shoulder at Aunt Louise. She'd been insisting lately that as his secretary she was paid to take notes and that any public scribbling on his part diminished her in the eyes of others. No doodling allowed? Was he the director of a major agricultural corporation or a schoolboy forced to obey an aunt's whims?

He looked absentmindedly to his right. Her eyes, wrinkled and half-closed, were ready for him; her nostrils flared as if to trumpet a call to arms. He wondered what had happened to his once kindly aunt. But he already knew. She'd been radicalized by his own dear wife, incorporated into a dress-for-success madwoman and trained in the manipulations of female office protocol.

When the nervous second accountant stood to speak, Charles wrote: ANDERSON'S WEAKLY REPORT. The young man held the papers inches from his nose as if he were smelling them first. "We've experienced a one percent drop on corn at Adams," he said.

Charles asked why, and O'Toole, the field inspector, raised a hand. "I think it was the seeds."

Charles asked if he had any documentation.

"I'd be willing to go with my intuition . . ."

"I'd rather you not," he said. "I want the paperwork on it and I'd like to see the germinating tests. That system is still so new to us. Maybe we'd better fiddle with . . ." He was conscious of Aunt Louise's menacing stare. How did she expect him to concentrate? But perhaps his annoyance was misdirected. Maybe he should be angry with himself for even caring how she felt. Finishing his verbal directive, he wrote the letters N.H.G.A., an abbreviation for Never Hire Great Aunts.

Charles shifted his attention back toward the tail of Anderson's paisley tie, which was all he could see of the accountant's upper body. The sheet of paper hid his face and the hand that held it was shaking. Charles asked for the details.

"We were gigged for moisture in the shipment to Atlanta and assuming that . . ."

"Excuse me, Anderson," he said and noticed the managers jerk to attention. It had been three years now since his expansion into a full-scale agricultural operation, but he was still impressed by the impact he had on the corporate staff, especially since they were all older than he. He'd have to jot down W.P.W.D. (Wield Power With Discretion), but for the time being, he concentrated on softening his voice. "I could see you better if you put your notes down and talked."

The managers shifted in their chairs. These meetings had grown longer since he'd purchased the Reardon land last year, and this week, with the acquisition of the Reardon grain elevator, they would only get longer. Anderson scanned his notes. Charles ran a hand along his chin, feeling the stubble and admiring it. He hadn't slept in two days but didn't feel a bit tired.

Still, he wouldn't mind a third cup of coffee. He peeked into a mug emblazoned in red with: YOUR FIRST FATHER'S DAY. Empty. This was the sort of thing that drove him crazy. If he rose to get more, someone would rush to fill it for him, and that would further aggravate Aunt Louise. But he couldn't ask her for more coffee, could he? Only last week he'd heard her complaining to Tamra about her heavy workload. He sneaked a glance at his new and improved aunt. Heavy workload, all right. Even the form-fitting skirt of her three-piece black suit couldn't keep her thighs from spilling over the seat of the chair. But he'd better concentrate. Anderson had his hands clasped over his stomach, as if waiting for his attention.

Clearing his throat, Charles said: "Give me the picture at a glance. This the only field down?"

"Yes sir," Anderson said. "We've recorded modest profits on fifteen fields this month."

"So what's the loss?"

"Rounded off at thirty-eight."

"Drop of?"

"Well, when we actually took a look at it . . ."

He rubbed his hands together. "Um, tell you what, Anderson. Why don't you give me a rundown each morning, say by ten?"

Anderson's gray eyes bulged.

Charles said it could be put in writing. "Sure, sure," Anderson said, his shoulders slumping with relief. He noticed Aunt Louise scratching under her Afro-puff hairpiece with a few of her press-on nails, while she used the other hand for writing. The pencil seemed to pull her fingers in a gliding motion, as if she were working her Ouija board. He sighed deeply. What he needed was a book on management skills. But had one been written on how to manage the Aunt Louises of the world?

"By the way, Anderson," he said, gesturing for the accountant not to pop up. "Give all those reports to Miss Louise. She can make sure I have them on my desk in the mornings." Her mouth spread into a smile. It was the same grin she had bestowed on him as a child, when he'd stopped at her house every marking period and she'd paid him a silver dollar per A. She was the aunt who'd insisted Pa give him week-long Christmas "vacations" at her house, no work allowed, and she was the aunt he'd promised that no matter where he went, she'd go with him.

"If there's nothing else," Charles said, about to stand.

His cousin, Bobbi, Cousin Johnny's silver-haired big sister, raised her hand. He'd hoped to avoid talking to her. She approached the slightest inconvenience like a catastrophe. It was okay with him that she didn't bother to stand. He'd always been "Little Charles" to her and she didn't seem ready to alter the relationship, no matter how many titles he gave her. Six feet tall and at least thirty pounds underweight, she wore brightly patterned dresses and was a chain smoker. "We're going to have to talk. Giving away money isn't as easy as it sounds."

That was typical. He'd brought Bobbi in to establish a foundation that among other things would fund cash-strapped soup kitchens, low-income housing, and a mentor program in inner-city schools. Bobbi continued: "And we still haven't decided on my assistant."

Only yesterday he'd assured her he trusted her judgment and had encouraged her to interview candidates and hire the one she preferred. "What's the prob——"

Bobbi cut him off. "I can't hire just anyone. It has to be someone who can handle a lot of stress."

Especially if she's working with you, he thought, but what he said was, "I feel certain you can——"

She interrupted again, saying vehemently, "For instance, if she's in the middle of an assignment and you just walk in the way you did yesterday, tossing papers down, demanding she drop everything else, that you've got to be helped that instant . . ."

So that's what this tirade was about. He raised his voice to drown her out. "We won't discuss this now." Was he shouting? At least one manager looked alarmed. Damn. A relative knew how to get to you better than anyone. Forcing himself to look calm, he added, "These folks need to get back to work," and he added to himself, "they sure don't want to listen to your complaints."

He checked his watch. Still enough time to beat Tamra home. That way he could cook dinner instead of having to eat whatever slop she poured from a can. Pushing against the table, about to stand, he said, "If there's nothing else . . ."

" 'Fraid there is." It was Ernest, his red-headed dispatcher who always spoke in monotoned shorthand. "Wilmington load. Turned over."

"Where?"

"Thirteen."

"Injuries?"

"None."

"Driver?"

"Eddie."

Eddie was Ernest's brother, and Charles thought that for someone whose sibling had been in a wreck, Ernest was far too calm. Something didn't fit. He tried imagining thousands of tomatoes crushed on hot asphalt, a tide of sauce, and grew increasingly suspicious.

From the time he'd purchased the Reardon grain elevator, he'd sensed a deepening level of resentment from whites. One bank official he'd known all his life had talked as if he was eager for him to miss a payment. There'd also been a lot of grumbling at that auction yesterday. Now this. An accident could drive up insurance rates, throw off shipment dates, take a truck out of commission for weeks. But would Eddie and Ernest actually risk their jobs to spite him? Had the accident been faked? He asked what the losses had been.

"Whole trailer."

His eyes fell on Pa's empty chair and he wished he were here. Only Pa could advise him in one silent, filial exchange whether Ernest could be trusted.

"How's Eddie?" He was stalling so he could devise a plan. Ernest smiled, emitting entire sentences in a rush. He said Eddie was fine, but the whole rig had come loose.

Could the fact that Pa had disagreed with him publicly over the elevator deal have something to do with it? Did the brothers view him as being so distracted they figured it was a good time to move against him?

"Okay," he said, standing, knowing his stature would add impact to his words and realizing everyone at the table was studying him. This was their first chance to see how he handled a crisis without Pa. He had to assume he'd be the only one in the room who'd know he would be acting, as he willed himself to envision Brando's godfather. "I want pictures."

Ernest glanced sarcastically at Anderson, who quickly looked away. Ernest shrugged: "No camera."

"The highway patrol will have one or police forensics will." He reached for his notebook, tore off a sheet of paper, and handed it to Ernest. "Maybe you should write this down. Number two: I want a report in twenty-four hours on Eddie's blood analysis."

Ernest, who had stopped smiling, clicked his pen.

"And Norm . . ." Charles said without once glancing away to address the petite Black man in tortoise-shell glasses. "Ask our carrier to get someone out there immediately and make a report. Then call the city desk of the closest newspaper in Delaware, find a coupla reporters, and offer 'em two hundred each to do their own investigations . . ." He tried to look as if he could see through Ernest and made his voice low and deep. ". . . So they can verify your brother's claim. He'll need that." He wanted to continue to make him squirm; he figured that even if the accident hadn't been faked, this could pay off. They would all remember he was not to be trifled with.

"Also, Norm," he added, "there's another hundred bucks apiece if those reporters call me tomorrow morning at seven." Flushed with the excitement of performing, he moved toward his seat.

Before he could sit, he heard Aunt Louise's voice.

"Excuse me, dear."

"Yes ma'am, you wanted something?"

She'd always had a girl's voice, he thought as he waited for her to blow her nose. "You have breakfast at the Lion's Club tomorrow from seven 'til . . ." She was trying to look over her wad of tissue and decipher one of the nearly illegible entries she'd made on his calendar. "Well, what duz it matter?" she said talking through her nose. "'Id doesn't quite say, but you'll be speaking about how you've turned your——"

"Yes ma'am, thank you."

He turned back toward Ernest, feeling his advantage had been blown into her tissue. Dammit. He ran through his orders: reporters at six. Blood analysis in twenty-four hours. Insurance report. Police pictures. "Got that?" Norm and Ernest nodded.

He'd been certain his instincts were right, until he saw the others staring at him, but not in admiration. What was it? It was difficult to read their faces. Anderson smiled reassuringly, and Charles sat down wanting to ask if there was any other business. The group watched him so silently he felt as if a spell had been cast over the room.

Had he gone overboard about this Eddie and Ernest plot? They'd worked for the family for years. Why would they cheat him now? Still, except for the worried smiles on their faces, no one talked. Even Bobbi looked more depressed than usual.

Aunt Louise slid his mug before him and patted his shoulder reassuringly. "Here you are, son," she said in the same tone she'd used years ago when his team had lost. Only this time, her tenderness implied that his behavior was okay, that she understood that he needed sleep.

"Jessie . . ." he looked at the delicate brunette he'd hired away from an investment firm in Richmond. "Ah . . . you'll have to walk down to the car with me . . . um . . . give me that futures report." She nodded okay, her eyes shining up at him.

Willie Smalls, still in dusty brown work clothes, raised his hand. "I ain't give you a rundown yet on the milk thistle at Little Rivers."

Charles shook his head and said he couldn't discuss it right now. But he warned Willie they should hold off on spraying and get some real aggressive boys with hoes and weed cutters out there. "Those airplanes are old and inaccurate. It won't take much of those chemicals on the half-section south of there, where we've planted . . . limas, aren't they?"

"Yeah, that's right," Willie said, "to turn those beans into mutants. If worse comes to worse a small field like Little Rivers can be sprayed from the ground until we get those new planes in."

Willie wanted to know what to do about Old Man Kohl's request to rent one of their refrigerator trucks. Charles found this last question frustrating. Maybe Aunt Louise was right and he just needed sleep. But what was wrong with wanting his employees to not look constantly to him for all the answers?

Determined to end the meeting, he stood, briefly answered Willie, made a quick suggestion that they all try to devise a plan for spinning rentals into a separate venture, and then silenced them by extending his left hand toward Cousin Johnny, the right toward Aunt Louise. Their palms spoke to him of their contrasting personalities. Johnny's grip was strong, the skin smooth and well cared for, despite his work as a crew chief. Aunt Louise's was fleshy and moist from years of Jergens.

Joining in a circle of hands, head bowed, he began: "Lord, here we are again. Seems like we're always asking instead of waiting to hear what you want. Certainly you're doing a lot more than ever we could dream of asking. Help us to be mindful of this and to remember the needs of others. Guide all of us, particularly Bobbi, as she helps the less fortunate 'til they can help themselves. . . . And keep us mindful that we are not only business associates but stewards of your creation. We'll have a moment of silence to add our individual prayers."

He asked God to forgive him for his pettiness concerning Aunt Louise, Bobbi, and Anderson, and he especially asked the Lord to do whatever was necessary to keep him humble, even if it meant more of the kind of foolish mistakes he'd probably made today with Ernest and Eddie. He wrestled constantly with the fierce pride he felt in his business and family. He thanked God for his unremitting energy, for Tamra, for their daughter, Joyce, and the child on the way, with petitions for a son.

At the amen, several managers rushed to him for signatures and last-minute advice. Jessie held onto his arm as she spoke, commanding his attention. "You know Mr. Lane" (how could he convince her to call him

Charles?) "someone should enter that information in a computer. I don't know how you remembered limas were planted in the section south of Little Rivers."

With the other ear, he listened to Norm's complaints. How did they think he could listen to them both simultaneously?

Still plugging away on his left ear, Jessie warned that Charles was the only one who knew the entire picture of what was growing, where it was growing, and where it would be stored.

Norm was saying, "Once we do get them going, umm, we can calculate more acreage per day, umm, faster drying, and umm . . ."

Jessie held up two hands in exasperation. "The rest of us only know bits and pieces of what's going where. A computer would give us access to the information and——"

Charles jumped in to cut her off, "Maybe that's the point, that I don't want everyone else to know what I know."

Without waiting for a response, he turned to Norm. "We should have gone with the four thousand. There's less maintenance required . . . the propulsion drive doesn't need belts . . . there's only one in the header drive." He told Norm to set up an appointment with him through Aunt Louise, and Norm rushed away.

Jessie didn't get the hint as easily. She was still carrying on about the computer system. "Your files could be protected. It's my job to . . ."

Cousin Johnny whispered in his free ear that they were short at Goodday field. Charles had asked to be told next time that occurred. These days he needed an excuse to get his hands dirty. But he'd promised Tamra he'd be home early tonight.

"Comin'?" Johnny asked.

He wavered for a minute. He didn't want to miss out on this. He hadn't been in the fields in months. Maybe there was a way to do this and spend time with Tamra. Turning to Cousin Johnny, he told him to get the truck and wait outside. He lingered in the circle of employees. He would never have admitted it but these had become some of his favorite moments of the week. His employees looked to him with admiration and it felt, he imagined, much like being besieged by fans at spring training.

He noticed Norm was standing awfully close to Aunt Louise. Was that old guy trying to flirt? Fighting off a grin, he couldn't help thinking, If they decide to go dancing she'd better first get rid of that Afro puff. Aunt Louise looked up, frowning as if she'd read his mind. She crossed her legs and stared, waiting for him to speak. The flesh between her knees formed a triangle of fat, and she wore white anklets, probably to keep her feet warm. This he found endearing. It was the one sign of softness Tamra had failed to eradicate.

"Do me a favor, Aunt Louie-Louie," he said. "Call Tamra and tell her I won't be home until after ten." He knew he'd made a mistake the minute she opened her mouth and chuckled.

"Last time you had me call your wife . . ." She gave the word *wife* extra emphasis, staring directly at Jessie, who had grabbed his arm again, "she said for you to make your own damn phone calls."

Jessie looked stunned. He shrugged. So what the hell? He was tired of playing Brando. "Okay, Aunt Louise," he said in a John Wayne imitation and winked at Norm. "A man's gotta do what a man's gotta do." Well, he thought, as he left the room, I asked God to keep me humble. Aunt Louise is on the case.

30

Tamra September 1982

WITH THE FILMSTRIP ending, she signaled for her assistant to turn up the lights and walked in front of the screen. The company logo of a giant ear of corn in a Superman costume now projected across her middle. She tried unsuccessfully to pull her jacket together. "As you have seen, gentlemen—and lady . . ." Mrs. Katsura tittered. She was the single woman traveling with this group of Japanese investors. ". . . Our company's development of super vegetables and fruit will enable farmers to adapt to the inevitability of increased temperatures in our atmosphere, and one day soon, we hope to offer more miracle produce like perennial corn that reduces soil erosion and breeds that return nitrogen to the soil. It's all quite exciting."

When Mr. Katsura, the designated speaker of the group, stood, she placed a supporting hand beneath her belly. This pregnancy had been so different from the first. In this last trimester it felt as if a fish tank had grown inside her.

Mr. Katsura began his question: "The soybeans, how drastic a temperature change can they withstand?"

She considered sitting but decided against it. These investors already seemed dismayed that she was working at this stage of her pregnancy. Over lunch, Mr. Katsura had asked pointed questions about Charles, as if they'd doubted that she had a husband. Even after Tamra's explanation, that she insisted on working, they seemed to pity her. The last thing she needed was to leave them feeling she was too weak to stand. She reminded herself to respond conservatively. The idea was to get them to invest, not scare them to death about the earth's warming trend. "Even if the average annual temperature increased four degrees and rainfall decreased ten percent," she said, "supersoy would thrive."

He interpreted her answer to his partners and she almost grew giggly thinking he might be prefacing all his sentences with: "This black whale up front says . . .". As Mr. Katsura turned to her for another question, she felt a tingling sensation in her breasts. Her mammary glands seemed unaware that she'd weaned her daughter months before. She wondered if Joyce was crying for her.

Mr. Katsura said: "Excuse me, but are we correct to understand you are uncertain the climates will continue to warm?"

She gestured toward a pile of brochures surrounded by a display of leafy cabbages, crisp peppers, huge red strawberries, a bushel of parsley—someone had overdone it with the parsley—and several giant ears of corn. "There's a body of evidence suggesting it will continue to get warmer. Take it from me . . ." Her hand slammed up against her middle. ". . . Higher temperatures are inevitable as long as the world's economies, especially in the developing countries, run on fossil fuels. As the filmstrip illustrated, burning these fuels increases carbon dioxide, which traps heat in our atmosphere."

This was followed by a buzz of voices, and she took advantage of the interval to turn the final segment over to Chip, the director of public relations. She felt the baby kick as she turned toward her guests. "I have so enjoyed my week with you."

Chip, a tall man in a plaid shirt, led the group applause saying, "We appreciate Ms. Wells-Lane's informed advice."

The guests bowed deeply. Worried that she'd topple over if she bent in return, she lowered her head and quickly reached for her attaché case and the gift box they'd given her at lunch time. It contained antique kimonos for two children: Joyce, as well as the baby boy they believed she hoped for. Mrs. Katsura stopped her at the doorway, whispering in her ear. "I have so much pride in you. I will tell my daughter of you."

Once in the hallway, Tamra realized it was already four o'clock. If traffic was bad she wouldn't have the time to freshen up before Charles arrived for dinner. But her feet dragged down the linoleum corridor. Nearing an open door, she recognized the voice of a reknowned plant geneticist. Tamra had scheduled this session with him months before her supervisor had suggested she transfer to a public relations job until she'd had the baby. Workshop participants were discussing the regeneration of plants from tissue cultures; something that actually requires a scientific background, she thought sadly. Pushing the gift box under her arm, she pretended to search for her keys, fearing condescending smiles from her former coworkers.

She'd take the emergency exit. It made for a longer walk, but after a week like this, when she'd felt more like a coffee hostess than a scientist, she couldn't bear passing room 104, where an associate who'd started work the same day she had now lead a team genetically engineering crops that would produce pesticides. She'd applied for the position but had been passed over shortly after her pregnancy had become apparent. She'd grown bigger a lot earlier than she had with Joyce.

The emergency door closed with a loud bang. Darn it! Her colleagues could believe what they wanted. She'd be back in the lab a few weeks after delivery. In the meantime, at least by being in the public relations department, she could keep updated on developments. And Chip did seem genuinely happy to have her there. Halfway across the massive parking lot she noticed milk spots on her blouse.

$$31$$

Charles *September 1982*

THE SKY WAS dark. Rain, perhaps. The cooler air was comforting through the fabric of his work uniform. He was afraid to relax too much in this passenger seat. Sleep threatened. So he forced his eyes open and watched Cousin Johnny's sharp profile and half-heartedly listened to his joke.

"So here this sister was in the dressin' room: big, fine mama . . . admirin' herself in this skin-tight red dress. The angel on her shoulder sex, 'Sista, save the money and give it to the church.' And the lit'l devil sez: 'Git that dress, Sista, the preacher's eyes'll pop out.'

"This gal listens to 'em both, musters up her courage, and sez . . ." (Cousin Johnny raised his voice to a falsetto) '. . . Git thee behind me, Satan.' Next thing she knows, ka-zaam! A lightening bolt! The devil disappears. But then here comes his voice again from somewhere . . ." (in a baritone) '. . . You right, sista. Looks pretty good back here, too.' "

Charles didn't bother to laugh, knowing Cousin Johnny didn't need the laughter as much as he needed the feeling of holding people captive. It seemed that all his life his cousin had supplied him with jokes about women and sex. Charles defended him to Tamra, saying there was more to him than met the eye, but he wondered.

Not that his approval made any difference when it came to Johnny's whoring ways. Folks had been preaching at Johnny all his life, but even now as he chuckled at his own joke, wiping the back of a hand across his mouth, it sounded like he had a tiny woman on his tongue and was rolling her around like a piece of candy.

The one time Charles had dared to introduce the subject of Johnny's sleeping around like a madman, Johnny had gone wild. He had accused Charles of thinking he was better than him because he'd been raised by his own parents instead of having to wait for the kindness of others, because he had an education, and especially because he'd been the one, not Johnny, to get the acreage. Charles had offered then and there to stake him in a farm of his own, but Cousin Johnny had just shaken his head like Charles was too ignorant to understand. Just as quickly he'd calmed down, apologizing, saying Charles had caught him at a bad moment.

Charles regretted taking Tamra's advice on that one. The next time she had started in on how Johnny would prove to be the family's instrument for self-destruction, he'd told her to drop the subject once and for all. What Johnny did in his spare time wasn't their business.

They passed a rusted cow shed and Charles watched as two men hammered at the new fence surrounding Widow Snyder's hock farm. She'd been making a lot of improvements on her property recently and he wondered if she planned to put it up for sale. He would check on that. He turned back to Cousin Johnny, asking his opinion on Eddie and Ernest.

"With white folks it never hurts to make sure," Cousin Johnny said, adding that Charles wouldn't have had this problem if he'd refused to employ white folks in the first place. "Those white boys'll turn on you in a minute."

This time Charles did laugh. "And a Black man won't, right?"

Cousin Johnny turned along a stretch of Lane fields. Charles wanted to ask details about where each of his workers were and what assignments they had this evening. But he knew that once Cousin Johnny got hold of his second favorite subject, white folks, he couldn't be swayed from it.

"Anybody'll rip you off, 'cept family maybe," Cousin Johnny continued, "but you got to realize how angry they are 'bout Mrs. Reardon selling you, not only her land, but the grain elevator, too."

Charles wanted to change the subject. He was tired of defending himself. Mr. Reardon had stipulated in his will that the land and elevator be offered to Charles first, at fair market value. What kind of fool would he have been to turn that down? And it had been Mrs. Reardon's suggestion that she keep the elevator off the market until Charles could afford to buy it. Cousin Johnny knew that, as did everyone else, but they seemed to enjoy looking for scandal. Someone had written Tamra an anonymous note suggesting he and Eve Reardon were having an affair. But that was one time having a wife who was different had come in handy. She'd hung the letter up over their bed and told him it would add to their sex life. Not that there was much of that these days, busy as he was. He felt a twinge of guilt about working tonight.

Cousin Johnny was laughing, saying that maybe Charles and Eve Reardon were having an affair. "Come on, man, you can tell your ol' cuz. What was she like? Did you get those big, creamy white thighs around your neck? And what about up at the top? She gotta lot of that, too, don't she?"

Charles pretended to be sleeping.

"What she say? How'd she do it? I bet when you was finished she called you mister."

A smile crept across Charles's face. "You are one sick Black man, but don't worry. I going to leave all those white women for you, and you can just keep spoutin' all that militant bull about how you can't trust white folks."

Johnny grew serious. "It probably wouldn't have bothered anybody that you got the land. Folks are used to the Lanes havin' land, but this elevator stuff . . ." He shook his head. "You won't find a white man in the neighborhood happy 'bout renting storage from you."

He noticed the new gas station was finally going up. "I suppose you've talked with every white farmer in the neighborhood, so you know how they all feel."

"If I were you I'd just watch my back, Little Charles."

He closed his eyes, signaling that he'd stopped listening, but his cousin seemed determined to shake him from his comfort. "And I'd make sure my wife and baby were safe, too."

He sat up quickly and found Cousin Johnny watching him. He realized Johnny had hoped for just this sort of reaction.

When they passed through Freeman's Run, Charles spotted Pa stooped over a mechanic working beneath a tractor. Johnny backed along the side of the road. Harlen looked up, his face without a trace of welcoming smile, and Charles knew he couldn't delay their conversation for another minute.

32

Tamra September 1982

BURIED IN THE usual assortment of bank statements and bills in the mailbox, she found a letter from Wadine, which she quickly tossed into the passenger seat. Later for that. The last thing Tama needed was to read any of the glittery details about her friend's life. Anyway, she was too tired to even tear the envelope open, so she rested her head against the steering wheel.

If only she could park right here and sleep. But she knew if she did, one of Charles's cousins or aunts or somebody with Lane blood was bound to stop and tell her how she should quit her job and take care of her babies and her husband, how if they had a man who worked hard enough for two people they'd be glad to sit back and be taken care of by him.

Fearful that she'd doze, she concentrated on a telephone wire where a bird remained, dead, its claws still attached to the line, creating a bizarre sight. The carcass had rotted away but the head and feathers remained intact. She watched, wondering what held it together, wishing it could defy its fate and fly off. Instead it stared sightlessly across the fields.

Maybe she should take a short walk. She'd gained fifty pounds, only about ten of it baby. But she didn't really have the time to walk. Charles might be home already, and she wanted to see Joyce, too. On the other hand, some exercise might clear her head so she could be a better mommy and wife. She'd feel it was worth it if it helped her to be even half as good-natured as Charles.

Pulling herself from behind the wheel, she started up the road, recognizing the sound of an augur depositing corn kernels into a truck. From a distance, she could just see the red grain bin and an operator's cab of an axial-flow combine. What she could not see from here was the small trailer in which she and her family temporarily lived. It was blocked by the old Reardon house, which could be seen from anywhere within walking distance. Stopping to catch her breath, Tamra studied the large, white structure that appeared to look proudly down its white, high-columned nose, over Charles's world. She was surprised the workmen they'd hired to renovate the house were just quitting for the day. Good thing she'd not driven in. Most of them had Lane blood and would feel obligated to stop and chat.

A field of clover tickled her ankles as she walked toward the newly completed and recently occupied farrowing house. She told herself that she was prepared for anything she might see, except the castration of infant pigs. She and Charles had hotly debated whether or not to circumcise this baby she was carrying if it was a boy. She was completely against the procedure and felt she didn't need any graphic reminders of how genitals could be brutalized by men.

Even before she could see the facade of the farrowing house, she smelled the rank animal scent. From the outside it looked like a massive red barn, but inside she discovered a gleaming, state-of-the-art birthing city, every bit as clean and disinfected as a hospital. An estimated four hundred sows were separated in units of ten to twenty, and, in keeping with stringent health guidelines, divided by feeders and eating creeps. The coarse-haired sows like slope-backed blimps, were boisterous and fidgety, twitching their snouts. Most were white-haired Yorkshires with the gray undertones indicative of the crossbreeding done to produce leaner, more healthy offspring. In five units, separated from other gestation areas, about eighty sows nursed piglets at the same stage of growth.

This, she knew from hearing Charles talk, was to ensure that the newborn not be exposed to bacteria for which they'd not yet developed immunities, as had the more mature pigs.

It looked like pig heaven in here, but she knew the residents paid a high price for luxury. Shiny baby pigs pushed and shoved for teats, which they first massaged with their noses, then hungrily sucked. Their small, sharp teeth had been clipped at birth so as not to irritate the sows's udders. As Tamra leaned over a sturdy cabinet, a sow snorted *"hurmph."* Tamra recognized this mothering noise, a sound of relief as the milk pressure eased in the udder and teats.

The blueprints had called for the doors of each major section to open onto the adjoining, fenced-in, grassy fields. Today they were closed, and she felt the chill of the air conditioner. Walking closer to the chalk board, she read the schedules for iron injections and teeth and tail clippings and noticed a worker scrutinizing her. Like many of the newer hands, he seemed not to know her. His feet and lower legs were shod in high rubber boots as he scraped away mounds of excrement. Outside the pen, it would be flushed through gutters to a lagoon system designed to keep dust, odors, and flies to a minimum.

One wall was lined with deep shelves that supported sacks of corn marked "Lane Inc.," and an extension ladder slanted upward beside a built-in, stainless-steel refrigerator. Charles had said the hogs would live better than they, and he'd been right. Not that she minded the trailer. Eve Reardon had moved only a month ago. Renovations were on schedule.

Across the sawdust-covered floor, two workers reached through a gate at the rear of a pen to assist an enormous sow that lay on its side, straining in labor. Tamra approached slowly as one of the men pushed up his sleeves and reached between the hog's legs and inside her body. When he brought his hand out, it dripped with blood, and he held what looked like a sack of mucous afterbirth. As she stepped in closer, the sack was gently wiped and came to life with four tiny spinning feet and a head, the eyes already opened. The hungry piglet, which had been placed near the mother's shivering exterior, would get a quick fix of colostrum, loaded with nutritious vitamins.

One of the men greeted her, touching his cap, and saying, "missus." She nodded, taking care to keep her mouth shut. She wanted to thank them for treating the sows humanely, to say that she understood how it felt because she too had given birth, and would again soon. Even if she had managed to get this out, she knew she couldn't say what else was on her mind, that that sow really wasn't so different from her or them, that in fact, they all possessed a striking singularity: a well-developed nervous system, and that yes, the sow surely felt pain.

If she had had the courage to say any of this, she would never have supplied them with a final piece of information, one that was sure to make them think her mad; that it was only due to mysterious factors that they had been born human and male, while this beast would spend its best days feeding young ones. She left after returning the workers' greetings.

Making her way back across the field, she paused at the trailer steps to stroke a kitten that had a fishing hook caught in its jaw. The cat seemed perfectly content. As she entered the trailer she heard only silence. The shades were drawn and the narrow hallway was without light. She listened for Joyce's cries but, still, there was only silence. Charles's Aunt Elbie sat before a television game show with the sound turned down and waved hello. Tamra could just make out her daughter's form.

Joyce's tiny knees were folded beneath her as she slept in a disposable diaper and T-shirt. Tamra carefully lowered her heavy body to kiss her daughter's cheek. She stroked the top of a sticky fist. She didn't want to wake Joyce but she couldn't resist this evening's touch, a nuzzle, this scent of child. She circled over the skin, inhaling as if drawing her baby back inside. Something smelled unpleasant, like the birthing house. Checking a tendency to be sharp-tongued, she looked inquiringly at Elbie, whispering: "How'd you get her to sleep?"

"I give her some real food," the old woman said. Tamra waved her toward the kitchen, away from the sleeping child.

"What's that I smell on her?"

Elbie smiled. "Reason she been keepin' y'all up was 'cause she was hongry. That child wanted more than watery milk and strained food somebody else put up."

Tamra kept the smile on her face. "So what'd you give her?"

"Grits and bacon grease."

She resisted a groan. How revolting. But she paced her words and said, "I appreciate that you care so much for Joyce." She had to force herself to continue. "But I think it's a good idea to keep her on that diet. In fact, I insist." It was getting increasingly difficult to keep the sides of her mouth up. "I, I told you that . . . when you gave her that candy."

Elbie gesticulated as if talking to a foreigner. "That child is so poor, that's why I give it to her. She needs the extra weight and it was *milk* chocolate. Milk is good for a baby."

Tamra's smile felt like a rubber band pulled too tight. Elbie reached over and tweaked the skin where Tamra had once had a waistline. "Honey Baby, with all that work and drivin', you done stayed too po' yoursef."

She didn't answer. She didn't feel she could.

"I fixed you some greens," Elbie said, pointing toward a large kettle on the stove. "They stinkin', ain't they?"

Ordinarily, Tamra would have agreed that they did indeed smell delicious, but tonight, the scent reminded her of the grease in her daughter's stomach, and she felt like retching. At least, thank heavens, Elbie hadn't given Joyce any of the greens.

"I brung you sumpin'," Elbie said, reaching into a cabinet, and held out a box of starch. Tamra stared at the package with the Indian maiden on the box as Elbie explained. "The woman I was raised up by give me some when I was pregnie. It'll give you extra weight."

She took a deep breath, studying the box as if she were considering taking a bit. But what she actually wanted was to get a better look at Elbie, stare into the old woman's kind face, and understand her better. She had to sneak a glimpse. Charles had warned her of her reputation among his family of over-scrutinizing people.

She'd often found herself surprised by many of the customs in this farming community, but this offer from Elbie failed to startle. She'd heard of women eating starch during their pregnancies, and in fact had read an article about it. The author claimed it had developed as a substitute for the mineral-rich dirt some West African and Gaellic women craved in pregnancy.

Opening the box and lifting out a bit of the white, dampish powder, she rubbed it between her fingers. It had the same claylike consistency of soil. Elbie pinched some starch and slid it into her mouth, gumming it. Watching her chew, Tamra remembered the author had called the women dirt-eaters.

She thanked Elbie for the gift and paid her for the week's work. Adding up the hours, sixty of them, made her feel ashamed; so much time away from Joyce. She'd have to wake her. They could have dinner together. Charles was due to arrive any minute. But Elbie interrupted Tamra's chatter. " 'Fraid that ain't so. I forgot. He phoned just awhile back, said he wouldn't get here 'fore ten."

This was disappointing, and she only realized Elbie was continuing to talk when she called her name. "Got a head rag I could borrow? Rain comin'."

Tamra rummaged through a dresser drawer and found a red silk scarf with a hammer and sickle that she'd bought at a flea market in Paris. It brought back a disturbing memory. She'd worn it one rainy afternoon and had just stepped onto the Metro platform when the Parisian police had picked her from a crowd, surrounding her. It had been a time of strong anti-immigrant sentiment, and they'd mistaken her for an Algerian or West Indian. She'd been shoved against a wall, French passengers slowing their steps, not one protesting this injustice.

The policeman pushed his face near hers. She'd been afraid to cry out, but when she had, words were her salvation. Suddenly recognizing her accent, the lieutenant inquired, *"Êtes-vous américaine?"*

Smiling, he complimented her on her French. There was no apology. Still, she was relieved. They would not search her. Her friend, from Gabon, tribal scars etched into her cheeks, had also been stopped like this but had been brutally searched. The lieutenant offered Tamra, who was still panting, a brief explanation. They'd mistaken her for someone else. She offered silent prayers of thanks. She was an American, respected, despite her dark skin. This comforted her only momentarily, this claim of patriotism to a country where she would be no more welcome by police than had been her friend, one of ten million dark aliens, in France.

Tonight, glad to hand over the scarf, she tied it beneath Elbie's chin and threw her arms about the old woman, surely startling her with this sudden show of affection. Again, she asked about Charles, her voice pleading. Had he said ten o'clock for sure, or was that a guess?

Elbie shrugged. Who knew? "But when he do come, let me tell you sumpin'. Don't you worry that man to death. He's got men's work to do. Go on, enjoy yourself some quiet time."

Elbie waved goodbye, moving toward her lime green Pinto. Charles had suggested they find her a newer car. She'd have to remember that. Roads were dangerous in storms. And after all, Elbie was family.

Tamra covered her sleeping daughter with a blanket, thinking it would be cruel to wake her. Joyce moved her lips contentedly, softly smacking them as if she'd just nursed. Her scalp had been oiled, and it glistened, each tiny square sprouting tightly braided thatches, like one of Charles's fields.

With a gallon of Breyer's in one hand, Tamra searched for her latest technical journal, then sat at the kitchen table. Dipping a spoon into the cold confection, she chewed bits of almond and read about the possibilities of genetically altered tomatoes that ripened only when the consumer wanted. There was so much to keep up with. She felt heavy with child. No time for a nap. She had to be prepared to return to the lab. But it was as if the baby inside, demanding a rest, pulled her eyes shut from within.

33

Charles September 1982

HARLEN SQUATTED AS he talked to a mechanic whose feet protruded from beneath the tires of a tractor. "Just hasn't been breathing right," he was saying.

Charles recalled when Pa had refused to let anyone else work on this tractor. His father was still a relatively young man, but it was as if he'd suddenly begun to age.

Charles waited several seconds for Harlen to acknowledge his presence. He refused to accept this chasm that had formed between them. Taking a wide step, he brought his toes close to Pa's. Harlen leaned on one of the massive tires caked with mud, and for the first time since Charles had told him of his plans to buy the Reardon elevator, Harlen spoke directly to him. "Meeting's finished, eh?"

"Yes sir."

A long pause followed. Cousin Johnny had cut his engine and the only sound was the clanking of the mechanic's tools. Charles reached out and touched his father's arm, saying he'd like to speak to him privately. They walked together for several yards, a long stretch of silence between them. Finally, Charles opened the conversation by saying he'd missed Pa at the meeting. Harlen whipped his head around, mouth agape. "What happened? Somebody need historical information?"

Charles asked him please, not to start again. Ignoring that request, Pa said, "I can't think of why else I'd be missed. You couldn't have had a question for me about the future of the company. You'd need a crystal ball for that."

Charles tucked his head down. During moments like these, when Pa acted like a balding, brooding child, he felt the need to be smaller. "You kinda got my hands tied, Pa. You don't participate 'cause you're sore with me. Yet you're the one who put me in charge in the first place." He lowered his voice. "I never asked for it. Then as soon as I pick up the reins, there you are sitting on my neck, telling me 'whoa, slow down, I wouldn't take that road. I wouldn't buy that if I were you . . .' Guess what, Pa? I'm not you."

Harlen put the tip of a finger to his mouth, like he'd been burned. "You're right about that," he said. "I never sassed my Pa in my life. This what you call being a corporate leader?"

Charles lowered his eyes. "No sir, I'm sorry . . . but I can't apologize for decisions I make about the farm."

Harlen's hand whipped through the air. "Don't call it that, it's not a farm . . . It's some sort of . . . agricultural industrial complex. But you'd better mark my words. A man can only do one thing right at a time. So choose. Is it farming or business? You got to make a choice."

"I made a choice. In fact, you made it for me, remember? I'm a farmer but farming *is* business. You once said something I never forgot."

"Glad you remember something."

"You said you were worried 'cause only ten percent of the farmers in this country were black. Well now you've got more of a reason to worry. There are two and a half percent now."

"So stick to farming."

"That's what I'm trying to do, with the elevator . . . and I won't stop there. I've got plans for a corn refinery and then I'll build a cannery, get together a logging and trucking business . . . You'll have to be with me or agin', but I'm not going to give up just 'cause my daddy don't approve."

Harlen moved off, as if the conversation were over. Charles caught up with him, chuckling.

"What the hell's so funny."

"I was thinking about that rabbit I got when I was five."

"I don't know what a rabbit has to . . ."

"You gave him to me for Easter, told me not to let him out of the cage, 'cause the dogs would get him. But I didn't listen.

"Dang fool probably got his tail chewed, like you're gonna."

"When I opened the cage, he wouldn't come out. Even when I carried him out, he ran back in."

"I suppose this story has a moral."

"You can't box a man in but for so long. I'm fighting for my life here. I don't want to be afraid."

Harlen stopped walking and rubbed his chin. "Son, a man ain't nothin' like a rabbit or there would never had been a Nat Turner or any slave with the nerve to fight back. We tried so often to run away, the slave masters made up a name for it. Did you know that? Drapetomania, an insane desire to run away." He shook his head. "Imagine that, they thought we were crazy for wanting to escape."

Charles laughed softly. "I'm feeling an insane desire to run from you and Bobbi and Aunt Louise."

Harlen jerked his head, amused. It was comforting to feel his father's goodwill again.

"What's that duo up to?"

"They stopped short of insurrection."

Harlen winced. "That bad, eh? Well, what you gonna do? After all, they're . . ."

"I know, I know, they're family. But listen, we've got a real problem." He filled Pa in on the trouble with Ernest and his brother, and the action he'd taken.

Pa listened without interruption, finally shaking his head, telling Charles he'd made a mistake, that though he didn't like the two brothers, he knew them to be honest. He tried convincing Charles to call off the investigation, to admit he'd responded without having thought the problem through. Charles said he'd consider it. What he actually wondered was how he could save face as well as apologize. He tried changing subjects. "I better get back to your nephew."

Harlen inclined his head toward Cousin Johnny, asking what his latest was.

"Why don't I just leave the jokes to him?" They walked back toward the truck. "How come you and Mama don't stop by anymore?"

Pa said, "You two are never home and we don't want to sit and listen to Elbie blabber. And . . . let's put it this way. We have the distinct impression Tamra would prefer we wait until she extends an invitation."

"No, man, that's wrong. She's got to get used to family dropping in. I'll talk to her about it."

"Wait 'til you move to the new house. It gets crowded in that lunch box you're in."

Charles agreed but said surprisingly enough, Tamra never complained about living in the trailer.

"That's 'cause she was so damn happy to get out of our house," Harlen said. He threw back his head laughing, and Charles joined in. "With her and Dalhia going head to head, it was bad enough, but when ol' Tamra found that snake in the shower . . ." They laughed heartily over this memory. Pa said he'd never met a woman so afraid of snakes.

Charles reminded him of Dick Gregory's joke, that if Eve had been Black, we'd still be in the garden. "Cause no Black woman's going to stand around and have a conversation with a snake."

Finally, they were on safe ground. Harlen seemed delighted to have someone he could safely gossip with about his strange daughter-in-law, and once started, he couldn't let go of the subject. "After she high-tailed it out of our house, how long did she stay in that fancy suite at the hotel?"

They'd reached Cousin Johnny, who'd apparently figured out the source of their laughter. Charles said she'd stayed at the hotel a few days. Johnny told him to stop lying. "She was there a week if it was a day. Then you got all hot and bothered and bought her that new trailer. Next thing I know she was pregnant again."

The laughter went round and round with Charles insisting she might not be enthusiastically adapting to country life, but at least she was determined to try. He said she met the crew every morning at the Reardon house and had them taking down the cabinets any place where a snake might get in.

Harlen said in wonder, "Think of it, a snake-proof house. Who's ever heard of something like that down here? You sure can pick 'em, boy."

Johnny chimed in. "That girl's all right with me. I'd like to have her fix me some of that ex-press-o and talk some French."

Charles smiled. He loved the sweet names of the foods Tamra had introduced to their breakfast table. Cappuccino, biscotti, croissants . . . Johnny's voice broke through his thoughts. "Now, she'll have to get used to bats or figure out how to keep 'em out of the attic. Tell her next time she runs off not to go all the way to the Baltimore Hilton. Shoot, I got me an extra room."

"I wouldn't trust you with my sheep, boy," Charles said.

Pretending to be insulted, Johnny said, "Maybe you got a point. I might be the sheepdog. *Woof, woof.*"

Pa's laughter followed them back to the truck.

Cousin Johnny and Charles now drove to the southernmost tip of the Lane holdings, where the land narrowed to a point and abutted the Nanticoke River. Goodday field, which until recently had belonged to the Reardons and had been left untended for the last year, was a pleasant surprise to Charles every time he saw it. Watching from the truck's passenger window, he surveyed the land with the eyes of an artist and a stranger.

Cousin Johnny maneuvered the truck over green mossy patches, on through a narrow path lined by hundreds of ragged weeds and pines. The land opened up clear, fallow, and silent, as if it had been waiting for him. While Johnny hunted in the back of his truck for tools, Charles jumped out, eager to walk alone.

He loved the feel of slipping back into the stillness of the land. He breathed in the tart scent of soil, saw that it clung to his boots. He admired an adjacent field, fecund with leafy crops. Lit by the late sun, the plants looked as if they flowed, row upon row, without beginning or end.

There was work today for nine extra hands and he found eight of them in the lean-to, sipping sweet, black coffee. It was usually the crew chief's job to give instructions, but Cousin Johnny hung back. The boss was here. Workers crowded in as Charles spoke. One task before them was to plow under a field of corn stubble. They usually did most of their plowing in the spring to lessen erosion, but this was different. They'd need Goodday immediately.

Turning to Herman Bestal, Charles spoke in respectful tones. Bestal had had his own farm once, and then had lost everything. Charles appreciated Bestal's willingness to help him out at such a busy time and didn't want him to think he was talking down to him. "Herman, what can we do about reducing the speed of the gear box on that cranky foraging system?"

Miss Anna Mae, the only woman in the group, raised a sun-parched hand. She'd worked for Old Man Kohl last season and he'd had a similar problem. If they slowed down their feed rolls first they could prevent overload from bunchy materials.

Charles trusted her when she wasn't drinking, and today her slurless speech gave her a sense of authority. Bestal backed her up. "She's right, and the heaviest volumes should be inched forward and that'll stave off any plugging."

Exhilarated, Charles looked from face to face in the circle surrounding him, mapping out his plans in clear, concise directions. Two of the workers were sent to the Navaho, where Harlen would join them. This was the first harvest when they would have excess hay; not only would there be enough for baling for feed this winter, they would also sell some of their hay crop.

Richard and a helper were to shovel through the dry corn and check for reddish mold. Moe Dean was to hook up the propane ring on the blower, and the rest would stay with him and Cousin Johnny. They'd work on the last of the corn harvesting and it had to be done tonight. Rain threatened.

Climbing into a tractor, Charles adjusted the seat and unbuttoned his shirt. The cabin had trapped the day's hot air and it would be awhile before the air conditioning kicked in. Up high, with an unobstructed, almost 360-degree view, he watched a shadow slip along the tree border. He thought it might be a doe heading for shelter. The digital tachometer on the instrument cluster signaled that all was well, and he started his work, happy to hear at last the sweet sound of chopping stalks, and kernels being deposited into the wagon.

By nightfall, he was drowsy and flipped on the radio. Ray Charles cut through the static and he tuned it in and turned it up, singing the words to "Hit The Road Jack," like a harsh rebuke.

He remembered his sister, decades before, prancing to this song. She'd been home with a friend and they'd pinned him into a corner, strutting in circles and mouthing the words like backup singers, pointing their fingers accusingly at him, as he'd tried impatiently to get around them.

A banging on his side window woke him and he jerked upright as Cousin Johnny, who'd climbed up onto the tractor, swinging from the hand hold, yelled loudly, "You coulda killed somebody . . . 'sleep like that."

He insisted Charles go home.

"I'm all right," Charles protested, then waited for Johnny to climb down before moving to his designated position. Thank God he hadn't hurt anybody. He would have to get some sleep, but it would have to be later. Right now this work had to continue.

Now that night had come, their lights shone out across the dark fields, like ships at sea. Directly in his path were a long-legged bird and a stout one pecking at insects along the furrows. With food sources diminishing in the bay and its tributaries, the birds seemed determined to find sustenance inland. Unintimidated by the noise of his tractor, the birds worked feverishly, separately, like tourists in for the hour to pick and pay. He steered around them, and slowing his tractor, carefully guided it while fighting off sleep. Charles worked the machine another two hours before sending a radio message to Cousin Johnny that he needed to get home. He'd wait for him at the truck.

34

Charles and Tamra September 1982

WHEN JOHNNY DROPPED him off, Charles rushed up the walkway. He'd spotted Tamra's car parked near the mailbox, a good walking
distance from the house, and he worried about whether there had been an
accident. He'd left home two days before at half morning, and had last had
a phone conversation with Tamra earlier in the day.

The Reardon house was dark and his Bay Retrievers slept against the
walls of the old smokehouse, their shadows outlined by the new moonlight,
tails touching. The slap of his boots on the path signaled them awake and
they rose in unison, panting like well-tuned engines. "Not now, boys!" he
whispered at the leaping dogs, their breathing so anxious he felt the warmth
against his legs. As he entered the dark, sleeping kitchen, the screen door
yawned, closing him in.

Tamra's head jerked up from the table revealing her dazed, sleep-starved
face. Melted ice cream had formed a pool on her technical journal. Joyce sent
out a confused wail, jumping up and running to him with upraised arms.
"Doo doo," she cried, the sharp stench of diarrhea on her.

Tamra rose with a hand on her forehead, saying, "It's all over the
couch." She pointed first at the brown liquid oozing from a corner of Joyce's
diaper, then at a trail of soft, dark mounds. The toes of one tiny foot were

hidden in another pile as Joyce reached for her father. He recoiled and Tamra dashed into action, first mopping the ice cream with a towel while Joyce clung to Charles's leg calling for her. "I'm coming, honey. Mama's coming," she said, throwing her soppy magazine in the garbage.

He flopped into a chair holding the screaming child an arm's length away and stared helplessly at Tamra.

"Charles," she yelled, "Can't you bathe her?"

"She wants you."

"And I want some help. It's bad enough you're never home. At least you could help when you are here."

He stomped toward the bathroom and she pulled the utility pail from beneath the sink, slamming the cabinet door. She was concerned about having yelled at him, but wondered when she would ever get the chance to come home and have someone take care of her because she was tired.

She moaned as she lowered herself to her knees and used a towel to clean up after Joyce. She'd have to be sure to apologize. But maybe first she'd actually have to feel sorry. Right now the thought of him just sitting there with Joyce as if he expected Tamra to handle the mess on her own filled her with resentment.

Filling the bucket with water, lemon juice, and baking soda, Tamra tried to recall how much she needed of each for this solution Aunt Elbie had once recommended. Tamra felt sure the stench had been made worse by a meal of grits and bacon.

Finishing up with the couch, she covered it with a plastic bag from the dry cleaners. If she watched Joyce carefully, to make sure she didn't get anywhere near it, it might hold the odor in. Smoothing the bag and tucking it around the cushion, she read the warning: CAUTION: NOT FOR USE BY CHILDREN MADE IN KOREA.

Opening the screen door, she felt warm, humid air move in. But her face burned as she remembered how she'd talked to Charles. By way of apology, when she opened a can of onion soup, she added a few teaspoons of imitation cooking sherry, something to make his meal a little more exotic.

A few minutes later, she listened as Charles, who, having emerged from the bathroom with a freshly bathed Joyce, sat on the couch reading to their daughter. "Fee, fi, fo, fum, I smell the blood of an Afro-American."

Tamra giggled looking across the room at the two of them. He returned the smile.

"Sorry I yelled," she said.

"And I'm sorry about sitting there like a big dummy." Joyce interrupted him, punching at his stomach, and he fell over in mock agony. Joyce squealed and chattered baby words as Tamra lifted her, covering her cheeks in kisses. The scent of baby powder and Sesame Street bubble bath clung to her. At least she'd had her bath for the night. Charles pulled the highchair over and she scooted Joyce in. It had been carved in maple by Cousin Johnny's father only weeks before he'd gone off to war. Vicky had used the chair, then Charles. Now Joyce. Tamra watched from the stove as Charles helped Joyce with her food and felt charged with love for them both. A moment later, Joyce's eyes filled with tears as her juice spilled out over her T-shirt.

Tamra swallowed her annoyance and carried her daughter back toward the tub while Charles sat at the table to eat. When she returned, she discovered him looking forlornly into his soup. For once he seemed to realize she was not in a mood to be teased. "Interesting flavor," he said. "What'd you put in this?"

She suggested he might prefer the greens Elbie had cooked and he agreed almost too eagerly. When the bowl was placed before him, steaming and pungent, he talked again, between bites, about the farm, what Pa had said, what had happened during the meeting. He was full of news and jokes and paused only to glance through the mail.

Calling her attention to an official-looking document, he held it out to her. She groaned as she opened it. It was a notice for jury duty. She began to voice her annoyance but saw that Charles was dropping off to sleep. Tamra decided not to notice. "This is too much," she said.

His eyes opened and he sat upright. "Don't worry. They won't put you on a jury."

She was determined to keep a conversation going, no matter how inane. He'd be gone before the morning's light and she wanted adult company. "What makes you so sure?"

He rubbed his eyes. "Just take one of your scientific journals with you. Those defense attorneys don't want a Black juror who can read, much less understand one of those."

She tried forcing a smile, but Charles's remark felt more mocking than good-natured. "At least that way I'd be using my science background for something," she said, and wiped food from Joyce's face and hair with a damp cloth. He moved over to Tamra, massaging her shoulders.

"I wish I could make you feel better," he said. "If the job makes you so sad, couldn't you take your leave a little early?"

"Would you consider leaving your business?"

"I'm not eight months pregnant."

"I'll never get back in the lab if they start thinking of me that way."

"Now that harvest is over, maybe we could hire someone to drive you back and forth."

"That would only call more attention to my pregnancy."

He looked over her shoulder, toward her stomach. "I think everyone has noticed your condition by now." He sat her down, slipped off her shoes, and tenderly rubbed her feet. She pretended to relax but inwardly cringed thinking that Charles would notice how gray her skin was with ash, how leathery her feet were now that she couldn't reach down to put lotion on them.

"Most of the weight has gone into my butt," she said.

He assured her that was quite normal. "You know why the camel has a hump, right?" She wondered if he could laugh about it if it were his body. He continued: "It's the same with African women. God gave them canteens back there, so they and their families could survive when they crossed the desert." She smirked as he added, "Sometimes, when I feel I can't take it anymore, with Pa fighting me or with Ronald Reagan's bureaucrats taxing the hell out of me, I look over at the back of you . . ."

He crossed the room in a ghoulish imitation of a woman. ". . . and you're saying . . ."

His good mood proved infectious. Tamra walked before him, rhythmically, swinging her rear end, "Daddy, this Bud's for you."

When they stopped laughing, he held her gently in his arms. "You'd be sexy in a nun's habit."

"*Ummmm*, kinky," she said wearily.

Tamra touched his face and apologized for complaining. "I'm just scared of losing touch with that young woman you fell in love with." She rested her back against his arm, thick and strong as a shelf, remembering a biblical line, "Sufficient is thine arm alone."

"I don't love you because of the way you look," he said. "If we were spirits in heaven I'd know you. One of those old angels might think it was the wind. But I'd know you from the sound it made."

"Oh yeah? What sound?"

"I'd just open a window and wait for you to scream: "Close it! The flies are comin' in.' "

Again they laughed together, and when they put Joyce down for the night, he held her and stroked her, loving her. Afterwards, she lay quietly, listening to his snores. She turned him on his side to quiet him and heard the scratching sounds of animals on the flatness of the roof, running jumps magnified by the steel of the trailer. It was a frightful, eerie noise that made her feel that if she stared hard enough, she'd see a stranger searching the room. She pressed into Charles's sleeping back and knew there were terrors from which even he could not save her.

She thought, at first, when she heard the ringing, that it was the alarm clock. He rose at such ungodly hours. But this was different. It came from a distance. She reached out to turn it off before it woke Joyce, but as she came fully awake she realized the ringing meant trouble and tried to shake Charles awake. As if trying to understand, he finally opened his eyes wide.

"Charles! Charles, do you hear me? Something's wrong."

Jumping up, he pulled his pants on. "It's the hog house," he said. She dragged herself upright, buttoning on a duster. "I'm going with you."

He ordered her to stay where she was, said it was a fire alarm and he hurried out. Creeping into the nursery, she found Joyce in a deep sleep. Tamra started out the front door but suddenly turned back. The plastic—she couldn't leave without it. Ripping it from the cushion, she rushed out.

He was running and already several yards ahead. The terrain looked alien at night and the unchecked wail of the alarm added to the harshness of the night. The dogs had run from alongside him, back to her, and they sat watching her silently, their eyes shining. She called out to Charles and he turned, slowing his pace long enough to wave her back toward the trailer, but she continued calling.

Holding the bottom of her belly, she tried to jog. It seemed at first an impossible effort. Her midsection was cumbersome but her feet picked up speed. She hesitated near the stalks in the yard, thinking that perhaps, if she cut through diagonally, she might catch him. He couldn't get hurt. Nothing must happen to him. She called out a few more times hoping she could force him back, make him choose between her and the farm. "Charles, please."

She entered the cornfield, the dogs barking madly. It was difficult to walk steadily through the rows, but she pressed on, and soon Charles's shouts came at her, up close, and urgent: "Not in there! Tamra! Snakes." She turned and ran out, realizing he'd come for her. Roughly, he grabbed her hand and they ran on, their shadows bulky and connected, the dogs at their heels. She felt him struggle to slow down so she could keep up with him.

The wail of the siren persisted, and smoke billowed from the building. A utility truck pulled up and she heard the shouts of men. Charles tried twisting his hand away. She resisted, but she could not hold on and stood panting as he ran off, his shadow swift in its now solo flight.

It took her several minutes to reach the building, gasping for breath. Someone had turned on the lights in the cavernous structure, and the sprinkler system had kicked in, raining water from the ceiling. The air was filled with smoke and the horrifically sweet scent of roasted flesh. With the alarm turned off, she heard the animals, hysterical and squealing, as they were herded through the sliding doors. Dead animals lay in a heap, and those still alive but too badly burned to move joined in a staccato of grunts and agonized wailing. She wondered how many had lost their young.

Three smaller fires burned, and the men fought these with the hoses she'd seen earlier. Holding her sleeve to her mouth, she rushed past a fire-blackened trough. Charles, who didn't seem to notice her, was bent over, inspecting something as Johnny wildly waved his arms. Charles stood, pointing toward the ground. Dear Lord, he was holding a gun, and she stepped back as he aimed at a shrieking pregnant Yorkshire, its belly torn open by fire. Layer upon layer of her fat sizzled as she was cooked alive. The gun exploded. Tamra flinched, covering her ears, and she watched the beings within the hog's belly squirm and struggle for their lives.

Cool water flushed between her legs. She thought she'd wet her pants. Then she knew. She'd have to tell Charles. He'd have to get Joyce. But she heard Cousin Johnny's words, loud and angry. "Don't be a damn fool, man. Of course it was them. I warned you. Coulda been *your* family. They always find a way to get back."

She tried yelling his name; but it came out a weak cry. She wanted to tell him, as she struggled for deep, calming breaths, that she needed his help, that he should forget about the damn farm, that their baby, their baby . . . wanted . . . to come.

35

Tamra *September 1982*

SHE STRETCHED OUT on the cool sheets, pretending to sleep, listening to the voices of those she loved. First her father's: "In Uganda and Kenya, this is seen as a blessing from the fertility gods."

Her thoughts were interrupted by the squeaking wheels of a baby cart. Of course, that was why she'd awakened. In only three days her body rhythms had adjusted to the hospital's nursing schedule. The cart's boisterous wheels were followed by the squish of a nurse's rubber soles moving toward her.

"*Shh!*" A rebuke, surely Virginia's. "Don't wake her, she's exhausted. I don't know how she's ever going to . . ."

Then Big Mama (*oh, her Big Mama was here*), "The same way we all managed. Why don't you bring the cart over here, honey, so we can *(squeaking wheels turning away from the bed)* ". . . see if I passed on some of my good looks."

Tamra waited with amusement as the others surely gathered around for Big Mama's pronouncement of beauty or lack thereof. "Well, the T-shirt on this one is cute. . . . And this one . . . you'd better keep him away from trees; he might feel a need to climb and swing."

"Oh, Mama!" Virginia said.

"Hello there. Can you see me? I'm Charles Lane. I'll be your father the rest of your———"

Virginia interrupted: "Had any time to name them?"

"We couldn't just name one after me," Charles began. "And we hate middle names. They only use those to identify serial killers. So this young man over here is Harlen. We'll call him H.P. And this other little . . . hey, look at that, they opened their eyes at the same time. Now Seth, this one, who looks like Sammy Davis, is named for you." The baby cried. Charles sounded awestruck as he continued. "Someone once said this was God's way of communicating that he hasn't given up on the world."

Big Mama: "Then God *must* be a man. Only a man'd put us through this much pain to send a message he could write in the sky or somewhere."

Charles, admiringly: "They cry in perfect pitch."

Tamra had noticed they always cried in unison, and there was nothing perfect about their noise. When she opened her eyes, the nurse pushed the double cart toward her. Tamra raised her back and pressed the bed's "up" button. The top half of her mattress rose to meet her spine. Her breasts, infected and sore, felt like sacks of rocks. "They slept three hours," the nurse said proudly and lifted one and then the other screaming, stiff bundle.

"What's there to cry about?" Charles called. "The sun's shining and a beautiful woman you've just met is about to stick her breasts in your mouth."

Tamra exposed her nipples through the slits in her nursing gown and crooked her arms into twin cradles. Babies positioned, her sons clamped their mouths onto her. She shut her eyes, biting down hard on her lip and steeling herself for the stinging pain as her milk was drawn into their mouths. She groaned softly, not wanting to upset Virginia, who had advised that with this sudden twist of events (twins!) she would be wise to abandon her plans to nurse. A guttural sound rose from her throat, and she curled her toes in anguish. It felt as if red-hot needles were being pulled through the flesh beneath her arms and on through her breasts to the tips of her raw nipples.

Despite the pain, Little Seth and H.P. sounded so sweet as they drank, like kittens eagerly lapping from a dish. But *"ooooohh,"* she groaned louder. It was astonishing that their little gums could cause such agony. Still, she wanted to see them again. They were so precious. Opening an eye and squinting down, she saw . . . was that Little Seth or H.P.? The yellow blanket was wrapped so tightly he was more tube than body. And with this scorching pain he was more like a snake, yes, two snakes with curved needles for teeth, double rows in the upper jaws, devouring her whole. She locked her eyelids.

When she could breathe again, she relaxed her toes and found Virginia and Big Mama watching with concern. Mother's love had to be genetically predisposed, she reasoned. How else could the species survive? Only love this powerful could keep a woman from flinging a gnawing baby from her tormented breasts.

And what was Dalhia doing here, anyway? Her mother-in-law, dressed in a vested black suit, parked herself on the bed. "Keep nursing. It's the only way to unclog those glands. I used hot compresses."

It surprised Tamra that her mother-in-law had nursed her children. Dalhia explained, "Only Vicky. Not Charles. They were born so close together . . . he didn't get his turn." She paused and looking demure, added. "I worried he'd grow up with a breast fixation."

Big Mama asked, "Why should he be different from other men?"

The nurse returned, saying the doctor had postponed the tubal ligation until Tamra had healed from the C-section. Tamra thought they should have performed it while they'd had her open.

"Actually," Charles said, "The postponement's not a bad idea. I want to discuss it with you, anyway." Tamra shot him a puzzled look and he returned the stare, obviously uncomfortable. Was there something wrong with the twins?

With the babies fed and sleeping again, the nurse suggested they be returned to the nursery. Virginia joined Dalhia on the bed, as if prepared to participate in the conversation. But Big Mama grabbed her arm, pulling her daughter up, saying that Tamra and Charles needed time alone.

Now that the last of the family was out in the hallway, Tamra insisted Charles fill her in on any troubling possibilities. Why would he want the tubal ligation postponed?

"It's just that getting your tubes tied is so final."

She smiled easily despite the soreness of her body and suggested he move in closer. She'd already thought it through. "Then I can stop worrying about my job."

"I suppose I have no say in the matter, like them not getting circumcised."

"Are you worried you'll feel old or less virile if we can't have more kids?"

"What do you mean *we, kimo sabe?*"

His joke fell flat. She straightened herself up, adjusting her gown. "This isn't something I'm willing to negotiate."

"This is a marriage, not a union meeting."

Her tone rose slightly. "And yet, what you really want is for me to produce babies for your business." (She thought of adding, "Why not just park me in the hog house?" but held her tongue.)

He said, "We could always hire a different sitter . . . I have a cousin . . ."

"Give me a break."

"Then we could hire someone from overseas. Heck, Paris, if you like. The house is just about ready. There'll be more than enough room. And as for your job, we could . . ."

Suddenly her body felt so weary. She didn't want a fight. "It isn't a matter of who we get. Sitter or not, children need time with their parents. Even asking me this is selfish. What *about* my job? Should I just sit on the farm nursing babies while someone else takes my place? Scientists are in their most productive stages from their mid-twenties to their early thirties. I only have a few years left."

"How much time do the boys have with their mother? It's troubling. The idea of you leaving the twins so soon . . ."

She argued that six weeks was more than enough time, that there was still a chance for her to be affiliated with a university, and that with all the new breakthroughs and technologies the scope of her work was unlimited. "We can identify two hundred thousand genes now. With tools for sequencing and synthesizing . . ."

"Maybe if I got home more . . ."

"Stop dreaming."

"You didn't marry a banker or a school principal," he said.

"Who am I, Aunt Jemima?"

"Look at other families, at how many kids they have."

"I don't want to wind up like those women."

He stood, insulted. "You think you're better than them?"

She wondered why it was wrong to believe that. But she didn't ask. Noticing how terribly unhappy he looked, she softened her voice. "You just don't know, Charles. Babies aren't abstract ideas. Each is a reality complete with ten fingernails and ten toenails to clean and keep clipped. And let's see, that's also two nostrils to wipe, thirty-six teeth per mouth . . ." She laughed wistfully. "Even when they're toilet trained they're still so helpless they hold their little bottoms up to be wiped. I can just picture myself being so confused when I get back to work that when I'm introduced to someone, instead of offering my hand I'll expect him to bend over."

There was a knock on the door. It was Cousin Johnny, and she pulled the blanket up to her chin, wanting to hide her bulky breasts and distended nipples from his insistent, hungry eyes. He wanted to talk to Charles and they went into the hallway.

She heard Cousin Johnny's voice through the door. "Yeah, I did, man. They weren't talking, insisted on waiting for you."

Then her father's voice, making Charles's decision easier. "They might be looking for signs of weakness. With the babies and all, you are distracted."

Charles returned to the room, concerned, she could tell, by whatever news he'd received. He said he'd have to go back to the farm.

"Oh Charles, we've had so little time . . ."

He sat on the bed. She felt teary at the thought of him leaving. He probably hadn't slept since those few hours before the fire. She cupped his face, prickly with beard, suggesting they temporarily shelve the discussion about more babies. They were still in shock over the twins. And feeling the strength of his arms around her shoulders, she was all the more aware of her own fragility. She needed rest, but not at the hospital, at home with him, tonight. Maybe then he'd sleep, too. "When you leave I'm leaving with you," she said.

He said that was impossible, that she'd need time to heal.

"And who's gonna stop me?" She pointed out that the babies were healthy and she was no longer waiting to have her tubes tied. Besides, she missed Joyce.

"I hope you're not coming home to be with me," he said. "There may be trouble over at the farm."

If he'd spit at her, she couldn't have felt worse. That farm made him so single-minded. She wanted to ask why he hadn't put a phone between her legs in the labor room so he could have taken calls between each of his son's deliveries. But she kept her anger bottled. "My decision has nothing to do with you. Get home when you can. Please don't leave me here."

When she told the rest of the family about her plans to leave, she was met with a wall of resistance, especially Virginia, who said, "This is suicidal. You've been cut up. Charles can come back after his meeting."

But Tamra knew he wouldn't return to the hospital tonight, and she pulled herself to her feet, dizzy. Virginia rushed to her side, saying she'd put a stop to this crazy plan. But Tamra whispered, please, she had to go. She was so lonely without him and she couldn't fight anyone else. She didn't have the strength left.

Virginia offered to go with her. No, Tamra said, and she pulled on socks. Her body was too sore for the nylon stretch of panty hose. Elbie would stay with her, she said, knowing that if her mother saw the clutter of the trailer she'd be up all night cleaning. Most importantly, she didn't want Virginia to see how Charles seemed to forget about her when he worked, long day after day. Looking helpless, Virginia finally agreed to her daughter's demands. "I understand," she said. And sadly, Tamra felt she did.

They spent the next hour in a flurry of details. By the time Charles pushed her outside in a wheelchair, she felt even more exhausted. From the car, she could just lift her arm to wave good-bye to Dalhia, Big Mama, Seth, and Virginia. But on the way home it wasn't the weariness or soreness that frightened her so much as it was the realization that in one hour she'd have to care for the babies who were in the backseat, as well as the child they were rushing toward.

By the time they turned left, near the hog confinement center, it was still light enough for her to recognize several pickups plus Mr. Russell's Caterpillar and a few unfamiliar Internationals along the road.

"Think if I get out here, you can drive yourself to the trailer?" Charles asked. She wondered what he'd do if she said no; she couldn't drive herself. He'd been distracted during the drive and she'd felt shut out. The crowd of white farmers Johnny had warned about had gathered before the hog confinement facility, and she was jealous that they, and not she, claimed his attention.

The men, some of whom had been leaning against the walls, broke from their tiny clusters to walk toward him as he stepped from the car. She shut the engine off, wanting to see what would happen. Their faces looked pensive. She wished she could see more of Charles than his back so she could get a better read on what Mr. Kohl was saying. He seemed to speak for the others, who stood behind, nodding their heads in agreement. When their talk ended, Charles shook Mr. Kohl's hand and was led to several stacks of crates.

Two men pried the containers open and lifted out one, then several more, young hogs. Charles was in profile, smiling, as were the others. Now she understood. The animals were gifts, replacements for those lost in the fire. It was interesting to know whites also felt a personal sense of shame when their own committed a crime. Maybe they'd even brought news on who'd started the fire, but she doubted that. State inspectors claimed to have found nothing, and Charles had said the sheriff had put little effort into identifying the arsonist.

When she started the ignition, the babies awoke, their twin screams startling in the quiet. Eager to hold them, she climbed into the backseat, momentarily puzzled over whom to comfort first. She still couldn't tell them apart. Which one had the nurse wrapped in blue? Uncovering a tiny wrist beneath a yellow blanket, she read the arm band. This was little Seth, his face like a rubber ball, eyes squeezed shut, with a mouthful of tongue, hollering for her.

Unbuckling him from his carrier, she lifted him, as hungry for him as he was for her. Leaning him on her shoulder, his mouth suctioning her neck and any expanse of open skin, she laughed, tickled by his fervency, and she stroked H.P., marveling at the wonder of them both. Two. Her love for them and the broad range of possibilities for their lives made her weep, the same salty water that filled the oceans, that had filled their sac, and all three were as one.

She spoke softly to H.P. "I know you want me to lift you, too, but I need practice. I don't know how to get you both up at the same time." As they wailed, she tucked Seth into her left arm and carefully lifted H.P., her hand weak. She rocked them together, their screams ceasing, her voice low, saying it was okay, that she had plenty of room in her heart for them both.

"You pulled an old okey doke on me. But that's okay, things are good out here. Just look." She lifted her arms slightly as if to allow them to see the scene at the hog house. Their lids were shut and they worked their lips, soothing themselves to sleep.

"See that big handsome fellow? That's your daddy over there, and look at how they treat him. They may not like him, but he has earned their respect. I've done a good job for you both on the daddy front." She cried again.

At the trailer, she was greeted out front by a grownup Joyce, in a black and white dress with a big red apple embroidered on the front. She'd waited on the top steps, holding Elbie's hand. Tamra rushed from the car, kissing her daughter's cheeks. It seemed as if months had passed. She wanted to cry again and didn't understand why. She wouldn't be left alone. Elbie agreed to stay overnight or until Tamra was rested.

The old woman put her arms around Tamra's shoulder, insisting on helping with the babies. Joyce fastened to her legs. Once inside, Tamra thanked Elbie for her hard work. The trailer had been scrubbed inside to a shine, and the clutter somehow minimized. The words exhausted what strength she had remaining. Leaning on Elbie, she did not fight the suggestion of a nap. Maybe the twins would be quiet for a few minutes. Joyce could sit beside her on the bed. She was teary again. Her hormonal system was in tatters. But what she really wanted, she admitted to herself, as she put her head on the pillow, was for it to have been Charles who'd helped her up the steps, carrying their new babies in his arms.

36

Tamra November 1982

SHE STOOD IN the master bedroom of the old Reardon house (she'd have to stop calling it that) and looked about her, trying to imagine the way he'd see it, now that it was complete. Of all the tasks required, she'd most enjoyed working with the restored photographs of Charles's ancestors. The aged pictures, now atop dressers and tables and along the walls, fit perfectly with this room's cracked marble fireplace.

So much was old in this room: the worn Oriental rug, the polished scroll-top desk, the four-poster bed, and the wide-planked wood floors. She'd insisted, no wall-to-wall, please. His slippers would be kept by the bed, and on chilly nights he'd return to a room lit by the glow of a fire. But first she must push back from the fireplace the wooden goose, a decoy that had lured so many from the skies.

Would the sheer curtains do for the winter? Was the chintz spread too coolly uninviting? She smoothed the bumpy coverlet for reassurance. Had she heard a car along the driveway? Rushing to the front window, she ignored the red and gold autumnal treetops and searched the quiet paths.

Had Eve Reardon waited in her own fashion from this room and also found disappointment in the quiet of the roads? Quickly she laughed at herself. She had never, even for a moment, compared their lives before.

Tamra had returned to her job at the lab, and there were, of course, the children and this house to care for. Eve Reardon had devoted her time to overseeing the house and servants and unlike Tamra, the chores she'd performed had seldom been rushed. She had also been unable to have children, a curse in this community for which other whites, rich or poor, had seemed unwilling to forgive her.

With no family to inherit their land or this sturdy house that sat on the edge of history, they had fallen into hands darker than the richest Chesapeake soil. The main section of the house had been built in the early 1800s by a wealthy farmer, but no slaves had labored here. Thank God for that. And as for ghosts, with Tamra and her family scheduled to settle in this very evening, the sight of their black faces would be enough to frighten away any Confederate holdouts.

Mr. Reardon, in one last jab at his wife, had written in his will that Charles was the kind of son he'd hoped to have. Eve Reardon had agreed. And it was at least a chance to retaliate toward her unforgiving white neighbors by leaving them a lasting gift: her house, her land, the grain elevator, all sold to Lane Incorporated. For this Tamra was of course grateful, but thoughts of her benefactors remained ambivalent. Mrs. Reardon had settled, of all places, in France.

The doorbell rang. She'd never heard it before. Chimes. It couldn't be Charles, though. He'd have used his key. Besides, the door wasn't locked. She walked down the stairs thinking maybe the children had awakened and Aunt Elbie had brought them over.

Passing the living room she glanced with admiration at a wall covered with her collection of African masks and a dozen oil paintings in bright primary colors. They depicted scenes of African Americans at picnics, graduations, athletic competitions; in song, in prayer; dressing hair; dancing; and en route to a schoolhouse. As colorful as they were, the room was dominated by a massive fieldstone fireplace, the flames within it claiming several small logs. She never passed without thinking of all the labor required to build it, one hundred and fifty years before, by workers carrying in stones one by one.

Tamra opened the door and was greeted by the stern faces of two white moving men. She and Aunt T.J. had spent countless hours searching furniture stores in D.C. for just the right sofas, and now they'd arrived. The shorter of the two men asked, "Is the lady of the house in?" Determined not to let him ruin her day, she pulled the door open wide, merely saying she hadn't expected him so early.

Even with two couches, the living room still looked empty. It would probably take years to fill it. For the time being, repositioning the sofas might help. "Just move it a bit to the left," she instructed. The short man, who seemed to be in charge, looked tired and about to complain. The sofas were obviously heavy. He set the legs down, rubbing the small of his back. "Let's make sure we got it right this time. You want it over there . . . by the barbecue?" He pointed at the fireplace. She pursed her lips, knowing full well he knew it was a fireplace, and not a barbecue grill.

Anger burned her cheeks. "Give me the invoice and I'd like your name, sir." She'd never bother to call his supervisor but it wouldn't hurt to have him worry about it on his return to D.C.

The men left, presumably for the paperwork, while she tapped her foot against the floor. Should she tip the other man, ignore the smart-mouthed one? No, that would be like rewarding the quiet one for not being overtly racist. They'd both lose out today.

A familiar voice broke through her thoughts. Someone was talking with the moving men in boisterous tones. "And so . . . when he and his old lady are at the zoo, a gorilla reaches out and pulls her into the cage with him. . . . This ape's puttin' his legs around her and the bitch's going crazy beatin' the bars, screaming 'what should I do?' "

Tamra knew that if it was a joke about a woman it had to be Cousin Johnny. She listened intently while he finished. "So this fellow said to his wife: 'Why don't you tell *him* you have a headache?' "

She spoke to the furniture movers. "Look, if you want me to sign something . . ." Cousin Johnny removed his hat, nodding his head of tight curls. The driver smirked as he extended the paper.

When she'd signed and was about to close the door, she stopped to examine Cousin Johnny's face, thinking it was probably that drooping lid that attracted women. It gave him an air of reckless danger. She asked what he wanted.

"You," he said. And he added slowly. "Charles sent me—in case you need me." His eyes flicked down momentarily toward her body. She was glad she'd kept her lab jacket on after returning home from work. She knew every word she spoke to this immature man would seem to be loaded with additional meaning.

"He isn't coming?"

"He can't . . . so he sent a man to do the job. The inspector's here. There's some problem with the seed corn. They're threatening not to take it, and he's got a gang rounded up waiting for him to lead a tree-felling over at Jimmy Macks." He laughed as if they were conspiring against Charles. "Says he's gotta be the one to do it and then————"

"I see," she interrupted, longing to ask him if he knew when Charles could get away, but that proved unnecessary.

"He might be gone all night, Cousin Tamra."

"Thank you for the message," she said and moved the door slowly, trying to give him time to walk away, but he remained in place, as if he wanted to be insulted. When she had closed the door, she tried erasing his face from her mind. What kind of man would make it his life's mission to flirt? Where had it gotten him, anyway? Almost forty and he was the only Lane in this neighborhood without an acre to his name. And it seemed every couple of years, some country girl was bragging that she'd had his baby. The mystery was that he'd impregnated them in the first place. A man like him didn't have a penis between his legs, it was a whip.

Enough of Cousin Johnny and moving men. If Charles wasn't coming she had to regroup. First she'd run down and get Aunt Elbie and the kids. She looked at her watch. The twins were probably still sleeping. She'd fed them only an hour ago, when she'd rushed in from work and pumped more milk. Her mind switched to Joyce. Would she be frightened sleeping in a new room? Maybe she would let Joyce sleep with her just for the night. The twins' bassinets would have to go into her room, anyway, so they might as well all be together.

Their first night in their new house and Charles would not be there. It was too annoying to dwell on. She started to leave but smacked her forehead in irritation as she remembered she must put out the fire downstairs. The one here in the living room was almost out, but the one downstairs needed to be tamped. Too bad for Charles, she thought. He doesn't know what he missed. Too bad for them both. She'd been looking forward to showing him the basement den. It was to have been a great surprise.

Downstairs she was reminded once again how much he'd love this room. The floor was warmed with a thick carpet, and a corduroy easy chair was poised before a television, its screen wide enough to catch every play of those baseball games he always said he loved. This room could make him slow down long enough to watch them.

Not everything she'd chosen had been practical. An old-fashioned, red Coke machine with the words DRINK COCA-COLA IN BOTTLES stood against one wall, and she reached up to unplug the circular neon sign, a red and green blinking EBONY BEAT that she'd hung on another.

She grew light-hearted picturing the delight on his face at seeing the finished den. Walking to her favorite attraction in the room, the jukebox, she hugged the machine. She'd found it in a failing diner in Richmond, but it looked as if it had come directly from a Detroit assembly line, with its chrome front grill, walnut veneer, and large letters boasting: SEEBURG 100 SELECTOMATIC. HI FIDELITY.

Each title of the handwritten entries above the selector numbers and letters brought back memories: "Sitting on the Dock of the Bay," "Stand By Me," "Tonight's the Night." Her finger lingered at "I Heard It Through the Grapevine," and fighting off a sense of timidity, she reached behind the machine, flipping the control switch. The jukebox lit up in red and white, clicking as she punched in H7. As the selector arm moved to the left, it crossed the row of shiny, black 45's, then paused. A record slid forward. At first only static grated on her ears, but then the needle worked into the vinyl grooves until finally the sound of piano keys like Indian drums introduced Marvin's plaintive cry, and she sang with him.

She snapped her fingers, moved her head, and followed her feet, unwilling, as was the rest of her body, to sit this one out.

Working up a sweat, she tore her jacket off, throwing it toward Charles's easy chair, and kept on dancing and singing, her high heels catching in the nap of the rug.

Swaying her torso, she felt the slimness of her body. This last diet had peeled off the extra weight, and she didn't miss it. She pranced until, at the conclusion of the song, she lifted her voice and her arms. But suddenly, she broke off, aware that someone now stood where only minutes before there had been no one. Spinning around, she was startled to see Cousin Johnny standing in the doorway, his trim body leaning into the frame.

"What are you doing here?" she demanded.

His mouth moved but she'd never hear him over the loud music. Crossing to the machine, she bent over self-consciously and pulled the plug. The needle dragged across the record. They'd told her never to do that.

"How'd you get in here?" she demanded.

He displayed Charles's car keys, asking, "Were you doing some kind of dance to keep the snakes out?"

"It obviously didn't work," she shouted and rubbed her arms. Despite having worked up a sweat, she felt chilled. Johnny, hands in pockets, looked around the room and whistled. "This is some little hot spot." It felt ruined by his presence. She walked toward the fireplace, feeling him watching her backside, and she closed the air vent with a snap.

"I've got to get to the kids. What was it you wanted?"

"Sorry 'bout just walking in," he said. "Charles couldn't call . . . phones ain't hooked up . . . I rang the bell . . . reckon you couldn't hear me." She felt so foolish having been caught this way, and by him of all people. She paused near the stairway.

"What was it you needed? I've got to go get the kids."

"I'll walk with you," Johnny said. Charles had sent him for the keys to his vault in the trailer. They were in his top drawer. Ordinarily she would have wondered what the cash was needed for but right that minute, something besides the embarassment of being seen by Johnny during an intimate moment was troubling her. She couldn't put her finger on it. Walking up the stairs, she thought her bottom must look like two, large, peach halves beneath her skirt. She wished she'd left her jacket on.

On their way out the front door, their shoulders bumped. "I'll give you a ride down," he said.

She insisted on walking the several yards down, not wanting to be inside Charles's car with Johnny. But it was more than his presence that made her uneasy. She rushed on as Johnny called, "Wait, I'll walk, too." She'd already started down, her feet unsteady in her heels, quickly putting distance between them.

There was that chill again, and now she had to hold herself. Her body shuddered uncontrollably. What could it be? Perhaps another breast infection. She was run down from too little sleep, her job, the house, waiting up for Charles; maybe the infection had returned.

She walked faster. There was a distance of a football field to travel and she'd have to take longer steps. She wished now that she'd accepted Johnny's ride. Something terribly wrong was disturbing her. The premonition was unlike anything she'd ever experienced. It pulled her toward the trailer. She felt Johnny's presence as he caught up with her, but she didn't speak. He asked what troubled her so.

She couldn't talk, not now, something, something . . . what? Would she laugh about this later? She breathed in as if smelling the air. No. She was certain now. Her milk rushed in. She was only halfway home and it was time to feed her sons.

A baby's cry came on the wind from an open window of the trailer. It relieved her, but for only a second, for as she hurried on she waited to hear something more that would allow her to catch her breath. And suddenly she knew it wasn't coming. There was just that unfluctuating cry of one son. Oh God, which son?

She stopped to tear her heels off, felt the slit in the side of her skirt as it ripped, and raced past Johnny, toward the trailer. She felt pain in her face, knew it was the skin pulled taut on her forehead, but she welcomed the hurt, for still there was that insistent and lonely cry. One son. "Oh God, oh God, please," she panted. Why couldn't she run faster? "Oh, Mommy's coming. Mommy's coming. Oh God." She could picture what was wrong. No. She couldn't let it in.

Finally she was at the door and tore it open. Joyce was on the floor, surrounded by blocks. She leaped up, crying as Tamra ran past. Aunt Elbie was in the hallway, two bottles of breast milk in her hands. She turned, a horrified look crossing her face. "Child, what is it?"

Tamra heard herself screaming but she couldn't close her mouth. It seemed to take forever before she raced around the sharp corner to her room, crawled over her bed, and stared terrified into the two basinettes. In one, H.P. beat furiously against the mattress.

She reached slowly into the other basinette, where Little Seth lay on his stomach, still and unmoving. She bent, panting, waiting, spoke in a rushed breath of prayer: "Oh God, oh God, oh God, oh God. Please, please, please, please."

She could beg no longer. Lifting him, she brought his hushed, unbreathing body to her breasts. His face, his eyes, his hands were without life, a bubble of spittle on his parted lips. Unsnapping her nursing bra, she brought him to a nipple. The baby's face remained cold, unstirring.

Frantically rubbing his lobes, his cheeks, she tried to stir him, warm him, slapped lightly at his body. "Oh please, God, please, please, please, please. Not this. Anything, God. Don't take him. Please, please, please, please, please. Not my baby."

There were hands on her shoulders. She jerked free. The voices of others. "Quiet," she begged. "*Shhhh!*" They tried to lift the form from her. "No, no, he's got to sleep. No, not this." She held on. She would not let go, kept begging them to be quiet, then realized it was her own screams she was trying to quell.

The hands pulled back. Released her and her baby. They were free again. Alone. This was the son, she was sure now, to whom she'd not spoken when in her belly. He'd been so silent. She hadn't known. She'd been busy. Now he was heavy and cold, grown tired of waiting. She could rock him, warm him, and soon she could speak again.

She heard springs on the bed as she rocked and someone horrible spoke: "Call Charles on the radio. Quick. The baby's dead." She held her son, thinking, This can't happen. She would never let him go.

When finally he did come she knew his hand in the darkening room. He tried to steady her, stop her from rocking. No one possessed that kind of strength. She heard her own voice telling him to leave, to go away, but there were no words. Snarls. He insisted on getting through. She knew because she heard him begging. "Let me in, Tamra. Let me in." But she could not. There was only room in this pit for her and her son.

37

Tamra November 1982

THE DOCTORS HAD rigged H.P. to an apnea monitor. It would buzz if he stopped breathing. His chest was wrapped with a cloth resembling an ace bandage that held in place rubber suction cups attached to the wires of a portable electrode pack. He would have to wear it for at least six months, the doctors said. Just to be sure, they said. She heard their voices in unison, a Greek chorus.

They assured her that even a baby whose identical twin had died of crib death was no more likely to succumb to the same fate than other healthy babies. There had been no way to predict what had happened to Little Seth, they continued. Sudden Infant Death Syndrome came out of the blue . . . usually babies who'd been carried full term . . . often boys under six months . . . born without signs of fetal distress. Crib death, they called it, as if the bed had died. Babies with insufficient air passages.

They told her to listen for the buzz, and she was always checking; her face pressed beside Little Harlen's, listening, listening for life, and when no one else was about, she woke him, shaking sleep from him, offering her breasts, both of them.

If he lived, and he must, she knew he would one day learn the story of his twin brother, always an infant, whose mother had danced while he died.

His brother, he would learn, was buried beside kin who'd lived their lives, made mistakes, and started over again. H.P. would blame her, she was sure, as the others quietly did. They'd whispered to her: This has never happened to anyone else in our family.

She awoke to a room filled with mourning. Startled that she had slept, she placed a palm on H.P.'s chest, felt the evenness of his breathing. Joyce slept beside them both in footed pajamas, a thumb in her mouth, a blanket in the closed fan of her fingers. Someone had given the boys birth gifts of toy firetrucks, and Joyce, who'd probably awakened when her daddy had left, had dragged one into bed with her. It lay tucked between her and H.P.

Tamra glanced at her watch. It was seven o'clock, time still to escape before any of Charles's family showed up to "help." They were all well-meaning, but she didn't want them in her life. She knew just where she wanted to go, to see Virginia and Seth, who still loved her.

She walked quietly to the bathroom. No shower today, perhaps at Mama's. The baby couldn't be left alone that long. A sponge bath would do. One of Charles's shirts lay on the tile floor a few inches from an open hamper. She lifted it by the collar, bringing it to her cheek as she had so many mornings since their marriage. She felt nothing. Her love was gone, burned away by his blaming, accusing eyes.

He pretended to still care about her. She knew how he actually felt, and she wondered if he too was awakened at night, when he did sleep, tormented by the same words she heard in her dreams. It was always her voice in the hospital explaining her theory of children's toe and finger counts. And always the dream ended in the same manner. He would follow her screams through the trailer, as he had that day, and he found her with their dead son. Pointing a finger, he'd say: "That's twenty less nails to clip."

She had stopped crying. There had been enough tears shed at the funeral. The infant gown had matched the lining of his coffin; that was the way it was done down here, they'd explained, and she had to choose the fabric, searching through swatches.

There were other intractable laws for dealing with death: always open-casket, however difficult for front-row mourners, or people might gossip, say he'd died of something contagious, disfiguring. It was a way of protecting her, really, they'd said.

And there was something else. Yes, it was a bit silly, they allowed, but they needed to tell her, for her sake. After the funeral people would gather at the house—By the way, they'll bring loaves of white bread, bologna, corn flakes, peanut butter; Accept them all graciously—and it was most important that she take care to welcome people through the front door. Of that she must be mindful. When she showed them out, always they must exit through the front, never back. Nail it shut if necessary, but don't allow mourners to bring more misfortune to your home. Death follows through the back door.

She pulled on a pair of wool socks she'd bought in London. It had been cold there, the East Indians snubbing her. She'd greeted the dark-skinned man behind the desk in the postal shop and he'd looked around, alarmed, lest his coworkers think them acquaintances. Today these socks will warm her feet. The floor was cold. A thick pile would have been nice after all.

She stepped into loafers, wondering if she should call her company today to resign or if she should put it off. She certainly couldn't go back there. Right from the start, everyone had seemed surprised about her short maternity leave; surely they whispered now. A baby needs its mother, they'd be saying. She hadn't needed the money, they'd say. Why had she rushed back?

Perhaps next year she'd apply for a job at one of the universities or maybe she'd return as a doctoral student. That would be something, wouldn't it? Work seemed to help Charles, he'd started right back. And he had never cried. The call could be put off until tomorrow.

She woke Joyce and then her son. They could get an early start, eat breakfast, and take off right afterwards. She insisted that Joyce hold her hand as they padded downstairs and Tamra guardedly carried H.P. with her free arm. They could fall so easily and be gone, just that fast.

When she did get Joyce's snowsuit zipped, her daughter struggled against it. Too hot, she complained. Tamra cupped her face with her hands. "You can take it off when we get there. Do you know where we're going?" The hood of her jacket was drawn tightly about her face, which was dominated by eyes too serious for a child; only the bangs were playful, three tiny braids resting on her forehead, satin rosettes clipped to each. "We're going to visit Mamma Two and Grandpa Seth. Isn't that good?"

Joyce bounced gleefully and Tamra held her shoulders to prevent a fall. Lifting her down, she saw Joyce's pockets bulged. When she reached inside, her hand closed over rocks, shells, pebbles, and a gull's feather. Her daughter snatched them back, her treasures. "We'll have to get you a wooden cigar box, like the one I had at your age. Maybe Mama Two still has my rocks. . . . I can show you the collection I gathered when Grampa Seth took me on nature trips." She marvelled at the truth of it. She had once been a child.

They walked beneath a massive tree, the fall leaves cascading on their heads and shoulders. Joyce stooped and lifted several leaves, comparing them, as if shopping for fruit. She was knee-deep in the pile. "Just one," Tamra instructed. Joyce chose one riddled with holes.

She told her daughter: "When there's time I can show you how to wax this so it always looks new." She helped her into the car and strapped her and the baby into seats. It was warmer outside than she'd anticipated, a late fall, and she wondered what that meant for Charles and his work on the farm.

They'd been in the car for twenty minutes and were just outside Salisbury when H.P. awoke, screaming, demanding to be fed and changed. She searched for a safe spot to pull over, and Joyce fought the restraints of her carseat. "Want to get out, Mommy. Out!" Tamra tried calming them both with her voice. It was useless. Joyce, behind the driver's seat, had wiggled down to reach just behind Tamra, kicking and struggling. "Stop! Stop! Want to get out."

She'd had her eye off the road for a few seconds before hearing the horn. It happened quickly. She'd veered across the line and a truck came at her. Brakes protesting, she cut sharply to the right, the car bumping to a stop on a narrow strip.

Joyce kept it up, kicking the back of her seat, and H.P. screamed, both oblivious to how close they'd come to a collision. She rested her forehead on the steering wheel, wondering if there was some part of her that wanted to join her son. They had to get the car off the road, she knew that. She was in no shape to drive. What had she been thinking?

Cautiously pulling back onto the road, she looked for a safe place. Minutes later, Joyce pointed to a spot they'd passed many times. "Circus," Joyce said.

It was an unpainted ferris wheel, a carousel, and a few other rusted rides, certainly no circus, but the parking lot provided a safe place to pull into. She freed Joyce from the seat, untying her hood and pulling off the jacket, seeing droplets of sweat across her small forehead. "Poor baby, I bet you were miserable back there."

She'd just begun nursing H.P. when Joyce opened the car door. "Circus, Mommy," she said. She bargained with her. If she would remain still just long enough for H.P to finish feeding, they'd get the stroller from the trunk and walk over for a better look at the circus.

At the ferris wheel they were warmly greeted by an elderly white man. "Any chance of riding just the merry-go-round?"

"She can ride the whole shebang if she likes," he said and introduced himself as a man with two first names, Uncle Harold Larry. He walked behind the ticket counter, as flimsy as a cardboard puppet theater. Joyce stood on tiptoes to pass a dollar through the open window of the booth.

Uncle Harold Larry announced each ride as if speaking to multitudes. "Step right up to the Mad Hatter's Teacups," he said and waited outside the creaky gate as his lone patron handed over a ticket. Joyce ran along the perimeters of the giant cups, finally nesting in a bright yellow one, and grasping the steering wheel with a look of expectation worthy of an astronaut. The cup circled, rising a few inches from the ground, the machine apparently too weary to travel higher. But Joyce threw her head back, laughing with delight. This was just what her daughter had needed, Tamra realized, a chance to laugh again.

When she'd ridden all four rides twice (Tamra said no to the roller coaster, even if it *was* for little people), Joyce begged for one last turn on the merry-go-round. But racing back from the ticket booth, ahead of Uncle Harold Larry, she fell along the cement ground. Tamra helped her up, and the old man patted her shoulders. The insulation of the snow pants had protected her knees, but Joyce sobbed, stretching out a hand, revealing the tiniest of scrapes.

For a fleeting second it was as if Tamra felt the same burning sensation in her palm. She led her wailing child to a bench, held her hand between her two larger ones, and instructing her to close her eyes, said, "I'm going to press and press and take your pain for you."

Joyce stopped crying when Tamra said, "Yes . . . I can feel your pain now . . . just a bit in the tip of my fingers . . . it's moving up . . . traveling through my hands, into my wrists, heading for my heart."

Joyce's voice cut through her own. "Is that true, Mommy?"

There was something new in her daughter's pitch and in her eyes. Was she witnessing the start of her child's critical consciousness? Did they really begin at this young age to question what others told them? Tamra asked: "Do you want it to be true?" Eyes unflinching, Joyce nodded yes. "Then it is," Tamra said.

Staring down at her palm, Joyce smiled. "The hurt stopped, Mommy. . . . Can I ride now?"

Tamra watched her run off and she held her breath, hoping Joyce wouldn't fall again. When her daughter was securely fastened onto the horse she'd chosen, Tamra buried her hands in her own pockets and felt a strip of paper. She pulled it out and saw that it was torn from a magazine. She didn't recall putting it there, but it had been a year since she'd worn this jacket. Unfolding the paper, she saw it was an article from one of her technical journals.

Slowly, deliberately, she crumpled it. Science had lost its hold over her. The way she saw it, Little Seth's death made a mockery of her life's work. She'd spent years organizing and analyzing data, trying to demystify life. At that she'd been successful, so much so that she'd taken everyday, ordinary miracles, like life, for granted.

And then there was this, this experience that could not be understood by scientific reasoning. Her son had died. How had she known before anyone else? And what of this invisible layer of skin? She couldn't see it, and it certainly couldn't be explained by Western scientific standards, but no one could convince her she hadn't felt the discomfort her daughter had experienced, that there were some hurts only she could assuage.

The more she thought about it, the more she realized the cruel humor of it. She'd invested all those years seeking solutions to seemingly intractable problems in the physical world when in fact no one, not even God, prevented disastrous events. In the end, human life was so fragile it hung on a thread of chance.

She was now certain that when it came to her children, she could hear and feel what others could not. And to her, that seemed perfectly logical. If an ordinary sparrow, possessing a brain only a fraction of the size of a human's, can sight from a soaring distance enough bugs and worms in the soil to feed her hungriest nestlings, it stood to reason that in a crisis her own brain could switch from complex thought patterns in the neocortex to a primitive form of instinct by which she could see or hear or feel whatever was necessary to nurture her children.

She'd been caught not listening. But she planned to never again misuse this strength. She would raise each child as if the survival of the race depended on it. They were that special, and nothing would stand in her way, even her own dreams.

Joyce called to her from the merry-go-round and she looked up, thinking, She expects me to be here, to wave at her, each time she travels back around. It suddenly didn't seem like too much to ask. Quickly she pushed the stroller closer, hoping the carnival music wouldn't be too loud for the baby. But she wanted Joyce to know that finally, she had captured her mother's attention.

Perhaps it wasn't too late. She could use this tragedy as a turning point to become a real mother, to keep the cleanest house, be wise and patient. She would be the kind of mother who would be there when her child circled round, waving her on reassuringly. Virginia did it for me, she thought, and then the high price of that constancy struck her. Quickly wiping away a tear, she saw Joyce's horse was circling back around. "Hi, Mommy," she called.

"Hello my dearest, dearest darling," Tamra replied but only in a whisper, for Joyce was already looking off, waving at Uncle Harold Larry.

38

Tamra and Charles December 1982

ON THIS DAY after Christmas, with gifts unopened beneath the tree, Big Mama phoned, insisting that Tamra give in to Virginia's demands. "She wants you to host that African whatchamacallit."

"Kwanzaa," Tamra said, "and it's not really African, just a holiday some man made up."

"Some man just made up Halloween and Valentine's Day, too," Big Mama said.

As always, she was impressed by her grandmother's wit. But she stalled for time. "I'd like to know when Mama got to be so African." She hoped this would at least elicit a chuckle. It didn't work.

Big Mama said, "You ain't the only one who lost a . . ."

Please, Tamra thought. She couldn't manage that conversation today. But she had no choice. The pain had surged in.

Big Mama continued: ". . . who lost a child. He was Virginia's grand-baby, too. It's been hard on all of us."

Her nostrils burned, a prelude to tears. She raised her chin, hoping they'd slide back into her tear ducts. "Okay, Big Mama. Call and tell her you accomplished your mission. I'll get busy cleaning. But I can't speak for Charles. He wasn't even home yesterday."

"He'll be there," Big Mama said, and she hung up. Tamra wondered when Big Mama had talked to Charles. And why have a celebration in a grieving house?

Tamra leaned forward as Virginia wrapped the last yard of African cloth around her head and secured the ends with tiny tucks. Then grimacing in distaste at the results of her efforts, Virginia complained, "I can't fix it the way our sorors in Accra taught us." The buzzer from H.P.'s monitor sounded, his infant cries joining in. Virginia had insisted that he and his portable crib be put in another room, that Tamra stop carrying him. He had twisted the wires and tripped the buzzer again. Tamra started for him but her mother intervened, saying, "I'll get him."

"He needs me."

Virginia quieted her with a measured look and enunciated. "Why don't you see what needs to be done in the kitchen?"

Tamra gestured impatiently toward the oven, where a Smithfield ham, doused in ginger ale, baked slowly. Along the range top, pots and pans sat crammed with foods of savory and invitingly reckless names: Hoppin' John, Dirty Rice, Jerked Chicken, Put Up Beans, Cracklin' Bread, and Spicy Peaches, to be topped off with a Fat Rum Bubba. Their lilting quality reminded her of a Gershwin musical.

"You two've taken care of everything."

Her mother hurried off. Tamra tried to trail behind, but like a traffic guard, Virginia spun on her heels, holding up a palm. "Will you please give me a minute with my only grandson?"

Discomfort hung between them while H.P.'s screams grew louder. She patted Tamra's cheek, whispering: "Baby, you'll have to stop blaming yourself or you'll go crazy."

In the living room, Virginia, regal in her African garb, paused before the tree, which was now fully decorated with lights, brown-faced angels, Santas, madonnas, and carolers, and lifted the bunched-up blanket and tiny, crying head that was her grandson. Tamra could just make out the wires to the monitor, as Virginia talked baby chatter, halting to glare at Tamra, who suddenly felt very much in the way.

When it was time to begin the festivities, they all sat at the low marble table that had been moved in front of the fireplace. There were Vicky and her son, Mark, Dalhia, Harlen, Tamra with her children, Virginia, Seth and Big Mama, but not Charles. He'd called to say he'd be late, to start without him. They sat low, on their haunches and knees, the fire warming their faces. Big Mama squirmed on the too-soft ottoman, insistent about not accepting the higher, more comfortable chair. Joyce reached to the center of the table, grabbing a peanut.

Tamra shifted slightly, readjusting H.P., who lay awake in her arms, cheeks puffed like a greedy squirrel. Taking care not to trip the buzzer, she rubbed his belly with her finger. Was that a smile? Miraculous! From the corner of her eye, she watched as Joyce held the peanut like a raw egg. Tapping the peanut against the table edge, she tried splitting it with two thumbs. Tamra reached to embrace her but Joyce was up, running to Charles, who had just hurried in and was still loosening his tie.

Dalhia had been unusually quiet, warned already by Harlen to be less bossy. But she spoke now, urging Charles to sit beside his wife. He ignored his mother and stood over Harlen, filling him in on the deal with International Harvester, the company his Pa had insisted he go to instead of John Deere. Charles whispered excitedly that Harlen had been right; they'd gotten sixty-four on the three-rower. Harlen shook his head, astonished. They'd made thirty thousand on an eight-year-old machine.

"He showed me something new with———"

"Enough of that," Dalhia hushed them and Tamra made room for him without looking up. She was uncertain about how to greet him, this reluctant griever, who had moved quickly on with life. "Make room," Dalhia ordered, nudging Harlen to the right and causing a volley of grumbles. No one except Virginia seemed quite sure of what it was they'd agreed to participate in. As if sensing their group ambivalence, Virginia began immediately by demurely suggesting Charles offer a prayer. While heads were bowed, Tamra watched Dalhia pick lint from Harlen's jacket. He brushed her fingers aside.

The prayer ended, Virginia read woodenly from a dogeared paperback book, and they each sipped from the *kikombe cha umoja*, a communal cup of juice. Charles passed it to Tamra with the now-familiar concerned and probing look. Had they been whispering about her? She felt she was saner than them all. She alone seemed to remember their lost son.

Joyce was fidgety and her grandmother spooned some of the creamy banana that they'd roasted in the fireplace into her mouth. When Joyce was settled, Big Mama permitted her to hold the stem of the cup while Big Mama pretended to drink. When it reached Virginia, her manicured hands trembled as she cupped the wooden chalice and brought it to her lips as if it were an elixir. Tamra wished she could give her whatever magic she hoped for tonight.

The cup reached Harlen, but before he could drink, Dalhia scolded him: "Save some for me." He pretended to hold a mouthful of juice, swish it like mouthwash, and empty it back into the cup. They all laughed except Dalhia. She was the last to drink, and did so cautiously, like a bird at a fountain, glancing pensively between sips at the others.

Virginia rearranged her eyeglasses on the flat bridge of her nose, running a finger along the arms of the frame to hook them firmly around her lobes. With the aid of a tiny flashlight, she read from a paperback book explanations of the items on the table. She pointed first to the basket filled with carrots, sweet potatoes, peanuts, cabbage, squash, and onions, the harvests of the fields, products of a unified effort. There were ears of corn, one each for the children, though Vicky's son could hardly be called a boy any longer. Mark had grown tall. He was a young man now, buttoned up in his shirt and tie, his lips moving occasionally, as he silently practiced the essay he'd written and recited last year for his school's Martin Luther King, Jr., oratory contest. Vicky had mentioned it to Virginia and his recital had been hastily added to the list of Kwanzaa activities.

Virginia explained that the colorful straw mat on their table was a reminder that traditions sustain them. "And the candles represent the seven principles we Blacks should live by."

Tamra almost choked at this. Her mother referring to herself as Black? She'd never thought she'd live to hear it. Virginia handed Seth the book but he looked away, speaking without notes. "These principles aren't new to us," he said. "Like the one about unity." He rapped his index finger against the table. "The fact that we all came together at a minute's notice is proof that our family is unified. And I don't know about any of you," he looked around questioningly, "but this doesn't seem like such a harebrained scheme, after all." He patted Virginia's hand.

"Think about it," he continued. "Hundreds of thousands of Black people around the world, seated at their own Kwanzaa tables, celebrating the spirit of unity. We're participants in the recreation of ourselves." Virginia smiled encouragingly as Mark lit the first candle and Seth discussed the remaining principles, which he promised to explain in the Kwanzaa story he'd created for this night.

When all the candles had been lit, Virginia handed out gifts of books wrapped in yesterday's Christmas paper. They were opened and admired and piled high in a stack. Joyce unwrapped a big glossy volume: *The Patchwork Quilt*, and wanted to have it read to her on the spot. Despite her protests, it was taken away and given back to Virginia, who held it while Seth drizzled honey along the cover, a practice borrowed from an ancient, Jewish ceremony. Joyce licked greedily at the cover as Virginia spoke. "We offer you this book, my grandchild," she said, "because reading is not only necessary, but very sweet."

"More, please," Joyce said, politely extending the book and seeming genuinely puzzled at the grownups' laughter.

When Mark stood, his Adam's apple bobbing, he explained that for his school's oratory contest, he'd written a letter to a mother from an imaginary boy who'd marched with Dr. King. Vicky added that he'd won first place. As the letter began the boy told of being hosed, clubbed, and chased by dogs, until, like the other marchers, he was taken to the Birmingham jail.

"My cell is over Dr. King's," Mark recited, "and at first I was sorry I'd joined in with the other protestors." Tamra was impressed by her nephew's passion. He reminded her of the Charles she'd known so long ago. "This place is dark . . . cold . . . and there are rats here," Mark continued, "but last night, while the others slept, I heard Doctor King praying. He said, 'Thank you God for these children. They've given me the strength I need to keep going, though my very life may be taken from me.'

"Mama, I heard him crying," Mark continued, "but I didn't feel sorry for him. He's scared like the rest of us, but he's not too scared to die for what he knows is right. I marched in his shadow yesterday and I'm proud of that. I made the right choice, Mama, and I believe one day, things will change. . . ."

Tamra felt a tap from Charles, who held H.P. and pointed toward the baby's bottom, mouthing the word "wet." She realized that not only had he never changed his son, he'd never seen him changed and was probably daunted at the idea of getting the suction cups reattached. She stretched her arms out for the baby, but Charles shook his head, pantomiming that H.P. was too wet. While Mark received congratulations on his speech they headed for the stairs.

Joyce stopped Tamra in her tracks, wrapping her arms around her ankles. She promised her daughter she would be right back, but Joyce hung on, whining. Dalhia, who had accused Tamra of spoiling Joyce, pointed a scolding finger at the girl. "You should be ashamed of yourself, a big girl like you carrying on like that, as much attention as you get."

Joyce's eyes opened wide and wet. Tamra stooped down, her face even with her daughter's. "Who does Mommy love?" she asked, part of a familiar and reassuring game.

Joyce brought her hand to her own heart. "Me . . ." she said, turning slowly, pointing at Charles, ". . . and Daddy, and H.P . . ." Pointing up, toward the ceiling, she added, "and God."

"Then you know I'll be right back," Tamra said. Joyce ran toward Virginia, who smiled maliciously at Dalhia. Tamra called to her daughter, "Thank you for being so cooperative."

As she started up the stairs she heard Dalhia grumbling. "And she thanks her for obeying."

Virginia snapped, "She was encouraging her."

In her bedroom, Tamra laid H.P. on the changing table, sponging him clean and powdering his belly, which had wrinkled beneath the wraparound bandage. Charles had dodged into the shower, saying he hoped it would revive him.

Moments later, he stepped out of the bathroom working the towel furiously along his body. Her eyes were drawn toward the coarse, circular hairs on his flat belly, and she was stunned to realize she had room for wanting him. He started toward her, dropping the damp white towel and opening his arms in welcome. She thrust the baby toward him and he pulled his son to his chest.

She watched them together, their bodies nude and cleansed, taut muscles against buttery softness, all that a man must be with a child of promise. She broke his spell over her by reaching for a suction cup. "Getting the monitor back on is easy," she said, "all you . . ."

Virginia called from the hallway, "Tamra, you two had better get down here quick. Vicky's running off at the mouth, ruining everything."

Downstairs, they found Vicky and Dalhia locked into an angry standoff, with Dalhia saying, to anyone who would listen, "I find it insulting."

Vicky said, "I'd think you'd be glad I was in therapy. We could all use it."

Big Mama cracked peanuts, watching the show with a smile. Dalhia was sniffing, "Well . . . what sort of things do you tell this . . . Is it a man or woman?"

"Man," Vicky said. Tamra realized she'd never heard Vicky speak up to her mother before and thought maybe the therapy had done her more good than harm.

Dalhia leaned into the table. "Is he white?"

Vicky smiled. "Everything I tell him is confidential."

Harlen wanted to know what kind of things she told this man.

"Like about when I was a girl."

Virginia, for once, agreed with Dalhia and turned to Big Mama saying, "I don't even remember my childhood."

"That's 'cause it was nothing special," Big Mama said.

Vicky seemed to be enjoying the spotlight. "Last week I told him about sitting on the back of the hay wagon." She looked at Charles for help. "Remember how much fun that was?"

Charles shook his head no. "Not for me. I was working."

Dalhia spoke up again, "Why would you want to spend your husband's money telling some white man about that?"

"He helps me interpret things." She looked desperately around the table for support. Tamra smiled encouragingly. Vicky started again, less sure of herself: "We'd follow behind the baler in a wagon that was piled high with hay, and I once fell and hit my head on that little piece at the back of the truck . . ."

"I don't remember that," Dalhia said.

"I was afraid to bandage it or even cry. I couldn't distract anyone . . ."

She looked at Tamra again for understanding, "A girl on a farm was useless. The only rule was stay out of the way and let the men do the work."

Tamra muttered, "That's still the rule."

Dalhia stood. "I'm not feeling very well. Harlen, will you drive me home?"

He turned to Vicky, "You should apologize to your mother."

Vicky said plaintively, "What'd I say that was so offensive?"

Now Tamra thought she sounded more like the Vicky she remembered.

"Your mother worked very hard to raise you," Harlen said.

"It's not how *hard* I worked," Dalhia interrupted argumentatively. "It's just that I know what it's like to have a mother who doesn't care about her children, who thinks some are smarter or more special than the rest, and I wasn't like that. Vicky could have come to me if she'd hurt her head," and she broke off, crying.

"Of course she could have," Harlen reassured her.

Tamra hoped they could get the evening back on track, especially for

Virginia, who for some reason believed this ceremony magical enough to heal their family. What most amazed Tamra was to see Harlen stroking his wife's shoulder. She'd never seen the least bit of tenderness between them. This sudden closeness was intriguing, especially since they'd only united to silence Vicky.

Seth inclined toward Dalhia and Harlen. "You two aren't going anywhere until I've told my story."

"Yeah," Charles interjected. "Don't ruin this, please. We've got a feast waiting for us."

His parents appeared to waver.

"Sit your maximus bootimuses down," Big Mama ordered.

Finally they relented and Seth scrambled to his feet and began to pace. Charles pulled back the table, dragging the couches closer to the fire, suggesting they make themselves comfortable.

$$\mathcal{39}$$

Tamra and Charles *December 1982*

"THIS IS THE tale of the first Black family," Seth began, and Tamra knew immediately he'd written this story with her in mind, that there was something he wanted to tell her about the loss of her baby that no other words could convey.

Seth continued his folk tale, "This was originally told to me before my birth, whispered on the wind. For you see, when the world was young, humans were first cousins to the wind, had skins of invisible colors, and spoke a language that sounded like rain falling."

He made a popping sound with his lips, like raindrops on a drainpipe, then told of a boy named Nia, "Which we've learned in Kwanzaa means a sense of purpose. His father died only a few days after Nia's birth, and his mother hoped her oldest son would grow up to be the leader of their people."

Seth said Nia loved running along the shore with his cousin the wind. Tamra settled into the couch cushions but quickly arched her back as she remembered that the couch had been delivered on that awful day. She had never sat here before tonight. Oh God, help me through tonight and tomorrow, she prayed, as Seth continued his story.

He said Nia, who enjoyed watching the birds gather in his family's fields, watched one day as a colorful flock pecked at seedlings. It made a spectacular scene, for with a rush of brightness and flapping wings the birds looked one moment like wild, unchecked flames, the next, like a field of dancing flowers. Soon this flock was joined by another group of birds as black, Seth said, "as the night when even a shining moon cannot break through."

He described the black birds' powerful bodies and coarse, wiry feathers, saying the sight of the two flocks intermingling was magnificent, each group enhancing the other, as the brightly colored creatures moved like rainbowed dancers against the ebony curtain of the darker birds.

"Seeing this," Seth continued, "Nia understood that colorful variations in God's creatures were no mere coincidence. The idea of many races, rather than one, was a direct offshoot of God's wisdom and *kuumba*, which means creativity."

Seth paused and Tamra watched the faces of the people she dearly loved as they listened with rapt attention. Seth explained Nia's dismay as the colorful birds, which greatly outnumbered the others, turned on the black ones, pecking and tearing at their feathers, driving them away. Nia, who had never witnessed cruelty before, chased behind the defeated flock, finally spotting one of the wounded, which he recognized from its fierce efforts in battle. This raven hopped about on one foot, weak and in need of nourishment. Nia offered a handful of seeds and his friendship, both of which were accepted. When the bird regained his strength, he talked to Nia, introducing himself as the Raven King, Imani, which means faith.

With afternoon approaching, Nia started for home. Little did he know how soon he would need his new friend. After a long walk, Nia approached his home, which was called Ujima, meaning collective work and responsibility. Nia and his family had worked together to fashion a dwelling from large stones.

Inside the house, he found the family's belongings had been destroyed and that his mother and siblings had disappeared. As he sat forlornly on his doorstep, he was joined by Imani, who said slave hunters had captured Nia's family and taken them away. He warned that they were searching for Nia too, and wanted to take the family's land, indeed their very spirit, from them.

Seth's face had looked heavy at the start of the evening, perhaps weighed down from the exhausting routine of the new substance abuse clinic he'd recently attended. But telling his story seemed to have reinvigorated him, for he moved gracefully as he spoke. Tamra was caught up in the narrative. She'd always considered his storytelling as moments that grace a lifetime. This story seemed even more special, for she remained convinced that although the plot seemed deceptively simplistic, he'd written it with her grief in mind.

"As Imani spoke, his flock surrounded him, and this time, Nia noticed a tiny crown on Imani's head. Bowing, Nia explained that he had to rescue his family."

" 'But not by foot,' Imani told him. Nia wondered how else, for he knew he could not fly. Imani said he was mistaken. 'The Creator gave birds wings,' Imani said, 'but humankind was blessed with a greater gift. Of all the creatures, only humans can dream.' He told him to call upon his cousin, the wind, and allow his dreams to lift him 'high and higher, until you soar.' Nia was doubtful, but Imani hopped upon his shoulder, restoring his faith. And calling upon the wind, Nia ran and leaped and soared."

Seth's voice lifted as Nia ascended. "He felt the wind move about him like dry, lapping waves, first against his cheeks, his hair. And opening his eyes, seeing expanses of field beneath him, he knew he was surrounded by a flock moving with the rhythm of *umoja*, which means unity. He learned in this spirit of *umoja* that each bird is responsible for the other. They all flew together, and through their long journey unity sustained them."

Seth described the intensity of the sun's rays on Nia's head and skin as they pressed on. Spotting the camp of their enemies, they circled high above. But as far away as they were, Nia recognized, even from this great distance, the hands of his mother, Kujichagulia, which means self-determination. A woman of great wisdom, when her children had asked what they should become, she counseled them to shape their own futures.

The flock waited for nightfall to begin the rescue. Meanwhile, Nia crept to a pond for a drink, and seeing his reflection, found the sun had blessed him, baking him a dark, earthy brown.

Seth gestured dramatically. "He touched his head, which had been bald, and found it covered in coarse, tightly curled hair, like a beautiful and enduring cap to protect him from heat."

The boy loved his handsome new looks, but worried his mother would not recognize him. Still, when night fell, he crawled on his belly past the night watchmen. Kujichagulia knew him at once.

"Well of course she did," Seth said, staring at Tamra. "A mother's love transcends all things physical. She would have known her son had she been blind." Tamra touched her heart. She understood.

Seth told of the mother and her children as they stole quietly from the camp and returned home by winged flight, they, too, receiving the sun's blessings. Back home, opening their door, they found strangers at their table who cried out in fear. Brandishing weapons and calling them evil, they chased Nia and his family away.

Nia's family did not lose hope, Seth explained. Reassembling in the field, they made a stew of wild onions and drew up a plan. They could take vegetables that grew wild in the forests, cook marvelous stews, and prepare salads to sustain them. And they could also make healing balms from roots and barks. This they could take to the cities and sell. Their plan was a form of *ujamma*, which means cooperative economics.

"As the family started off," Seth concluded, "Imani swooped down to tell Nia he was proud of him, that he'd accomplished his mission as only a prince might have. He told Nia, 'One day, tell your children of me, that you have become like a son, my Raven Prince, and assure them that they are descendants of royalty.' "

He cautioned Nia that their journey would be filled with heartache and would take them to many lands where they would be turned away. He counseled him to keep his family with him, and in the spirit of Kwanzaa, celebrate the harvest of his people.

Seth said, "Nia thanked God for the gift of dreams, which no one could take from him, and which he could use to chart his new course. He would teach his children that with those dreams they could reach and aim and see as high as the sun that had blessed them. They turned their faces to the wind and walked on."

As Seth ended the story, the room was silent. Tamra felt deeply affected. The other guests thanked him for his gift of story, assuring him it had been a perfect ending for their first Kwanzaa.

But Virginia begged their indulgence, saying she and Seth had learned a lullaby in Africa that she hoped they might sing in closing. She hurriedly passed out song sheets.

Charles was the first to sing the unfamiliar words, cautiously at first, and then more confidently when his sister contributed her timid alto. "*Al-lun-de, Al-lun-de . . . Al-lun-de, A-lu-ya.*"

They repeated the words, embroidering them, as the others began, frowning and laughing over the foreignness of words such as *zjay-poo-wah, yay. Yay, koo-saw.*

For all their newness, the words drew Tamra in. She felt she'd heard them before or at least that she had felt the peace of this hushing declaration of love, as if in another life, at day's end with blazing fire; a warm reassurance of mother's song: *"Mahn-day ah-kwa-ka, ka-kwa mahn—day."*

She fully understood the promise of Seth's story, that no matter how high up in the sky, a child could look down and recognize his mother, and she opened her mouth and sang, *"Ai-yai-yai-yay."* She wanted her boy who was gone from them to know he'd not been forgotten. Raising her voice, she watched the faces of the women singing with her, Dalhia and Vicky, Big Mama and Virginia, and seeing them, imagined the first women who'd sung this song.

Beaten and thrown onto ships, had they sung these words even when chained to faraway children? *"Mahn-day ah-kwa ka."* And in the new world, had those who survived sung to infants born of rape? What of babies, white, on their breasts? Had they received these crooning words of love? *"Al-lun-de, Al-lun-ya . . ."* At auction blocks, had their children been granted a moment's pause for brief good-byes, small hands on mother's legs, wet, tearful kisses? Or had there only been this, mouthed for memory's sake: *"Zjay-poo-wah, yay. Yay, koo-saw."*

She prayed as she sang, her eyes closed, that despite evidence to the contrary, a world existed where her son and all lost children could grow and laugh and listen like darling little rogues. A hand touched her shoulder, and without opening her eyes, she knew the feel of it. It was Charles. She saw that his arms were empty, and that all about her, her family wept and sang to their lost children. She knew they mourned but she could not comfort them. Their voices were drowned out by her husband and the words he spoke. "Don't shut me out again, Tamra," he pleaded. "Come back. We need you." And this time, as she moved into him, it was as if a canal had opened, and she rode to him on her tears.

40

Tamra and Charles *April 1986*

SHE'D TIMED IT perfectly. The news update had just started. The announcer said Prince Andrew would marry the red-headed commoner, Sarah Ferguson. As Tamra dipped the rag into a pail and squeezed a fist of suds, she remembered her own wedding. Now that the kids were a little older, it would be nice if she and Charles could get away for a second honeymoon. Then she laughed at herself. She'd been watching too many soaps. In their nine years of marriage they'd never taken a real vacation.

She applied extra pressure to the dirt lodged in the capillary-like crevices of the linoleum. The grime resisted her efforts and she squeezed on lemon juice, dusted it with a sprinkle of baking soda, and scrubbed again. There. Much better. But she couldn't allow herself to pull back and admire the glistening cleanliness while she still had a chance of beating her best time of two-thirds of the floor being finished by the resumption of "All My Children." The Balenciaga gown Erica had purchased had been delivered before the station break. It was outrageously expensive but Erica deserved it. She'd been through hell.

Should Tamra check the porch? H.P. and Joyce were awfully quiet out there, but when she heard giggles, she continued scrubbing. Juice from their cherry ice pops was probably running down their arms by now. Uh oh, there

was the familiar saxophone solo signaling a resumption of the show. She'd
never make it. But she couldn't look up: five more squares. The floor had to
be finished during the ice pops. Later she'd have seventeen minutes, one side
of the "Velveteen Rabbit" tape, for the hall bathroom floor. *"Eeeeeeek!"*
Engulfed by weakness, she looked up. Erica tried on a frumpy dress, five sizes
too big. I could fit into that, she thought, and scolded herself for not
cushioning her legs, which now ached. She forced her chin back down
toward the floor. Suppose H.P. didn't take a nap again this afternoon. She'd
be sorry then that she'd wasted even a minute.

"Mommy, here comes Daddy . . . *Daddeeeeeeeeee!"*

Now, what was he doing home in the middle of the day? Maybe he'd
actually taken her speech to heart. She'd been waiting for him this morning
when his alarm went off; she had kept herself awake all night doing the
chandeliers (a solution of Polident dissolved in hot water left them sparkling).
Everybody has to work, she'd told him, but he was destroying their lives.
The children were growing up. Joyce would begin first grade this fall, but
how could he know? He was never around. How did he think it felt to realize
that if she dropped dead tomorrow even the toilet paper wouldn't be
replaced?

"You worry too much about anuses," he'd said.

Maybe because I'm surrounded by them, she'd grumbled. It was childish, she'd admitted, but he hadn't heard her, anyway. She'd really let him
have it this time, and maybe, for a change, he'd heard her. But if he planned
to turn over a new leaf it would be better if he'd waited until her show was
over. Remembering Erica, she looked up and laughed aloud.

What was that girl up to? She'd never get away with it. Phoebe was
bound to notice that Erica's gown was made of the same fabric as the drapes
in the mansion's living room. Boy, did she look good. She touched her own
hair. Darn. There hadn't been time to comb it. Perhaps she should get off her
knees before he walked in. But then, maybe not. Letting him see her like this
might be better than a thousand words. His "bride," as he always called her,
his own personal geneticist, down on her knees, practically dressed in rags,
scrubbing the floor.

In Erica's daydream, her latest beau ran a finger up her black, silk-
stockinged calf. She could have him . . . if only she could keep Phoebe quiet.
When the door to the hallway opened, Tamra bent lower, working feverishly, and listened cautiously to Joyce and H.P.'s chatter. He wouldn't let
them in with those ice pops, would he? She wanted to call out and stop them,

but she couldn't risk being caught with her head raised, giving him the impression that she was mindlessly staring into the set. Better to chance her children actually obeying. She scrubbed on, amused by her daughter's patter.

"Daddy . . ."

"Yes, hon."

"Let me see your muscles."

"Can't take my jacket off now."

"Mommy says women are stronger than men."

"Oh, she did, eh?"

"*Umm hmmm,* said men weren't strong enough to have babies."

He laughed at this. "Don't let her confuse you. There's a difference between strength and capability."

Her soap had faded to the L'Oreal model running fingers through blond tresses, a commercial she hated. The model explained that the product cost more, but she was worth it. Tamra slapped the rag to the floor.

"Tam?"

"In here," she called sweetly, thinking how wonderful it would be if he took off his suit and they scrubbed side by side. He would say he was sorry he'd ignored her and failed to show his appreciation all these years, that only she and the children mattered.

"The kitchen's right this way," he said.

She paused, frowning. Who was he talking to? Who could it be who was unfamiliar with the layout of the house? She froze as he entered, too embarrassed to tell him the floor was wet. He stood in the doorway, easing his daughter down.

She looked across the floor, a world away. He wore a seersucker suit, without wrinkles. It was from England. He'd never had suits for separate seasons before, he'd said. But she wondered if he knew, as he stood there, that he no longer looked like a farmer. He didn't even have dust on his shoes, the handsewn toes of which pointed into her world.

Joyce had pulled her headband over her ears and it held her thick crop of braids like a carton of black asparagus. Red juice stained her sundress, and ice pop sticks dangled from her hand. Before Tamra could wonder what had become of H.P., he squeezed his dark head between Charles's legs, displaying a cherry tongue.

Another head, this one not a child's and not familiar, was looking shyly over Charles's shoulder. She was a teenager, whose pale, indistinct features and limp, brown hair identified her as a Rowan. Everybody knew them. Poor white trash. The men, public drunks who always worked someone else's land, their women laboring by their sides or taking in laundry. And they married cousins, had child after child, giving birth to their own blood. None of this history had ever mattered to Tamra before as they lived fields away, in the squalor of Honker Cove. So what was this Rowan doing in her kitchen, dressed up in a too-tight acetate dress and high heels?

"I have someone I want you to meet," he said. She tried to communicate annoyance by smiling in confusion. H.P. ran toward her, leaving wet, ghost-like prints across the floor, shoelaces dragging. She put her arms protectively around him. "This is Cassie Rowan," Charles said, and he stepped aside, encouraging Cassie to move in for better viewing.

The girl dipped uncertainly. "Pleased to meet ya, ma'am." But her nervous smile turned to one of camaraderie as she pointed toward the black-and-white television set where Erica was force-feeding canapés to Phoebe. "That's my show, too," she said.

Charles beamed.

"I only watch it when I'm working," Tamra said, and she got to her feet, lifting H.P. to her hip.

Joyce piped in, "Cassie's gonna work for us."

Tamra looked questioningly at Charles. At least, she thought, he had the good sense to sound embarrassed as he explained. "That is not necessarily true, only if your mommy wants her to . . . er . . . help her out around here . . ."

H.P. clung to Tamra like a koala. Charles walked toward her and kissed his boy's cheek. "I want you to get down and be a gentleman." She resented his attempts to raise the kids the way his mother had raised him, like a toy soldier, and she was grateful that H.P. held fast, his grip tight at the back of her neck.

"Put him down, please," Charles said firmly. Not wanting to make a scene in front of the kids, she grudgingly complied. The boy struggled against being put down and wrapped his arms around her waist, trying to climb back up her trunk. Charles gently turned his son around and spoke in soft tones. "If you want to be a man like Daddy, learn to say hello properly." He introduced him to Cassie, who shook the boy's hand while Tamra wondered how the girl expected to work with those long nails.

Charles continued. "That's right, now how about looking up and saying, 'It's nice to meet you'?" Cassie giggled as the boy mumbled something vaguely coherent. When he scurried back to Tamra and she lifted him, he whispered: "Am I going to be a man like Daddy?"

"I suppose," she shrugged.

"Do Daddy's make doo-doo?"

She took advantage of their laughter to suggest a private conversation to Charles. "Joyce, maybe you can show Cassie your turtle."

"He's boring," Joyce said.

H.P. spoke shyly to Cassie. "I have a jar with a mommy-longlegs in it."

His sister corrected him: "That's a daddy-longlegs."

Tamra reached on top of the refrigerator, saying to Joyce: "Here's that book Dalhia sent." She handed it to Cassie.

"It doesn't have pictures. I want a real book," Joyce whined.

Tamra was about to remind her to use her "nice voice," but before she could, Charles pointed toward the stairs, saying only, "up!" H.P. scurried up. Joyce took one step at a time. Cassie seemed to believe getting the job was dependent on winning Joyce over. She held up a brown doll from the hall table.

"What's your doll's name?"

"Aretha," Joyce said, stomping up the stairs.

"Ooh," Cassie said. "I think this doll jes burped."

"She makes gas, all right," Joyce said, "but it's not coming from her mouth."

Persisting, Cassie called to the top of the stairs, "Want I should bring A . . . A . . . Aretha up?"

"You may if you like. But I'm fed up. She doesn't appreciate anything I do."

Tamra clicked the television off and Charles followed her to the porch. If they were going to fight again, she didn't want an audience. Charles pointed toward the upstairs floors. "Tex's sister."

She nodded for him to continue.

"She's a Methodist."

As if that mattered. Most of the people around here were. She waited for him to come up with some logical excuse for bringing this girl into her home.

"I realized you had a good point. You do need somebody else around here . . . who's not my cousin or aunt."

She broke in. "Not *somebody*, Charles. *You*."

"You know I can't sit around here and hold your hand."

"Is that what you think I . . ."

"Just hold on a minute. I listened to you this morning and for once in your life I'd like you to try and respect me."

Tamra clamped her mouth shut.

Running a finger beneath his collar, Charles turned toward the yard, which, in its summer perfection, looked to her as if it had been created in an art studio. Sky, watercolor blue, a toy tractor with monster wheels rotating between rows of green noodles, and closer in, pink popcorn trees, a bush of butter slices, and a green felt lawn fenced by red and white crepe paper tulips.

"I work hard, damn hard," he said. "And I do it for you and the kids."

"Great! If you do it for us you have my permission to stop. Let's sell it all and move some place that doesn't require all your time. I didn't ask for a maid. I want something simple, a one-hundred-percent husband. Not someone who zooms in for pit stops."

"With you, it's more like reconnaissance flights. Who'd want to come home to this?" He started down a porch step.

She grabbed at him, caught hold of his jacket, and thought she heard a rip. "I'm not a customer phoning your office. Don't put me on hold. You pop this girl in on me and wonder why I'm angry."

"You're always angry. No matter what I do to make it right, I'm wrong."

Glancing toward the upper story, she lowered her voice. "I thought of you this morning when the kids and I were reading *Peter Pan*. Wendy says to Peter, 'Since I'm going to be mother, how about if you're the father?' "

Charles crossed his arms and watched her. Why had she used a child's story to make her point? She decided to continue nevertheless. "But ol' Peter was smart." She held her chin, rubbing it as if in deep thought. "He waited a minute and said, 'Well, all right, Wendy. I'll be the father . . . as long as it's only pretend.' " She jabbed her index finger at him. "And that's what you do. You only pretend to be a father and a husband."

He shook his head. "I know I don't give you the time you deserve. But do you realize how many farms are going under?" He paused. Tamra glared at him as he began again. "I should have listened to Cousin Johnny. He thought if I took you up in a helicopter so you could see our holdings, gave you some idea of why I'm always . . ."

"Cousin Johnny? This is who you turn to for marital advice? The man who took his date to a restaurant and ordered lion?"

Charles bristled. "Anyone could have made that mistake. Pork loin reads like . . ."

"I'm less worried about his intelligence than his morality." She took a deep breath, forcing herself to calm down. "If you love me so much, do one thing. Come home tonight, have dinner with us. It's not just the kids, Charles. I'm lonely. Yesterday someone called with the wrong number and I tried keeping him on the phone so I could have someone to talk to."

He smiled suddenly. "Then this is it. Cassie could help out, and be a companion."

"She's no more than fifteen or . . ."

"Fourteen in November, but . . ."

". . . and needs to be in school getting . . ."

"They put her out." He tapped his head, whispering. "Somebody forgot to put the sausage on her biscuit."

"Some companion!"

"She doesn't have to be a genius to clean floors."

She put her hands on her hips. "You're perfectly correct. You don't have to have brains to do what I do. I'm a housekeeper, and only occasionally, when you bug me about getting pregnant, your lover. None of which requires more than a ninety IQ."

"You know that's not what I . . ."

She glanced back at the door to make sure no one would overhear her. "If you owe Tex a favor, fine. But why not the cannery? She'd be perfect. One of those uniforms would cover those . . . clothes. I don't particularly want her in my house. Those people live like . . ."

"So that's it," he said. "She doesn't have the benefit of your family ancestry. Po' white folks never learned to clean up after themselves, right?"

"Sssssshhhhhh."

He walked closer. "Now, in a family like yours they learned to clean splendidly—at Miss Lizzie's house."

She held her forehead. "First it's my intelligence and now my family. I'm . . ."

He cut her off by pointing out that she was always making some negative reference to his family, especially his mother, and he added that her attitude about Cassie was typical of the way she looked down her nose at everyone who hadn't traveled the world and been educated abroad. "And you're teaching our kids the same . . ."

The front door opened, and Joyce, looking conciliatory, stuck her head out. "Let's hug each other and pretend we're in love," she said, moving toward them.

Tamra hoped to convince Joyce they hadn't been arguing again. She looked lovingly at Charles. "I worry about Daddy. He doesn't even get five hours of sleep a night."

Charles smiled back. "How many husbands earn an average annual return of 13.8 percent?"

Tamra whispered. "Explain those figures in a way that someone with a low IQ, like mine, would understand. How would that figure translate if, say, you were to drop dead tomorrow?"

"Are you and Daddy having another debate?"

Tamra smiled at Charles while answering. "Daddy calls it nagging. But nagging him is my job."

He smiled back. "With you it's more like a calling."

Tamra to Joyce again: "I thought you were listening to a story."

"Heck," Joyce said. "I can read better than she can."

"Ssssshhhhh." Tamra hissed.

He gave Tamra a what-did-I-tell-you look. Joyce grabbed for his forearm. "Let's wrestle, Daddy."

He raised his arm, as if checking to see if his jacket had been torn.

"Come on, you promised," Joyce said.

"You're getting too big for that," he said.

Tamra couldn't resist interfering. "It's healthy for kids to wrestle with their fathers. They learn to set boundaries when they tell someone who's bigger and stronger that they've had enough, and when to stop. It trains them for leadership roles."

"You can always tell when your mother has some new psychology tips from Aunt Wadine." He smothered Joyce's neck in kisses and hoisted his giggling daughter to his shoulders. Tamra watched them, remembering Seth lifting her this high, this lovingly. Joyce squealed with laughter as he put his hands beneath her armpits and swung her toward the porch ceiling.

Tamra held her mouth. "That's too high, Charles."

"I'm training her for leadership."

When he put her down, Joyce asked why Tamra didn't like Cassie.

"I didn't say that!"

Charles stooped to meet his daughter at eye level. "Your mother doesn't know whether she likes her or not. You know, people are a lot like those black and white boxes of cereal we bring home when we shop at that big supply store. Remember those packages you weren't sure about? They looked alike so you couldn't tell from the outside which one held something you'd want."

Tamra hated it when he corrected her through the children.

"People are like that, too," Charles continued. "You can't tell what they're like until you sample what's in the box."

Cassie pushed the door open. "There you are," she said to Joyce. "We looked all over for you. A little thing like you could git lost in that big house." She looked toward Tamra. "It's like a palace, Mrs. Lane, and you keep it so clean."

It was gratifying to have her hard work praised. She noticed H.P. held Cassie's hand rather than running toward her as usual. She felt jealous but realized Cassie might be helpful after all.

At any rate, having her around had to be easier than working with one of Charles's well-meaning relatives. And maybe this extra help could free her to keep the house as clean as she'd always wanted, and give her more time with the kids. Maybe . . . she'd see.

"Can I walk to the mailbox?" H.P. asked Tamra.

"You may, if Cassie goes." She turned toward the girl, their eyes meeting.

"When I grow up to be six," H.P. said proudly to Cassie, "I can walk all the way to the mailbox by myself."

Tamra wondered how Cassie would walk that far in her spike heels. Charles must have noticed also. He offered to drive Cassie and H.P. down, and said they could walk up.

Joyce started to run off, but Cassie caught her arm, taking a pencil from the girl's pocket. "Fall on this and you'll git lead poisnin'."

Joyce looked toward Tamra, who only last week had explained that lead was no longer used in pencils. For once, Joyce held her tongue, not bothering to correct Cassie as she ran off, calling over her shoulder to her brother, "H.P., can I take your Big Wheel?"

"No," the boy answered. "It has my germs on it."

Joyce changed directions, moving now toward her bicycle. The mist of summer heat and the grassy fields behind her made her look as if she were surrounded by a green aura. "I'll race you guys," she called to her father, who was helping the others into the car. "Look, Daddy," she cried, throwing a leg over the bicycle seat and pointing toward a wheel. "The tires have nubs in them to tickle the road," and she sped off.

Charles smiled. "Fix something good, Tamerlane. I'll be home for dinner."

As they drove off, a back window slid down, and H.P.'s head popped out. She'd have to talk to Cassie about seatbelts. But for the moment she had another concern. The car was a few feet behind Joyce and would pass her in only seconds. She knew her daughter would not concede defeat. Even now, she stood, pedaling, her brown legs pumping like pistons.

H.P., his head still hanging from the window, poked out his tongue, calling: *"Na na na na nah."*

It struck Tamra that she remembered this chant from children in the streets of Tokyo, and Lagos as well. Could it be a universal taunt, a recognizable pattern of mean-spiritedness that humans come by naturally . . . and hone as adults in the privacy of their marriages? Charles had once encouraged Tamra's high spiritedness, yet now it seemed to be one more aspect of her personality he disliked. In his own way he felt for her soft spots and jabbed.

Charles hadn't slowed the car down as she would have, so Joyce had no chance of winning. But her daughter pumped on in the isolation of her race, down the stretch of driveway, going the imaginary distance against the car that had long since passed.

Spirited girls seemed to pay so dearly that Tamra wished, just for the moment, she could reach down that wide expanse of green and pull her daughter back inside her womb, where she would live suspended on her breath.

Charles's car was only a flash in the sun and his mind was probably already back at the office, but at least he was coming home for dinner. Maybe there was a chance for change. She checked her watch. With Cassie to watch the kids, there just might be time to try out that mushroom recipe. And she'd bake the rockfish Harlen had brought over this morning and perhaps do her hair and put those new sheets on the bed and shave beneath her arms and her legs and . . .

She turned, rushing across the porch, into the house and up the stairs to plug in her hot curlers, take a quick shower, and slice the mushrooms. Oh, they'd need some wild onions, too, and this summer she was rich in them. Out back, near the old well, there were shoots and shoots of potent garlic onions.

41

Tamra and Charles April 1986

"MOMMY," H.P. CALLED from the tub. "Turn off the water. There's a wowt, you know."

"I know there's a drought," she said, sliding the shower door open and twisting the faucets off. "Would you like me to bathe you?"

He shook his head no. "You do not have permission to touch my body."

"Make sure you're thorough," she said, a bit annoyed but not under-standing why. After all, she'd been the one insisting they learn to take charge of their bodies. Maybe it was just that he was growing up so quickly. One thing was certain, she didn't have any babies left. Over the sink, Joyce stared at her reflection and applied a coat of Strawberry Shortcake lip gloss.

Tamra brushed her own thick head of hair. She'd set it on hot rollers and it now fell beneath her chin, thick and nappy. She watched from the corner of her eyes as Joyce ran a finger down the bridge of her tiny nose. "Mommy . . ." she began distractedly.

"Um hmm."

"Does God have an eraser?"

"What do you mean?"

"When he makes a mistake can he just wipe it out?"

"Everything God does is intentional. God doesn't make mistakes."

"Ohhh," Joyce said, squeezing her nose between her fingers, as if trying to render it less broad. Tamra watched with concern, wondering if she'd been the one who'd made a mistake. She'd insisted on not following the local custom of sending Lane children to the mostly Black school, where so many of Charles's aunts and cousins taught. Joyce's private school was forty-five minutes away, but it was led by a woman who'd trained at the Waldorf schools. They had more of an international outlook. Unfortunately, few of the other students and only one teacher were Black. She framed her next words to Joyce carefully. "Do you think God made a mistake with you?"

"I don't know," Joyce said.

"Come up here," Tamra said, patting the counter and helping position her daughter. She pointed toward the mirror. "If anyone made a mistake, it was me and Daddy." Joyce watched pensively. "We knew God would make you from the same earth God uses to make everyone else, but Daddy asked God to throw in a few ounces of chocolate. You know how he loves chocolate. And I wanted you to have nice full lips, so when you said 'I love you,' you could kiss every word as it came out."

She ran a hand over her daughter's head, which had been twisted into a high, nappy ponytail. "And both of us begged for you to have special hair. God said yes to that, too. When I touch it, it wakes my fingers and makes them dance."

Lifting Joyce to stand on the stool, she added: "And we promised God we'd keep a check on the most important part of you, what's inside." Patting Joyce's slip, she pressed her ear to her heart, as if listening. "Yes, it's there," she said mysteriously.

"You didn't really hear anything, did you?"

"Of course I did. Your heart beats so surely, I know you'll stand up for what you believe in."

"And my heart says you're the bestest mommy in the world. And I'm going to be the best girl tonight, so when Daddy comes home he won't get angry with you, 'cause of me."

"Oh honey, Daddy and I don't argue because of you."

Her daughter looked doubtful, but just then H.P. interrupted, running from the tub, for the toilet, one hand holding his stomach, the other clutching his favorite miniature race car. He'd had a bad case of diarrhea and from the gaseous outburst made as soon as he touched down, he didn't have a second to spare.

Tamra and Joyce were rushing out when he screamed. "I dropped my car!"

He stood and pointed at a vague spot in the brown, malodorous liquid. Tamra assured him they would buy a new one, but he was inconsolable, his mouth ovaled and screaming as if he were displaying his tonsils. *"I want my car!"*

She hesitated, trying to convince herself that excretory matter was only made up of bilirubin, dead bacteria, and mucus, that it was no different from the feces she'd once changed several times a day in his diapers, but none of this worked. Closing her eyes, she plunged a hand in the cold, lumpy water, and was grateful when finally her fingers hit up against the steel of the tiny car. She fished it out and wrapped it in toilet paper. It would have to be sterilized, but at least H.P. had been quieted.

Cassie knocked, saying she'd put out clean underclothes for H.P. Her son raced out, leaving Tamra, as she washed her hands repeatedly, soaping them, rinsing and beginning again. Joyce said, "That was the grossest thing I've ever seen in my entire life."

Tamra ignored her. She wanted to sterilize the sink, and reaching down into the cabinet, grabbed a can of Ajax. A stinging slap hit her upper thigh. Furious, she spun around, grabbing her daughter's shoulders. "Why'd you do that?"

"I wanted to see the fat shake," Joyce said. And Tamra knew what she wanted to see: her daughter's eyes rolling back in her head when she hit her. She was so angry, she felt as if steam poured from her ears. Counting slowly to herself, she pictured the serenity of the pond, only a mile away, where the fish swam quietly. She pictured herself as the calm, confident mother she wanted to be. It worked. Telling Joyce through clenched teeth that it was never acceptable to hit, and to take a fifteen minute time out to consider her behavior, Tamra walked away.

She was startled to find Cassie in her bedroom. It would take time to get accustomed to her being in the house. The girl had positioned herself Indian fashion on the floor, surrounded by Tamra's lingerie, much of it never worn.

Tamra had hired her, temporarily at least. Her references were acceptable. She'd suggested that Cassie walk around, open cabinets and drawers, familiarize herself with the layout, and come back tomorrow ready to work. But from the looks of it she was too eager to please to just sit idly. This drawer had been in chaos for years. Cassie removed each piece, folded it carefully, and stroked the top of the piles.

Tamra pretended to search for earrings, but she couldn't resist this opportunity to study the girl. She'd been around white girls before, but never in America; not alone with them for sure, and certainly not in the private confines of her life.

She looked closely at the skin on Cassie's arms and knees, skin that only decades before had been considered so special that if a Black boy had dared to kiss it, he'd have been hung. If Tamra's family had moved next door to it, they could have been burned out. If they'd fought for Tamra to go to school with it, their church might have been bombed. Even now, this pale flesh was still so cherished, so preferred, that her daughter, raised in a home with love and adoration, in a community of Black achievers, measured herself against it and felt herself wanting.

She thought all this as she screwed her diamond stud into her lobe, but she was unable to feel the old rancor. For there Cassie sat, a young girl with long fingers and rusty knees and a scar on her elbow. An overdressed and unsure girl. She'd not been given the least signal of welcome. Yet she'd looked around and found the one area in Tamra's life that most needed caring, her lingerie drawer, always neglected in favor of doing for others. She'd sensed it, and for that, Tamra knew she could forgive this girl.

When the doorbell rang, Tamra rushed downstairs, sashing her robe and pulling it tightly to her before opening the door to Cousin Johnny. As always she bristled at the sight of him, and she clutched her robe as if warding off his spell of evil. He smiled, saying he had a favor to ask. " 'Fraid to let me in?"

"As you can see, I'm not dressed."

He grinned in delight. "Oh yes, ma'am, I can see that."

She'd always remember with shame that he'd seen her dancing at the hour of her baby's death. Because they'd shared that ugly secret, she felt he sensed something in her that was beastly. She hated her body responding to him at all, but it did. His predatory manner made the tips of her nipples rise beneath the cotton robe, and on this miserably hot day, she wanted him to slide to his knees and gently lift her hem. She wouldn't need to pretend she liked him, just stand there, catching the breeze as he searched for her only cool, dry spots, the uppermost inside hollows of her thighs. What would a man like this do with a woman like her?

Worried that she'd groan aloud, she asked sharply, "What do you want?"

"Kinda embarrassing . . . but being we're kin . . . I got a date with the vet. . . ." He held a finger up, as if prepared to stop her if she spoke. "I ain't asking for tonight . . . I know Charles gotta be home . . ."

Her irritation increased as he said, "I just thought you might give me some pointers on how you use your knife and fork."

She didn't understand, and perhaps the confusion showed.

"You don't eat like everybody else around here. I mean, I know how to do tricks, like when you hit the end of the fork and it flies up and lands in your hand. . . ."

She cleared her throat and he continued. "You turn your hand backwards . . ." He twisted his hand, imitating the way she held a fork.

"Oh that," she said, smiling despite her annoyance. "That's just something I picked up in Europe."

"Yeah, but I like it . . . it looks so refined."

She reined in her smile. She had been leaning toward him and realized it would be so easy, in her loneliness, to give in to him. For the moment, he was looking past her, sneering. She turned and saw Cassie on the bottom step, eyes downcast. Tamra arched her body back, clutched her bathrobe, and attempted to introduce them. Cousin Johnny said they already knew one another.

Cassie agreed, they'd met, and she added in the same breath, "It's pret'near time for me to go."

Not wanting to be left alone with Johnny, she made an excuse to delay her. Cassie walked to the kitchen, with Cousin Johnny predictably watching the rear of her snug dress. He turned his attention back to Tamra, smiling. "So can we do it?"

She said curtly, "I haven't time. I have to go . . . now." He stepped back, still trying to force this last message through the door. "You know you should try to make time for me, Cousin Tamra. We got a lot in common."

She'd closed the door but she was sure he could hear her through the open window as she laughed, loudly and with bitterness, at these last words. And she knew, as she watched him stalk away, that she'd made herself a terrible enemy.

She'd waited for Charles to drive up before broiling the fish, and now, as she removed the pan, the almond bits crisp and darkened, she called her family to dinner. They ignored her completely.

They were in the next room, Charles in shorts and a T-shirt, laying on his back. The children took turns at sliding down his calves as he slowly raised each child up, and then quickly let each down, in an exhilarating drop. As Tamra stood holding the hot platter with a cooking mitt, she wished their lives could always be this way. The children screamed in excitement and fought for turns.

"I'm so glad you're home," Joyce said, hugging his neck. "It's like a party with a hundred people for a million years."

"Okay," Tamra called, "this fish will get cold."

Joyce pulled herself to her feet. "I hate fish."

"That's not nice," Charles said. "Your mother worked hard to prepare this dinner."

"I was just saying how I feel. Mommy likes us to say how we feel."

At the table, Charles said grace and H.P. added, "Thank you, God, for making flowers and for a daddy who makes vegetables."

"Amen," they said.

Tamra opened the lid of the tureen, dishing the creamy soup into two-handled bowls. When Joyce voiced her disgust, Tamra called her name warningly and told her to sit down.

"I'm not standing. I was walking backwards slowly."

"Joyce," it was Charles. She sat, lifting her spoon.

Even with the children overexcited, it was pleasant to see them eating from her favorite china. The crystal goblets were filled with sparkling cider and the candles flickered.

Charles announced he'd been appointed chairman of a foundation that would work with other farmers to restore the river and the bay "to the way they were when your grandpa was a boy," he told the kids, and went on to explain the problem of nitrogen and phosphorous runoffs. Tamra's smile felt plastered to her face. As much as the bay and its tributaries needed attention, she was sorry Charles would be getting involved. This new responsibility would only make him busier.

She tried ignoring H.P., who held a mushroom slice to his nose, pretending he'd sneezed it out. As if disappointed by not getting a response from his mother, he frowned as he chewed a carrot, asking her, "Why didn't you cook these all the way?"

"We need roughage, honey."

Charles rubbed his stomach. "*Mmmm mmm* . . . what a word. Work all day, come home, say, 'I'm starved. Let me at some roughage.' "

Dour-faced, Tamra explained where the food went when they swallowed. "Our body is so efficient it's miraculous. No factory can be built that works as well. Thousands of chemical processes take place inside us when we swallow——"

Charles interrupted to say that Tamra reminded him of one of his aunts, a school teacher who had always had something for him to learn. She knew the aunt he referred to, a long-nosed spinster type. He'd once laughingly pointed her out in the yearbook. She sat quietly watching him eat, his head bent close to the soup dish. She wished she could tell him he reminded her right now of a fly about to regurgitate over its meal.

Tamra thought surely the children could feel the tension despite the jokes, and it seemed to add to their misbehavior. H.P. suddenly asked: "What does a woman's volvo look like?"

A sisterly correction: "That's vulva, idiot."

"Read my lisp," H.P. said.

Charles abruptly cut them off, slamming his fork to the table. "Enough of that!"

Tamra corrected her husband: "We like to ask shocking questions. I've told H.P. it was okay as long as they're asked in the house. It's a stage we're in."

"Oh, we are, are we?" Charles said, sarcasm lacing his words.

Not willing to be outdone, Joyce faked a burp, loudly, and extended her bowl, shouting, "Please pass some more vomit!"

Charles's fist pounded the table. "I've had enough."

When Tamra ordered her to take some time out, the girl moved sullenly out of the room, hurling back at her, "I'm so angry with you, Mommy. I'm going to put a thousand snakes in your bed."

Tamra, impressed as always with her daughter's spirit, held back a smile. "But I'm afraid of snakes."

"Then you'll learn to live with them."

Tamra could tell from the look on Charles's face that she had another lecture coming. The only thing she didn't know was whether it would be now or later. She watched him push the cold vegetables around his plate, and then he threw his napkin down in disgust. "That girl needs a good spanking."

"There's nothing good about a spanking," Tamra said.

"We don't exactly agree on everything, do we? I'd have more faith in your methods if there was some sign of progress."

She served herself some of the fish and said, "Don't slouch, H.P." But her words were ignored. He was falling asleep. She chewed quietly. Too much salt on the fish. Calmer now, she offered an explanation of their daughter's behavior. "She's excited that you're home."

"Right," Charles said, "blame me."

"You know that's not what I meant, but kids get thrown off. She's not accustomed to having you here. This talking back is only a stage. Beat her or shame her and we destroy the best of her. But I can understand how someone like you, a strong disciplinarian, might find her behavior almost insane."

"More like premenstrual."

H.P. had nodded off. It was only five-thirty. If she let him sleep, he'd be up before dawn, and she couldn't start her morning chores. Then again, if he slept an hour, maybe they could take an after-dinner walk. She watched her son's head bobbing toward his folded arms. He was probably trying to block out all the tension. She wished she could wave a wand to create a happy home for him.

Looking at Charles she whispered, "It really isn't so bad that they stomp their feet and yell a little. It may be annoying to us, but trust me. They'll grow up to be a lot healthier for it. Home is supposed to be a place where they feel safe enough to share their feelings, and they probably feel scared about us. That's what they're trying to communicate. I wish you'd stop joking all the time and share your feelings with me."

Charles walked around the table and lifted his sleeping son. He turned, as they left the dining room, smiling sadly at Tamra. "Baby, I love you, but I don't know what in the hell you're talking about."

Alone in the room, she looked across the table, crowded with plates of food, and forked the scraps into a pile. H.P. had left a food stain on the table cloth. She'd better boil some water to dip it into before it set. The house suddenly seemed so quiet. She knew Joyce, who was seated on a stool in the kitchen, would never say outright that she was sorry. She was like her father in that regard. But Tamra guessed that at that very moment, Joyce was piecing together questions for an intellectual game that almost always worked her back into a good mood. She knew she'd guessed correctly when Joyce called out the first question.

"Mommy, why do we have to wash fish before we eat it?"

Tamra never responded right away. That was part of the game, and if she waited, she knew Joyce would manufacture a more sophisticated question. Tamra blew out the candles and scraped wax from the silver candlesticks. She would put them in the freezer for a few hours. The wax, when frozen, could be lifted off.

"Mommy, how do people in Alaska heat igloos?"

As she walked toward the refrigerator, she saw Joyce searching for a question. "Mommy, is there a cartoon heaven for the animals who get killed on TV?

"Mommy, is there any clock so big that if it stopped, it could keep the night from coming?"

The freezer door was open, vapor blowing into her face. Ordinarily she would have been concerned by this waste of electricity. But she was caught up in thinking that she could almost hear her daughter's brain working. She regarded her children's intelligence, and her role in teaching them systematic reasoning, one of her greatest achievements. She'd spent dozens of play hours teaching them to think and reason. She believed that as African Americans, raised in a country where their self-esteem would endure daily, rigorous assaults, their only defense would be fully trained intellects.

She quickly ran Joyce's four questions through her mind noting that they were progressively more sophisticated. The first two, about fish and igloos, had to do with practical reasoning, questioning dietary and housing conventions. The third, regarding cartoon characters, sounded simplistic enough but was actually theoretical and metaphysical in nature, concerning the fate of natural order. And the final question, about the clock, well, her undergraduate philosophy professor would have been amused by it's Kantian bent, for it queried the space and time formation of the intuition.

Marvelous, Tamra thought, feeling certain another provocative question was at this very moment being formulated in her daughter's head. But which question, she wondered, as she shut the door on bags of crinkle-cut fries and English muffins; which question would tie these disparate subjects together?

Before she could produce an answer of her own, Joyce's voice sailed forth. "Mommy . . ." Tamra held her breath in anticipation. "What does Mr. Rogers look like with his clothes off?"

She turned from the freezer in a fit of giggles, wrapping her arms about her daughter's neck. "I have a question for you." The girl looked up into her face, unintimidated, ready, Tamra could tell, to start those brainwaves rolling. "Do you think I'm supposed to love you this much?"

Joyce paused, giving the question full consideration. "Even more, Mommy . . . even more."

42

Tamra and Charles April 1986

SHE HELD UP the rolling pin and ran her finger along the surface. *By any means necessary* . . . She was determined to get along with Charles. Dusting the almond bits from the wood, she tucked it into a drawer.

His voice sailed in from the next room, where he talked on the phone. "Listen, man, I want you right up front, and if you get any hint they'll vote tonight, let me know. I'll be damned if I'll just sit back and accept this."

From the kitchen window, she watched Joyce move busily about her playhouse, probably doing her play dishes and scolding Aretha. Tamra untied her apron and walked into the den, smiling at Charles. He didn't seem to notice. He was worked up over this county water diversion plan that could flood one of his fields.

Placing a mint on her tongue, she slid onto his lap, and applied playful, popping kisses to his neck. He moved his eyes in mock delight. "Okay man, I'm hanging up. There's something I've got to take care of."

Her mouth was on his long before he'd placed the phone in its cradle. He plowed a hand beneath her skirt and up her thigh. She resisted. "Charles, I want us to talk."

"Let's talk upstairs."

"No, I mean talk the way we used to. Try not to think of me as Mrs. Lane."

"How do you suggest I do that?"

She asked him to stand and turn his back to her.

"Close your eyes and picture the person I used to be."

He turned, reluctantly, holding his hands over his eyes.

"Okay, what now?"

"Can't you remember me? I've got a scintillating wit." She tried to sound sexy, "I'm filled with passion, and oh, yes, I'm tall and thin. And since nobody wears contacts yet, I've got glasses, and . . . my lips are full."

"Umm, let's see, Woody Allen?"

"You big silly." When he spun around, she fell into his arms laughing. He sat, pulled her back on his lap, and fumbled with her buttons.

"We're not through talking," she said. "Tell me something, anything."

"What?"

"Like . . . how much you love me."

A groan. "Not that again."

"You can never say it enough."

He pretended to bawl. "Fifty years from now, when the hospital attendants push me out on an operating table, prepped and drugged for my quadruple bypass . . ." He held his chest, feigning weakness. ". . . You'll be in the hall sobbing, throwing yourself on me: 'Charles, Charles, just tell me one more time . . .' "

They hooted over this. After a while she said, "But don't you think about me when you work, things like how you want me and how you couldn't live without me?"

He said, "Mostly, I think about how I can't get you to shut up."

She played with the buttons of his shirt. "Remember that camping trip we'd planned?"

He pulled her hand away. "Let's not get into that. It wasn't my fault the hail beat the stalks down. I don't control———"

"Give me a chance," she said and realized that more and more often these days she thought of Charles as being like the kids' Transformers, toys that switched, with a sudden twist, from kind-faced dolls to menacing war planes.

"I wasn't nagging you about that trip. I just didn't want the tent to be wasted. I put it up . . . in the bedroom."

He nuzzled her neck. "If I get in it, will you talk dirty to me."

Checking her watch, she said, "Yes, but later. I've got to wake H.P. I thought we could go for a walk."

He stood suddenly, forcing her to her feet. "Let's go."

"Charles, don't be angry. The kids need to spend some peaceful time with all of us together." Ignoring his sarcastic response, she suggested that he get Joyce to show him how she'd arranged the playhouse, and he walked quickly toward the door. There was nothing she could do about his disappointment. With a load of housework scheduled for the early morning, if H.P. kept sleeping, it would never get done.

At least Charles was outside. When H.P. awoke from his naps, it was like fighting a tiger. She hadn't wanted to give Charles more to complain about.

As usual, H.P. had burrowed under his comforter. She called his name. When he failed to open his eyes, the old fear rose up. Frantically, she shook his shoulder, and he woke, screaming in protest. She tried clasping him to her, but he was outraged at being awakened. Fighting to return to bed, he tore at her clothes and hair. She kept at him with comforting words, humming and rocking him until he was fully awake and calm.

H.P. insisted on wearing his pink sneakers. Joyce had outgrown them and H.P. had demanded he be allowed to keep them. Ordinarily she wouldn't have minded, but tonight she worried Charles would tease him.

By the time they walked outside, his tears had ceased. Charles would never have to know about the scene upstairs. Together, the four of them started toward the bush, she and H.P. up front, Joyce and Charles behind. "Those are some cool shoes, son," Charles called. And that was it. Tamra was relieved.

"Daddy, what if there were no people?" Joyce asked.

"The land would be as it was, pristine and unspoiled."

"What if there was no land?"

"Then there wouldn't be people," he said. "We need the land, but it doesn't need us."

They moved on quietly, between the tall trees, down the dusty deer paths, into "the bush," as Charles and Vicky had called it. It had always been a forested area, and once, Reardon land, though the Lane children had been invited to enjoy it. Running for several acres, it abutted the west side of the house. As much as Charles loved developing land, he had guarded the Reardon tradition, leaving it as it had been for centuries. There was a sacredness about the place. Once inhabited by families of Native Americans, they'd left behind remnants of their lives: pieces from a wooden bowling alley, bits from cooking utensils, and religious relics. As a boy, Charles had unearthed a collection of arrowheads, which were now housed in a drawer.

At the age of six, he'd been taken away and taught farming, he was telling H.P. And he pointed to a patch, where once his sister had had the time and leisure to plant a flower garden. She'd tended it carefully but quit when she found even the hardiest breeds failed to grow.

Tamra listened to this edited version of the story. The rest he'd shared with her a long time ago. The details had not only left her unsmiling, but she'd scolded him about his part in Vicky's failure. She knew he wouldn't share it with the children tonight.

Vicky's efforts had been defeated because Charles had passed through, on his way home from the fields, and would urinate on his sister's plot. One day Mr. Reardon had caught him, and knowing Charles would be beaten for this trick, he'd kept it a secret between the two of them.

Tamra sensed Charles had already told their son, for it had become H.P.'s favorite watering spot. Even now he said, as they approached the site of Vicky's failure. "I have to pee, Daddy."

Charles walked him behind a tree.

"Look how far it can go," H.P. bragged. Father and son laughed brashly as a long stream of urine hit the dry ground. His Arc de Triomphe, she thought, listening to their brutal laughter.

She moved briskly through the shaft of late sunlight tunneling through the trees. Above her, thin trunks creaked like the knees of old giants as they moved in the wind.

Joyce yelled for Tamra to slow down.

"Catch up with me," Tamra called.

"My shadow's too tired to run."

"Mine can't be stilled."

Joyce scolded in tones of disappointment. "Good mothers don't leave their children behind."

But Tamra hurried on, wanting to reach the pond before the others arrived. She had to flee, if only temporarily, to protect herself from the stinging bite of disappointment she felt regarding their imperfections. They were all she had, the sum of her achievements. She wanted, on evenings like these, to see them as something beyond merely human, see them instead the way she might years from now, when, looking back, she'd say longingly, "My, how the time flew," their scoldings, their crassness and petty cruelties forgotten over the distance of time.

Nearing the pond, she saw a white rat scurry for cover. Schools of silver fish performed precise routines. The ducks moved in closer and she tossed crumbs pocketed from her table.

She'd expected the quacking to bring the children running, but she heard from the bush their shouts of rapture. Retracing her steps, she found them at a tree that had been half-felled by lightning. Charles pulled it back and forth like a swinging teeter-totter. As H.P. rode cowboy style, Charles warned her to step back. "Hold on!" she yelled unnecessarily, for his arms and legs hugged the trunk as Charles, giving his son the ride of his life, raced furiously by. When the children were done, they turned to their mother, insisting she ride, too. She approached with trepidation. But once on, she yelled as gleefully as any of them. They tried together to push Charles but even as a team were unable to budge the trunk more than a few slow feet.

Panting breathlessly, they started for home, the boy riding his father's shoulders, Charles's free arm about Tamra's waist, their daughter pressed into her side like wet clay.

Trudging up the slope to the house, they stood together, arm in arm, watching as the fog rolled in.

"What's fog?" H.P. asked.

"Dusty rain," his sister said.

H.P. turned in another direction, pointed out toward his father's latest treasure, the cannery, where smoke billowed from its chimney, and asked, "Are you making clouds, Daddy?"

At the house, the children rushed upstairs to get their teeth brushed. They knew their father would play his game. He stuck a piece of blue Silly Putty on his nose and donned fake wire glasses. Opening each mouth wide, he brushed their teeth while finding clues to what they'd eaten. "Yes," he started, "there's a piece of chocolate cake with spinach icing."

"*Naaaw*, Daddy," H.P. said with an open mouth.

"Then I've got it." He'd switched to a mock British accent. "This appears to be one of the forty species of mosquito that carries life-threatening diseases. Yes, I can tell from the proboscis, it's of the deadly anopheles variety."

When finally tucked in bed, the children hugged him once, and many times again, and then he left to answer the phone. Tamra had rushed them into pajamas, saying prayers, pulling blankets up to chins. Joyce was asleep even before the amens.

H.P., fighting sleep, cried for a bottle, the first time in years. No bottle, Tamra said, reminding him he was far too big.

"When I'm a baby again, then may I?

"We'll talk about it tomorrow.

"But the sun's still out."

"It's daylight savings time."

"It's not my fault God keeps changing the time."

She rushed to her bedroom, prepared to tease Charles away from his call. She didn't have to. He excused himself, hung up, and turned toward her. She gestured toward the tent. No, he said, he had a better idea. Reaching to the top of a closet shelf, he handed her a set of radio headphones, pulled his on, and gestured for her to do the same.

When they'd tuned in to the same station, he drew her to him in a slow, graceful dance. She let her head fall onto his chest. Next, they turned to a faster-paced tune. He jerked his shoulders, enjoying the music.

"Come on, move," he mouthed, and she tried dancing, but the more she tried, the heavier her body felt. There was one tear on her face, followed by another. Charles ripped off their headphones, looking genuinely concerned. "What'd I do?"

After much prodding, she shared her dreaded secret. On the night their boy had died, she'd danced. Johnny had been there.

Charles cradled her, rocked her, just as, only a few hours before, she'd rocked their son. "You did nothing wrong," he assured her, calling her the world's best mother, best wife. "My life is graced by you." He kissed her hand, and she opened her eyes, saw gray hair at his temple. "I love you, I love you," he repeated.

She felt that love and was comforted by it. The room had grown dark, and still he held her. No one else knew or loved her as well, and she returned his kisses, thanking him for that.

They undressed, and before climbing into bed, she grabbed the flash-light from their camping kit. Slipping it beneath the sheet, she shone the light between his legs. Gently touching the tip of him, she watched, entranced. The smooth-skinned column swayed as if charmed. She wondered if men understood that the true allure of an erection, for all its thrusting shape of weaponry, was the soft, feminine, almost pleading curve of it. He whispered, "Light shineth in the darkness for the upright."

He climbed onto her, the flashlight falling with a thump. His finger traced the outline of her breasts, tempting the nipple. She invited him inside, but he said no, that tonight she must beg. This aroused her all the more, and teasing inside the back of him, she insisted. It was he who would plead.

When the phone rang, they did not answer it. Rough and unschooled, it was Cousin Johnny's voice over the answering machine. "Hate to interrupt," he began, and continued, saying the commissioners would vote tonight on the water diversion plan. "Charles, you'd better come quick," he finished, and he laughed.

She had suggested turning the machine off, but it was too late. Johnny's voice did not belong in her bedroom, not now. So she begged, "Charles, please, get inside me. Don't make me wait. I want you now."

He entered her. And she knew. She had to have him, drooping eye, and all, the baseness of him. In her. On her. Rolling.

They lay spent, but the night had not ended. She could tell because he refused to let his body rest and was prepared to spring away. His shoulders said what he must do. When he walked to the bathroom, showered, and emerged fully dressed, she knew what she had to do. Not after tonight, he couldn't. Not leave her like this. She leapt up and was on his back, laughing at first, but when he struggled, she scratched him, ripping buttons from his shirt.

They were fighting like this when Joyce threw the door open, and seeing them, she cried. Tamra climbed off him and Charles led their daughter back to bed, promising it would be all right.

Tamra lay there, still naked, too ashamed to face Joyce. She heard Charles when he crept down the stairs. But he need not have feared another encounter. The fight was gone from her.

43

Tamra October 1990

SOUTH OF WALL Street a group of young people carry large backpacks and crowd a storefront, talking excitedly in a language she thinks might be Dutch. Smiling awkwardly and shouldering her way around their packs, she stands on tiptoes to see the object of their attention. A window dresser clothes three mannequins in thermal underwear.

She studies the young faces in the crowd, unable to decipher from their body language the reason for their fascination. But before walking off, she glances back one last time and realizes the mannequins are actually mimes: stiffened and unblinking despite the dresser's maneuvers. As she leaves she hears the crowd's applause.

There are signs for the Staten Island Ferry and she is about to cross a wide street where a park is filled with tourists and merchants hawking green foam liberty crowns. Only a few feet from the traffic light, a man in clerical robes with an enormous wooden cross about his neck sets up a table outside a commercial building. He hands her a flyer: "When Life Gets to Be Too Much . . . New York's Most Unusual Church." There is also a photocopy of the first few paragraphs of a story from the *Post* repeating the claim that there is no other church like it. She watches as others greet the cleric, enter through the open door, and stop to sign in at a guard's table. The traffic light has changed several times and the park filled with tourists awaits, but curiosity has claimed her.

Room 176, the guard says, and she boards the elevator, her eyes again on the flyer: "When life gets to be too much." She gets off on the first floor and locates the door numbered 176. There's a buzzer to the office and two handwritten signs. One says, "Weight Watchers Begins at 3:00." The other announces: "This Is Our Father's House." An elderly woman with wire-framed glasses and a smock over her dress ushers her toward the front of the room, but Tamra insists on the back row.

The small room fills with people who wind their way around folding chairs. Curiously enough, large, white, utility buckets lined with garbage bags are spaced throughout the room. But that's not all she finds odd. There are boxes of tissues on some chairs, and up front, in a cleared space, a large exercise mat is open near a scattering of baseball bats.

At the front of the makeshift altar, the cleric she has seen outside signals it is time to begin. A woman rushes in, sliding past Tamra to an empty chair.

The Reverend Pascal Lamb introduces himself and opens with: "God says it's time to get this show on the road." When the group quiets, people raise their hands, eager to be heard.

The first speaker says he met the Reverend Lamb at Macy's, right after he'd been laid off from his job as a shoe salesman. He says his wife left him after he lost his job. "Every night," he continues, "I go home to empty rooms. On the streets, I pass people I'll never know. I try to meet companions, but no one seems interested anymore in genuine love. Every day I pass people who have love but who don't deserve it. I don't know why God has given me a life of loneliness. I want to accept it, but there can be no greater burden."

A tear spots her cheek and this embarrasses her. The tawdriness of it all, an out-of-work shoe salesman with no wife, confessing to strangers. During the next hour others speak, a thin woman whose ungrateful daughter is on drugs, a dance instructor who is growing deaf, and a fireman who resents his supervisor. Like the woman on the train, their voices start out low, but as the hour wears on, sadness overcomes them. Many others are crying softly, tissue boxes passed along the rows.

The Reverend Lamb points to the fired shoe salesman and the woman with the junkie daughter. "The holy spirit is within you," he says, beseeching them to bring "it" up.

The shoe salesman stamps his feet, and throwing his arms wide says, "I

286 / BRENDA LANE RICHARDSON

feel like vomiting." A white bucket is passed his way, and Tamra no longer wonders what it is for. The unappreciated mother screams, grabs her midsection, and kneels, her head hidden in a bucket. The woman who sits nearby pushes a bucket toward her. Just ahead a man pushes a finger down his throat, his pent-up problems apparently resisting the light of day. All about her people gag and retch, and the room has the scent of newly disgorged matter. Tamra stands to leave, fearful Reverend Lamb will point his finger and call her back, demanding she tell her story.

Outside, she walks purposefully to the park and sits on one of the only empty benches, glad to have fresh air to breathe as she watches the movements of those about her.

She is there for a while when two women with foreign accents happen by. One points toward a small stone restroom in the center of the park and tells of having walked in on a woman who had given birth in a toilet stall. "She was quite nude, blood all about, washing herself calmly at the sink, the infant screaming on the floor."

Recalling her own experiences of being surrounded by love and familiar faces, generations strong, each time she has given birth, the details the tourists discuss seem especially grisly. A public toilet in lower Manhattan? A cruel, cold place for a birth. Her picture is enlarged as she notices the old men in dusty clothes who lay about on the lawn like scattered leaves. The sight of them along with her experiences in the church and the screaming woman on the train have left her with a profound longing to reconnect with her own history. She knows she must leave, not just this park, but this city.

She has heard from many New Yorkers of the energy and life in this city, and all along she has assumed it was her lack of sophistication that has blinded her to it. She has visited museums, made trips to the ballet and opera, shopped in dozens of tiny stores with fashionable clothing stuffed onto racks, heard Broadway musicals that left her tapping her toes, and she has taken a dizzying ride to the top of the tallest building, up to a buffet lunch, where the city sat at her feet. But all she has felt is despair.

This is not her home. And she needs that and her family. But how can she will herself to be different when she returns? Maybe the mannequins in the store window have provided a lesson. Like them, she must remain quiet and unblinking, offering peaceful acceptance of the way things are and will be.

She will learn to live that life because she knows no other. Indeed, as a scientist she'd learned there was really no such thing as discrete particles or isolated electrons. Instead there are fields, patterns, networks and relationships. All along, her relationship to her community has been fundamental. Her vision of who she is is rooted in communal memory, passed down over generations and deeply embedded. Apart from it, even the simplest thoughts seem unintelligible, the smallest pleasures unattainable.

It's time to give up on fighting for change, she thinks, as she pictures the flowers that will bloom in her yard next spring, blossoms that flourish from year to year, cuttings from roots lovingly sent to her or hand carried from Virginia's or Big Mama's or the yards of her maternal aunts or cousins. Without talking but standing tall in the breeze, the flowers will remind her each day that she is an extension of a family.

44

Tamra and Charles *August 1988*

THIS HAD TO be the way a rock star felt minutes before a concert, when upon opening the case to his only guitar, he discovers the instrument has been damaged beyond repair. Tamra shook her head regretfully. In less than two hours, hundreds of members of Charles's family would arrive for their family reunion. They hailed from around the country, a few from overseas. And most were either students at prestigious schools or retired from or actively involved in jobs that took her breath away. It promised to be more like a N.A.A.C.P. image award ceremony than a family reunion.

A robin flew up to the window over the sink, perching briefly on the sill, straw in its beak. She watched until it flew off, then reminded herself to concentrate on more practical aspects of the day. She and Charles were supplying the house and grounds for the festivities, and his cousins had planned all the other details. She hoped she could remain as much in the background as possible.

"A little nervous?" Vicky's voice broke through her thoughts as she realized she had rinsed a tea towel, not lettuce leaves.

"Don't let these folks intimidate you," Vicky continued. "I'm no college president or acquisitions specialist myself and I never even had a career. At least you had one."

Thanks a lot, Tamra thought. Vicky said she'd given up on trying to impress them years ago. "One of our cousins has two doctorates, one from Harvard, the other from M.I.T. . . . ." Vicky held her fingers up, ticking off Beverly's other degrees. "And a law degree from . . . I forget where . . . I think it's Columbia or something. She's brilliant and beautiful and raised two perfect daughters. . . . Brown and University of California, Berkeley. See what I mean?"

Tamra tried to think of what to say if someone asked her what she did. Last year she'd started a countywide science program for girls. But this volunteer, two-day-a-week job was run from a converted broom closet at the local high school. These weren't the kind of people who'd even blink at an effort like that. They'd think, well of course, she does something, but was she written up in *Time* or *Ebony?* Has President Reagan invited her to the White House, thanked her for her social contributions?

At least Vicky could always refer to her son's accomplishments. Mark was on the dean's list at Stanford. As smart as Joyce and H.P. might be, they were only six and eight.

"My point," Vicky continued, "is that degrees don't make the woman. I know who I am and I like myself." She wondered if her sister-in-law had memorized that speech, but then chided herself for her mean thoughts. Charles's sister really did seem, well, different, in a good way, sort of. She was certainly bolder and far more extroverted.

Her only complaint with Vicky was that she was always urging folks to go into therapy, when the truth was, it may have done her a disservice. She'd divorced her husband a year ago, remaining tight-lipped about the specifics. The few times Tamra had met Stanley, he'd seemed nice enough. And maybe, if Vicky had been patient, he could have changed whatever it was that bothered her so much. She carried on about him being "anal retentive." But what difference could his being cheap make to Vicky? Charles had made her, and everybody who owned shares in Lane Incorporated, wealthy many times over.

She sneaked a look at her sister-in-law, whose head was bent in concentration as she rinsed sand from the vegetables. Although Vicky's hair swung forward covering much of her face, the part Tamra could see didn't look unhappy, she conceded.

She had several questions for Vicky about therapy and what it was like being alone after all those years of marriage. But there wasn't any time, and certainly no privacy. Reunion organizers had been walking in and out of the house since early morning. They'd arrived two days before with stacks of suitcases. And while most of their tasks were complete, Tamra's were not. The bedrooms needed work. As soon as she and Vicky finished the salad preparations, she'd have to rush upstairs and put last-minute touches on the kids' rooms. Where was Cassie, anyway? She'd been due a half-hour ago and was usually prompt.

Joyce ran into the kitchen accompanied by her young cousins, Christina and Sabina. All three had insisted on dressing identically, from their blue striped short sets to the four strategically placed braids and colorful hair clips. Gathering her cousins by the back door, Joyce encouraged them to laugh loud enough for the dog, Muddy Waters, who sat just outside, to hear them.

The girls shouted, and soon the beagle Charles had given the children for Christmas could be seen through the door's window, leaping wildly in the air, his long ears flapping with each bound.

"Good Lord, what's wrong with that dog?" Vicky asked. Tamra said she should have seen him before the vet had given him some valium. Vicky shook her head, grinning. "Try slipping a few of those tranquilizers into Charles's supper," she said. "Then you could tell everyone he disappeared. We'll drag him to the attic and you can visit him twice a day to serve him supper and dessert, if you get my point." Vicky did a little dance. "Your *loooove* slave." When she'd stopped laughing, she leaned toward Tamra, whispering, "Is he still working that crazy schedule?"

It was no laughing matter, Tamra thought. He was worse than ever. Regretting she'd ever confided in Vicky, she looked away toward Joyce, who remained near the door, teaching a hand jive to her cousins from Omaha. Tamra couldn't remember when she'd last seen her daughter this animated and cheerful.

"Grandma, grandma, the doctor said . . ." The girls' hands moved at an ever-quickening pace. There was something about Dalhia's family that was almost intoxicating for the Maynards. Meet one of them individually and they seemed reserved and aloof, not unlike Dalhia. But put two of them together in a room and it became a party. It was like watching an enchanted forest when the spell is broken. She thought she might be one Lane who understood her father-in-law's sense of being an outsider. One did not simply marry into this family. You had to be born into it.

Christina and Sabina raced toward the door.

"Walk," Vicky commanded.

They slowed immediately, saying, "yes ma'am." Tamra was always impressed that although they would never have answered adults like this back in their hometowns, as soon as these kids came south, "yes sir" and "no sir" became an automatic reflex. She had found that she, too, immediately switched to being deferential when addressing older African Americans.

Joyce tugged at Tamra's blouse. "Let me see you smile, Mom." Tamra did as she was told, while her daughter scrutinized her face. Joyce then instructed her to stop smiling. When Tamra did, Joyce asked, "How come when you stop, the lines stay there?"

"I'm getting old."

"Are you sad, Mom?"

She told her she was fine and to run along and enjoy her cousins. Joyce made a dash for the door and Tamra heard her collide with Charles. As was his manner, he comforted Joyce by teasing. "Don't worry, honey. I just knocked your frontal lobe off. You didn't use it, anyway."

In the kitchen, he said he'd been told there was more meat inside for the grill. Tamra didn't know many of the details about what was where. The cousins had organized the entire affair, and Charles's godmother had arrived last night to supervise final preparations. Vicky told him there were several racks of ribs in the spare refrigerator. "I've been marinating them all night in soy sauce," she said.

When Charles returned from the back room, he dangled one of the ribs in the air. "This meat looks like it's from Chernobyl."

She was glad to see that same sense of joy in him. He deserved it. This was his day as much as anyone else's. Now he could show all his big-city cousins what he'd accomplished. On his way out, he called back, saying Cassie was outside helping with the charcoal. When the door opened, she heard Joyce's voice, leading a double dutch routine. "Down, down baby, down. I love you so . . . sweet, sweet . . ."

Tamra looked up to discover Vicky staring at her. "How can you stand having that white girl underfoot all the time?"

"She's certainly not underfoot," Tamra said. "And as for——"

"Not very smart, is she?" Vicky said. Tamra felt uncomfortable with this conversation and tried to cut Vicky off by saying she had work to do upstairs. But her sister-in-law persisted. "Last night she was reading a *National Enquirer* and there was a story about a man with two tongues. You know what a smarty-pants Joyce is. She asked her if she thought that meant he could speak two languages at the same time. And girl, you know it took a while for Cassie to figure out she was joking!"

292 / BRENDA LANE RICHARDSON

Tamra felt trapped, realizing Vicky assumed that because Cassie was white and uneducated (which in this family was akin to being a leper), she could say whatever she wanted about her, no matter how derogatory. But that wasn't okay with her. In the two years they'd worked together they'd become, well, friends. Weren't they? But Vicky was her friend, too, and her only real ally in Charles's family. She felt obligated to hear her out.

"Joyce pointed to another story about a woman who delivered ten pairs of twins at the same time. I didn't think anything about it, until I heard Cassie say, 'She sure musta been big.' "

Tamra frowned. This couldn't be tolerated. "As a mother, no matter what material gifts I've given my kids, I'd feel I had done an inadequate job if I hadn't also taught them the importance of respecting everyone, especially someone who might be different. I wish I'd been there to hear Joyce. I'd have . . . well, Cassie is not dumb. She's naive. But that's refreshing. And she doesn't have a mean bone in her body. She'd never let anyone say a word against me."

Vicky looked concerned. "You really trust her, don't you?"

"Like family," Tamra said sternly, and excused herself, saying she had to get ready and wondered if she'd ever been that hateful.

By the time she'd reached the middle of the stairway, Cassie had walked in the doorway with sunshine streaming through her skirt and a black smear across her T-shirt. She looked at Tamra apologetically.

"I shoulda wore a apron," she said.

Tamra offered to find something in her closet, and she added with a grin, "Wait 'til you get upstairs. You won't believe the kids' rooms." They ran up. There was something about Cassie that made her feel like a friend had come to play. They worked hard, but they could get silly. Charles had surprised them one afternoon by walking in when they'd been singing "Stand By Your Man."

They'd worked together so often by now that it was no longer necessary to discuss what they would do. In H.P.'s room they stood on either side of his bed, and holding corners of the sheet, shook the sand off, whooshing it down, tucking the corners along the sides, making hospital folds. They moved across the rug retrieving toys and tucking them back into the color-coded containers stacked along the walls. They checked to see if H.P. had remembered to feed his pets. There were five tanks and cages in all. The hamster dishes were empty, and the water bottle had to be refilled. Next, they shelved books. Only she and Cassie knew which volume belonged where. H.P. still liked being read to but didn't want his friends to know, so picture books were up high. Science, poetry, geography, and other non-fictions were eye level, for easy reaching.

They worked quietly, restoring first his room, then Joyce's. Joyce usually did it herself, but five girls had shared the room last night. Finally, they finished up with the bathrooms. When they'd completed their tasks, Cassie held the laundry chute open while Tamra stuffed in damp towels. She quipped: "If we are truly creatures who evolve, why don't women have five hands?"

Cassie had a blank look in her eyes. Tamra blamed herself for strained moments like these, like she was lording her education over Cassie. She chattered uncomfortably about the tours, ten passengers at a time, which Harlen and Cousin Johnny were giving out-of-towners today.

Cassie looked like she had something she wanted to say. "I brung you a sack of sweet onions my Uncle brung me from Vidalia. You kin only git 'em this one time a year."

She thanked her. Cassie had started bringing her gifts like these since last month, when she'd caught Tamra crying. In true Henry tradition, Tamra had taken a clump of flowers from her yard over to Dalhia's. Her mother-in-law had left them in the sun to die. It seemed the kind of slight only another woman would have understood. The next day, Cassie arrived with a clump of daisies. She and Tamra had planted them in the front yard and Cassie returned home with a cutting of lavender.

They searched Tamra's closet for a replacement for the girl's soiled outfit. Most of the items were several times too large, but they settled on a yellow shirtwaist that could be belted in, and Cassie struggled out of her tight clothes.

"Too hot for pantyhose," Tamra said, opening a drawer. "But a cotton slip would be perfect." Handing it to her, she saw Cassie wore a see-through bra. Her breasts were heavy but didn't sag, and they had delicate pink nipples. From the sides of matching bikini underpants, a dark patch of hair protruded.

It struck Tamra that this was the kind of outfit a man would choose for his mistress. With her clothes off, she was downright lovely. Searching for words, Tamra complimented her. "You look fabulous. Good for you, girl." Cassie flushed crimson.

Worried that her bewilderment stemmed from a sense of guilt, Tamra felt it important to say something. "Are you wearing those for . . . somebody special?"

Cassie's face flushed darker, as she hurriedly pulled the slip over her head. She hadn't answered the question. Fraught with unexpressed emotions, Tamra moved quickly to the bathroom. She worried that Cassie didn't have a mother of her own and even if she had, it wasn't likely one of those Rowans could give her decent advice about premarital sex. She wasn't yet sixteen. But, she conceded to herself, in every other respect Cassie was womanly. With a body like that, combined with her naïveté, danger seemed imminent.

Determined to talk to her, Tamra returned to her bedroom, where Cassie was considering her reflection in a floor-length mirror. Even with the belt, the dress was huge but far more flattering than those out-of-character motorcycle girl clothes she favored.

"You look lovely," Tamra started, and she lifted Cassie's hair from her cheeks. "I wonder if you pulled it this away . . . There, look how pretty. I might even have a ribbon . . . you know, in that basket?"

Suddenly Cassie had her arms about Tamra, clumsily catching her off-guard. She reached, brushing her mouth against Tamra's chin. Quickly recovering, Tamra hugged her back, and they stood there a few uncomfortable seconds.

When Cassie pulled away, Tamra hated disturbing their first real moment of affection, but she felt that if ever there was a need for candor, this was it. "You can tell me to mind my own business if you . . ."

"Oh no, ma'am, I'd never say that."

"Do you have a . . . gentleman caller?"

Cassie hung her head.

She assured her if she ever wanted to discuss him, she'd be there. She also tried warning her that she was too young to get tied down, that she should consider mastering a trade.

"Mr. Lane and I would help you with that, you know."

Cassie's eyes were wet. "Oh, please . . . I wouldn't wanna leave here for all the world."

"I wouldn't want you to either, but . . ."

"I already've learnt so much from you, like when you taught the kids 'bout that lightening. Les see . . ." She held her hand up, as if this was something she'd been practicing. "A buildup of electricity on the raindrops . . . wait . . . buried within a cloud."

Tamra nodded, impressed that Cassie had retained the information. "You're making my point for me. People have been telling you all your life you weren't smart. That's just not true. There are a lot of different ways to be smart. A girl like you could get some training . . ." She laughed nervously, gesturing toward Cassie's clothes, ". . . permanently borrow a few of my clothes, and if you got away from here, you could have the world eating from your hand." She felt she was telling a slave how to escape on the underground railroad.

"Yes, ma'am."

She thought she might as well speak Greek. Telling a Rowan she could make a better life for herself must have bewildered Cassie. Tamra wondered if Cassie ever considered her naive. Besides, who was she to lecture someone on living life to the fullest? She excused herself by saying she'd have to get dressed herself. It was getting noisy downstairs and people would be expecting her.

When she and Cassie walked down, Tamra was greeted by a number of Charles's relatives, many who'd recently returned from the tour of the land and facilities. Admiration was written across their faces. One of Charles's aunts, who rubbed her neck with a damp, white hankie, said she planned to get her daughter-in-law, who was an editor at the *Washington Post* to come see this. "I've never seen Black folks with something this grand, not in agriculture," she said.

Tamra and Cassie walked to the back porch. Cousin Johnny had his back turned to them as he stepped out of his trousers, revealing a pair of slinky black running shorts and legs corded with tendons. He was getting ready for the three-legged races, and of course, she thought, with resignation, he was telling a joke.

". . . Complained the potato hadn't done a damn thing for him 'cause the girls were still ignoring him. And I said, 'Man, you missed the point. The bulge wasn't supposed to be at the back of your pants!' "

As the two men he'd been entertaining laughed, she whispered to Cassie, "I can't stand that man."

"Really?" Cassie said, looking doubtful. Tamra wondered what that was supposed to mean. There was no time to inquire. Cousin Johnny was introducing her to the two men, pointedly leaving out Cassie. Tamra pulled her into the group. One of the men told Tamra that when they'd driven up the hill, his youngest son had asked if they were at the White House.

Virginia was suddenly at her side, flushed and triumphant. "Don't you do any more work," she scolded, "the kids are fine. H.P. has your daddy cornered. He's so cute. He made a list, trying to stump Seth. Now you go out there where you belong. You deserve this." She pointed toward the crowd.

Scores of guests were lined up at food tables, while others greeted one another for the first time in decades. She wanted to tell Virginia how she felt, but she had found that confiding in her mother was like sniffing the tiny pink roses climbing the trellis. The scent was lovely from far away. Up close it could overwhelm. Virginia urged Cassie toward the kitchen and waited on the porch, smiling as Tamra walked into the crowd. If she could locate Charles quickly, she planned to attach herself to his arm.

The groups looked like clusters of well-dressed birds, with many guests seated on benches near long, white tables that were covered with platters of shrimp, stuffed striped bass, steamed crab, sizzling fish cakes, green salads, and roasted corn. One woman with black, fishnet gloves, daintily held an oyster to a man's mouth, insisting he slurp. Beside them, a woman looked unsure about whether to devour the softshell crab before her with a knife and fork or whether to simply break the pieces off by hand. Between mouthfuls, family members alternated between talking and listening, their faces shaded from the fierce sun by pink and white umbrellas. The teen-age nieces and nephews Dalhia had chosen to serve moved busily through the crowd.

Some of the women, who'd decided not to dress casually and instead wore dresses with wide skirts and fashionable hats, had gathered in the most dramatically decorative spot on the property. They sat on a long extension of rough-hewn benches built beneath a bower of wild grapevines, the latticework threaded with leafy, climbing shrubs, bits of shadow and light embellishing clothing, faces, and limbs.

Charles would not be easy to locate. The crowd was massive. One of the few faces she recognized was Cousin June Bug's. He was on grill duty, clutching a brown paper sack that, she was sure, contained a contraband beer. She waved hello and wondered if he, too, felt overwhelmed by this crowd. A few years older than Charles, he'd once owned a thriving oystering concern. Now, with the biological health of the bay and its tributaries in decline, he, like so many watermen, had a failing business. The only boat remaining from his fleet was a creeking wooden skipjack.

She paused at a table where a thick-necked man with an old-fashioned Afro, a beard, and fat cheeks laughingly pounded a young man's back. "You don't even know who John Stuart Mill was."

"Do too," the young man shot back. "He's the guy who wrote 'On Wandering Brook.' "

His tormenter said, no, that Mill had been a philosopher.

"That's what I meant," the young man insisted. "He wrote an essay philosophizing about why his old lady, Brook, wandered all over town."

Amidst the laughter, Tamra introduced herself, and the wife of the bearded man extended her hand. She wore her graying hair parted down the middle, the ends of the braids meeting at the top like a Swiss maiden's. Tamra had seen her picture in *Jet*. She was an architect who'd been raised in Salisbury. (Seth, she was explaining, had been her principal.)

Tamra excused herself. She'd spotted Charles only a few feet away. He was part of a crowd clustered around Dalhia's father. Though in his eighties, Dr. Robert Maynard still looked very much the college president. He had a thick, white thatch of hair and a face alive with discerning eyes. Several years ago, Jimmy and Roslyn Carter had hosted a ceremony highlighting Dr. Maynard's achievements, and it had resulted in a PBS documentary.

Surrounded by his children, great-grandchildren, and grand-nephews and -nieces, many of whom had his high cheekbones, Dr. Maynard talked into a microphone. Vicky's son, Mark, was producing a documentary of his great-grandfather's life. "It was in 1923 and the administrators of the law school said they didn't want Black boys. They had accepted me sight unseen and had assumed I was white. So they offered me a deal. Paid me to go elsewhere. If it hadn't been for them, I could never have afforded to go to law school at . . ."

Charles was engrossed in a whispered conversation with Vicky, while Dalhia busied herself straightening collars, plucking lint off jackets, and smoothing down heads of hair. She'd made herself the official rounder-upper of people to be interviewed. As Tamra passed, Charles caught up with her, grabbing her hand. There were cousins he wanted her to meet, and he led her toward one of the groups.

One man was telling the others about a recent interview he'd had before a senate subcommittee. "The chairman read directly from his notes and after one question, he apparently forgot to stop reading whatever his aide had written for him. The chairman kept talking, said, 'If his answer is yes, ask him . . .' "

They interrupted their Capital Hill stories to compliment Tamra on the perfection of the party. She'd explained she couldn't take credit for any of it, that it had all been carried off by a committee of their cousins, and they soon turned back to Charles for a serious conversation, lamenting the end of the oyster industry in Nanticoke.

Tamra only half-listened. Her attention was drawn to one of the cousins she'd met on the porch who was talking about a woman he'd dated who'd been "hung up on her cat."

"This was a yuppie cat." he said. "Had it's own exercise room and climbing equipment. All he needed were some shades. She even cooked dinner for him. When this dude finished eating I expected him to pounce on my chest and say, 'Meow, brother, where do you keep the toothpicks?' "

She pulled away from Charles, wishing she could go back to the house and spend the rest of the day in the kitchen. It wasn't that she felt intentionally ignored. These people were simply so glad to talk to one another, there was little enthusiasm left for getting to know her. And getting involved in their conversations required the kind of self-confidence she no longer possessed.

Tamra started toward Seth and H.P., but when she passed the group of stylishly dressed women, they insisted she sit with them. They'd been complaining about the difficulty of finding suitable partners. The tallest woman, dressed in an orange sleeveless dress, wore her hair in a blunt cut wedge, and a pair of black-framed, cat's-eye glasses dominated her face. She waved her hands in disgust as she said, "In my town, you learn to read between the lines. Says he's a zoologist? Look for him in a uniform cleaning the cages. Says he's an international business consultant? Then that's one more Negro with a business card and lots of frequent flyer miles."

She put her arms around Tamra. "I want to be just like you when I grow up." Tamra found that amusing. This was the cousin with her own advertising agency in Chicago.

One of the others, a petite woman who practiced pediatrics, asked Tamra for words of wisdom. "I look at your life and some of these others with these good men, and I wonder, What did we do wrong?"

When no one said anything, Tamra realized she was actually expected to answer.

"I'm not quite sure what to say," Tamra said.

"Just tell us how you did it," insisted the doctor. "The only thing I seem to run into is married men. But because of my religious convictions, that rules them out immediately."

"Stop lyin'," Cat's Eye chimed in. "From what I've seen you with, the only man you'd rule out is someone who's a wife-beater, a flasher, and . . ."

Someone piped in, "And he'd have to steal all her grandma's money."

Tamra forced herself to jump in. "Charles and I have known each other since we were little kids."

The pediatrician struck a reflective pose: "Why didn't I think of that? How old did you say your son was?"

When they'd stopped laughing, she assured Tamra that she did indeed have darling children. "Especially your little boy. I told him I was a pediatrician and he said he wants to be a gynecologist—because he likes women."

Tamra scowled. She knew he'd gotten that from Cousin Johnny. But at least she felt she could loosen up somewhat, especially as they took turns explaining about their lives. The other professions represented in this group included an economist and an astronaut-in-training. They seemed stunned when Tamra told them she'd once had a job. But forget work, Cat's Eye added, "It ain't all it's cracked up to be." Each of them agreed they'd be willing to swap their lives with her for a man like Charles and a house like hers. She wondered if they thought the house and the marriage just took care of themselves. But she listened, giving in to the lies they believed about her life.

Cat's Eye said: "You're lucky to have found someone normal. It's like I have a sign around my neck that only the sickies can read, says: 'Pick Me.' "

"What happened to that one I met when I visited you?" the pediatrician asked.

"Oh, he had a problem," Cat's Eye said, and bending toward the pediatrician she told the others, " 'scuse us for a minute," and began whispering.

The pediatrician grabbed her stomach and bellowed. "You shoulda stuck with him for a while. They're developing condoms with suspenders attached."

Someone else said, "I heard when they have that kind of problem, they work harder."

Cat's Eye shook her head: "Then this one needed overtime."

Someone else screamed, "And forget vacation."

Their table was so rambunctious Tamra had to pull herself away. She still had so many guests to greet. Moving through the crowd she heard delicious snatches of conversations:

". . . I wouldn't want to roll back the clock legislatively on abortion. It's just that when we were young we understood it was an act involving moral judgment. Today kids don't even blink . . ."

". . . I go to the projects in my tux to pick this kid up for the Met. Cop asks me what I'm pushing. I say eighth notes."

". . . I was so glad to have moved there, ran over to the track . . . it's a block away . . . and these two little blond girls looked up from the sandbox like I was E.T.'s ugly brother."

Someone tapped her shoulder. It was Charles, who said not to leave him again, that she looked like one of the lost sheep. He had someone else he wanted her to meet, another geneticist. Tamra warned him not to mention her scientific background, that six years out of the field made her a dinosaur. He said it was too late, he had already told them about her.

His young cousin, Fahiza, wore tight jean shorts, a baseball cap, and a T-shirt, that read "International Congress of Genetics, London." Her specialty, she said, was genetic fingerprinting, and she introduced her fiancé, Sanjeev, a doctoral student, who had been born and raised in New Delhi. Charles tried maneuvering the conversation around to Tamra's years of research while she tried quieting him. But she needn't have worried. Fahiza was busy explaining the importance of her own work.

As her monologue continued, it became obvious that Sanjeev was impressed with Tamra. He watched her with interest, especially as Charles cut Fahiza off to brag about Tamra's work in France. Sanjeev insisted on knowing more about Tamra, asking loudly, "What is it you do now?" Tamra felt everyone was waiting for her answer. Charles spoke for her.

"She's home with our children." When the quiet continued, he sped up his defense. "She's a wonderful mother. At lunchtime, our kids find notes or raps or sonnets written on their napkins." She squeezed his hand again but not because she wanted him to stop. She appreciated his praise.

He continued, saying that when the children were very young, rather than scolding them for being forgetful, she had paid each a dime a day when they returned from school with one of their sweaters or jackets. She hadn't realized he was even aware of any of this. Before she could cut him off, he started up again. "When they argue, she gives them a few minutes to settle it themselves. It teaches them to resolve conflict. Thanks to her, no matter how terrible they were, our children have never been spanked. And they're great kids."

"That's enough," Tamra said.

Fahiza also tried to interrupt, detailing Sanjeev's gene altering research. Charles refused to be stopped. He told about an unusual punishment Tamra had created when the children were young. "She'd put something secret in a bag and let the one who had obeyed look inside. And, here's one more. Let's say H.P. starts playing with something that belongs to Joyce. Rather than demanding it back, Joyce has to suggest a time frame, of at least ten minutes, telling him when she'd like to have it back."

Sanjeev seemed to hang on to Charles's every word, all the while watching Tamra. She whispered to Charles to quit, said he was boring their guests. "Why can't I brag about you?" he asked. Before she could respond he'd moved on to the science program she'd originated. "Not only to encourage girls to be scientists, but she says it's important for the kids to see her in a leadership role." He was finally winding down. "So I guess what I'm trying to say, Sanjeev, is that she's a gifted mother." He looked tenderly at Tamra. She was so deeply affected she couldn't speak.

"A gifted mother . . . that's cute," Fahiza said, obviously unimpressed.

But Sanjeev stared intently into Tamra's face. "I find you admirable. You gave up your life's work to be with your children."

Fahiza patted his head. "I'd better get him out of here before he falls in love. He wouldn't mind having a woman willing to stay down on the farm and make babies."

Tamra wanted to slap her impudent face, but Charles stepped in, first shaking Sanjeev's hand good-bye, then turning to Fahiza. "When I look at you, I can't help but consider the genetic possibilities. If you'd had a mother like Tamra, you wouldn't have only been smart, you might have even been human." He and Tamra walked away, their cousin now silent.

Tamra said, "I'll never forget that you defended me."

"Why would you think I wouldn't, honey?"

A well-wisher interrupted, and as they talked, she squeezed his hand in gratitude.

Vicky passed, saying those ribs she'd marinated were almost gone and that they'd better hurry if they wanted to taste them. Charles whispered to Tamra that he wanted to fix her a plate, serve her for a change. But it would be awhile before they ate. The crowd pressed in, congratulating them on their spread. Once again she only half-listened to the compliments. After so many years of seclusion, she found the conversations compelling.

". . . So I can study people raised in group situations, like tribes, a *kibbutz* . . . Palestinians, people raised without a primary figure. My guess is they have no emotional boundaries, they're proteans, without emotional syntax . . ."

". . . But all the photos this white boy sends back from Port au Prince

are static, boring. I mean, there's only a coup happening, man. We can't
figure out what the problem is, then we learn he never left his car . . . afraid
to get his ass out."

". . . Now they're having 'Black parties.' Know what that means? White
folks dressed up in loud clothes, big earrings, carrying ghetto blasters, and
talking the way we're supposed to sound . . ."

"She was a dominatrix . . . yeah. Men would come into the club and
she'd urinate, defecate on them; tie them down and beat them with whips.
. . . Are you crazy? You know there ain't no Black man willing to pay a
woman to kick his butt. He can get that at home for free."

At one table, Dalhia and Charles's godmother were huddled together.
But she didn't know how they could hear each other. Across from them,
conservatives had lined up against the more liberal faction, and they practically shouted at one another.

"All our lives they've told us we aren't smart enough; didn't have what
it takes to make it, so why would we encourage these special programs? You
mean to tell me they're going to admit my boy, even if his grades are lower
than some white kids? Think of the message. I wouldn't have it. He's no
victim."

"You think everybody starts off like your son? That each of these kids
has a mother and a father who work as surgeons? The cycle of racism has
hit some of our people harder than others. It's easy to forget that when
you're driving around the ghetto in your Mercedes."

She looked around for Charles, but he'd been swept away again into the
crowd. To her right, two more guests debated Black issues. One, a young
man in a vest and cotton cap, claimed that Black men had been taught early
on in America to capitalize on their sexual prowess. "They intentionally left
this out of *Roots*, but it's true. The slave who was fed best, treated kindly,
and even got to sleep in on weekday mornings was the one who impreg-
nanted the most women, so that's . . ."

He was interrupted with an angry blast from a young woman in a halter
top who pointed her finger and shook her head as she spoke. "I don't want
to hear that crap about slavery and what the man taught you. You're always
looking back to the nineteenth century for an excuse, no matter . . ."

Her debator cut her off, laughing. "Yeah, that's right. You're like the
rest of America. Don't want to hear us connect any of our behavior to
slavery. We're not suppose to look back, right? Yet, let some ol' gal hobble

in here talking about her roots dating back to the Mayflower and you'd probably . . ."

Progressing alone toward the food tables, she spotted a group of Charles's teen-age cousins, who chanted raps and swapped news about their lives. One young man described his girlfriend's coif: "like Whitney Houston's with a Janet Jackson twist."

A few feet beyond, a man who worked as an English teacher said he'd broken off with his "lady friend" because she had too many kids. "I'm reading Langston to her and halfway through, one would invariably begin bawling. I called it *poetus interruptus.*"

Virginia, who seemed to have found her niche in this crowd, was sharing details about the volunteer work she and her sorors performed at a hospital: "The patient was still alive but his family had the drapes drawn, candles burning, and they chanted in a foreign language. Seth said, from what I told him, it sounded like Farsi. When I opened the drapes, put the children on his bed, and asked him if he wanted something to eat, he sat up and ordered cherry pie for lunch. He was dead before it arrived. But at least he'd been smiling at his grandkids and the sunlight streamed into the room."

Under the beech tree, her son still huddled with Seth, just as Virginia had described them. Her father looked thin and drawn. He'd been through the rounds of another clinic. This was the fourth one. A cunning and baffling disease, they had told him. He wore a blue fishing hat to protect his bald head from the sun and he winked at Tamra as H.P. read aloud from a wrinkled sheet of paper. He and his cousins had come up with twenty questions that they thought might stump his grandfather. Right now he asked why, when airplanes fly really high, they don't cast shadows.

Seth didn't pause before answering. "One way of looking at it is that the light at that distance curves around the plane and . . ."

She wanted to visit with Big Mama, who was only a few feet away, but Charles rushed up and grabbed her elbow, pulling her through the crowd, excusing himself from the greeters, saying if they didn't get to the food table everything would be gone. Despite his determination, they were stopped continuously.

Mark, with his video crew following close behind, said he'd been searching for Charles, that he'd interviewed everyone but him. Charles insisted Tamra be included. A bench was set up for her comfort, and they sat with the grand white house looming behind them.

Only a few feet away, Johnny, still in his black shorts, danced with one of his cousins. As Charles brought an arm around her shoulder, she forced herself to look away. Her nephew, the director, signaled the cameraman to begin.

While Charles spoke, her eyes wandered back into the crowd. Two people in particular captured her attention. The first was Joyce, who tugged at the sides of her mouth, communicating to her mother that she should smile.

The second was Cousin Johnny. He'd stopped dancing, and he wasn't smiling at all. But he too communicated something without a word. The look was threatening. At first she wondered why none of the others were as alarmed by it. But as she watched him, their eyes locking, she understood. Johnny knew how to tune in to a deeply hidden reservoir inside her, a lustful, ugly place. And he spoke a language that only they could understand. Right now he was telling her something that could change her life, and his words were simple and easily understood. He said, without uttering a sound: "I'm gonna get you." And she heard him.

She moved in closer to Charles, who absentmindedly stroked her hand.

45

Tamra and Charles *October 1990*

ON THE DAY that she left him, her heart worn smooth and chilled like a stone beneath rushing water, the morning began in a swell of pleasure. He had come in, bragging about a deal with the Italian government. They'd go together. Ten days, he'd said. And he wanted her.

She was sleep crazed. The early afternoon had been spent with Joyce's Girl Scout troop, and later, she'd chauffeured H.P.'s Little League team. She and Charles had sat together, then gone their separate ways. He'd left to negotiate this business deal. He now murmured, ". . . soybeans, big, big deal."

She wondered as he kissed her back, slipping the gown from her shoulders, if Italian women would be drawn to Cousin Johnny's bragging. Here, in this bed, she'd given herself license. Johnny was in her, dreamed up from the loneliness of her bed. When she'd awakened, Charles was on her, in her, and she'd pulled him closer, drawing blood from her lip, cancelling the dream.

They'd been sleeping only hours when the phone rang. She'd thought the call would send him off into the morning, an emergency, the elevator, a truck, the plant, the hogs, anything but this. Sitting up in bed, she watched him talk into the phone, feeling he was still inside her.

"When?" Charles asked. "I've been looking for him."

She was thanking God for his goodness, his rootedness, was grateful she'd not given herself away. She'd end these dreams. This was not something a husband could understand.

"I'll be right there," he said, and hanging up, swung his legs over the bed and stood.

"I suppose it won't make a difference if I remind you that you only arrived home a few hours ago," she said, still warmed by him.

He didn't offer apologies, and this made her certain something terrible had happened.

"Got to shower."

"Charles, what is it?"

He walked toward the bathroom. "Johnny's in jail."

Good, she thought. She asked, "Why?"

"Six counts of statutory rape, twelve sodomy, one of endangering the welfare of a child."

"Who?" she called to him, but the shower drowned out her words. Rushing to the bathroom, she insisted on an answer. His face was like a mask through the frosted glass of the stall.

"You won't believe who it was," he said.

"Tell me."

"Cassie."

"Charles!"

"After all we've done for her."

She walked into the bedroom, reaching for a robe. She was feeling ridiculous without clothes. Her mind locked into place. Cassie, hurt. She'd have to go to her, but she felt old and frozen to the spot. As Charles hurriedly dressed, he added, "I've got to get down there. Will you try to get hold of Uncle Bradford? Tell him what happened. I'll bail him out. Statutory rape. Such foolishness."

"Charles, you *can't* help him."

"Don't start."

"Charles! This isn't the first time, remember? When we were kids . . . Cindy? Your family helped him then, too, and look what has happened."

She grabbed his arm, but he shook her off like an annoying, yapping dog.

"This is worse. Johnny's more than twice her age."

"You don't know about these kind of women."

"What kind?"

"All that makeup, and the way she dresses."

"Oh my God, Charles. You're scaring me. You can't be saying she deserved this?"

"I'm saying, number one, he's family; number two, he's my crew chief; number three, I'll be damned if we take her side against his."

"What about the side that's right?" She tried to find his reasonable center. "We'll go together. Johnny or Cassie first?"

"Not Cassie."

"Charles, she has been part of this family. We've worked together, sweeping dirt back outside when it's come in, placing gifts under the tree. She's my friend, just as you hoped."

"Then why didn't she come to you?"

"I don't know. But I want you to hear me. I don't ask for much."

"Neither of us goes to her. Do you hear?"

She spread a hand across her forehead, trying to understand. "Are you forbidding me to go?"

"What if I am?"

"And what if I tell you that if you go to Johnny, it'll be the last straw?"

"I'm not going to listen, for the thousandth time, not today, to your litany of . . ."

"I mean it, Charles. I've put up with a lot, and I don't ask for much. If you do help him . . . I will leave."

"You came into this marriage ready to leave me."

"I will, I'll . . ."

He left the room, slamming the door behind him.

When she stepped from the shower, she could hear him in another room, roaring into the phone.

In Joyce's room, she found her daughter in bed watching *The Little Mermaid* on the set Mama Two had insisted on giving her for her years of being on the honor roll. Any other morning, she wouldn't have minded this video. But today, with it's light-hearted theme about a woman giving up her body, her family, even her voice for a man, Tamra objected. But only to herself. Maybe the music had drowned out any shouting.

"Can you get in bed with me?" Her daughter looked up and asked.

"I need you to watch H.P."

"H.P. doesn't need watching."

"Get dressed," Tamra said.

She'd started for the door, but turning back, noticed Joyce hadn't budged. "And do it now!" she shouted, closing the door to the fear on her daughter's face.

She discovered that H.P. was already up, his comforter thrown across his bed. He only made it up on Saturday mornings if he planned on being away for the day. He hated being sent back "like a baby" to tidy his room. But where was he? Surely Charles wouldn't take him to the jail.

Downstairs, she made herself instant coffee. Reaching into the refrigerator for milk, she saw the bowl of corn Joyce had cobbed. Breakfast was to have been pumpkin corn cakes with warm maple syrup. Shoving the bowl toward the back of the refrigerator, she slammed the door.

"How come you're drinking from my Michael Jackson cup?" It was Joyce, fully dressed. Tamra stared into the steaming cup.

"It's okay," Joyce continued, as if fearful of her mother's mood. "It's okay, because I want to share my stuff with you and Daddy and H.P. and Cassie. She's in our family, isn't she?"

She'd overheard something, Tamra knew, and she also knew her arms would be insufficient for comforting her. She offered them anyway. "I know you're confused. I am, too. Let's take a deep breath, together, like we used to." Joyce leaned into her. Tamra thought about Cassie and that the girl had no one with her to reassure her. Cassie deserved to have that. "No one is angry with you. Cassie has some trouble and I'm going to see about her. Do you feel okay about me leaving now?" Joyce nodded yes.

Tamra pulled a sweater on as she said, "I'll be back in a bit. If you find your brother, walk with him to Dalhia's. And put on shoes, hear?"

She shouted unsuccessfully for H.P. while she walked toward the station wagon and hoped Joyce would remember to put on shoes. Ahead of her, Charles was just starting to pull out of the driveway but instead drove his car alongside hers. Rolling her window down, she searched again for his reasonable center. "Don't you at least want to hear Cassie's side of the story?"

His window slid back up as he spoke, the end of his sentence fading away. "It's your name she's ruining, too." He turned his car toward town, and she headed in the opposite direction toward Honker Cove.

At Head of the Creek, H.P. rode up on a small open tractor. She'd always hated that he drove at such an outrageously young age. He stopped directly before her, as if allowing her to admire his International Gas Cub Tractor. Watching him, she was astounded by the lack of fight in him.

Both children had been given a choice. Joyce thought it a wild joke when asked to consider being a farmer. This child, her husband's son, whom they'd made two of, sat alone this chilly morning atop a workhorse designed for hauling, plowing, hitching, and digging because he wanted to. No, it was more like he demanded it.

They didn't speak. No need to. He waved proudly from his perch, and she, back to him. Joyce had been right. He didn't need to be taken care of. They drove off in separate directions.

Tamra had never visited Cassie's house before. Cassie had always insisted on being dropped off on the main road. Stopping at their familiar drop-off point, Tamra parked the car. The back roads were unpaved and looked too muddy for driving. She walked briskly along the path, almost glad her brown suede boots were being ruined.

She sighed, recalling moments when she and Cassie had laughed together, and tried to chase the memories away. They made her feel so foolish. Here they'd had these girlish conversations, with Tamra offering advice about the importance of women keeping their bodies clean, and how to make special meals for a man. "Look," she'd told Cassie, "frying's all right, but this is how you keep him healthy." How she must have laughed. And what had Cassie guessed about Tamra's feelings for Johnny? It was too horrible to even contemplate.

All this time, Cassie's mysterious gentleman caller had been Johnny. She was sick picturing them together. Her head ached in remembrance of the closeness she'd thought she and Cassie had had. The more her brain called up apparitions of their past, the faster she walked.

Tamra was in a clearing now, passing closely standing shacks. One was only a roof with a few vertical planks attached, and a faded sign read, "Deaks Auto Repair." Nearby, three rusted cars sat abandoned. Another shack was surrounded by a fence of innerspring mattresses, held together with baling wire. She crossed a stream and smelled septic tanks. At one dwelling, a girl and her mother sat on their three-step porch, breakfasting on white bread.

One house, a white A-frame with two neatly trimmed decorative bushes on either side of the front porch, stood apart from the others. The roof had been painted a bright red to match the walkway, and it had a cement lawn, painted green. Tamra hoped at first that this might be Cassie's home. A mutt trotted from behind the house and barked fiercely. A young man poked his head out the front door to see the cause for the barking and then spit on the front steps.

Tamra paused at a five-foot post topped with a yellow and orange plastic daisy spinning in the breeze. She knew in her heart that this was Cassie's home and felt certain she'd guessed correctly when she saw the familiar straw wreath on the door. Last fall, Joyce, whom Cassie fondly called Little Sister, had made this wreath as a housewarming gift. It was decorated with bits of lace, dried flowers, and the decapitated head of Joyce's old doll. The house proved to be more trailer than house, with a back section that had a crude wooden extension.

Tamra knocked and heard the echoes move the length of the structure. When she turned the knob, the door opened. Calling Cassie's name, she glanced back to the clearing and saw the man who'd come from his A-frame watching her. Frightened, she stepped into the unfamiliar dwelling. As still as it was, she sensed Cassie's presence. Despite a crowd of shabby furniture, the small front room was shining clean ("Good for you, girl," she'd always said to encourage her.) Here and there she recognized gifts she and the children had given Cassie.

On a shelf of a bookless case sat a stagecoach clock, the driver's copper arm moving up and down, steering his team of horses through time. She and Cassie had found it in the attic. Cassie had seen the clock and been amazed at Tamra shunning it.

On the floor two lambskins that had warmed the twins' cribs now served as tiny rugs; a set of designer sheets, a birthday gift from her to Cassie, were now curtains. Another corner was filled by Joyce's old writing desk, the top clear except for a toilet paper tube. In a moment of levity, Joyce had covered the tube with tiny pictures from an issue of *Smithsonian.* Tamra had taped a spring to the bottom and written in careful hand, "pop art."

Looking around, she understood the special attraction that Johnny, a man who'd had his choice of so many different women, black or white, had felt for Cassie, and why he'd risked so much. He'd seen the closeness between Tamra and Cassie and had known he could use Cassie to make good on his threat. Tamra buried her face in her hands recalling that she'd considered Cassie a friend. But she'd been wrong. Cassie was more like a daughter to her. Like the child she'd lost, this was one more she'd not recognized as her own until it was too late. Cassie had watched Tamra's life, nodded when she'd heard her woes, and never told any of her own.

She ignored her lingering misgivings about wandering uninvited through the house and walked into the only other room, a bedroom, where in one corner, a hot plate and a sack of rice sat atop the pile of books she had given Cassie. Across from them, on a mattress, the sheets half on, half off, sat Cassie, knees drawn to her chin, eyes wide, studying Tamra. They watched one another, and for once, Tamra had no advice. No speeches. She'd started her search without preparing for this moment.

"Have you eaten?"

"No, ma'am."

Shall I get you something?"

"No, ma'am, no thanks."

Then this from Cassie: "I didn' have no way to tell you."

"But tell me this. . . . Did you wa . . . . Did you like him?"

"Yes ma'am, I mean, no . . ."

"Did you want him, Cassie?"

"He'da bin aright if he'd never come 'round threatnin' me."

"Did he force you?"

"Johnny didn' have to force nobody."

Yes, this Tamra understood. He had a way of making a woman want him, even the proudest woman.

The girl was out of bed, touching Tamra's sleeve. "You believe me, don't you? I wouldn't lie to you. You're the first person bin so good to me."

"I haven't been good enough."

"I never tol' nobody. Johnny said he'd make you fire me, said you'd always side with your folks."

Johnny had been right. Cassie couldn't come back to the house now, and he'd been right about Charles, too. He had sided with Johnny.

She wanted to ask if he'd mentioned her name and was mortified at her own shamelessness and vanity, even now, when Cassie had been through so much.

"Why the police? Why not tell me?"

"Sheriff Watson . . . he said he'd run me outta town if I didn'. I knowed the minute I signed I done the wrong thing." She wrung her hands. "Please don't hate me. I couldn't stand it. I really look up to you."

"Cassie, I have a little money tucked away that was a wedding gift. I'll leave a number where you can reach me. Say the word and it's yours, so you can get out of here. I can't make you go, but if you've learned anything from me, I hope it's this: When it comes to people, don't look up to anybody. Look only eye level."

They crossed to the mattress, and pushing it away from the wall, Tamra began to make the bed. Cassie joined in and they raised the sheet high and whooshed it down.

The task completed, she tucked Cassie in and sat low to the ground, the girl's head in her lap. "I'm so sorry, Cassie," she said, too cowardly even then to admit her own culpability: Cassie had been made to pay for her undiminished pride. She'd hoped for a while, especially after the loss of her son, that she'd been successful at stamping out some of her arrogance. But she'd remained puffed out, even without the fancy job title. She'd resisted her efforts of self-reformation. Charles had once said her kind of pride and self-concern distorted the way she saw life. And he'd been right. As long as she'd continued thinking of herself as better than Cassie the relationship could only be one-sided. More than anyone, Johnny had understood this and he'd preyed on her arrogance to bring her down.

Charles would never understand. They knew one another now only as occasional lovers, carefully stepping around the anger that could be so easily detonated. All along she'd been willing to give up so much of herself, while accepting that he wouldn't change even his impossible work schedule. He bought her gifts, held her hand in public, and when she reminded him, told her he loved her. She believed he did, but what good was that if in the end, when it mattered, he hadn't cared enough to make this one sacrifice for her? His decision today had strained their marriage to the point of breaking. Leaning her head against the wall, she stroked Cassie's cheek until the girl slept.

46

Charles October 1990

THE WAY HE sees it, this situation has multiple layers of irony. Perhaps first and foremost, that except for a one-hour break this afternoon, when he'd tried to convince Tamra not to leave, he has spent hours in this jailhouse, while Tamra has flown first-class to freedom. And he hates even considering the irony that Lane Incorporated had been a major contributor to the sheriff's building fund. Charles looks around the fancy new reception area, well-illuminated by half-lidded recessed lights, its space partitioned by bulletproof glass, and wonders which of his harvests paid for these recent improvements.

From this spot, Sheriff Watson could be seen in his office talking into the phone, feet propped up on his desk. The sheriff had sent word out that he was tied up on pressing calls, but Charles thinks it's more likely he's talking to the receptionist.

What is it about him today? Tamra had run from him when he'd gone home to talk to her. And now the sheriff, who has known him since he was a child, is avoiding him. It isn't as if he has a history of violence. The only serious fist fight he's had in his life was with Cousin Johnny . . . over Cindy, and even then, how was he to have known about her pledge to Johnny? She certainly hadn't mentioned it to Charles on that class trip. He remembers her fondly, but when he tries to feel something about her, all he sees is Tamra.

Why couldn't he have loved someone less troublesome? And why does he have to sacrifice, once again, what he most wants? Besides, there's no getting around it. No matter how it's viewed, Johnny was dead wrong. Cassie is a kid. Of course, it isn't as if Sheriff Watson couldn't have called him in to settle things quietly.

That, of course, would have limited the damage, and that wasn't what "they" (whoever "they" were) wanted. But he wasn't angry with the sheriff. Watson had done precisely what Charles had: sided with his own. The idea leaves a bad taste in his mouth, and he concentrates on the big-shouldered brunette behind the desk. She laughs too loudly into the phone, her finger idly tracing the state shield embroidered on her shirt sleeve. He has known the inscription since childhood, Lord Baltimore's favorite saying and the state's motto, in Italian: *"Fatti Mascolini, Parole Femminine"*: "deeds are masculine, words are feminine." Some things never change.

He and Johnny had been tied together by the same great-great-great-great-grandfather Moses Lane, who'd come to Maryland a hundred and sixty years ago, hired blindly by the Baltimore and Ohio Railroad for his engineering expertise. He'd shown up with that dark face, a head of kinky hair, and suddenly the job had been filled. He'd stayed on despite the danger of slave hunters. Big money could be made behind the scenes, work in design and building of the first American coal burning steam locomotive. Peter Cooper had received the credit, but Moses Lane had discovered the beauty of the Chesapeake and he'd held on to a piece of it and a dream. They'd fought him then. They were fighting him now. That was not something Tamra would understand—that Johnny wasn't in jail simply because of Cassie. The sheriff didn't give a damn about Cassie Rowan. Instead, this arrest was the work of a group of cowards taking pains to remain anonymous. They were trying to destroy the Lanes because they viewed them as being too successful for African Americans. It was the same resentment many whites had had toward the Lanes for the last century and a half.

It just went to show that right or wrong he was supposed to bail Johnny out. They were tied by blood to Moses Lane, and had been, long before marches and legislation had brought "sweeping change." All these years later, here he sits, viewed by some as the same Black boogeyman they'd seen in Moses Lane. He'd been a fool to think change had occurred. Racism now. Racism tomorrow. Racism forever. And with a bitter smile, he translates the words into Latin: *racismus nunc, racismus cras, racismus in saecula saeculorum.*

It is a motto he'd like tattooed over his heart. That way, when his children bury him, they will read and understand the necessity of holding onto one another, even to the weakest link.

The phone rings in a distant office, startling him. The quiet of the reception area has allowed him to think. He remembers a story about his father's father, and how, like Cousin Johnny, his actions threatened to tear the family apart. Now the incident is only a footnote in the Lane archives. From what he has heard, it occurred sometime before the forties, before Grandpa Lane had handed over all the land to Johnny's father. Grandpa had had lots of money and little faith in banks, and so had had hidden cash reserves when the Depression hit. In fact, he'd been the one farmer in the area able to buy land.

When the harsh economic climate ended, Grandpa Lane's holdings were extensive. And it wasn't too long before he insisted, despite familial advice to the contrary, on building a new barn. It was going to be the largest, most efficient structure of its kind in the state. Red and cavernous, the barn rose on its foundations at a time when neighbors still struggled to feed themselves. Locals had named the structure "Lane's Folly," and some members of the family had been so furious over his display of wealth that for a long time they refused to have anything to do with him.

Surely it had been interpreted as divine action when Hurricane Hazel came through in 'fifty-four and in one furious twist tore the barn from its foundation, smashing it.

Charles had heard about it from Pa, long after Cousin Johnny's father had died and his mother had run off, abandoning Johnny and Bobbi, and long after the land had gone to Harlen. Charles had asked Pa if he ever considered rebuilding the barn, and Pa had shaken his head no. He said the problem was that to Grandpa Lane the barn had become more important than its purpose, which was simply to house animals. Grandpa Lane had made the mistake of investing too much in something that could so easily be destroyed. In doing so, he'd lost sight of what truly mattered, the structure of his family and his relationship to God and his neighbors. No, Pa had said, only the foundation would remain to remind them all of the absolute certainty of what was most important: God and family.

What Pa hadn't explained was how a man could separate the good from the bad in your family when you found yourself on the wrong side of evil. Tamra was his family, too, and yet he'd been foolish enough to let her go.

Cousin Johnny, dressed in a shiny, gray shirt, a new diamond stud in his ear, is led by a deputy through a door. Charles recognizes the deputy. He and Johnny golf together. The man is grinning like a schoolboy at Johnny, who, even now, is telling a joke.

"I'm pulling my pants up when she hands me a dollar. I said, 'That was a nice treat, but what's the money for?' Said it was her husband's idea. She'd asked him what I should be paid for the work. He'd said, 'Screw Johnny, give him a dollar.' "

Charles walks briskly toward the front door, and Johnny rushes to catch up.

Back in Nanticoke, after a silent ride, they pass Johnny's driveway. Charles ignores his protests to stop, that he has to get home, take a shower and shave, get the jail off of him. Charles continues driving toward his own house, which he knows is empty of his wife and children.

"Hey, slow down," Johnny says, as they drive perilously up. It is a demand that only propels them faster up the hips.

Charles slows for a minute to point at a field where they'd grown tomatoes. They'd boosted their yield every year with the right mix of fertilizers and an efficient rotation schedule. But today he's thinking of something other than profit, and he says to Cousin Johnny: "Remember that fight?"

Even now, in his fury, Charles is thinking that one of the best aspects of family is that you can speak in code. One word can elicit memories. Johnny laughs. "Sure I remember. I whipped your ass, boy."

Johnny had whupped him, soundly. And then they'd both been beaten by Pa. It had been years ago. Charles was smaller and less devious than Johnny, who'd fought his way through school. Pa had left them to supervise the pickers, and when Johnny goaded him about Cindy, they'd fought. Charles had been humiliated, tomatoes crushed in his face and hair. Pa had come up quick and silent, beaten them both for fighting in front of Whites, and for worse, he'd said, blood fighting blood.

Now driving toward his empty house, Charles feels he has been whupped again, in front of those same White fieldhands who'd resented taking orders from two boys. But he hasn't broken the family promise. He has remained true to his cousin, at a great price. He pulls into his driveway, telling Johnny to get out, that he wants to show him something.

"This better be good, man," Johnny says.

"Oh, it's good, all right. Maybe you and one of your women can laugh about it tonight." He spreads his legs, like he needs to balance himself, and he points out toward his land, heartbreakingly lovely. "Get a good look at all this," Charles says.

"Spare me your self-righteous bullshit, please, man."

"I'm only being hospitable," Charles says. "I want you to get a good look, from up here, 'cause you won't see this view again."

"You mean to tell me you're gonna turn against family over some piece of White . . ."

Charles is still pointing, only now his finger is in Cousin Johnny's face. "If I'd turned against you, you'd still be in there and I could see to it you'd stay a long time. But we both know this is between you and me, and it ain't about no white or green or yellow. This is about my home and the sanctity of it. When I invite you inside, that invitation is based on trust. You violated that, man, and I ain't givin' you another chance. So that's it. You walk through my door one more time . . ."

"And what?" He moves so close Charles can smell last night's cologne. Johnny says, "Go ahead. Whatcha gonna do, man? Same thing you did to me in the tomatoes?"

"*Nooooo*," Charles shakes his head, his face telling a lie, 'cause he'd love to wipe the ground with Johnny, but he won't and he tells him that. "If I did, I'd whup your tail too short to shit." He laughs, "And I'd like it. But it's enough to know my house and the people who live or work or play in it are off-limits. You can't walk up and down the aisles in this house like it's a K-Mart. Call me Mr. Bouncer, because I'm throwing you out of here. Come up again and you're gone, for good. If there's another scandal, out for good. No job here, no job in all of Nanticoke. And you can walk your damn self home."

Charles starts off toward the steps leading up to his house but he turns as Johnny screams, "You can't get away with this!"

"It's our fault, mine, too. We've let you get away with garbage all your life. Your daddy died. Your mama left you. That's terrible, man." (And he shouts) "But get over it!"

Johnny hasn't given up yet. "In all your spoiled, sweet-ass life, you have never heard me talk about my problems. You're the problem. This land woulda been mine. All of it shoulda been mine."

"I used to puzzle over that myself. Fate seemed so cruel that I, someone who didn't want it, should wind up having it. But I don't have to wonder anymore. Fate ain't cruel so much as it's wise. If you'd gotten the land we wouldn't have it anymore. 'Cause you'd have fucked it the way you fuck everything else. . . ." He lowers his voice before saying, "I expect you to remember what I've told you about this house." He lifts one shoulder higher than the other, adding a sudden twist to the old family saying. "Whatcha gonna do? After all . . . I am the boss."

He walks up the steps into the house. Discovering Tamra's note, and without reading it, he tucks it inside his shirt pocket. He plans to find his children. They've got to be needing him.

47

Tamra October 1990

NOT UNTIL THE cab pulls up to Wadine's does Tamra remember that this is the afternoon of Shisheemay's party. At the door to the building, a woman in a harlequin suit hands balloons to little girls in party frocks who pass beneath the awning. They are accompanied by their parents or housekeepers. Tamra waits with them at the elevator. She only takes the stairs when Wadine is there to insist.

As the elevator ascends, the guests are tightly packed in with the balloons, which give off a sweet, rubber scent. The mothers exchange pleasantries, and in the rear, three Black housekeepers stand silently. As the apartment door opens, Mrs. Twichell looks relieved to see Tamra among the crowd. She nods toward Wadine. "She bin askin' 'bout you."

What Tamra would like to do is politely greet her hosts and make a quick beeline to the guest room. Now that she has decided to return home, she'll need to make a flight reservation. But it is not easy to escape. Wadine and Stephen, though occupied in their roles as hosts, greet her enthusiastically. Tamra finds it difficult to return her smile. After what she has seen this morning, the opulence of the party overwhelms her.

One clown, dressed in gold lamé, poses with young guests as Wadine snaps photos with a buzzing Polaroid. Another clown practices "Happy

Birthday" on the piano. In the garden, a magician performs tricks with shimmering bubbles the size of a man's head. The bubbles hover, while the magician adds small, then longer, trembling ovals, transforming them into dogs and teddy bears. They sail out toward the East River.

The dining room table is covered in white linen, with two dozen gold-rimmed china place settings and ceramic rabbits in various poses, their baskets loaded with pretzels, grapes, raisins, and nuts. Colorful strips of ribbon hold bobbing helium balloons to the backs of chairs.

"Thank God you're here," Wadine says between snapshots. Tamra thinks these simple words of concern are what the fired shoe salesman longs to hear; what the newborn in the park restroom may never hear. She smiles gratefully at her friend, noticing for the first time the skintight jumpsuit Wadine wears in sharp contrast to the suburban-styled mothers settled about the room on couches, along window seats, or standing in small groups. Most of the mothers, Tamra notices, are White. There are twenty-four children, four Black, and from what she can tell, all of the housekeepers are Black.

Another African-American girl has entered, but unlike the other guests, she is dressed in a stiff, blue lace dress. Peering at the revelers through Coke-bottle glasses, she must notice she's the only girl not wearing a calf-length, autumn-flowered dress with a crisp, white collar. It's as if everyone, except this child, has been told to shop at the same store. Tamra introduces herself to the girl's father.

He says he's Tyrone, Wadine's big brother, and they share a hug. He'd been a high school football star, and she'd developed a mad crush on him the night he'd played the piano in the talent show crooning, "There's a Moon Out Tonight." That same year she and Wadine found condoms, which they'd filled with rice, at the back of his drawer.

Tyrone's face is thicker and less confident than she'd remembered and she wonders if it's New York or just getting older that has changed him. He apologizes for his gray uniform. He's working today, he explains, and adds that he has his own emergency refrigeration repair service. He introduces his daughter, who has remained by his side. At home, he says, he has a mantle covered with her honor roll certificates. Samantha attends a Catholic school.

"In Bedford-Stuyvesant," he says, and quickly adds, "that's several stops away." Before she can comment, he explains, "We can't afford this neighborhood."

She feels he is criticizing Wadine, and she remembers that on the day he'd found the riced condoms, he'd ripped pages from Wadine's diary and passed them out among the football players.

Tamra hastily bids good-bye to Tyrone and calls out to Stephen's brother, Kenneth. Although they have never been introduced, she recognizes him immediately. The resemblance is extraordinary, she tells him. And he introduces his partner, a stocky young man who insists she visit them while she's in New York. As Kenneth talks, she has difficulty reconciling his appearance as a conservatively dressed, middle-aged banker with the picture Wadine described of a man on roller skates wearing a tutu and a sequined mask. She wonders if he was relieved that his parents saw him in costume and thus allowed him to avoid the burden of singlehandedly running a family business.

Overhead lights are dimmed and the cake is brought in as the girls crowd around the table. Tyrone's daughter stands nearby, the party favors reflected in her lenses. Wadine positions a tiered cake before Shisheemay, whose face is filled with expectation. Vinyl magician hats have been provided for the guests, while the birthday girl wears a golden crown. When the singing ends, she sucks in her breath, prepared to blow. Wadine and Stephen hold hands. "Make a wish," Wadine calls.

With one strong gust, Shisheemay douses the candles and is applauded. A best friend inquires, "What'd you wish for?" But Stephen wags a finger. "She's not supposed to tell."

Shisheemay has other ideas and calls past him, "I want a pony with a rainbow saddle, and . . ." (this quickly) ". . . I want to be White."

Tamra steps in. Has she heard correctly? But she has only to glance at Mrs. Twichell, who shakes her head disapprovingly, and Tyrone, who leads his daughter away from the table. If the other parents have heard, they are not fazed. The children want cake. Wadine places the silver cutter in Stephen's hand, motioning for him to take over. Tamra hears the last of his explanation. ". . . Just a child talking." She watches her best friend make her way smilingly through the crowd, slowly toward the conch shell stairway, and then dash up. Tamra follows, and on the third floor, she knocks at Wadine's door. Without waiting for a response, she walks in, recalling that only a few weeks before, she had entered a strange bedroom in search of Cassie.

Wadine and Stephen's room has only a large, pillowed bed and two night tables with lamps. The adjoining dressing area, study, and baths cannot be seen from where Tamra stands. The most notable difference between this and the other upstairs rooms is that this one is flooded with sunlight. Here and there, on the walls just below the ceiling, there are large scallop cutouts of glass, and sliding doors lead to a smaller, terraced garden, its walls, like the one below, topped by high, double barbed wire.

Wadine is stretched across the bed, and Tamra tries lifting her head to comfort her, but her friend resists. Tamra settles for stretching out, saying with mock gruffness, "Move your big butt over," and begins to speak by posing a question. "What if I tell you she'll grow out of it?" Wadine does not respond. "Come on, Deenie, this isn't a big deal. I wanted to be Darlene and you wanted to be Annette, remember? And that Chinese restaurant on Mechanics Street? Jennifer Wong? She had to work so hard. . . . All those dishes. But she had that long braid down her back. We would have been her, too, no matter how many plates. It's part of the African-American experience. But we got over it."

Wadine keeps her face buried in her hands as she talks. "I'm going to tell you something I wouldn't tell anybody else."

"Shoot, my sister," Tamra says, her voice more confident than she feels.

Wadine's eyes look smaller, the way Tyrone's daughter's had seemed. "I'm not crying because Shisheemay wants to be White. It's because I wish she were. She'd never have to go through what we have."

She speaks to Wadine in a whisper. A whisper is all that is necessary. Their faces almost touch. "As a mother who's also raising children in the middle of this desperate and unconfirmed war, let me remind you that if you really feel that way, she probably knows that. So I can only offer one suggestion to help you help her: Get up, walk over to that balcony, and jump the hell off."

Wadine seems to be searching her face, to see if there's a punch line. Realizing one won't be forthcoming, she stands. Tamra worries for a minute that her friend might actually follow her advice. Maybe she guesses what Tamra is thinking. Wadine points down the corridor. "I'll just go and wash my face."

She's only a few steps away and halfway down the hallway before she pokes her head back around the corner, smiling miserably. "Thanks. I needed that."

Tamra salutes. Alone in the sunny room, she wants to scold herself for not being a better friend. Wadine had, after all, offered this in confidence. But she's too concerned with Wadine's spirit to care whether or not she has been rude. Her mind is drawn back to Atunay's noisy posturing about who he is and the strict standards by which he judges his mother. Maybe there is a connection between his clamor and the silence of the old folks in Salisbury. After word had spread around about who Wadine had married, the old guard had simply stopped talking or asking about her. Tamra had been startled by the uniformity of it. Worse than if she'd died; it was as if Wadine had never lived. But now, as Tamra sits waiting for her old, dear friend, she has the troubling sense that she understands their logic. She imagines a dark sky where indeed, a star flickers out, and she wonders if Atunay sees what she does, and shouts in desperation to keep his mother from fading away.

48

Tamra October 1990

WITH TEMPERATURES PLUNGING into the teens, October has turned suddenly and cruelly into winter. Only yesterday she'd seen homeless men stretched out in the park, but last night, according to a news report on the car's radio, "Police were called in as fights broke out over floor space at Grand Central Station."

This morning, the day before she will return to the Chesapeake, she has borrowed a warm coat from Wadine, who has insisted Tamra accompany her to her office.

"Good-bye, Aunt Tamra."

It's too cold for Mrs. Twichell to walk Olu and Shisheemay the four blocks to Grace Episcopal School. Wadine climbs over Tamra, her fur brushing against Tamra's calf. As the car door opens, a glacial blast rushes in and she watches Wadine wave good-bye to the children. She's annoyed with herself, once again, for allowing her friend to talk her into doing something she does not want to do. Tamra will spend the day in the Bronx when she would have much preferred to be in the Village, to shop at lunchtime with Kenneth and his partner, the manager of an "intergalactic" toy shop.

Instead, she'll be sitting in Wadine's reception room while her friend works at repairing broken marriages. Phillips ushers Wadine back inside, and feeling the stinging air again, Tamra shivers, remembering Virginia saying when she felt a chill that it was "as if someone had walked on my grave."

Wadine is talkative, allowing her few opportunities to even glance out the window. And almost too quickly they have arrived. They glide past a Kentucky Fried Chicken's massive face of the Colonel, and a bus stop, with a crowd waiting, where one small child eagerly points toward the limousine.

"This is it." Wadine says, indicating a brick, semi-attached building. As they climb from the car Wadine explains how she gets to use the building, rent free. Members of the housing authority, administrators of the property, had initially mistrusted her intentions. In the Heights she'd charged clients two hundred to three hundred dollars an hour. Here, she says proudly, she provides free marriage and family therapy.

"They obviously realized I was serious," Wadine continues, pulling several keys from her bag and unlocking the barred gates. "The second day I was open, one of the administrators brought his wife by. They're still my clients." Tamra notices Phillips settling into his seat, his whipping stick ready for attack, and she wonders if he also carries a gun for protection. Five locks later, Wadine has the doors open.

She leads Tamra into a small outer office furnished with two well-worn, corduroy couches, a coffee table with cigarette burns, and a litter of magazines: *Black Enterprise, Ebony, Jet, Essence,* and *The African American Scholarly Review.* The walls are covered with colorful posters. In one corner of the room, a television sits amidst a scrambling of toys.

"My home away from home," Wadine says, a statement Tamra thinks rather pretentious coming from a woman who owns three houses.

She scolds herself once again for being judgmental but realizes she does feel defensive this morning, separated from her friend in a manner she can't explain. They'd seemed so close yesterday after the party. But there is something about being here that makes her uneasy. Brushing aside these feelings, she pokes her head into Wadine's office and asks for a tour.

Just outside the door, what looks like the speaker from a small stereo set proves to be a sound machine. Wadine explains that it reproduces the sounds of ocean waves to drown out conversations from her office that might be overheard by clients in the waiting room. Tamra asks why there is no couch for clients to stretch out on. A couch, Wadine explains, is for psychoanalysis. She's a marriage and family therapist. Tamra would love to sit in on one of these sessions, seeing her old friend in action.

It's not long before a dignified looking African couple arrives for the first appointment. The wife is much the taller of the two, and the husband speaks with a heavy accent. A bronze medallion swings from his neck. Tamra wonders what his homefolk would think of this intimacy with a stranger.

Throughout the morning, as one couple after another enters and departs, she speculates on the nature of their problems. By noon she looks forward to lunch with Wadine, who has reservations for half-past one at the restaurant of an old acquaintance, B. Smith. Located in the theater district, it is a fashionable, Black-owned establishment.

As the last couple to enter Wadine's office leaves, Wadine emerges with an exhausted grin. She's wearing a hound's-tooth suit that stops just at her knees, and like all of her clothes, it fits as if it had been tailor-made for her. It probably has been, Tamra thinks. Wadine looks impatient as she explains that the next clients are holdouts from her old practice in the Heights, and that they are usually punctual. "They work in midtown," she says.

Tamra doesn't know why, but she's becoming increasingly irritated as Wadine, who's back in her office, lifts the receiver and presses several buttons. She speaks in an unusually loud voice. "Operator, I'm trying to get through to a car phone." She supplies the number. "This is Dr. Drake calling."

Doctor Drake, that's the part of the image Tamra's uncomfortable with. She turns her attention back to the television, where a man in lederhosen leads viewers through an Octoberfest menu. "The cabbage should be translucent," he is saying, but her attention is on Wadine, who continues shouting into the phone.

"Well, if the traffic is that heavy, we should reschedule. You'll never get here in time. And I have a luncheon appointment waiting." Tamra feels like a Chesapeake crab waiting for Wadine's fork.

Her friend returns to the waiting room. The traffic is heavy, she says. They won't make it today and maybe Wadine should cancel her and Tamra's midtown luncheon reservation. No sense driving into trouble. Tamra eyes her suspiciously and says, "I saw a White Castle not too far from here and we could——"

Wadine interrupts to ask what's troubling her. Only she doesn't just ask Tamra. She stutters. "W-w-w-why'd you have that strange l-l-l-look on your face?"

Tamra's suspicions are confirmed. As a girl, Wadine had always stuttered when she'd lied. That had made her a terrible liar. And this, this is too obvious. Tamra asks: "How is it that I'm sure this is a set-up?"

"What are you t-t-t-talking about?"

"Well, think about it, Deenie. You've stopped asking me questions about my marriage. Then you insist on me coming up here with you . . . and now this couple suddenly can't make it, and guess what? You're stuttering, or haven't you noticed? And something tells me your next line is going to be that you have the whole afternoon free."

The idea of Wadine stuttering is even more unnerving to Tamra than this thwarted conspiracy. Wadine had worked for years to control her speech.

"I w-w-wouldn't think of giving you uns-s-solicited advice."

"That's what I'd say, but I could probably say it a helluva lot better."

"You still like a good fight, don't you?"

The stutter is gone, just that quickly, and its sudden absence lends Wadine a certain authority.

Tamra says, "If I answer any more of your questions, will I get a bill in the morning for two hundred dollars, or is this a Bronx freebie?"

Wadine turns away. "I don't understand what's going on with you. Soon as we walked in here, you copped an attitude."

"Copped an attitude," Tamra says, rubbing her chin sarcastically and speaking in a mock accent. "Is that psycho-babble for a show of resistance?"

"Tamra, don't do this, please. It's been good having you here. I don't want to fight."

"Neither do I," Tamra says, "But . . ."

"What is it?"

"Tell me who I'm talking to, my friend or Dr. Drake?"

"Who do you want me to be?"

"Hmmm. Let me consider my choices. There was the Deenie I saw yesterday, but she's got problems of her own, so she wouldn't dare offer me advice. Then there's Dr. Drake. She works hard for free to stave off guilt about living in luxury while a lot of Black folks are on the street starving to death."

Wadine looks torn between sadness and anger. She puts her palms together and brings them toward her mouth in a prayer position. "I've always thought it more than a coincidence that the two of us wound up on the same block in the same backwater town just a couple of doors apart."

"You do, eh?"

"And that we didn't have any sisters of our own, but we grew as close as sisters. And sisters don't even have to tell each other when they're hurting. They can feel it, and I want to help."

"Sounds unethical to me."

"Damn the rules if I can help you. I love you, Tamra, and I don't want you to go back like this. Won't you just give it a try?"

Wadine's unrelenting need to question her has finally crossed the line for Tamra. She walks into her office, determined to shake free of this adolescent chuminess. With a concerned look, she slides into one of the client chairs. "You're right, Deenie. I do have something that's bothering me terribly." She wrings her hands. "And it has to do with my marriage."

At first Wadine seems thrown by this sudden reversal but nevertheless is eager to help as she sits behind her desk. "Go ahead."

Tamra groans. "It happens when I'm in bed with . . ."

"Go ahead."

"Well, it happens when Charles climbs on top of me and I . . . I start seeing . . ."

"What is it?"

"I look over at the window, and I see . . ."

Wadine, who looks confused, reaches for Tamra's hand.

Tamra says, "I see Elvis Presley singing 'You Ain't Nothin' But a Hound Dog.' " She shrieks at her own joke. Wadine looks stunned and hurt. Tamra, embarrassed by her own sophomoric humor, apologizes but cannot stop her nervous giggling. "I really had you going there for a while, didn't I?"

Wadine opens the top drawer and pulls out her office keys. She stands, turns out the lights, and walks into the reception area. "I think there's still time for that lunch," she says.

Tamra trails behind her.

Wadine says, "I bet we could also round up Kenneth and Bob if we call from the restaurant. They love spur-of-the——"

Tamra stops Wadine from turning out the lights to the outer office. "I'm sorry, Wadine. I hurt you."

"I'll get over it. Hey, I can't believe I was stuttering again. It's been . . ."

"Deenie, please stop. I hate us like this. I know it was silly, but I couldn't resist . . ."

"Let's do lunch." She flicks the switch, and the room is dark. Tamra sees a crack of daylight from under the door.

"If you go back in there with me, I'll try . . ."

Silence.

"Deenie? Please answer me."

Silence.

"I really want to."

Wadine's voice is thick. "I know you do, Tam, but there's one rule."

"What's that?"

"If we go in there, I'm not Wadine anymore. I'm Dr. Drake and hurting me is off-limits."

She seems to understand Tamra's acquiescence, and taking her by the hand, Wadine leads her through the dark and into the room she has tried so long to avoid.

49

Tamra October 1990

THEY HAVE BEEN together in this office for what seems like hours and Tamra has found it easy to talk almost nonstop about subjects as diverse as her marriage, Cassie, and Cousin Johnny, even her disappointments concerning her career. Through it all, Wadine has listened sympathetically, interrupting only occasionally to ask a few leading questions. It amazes Tamra how much anger she still feels even though so many of the incidents occurred years before. She's just so angry with Charles.

"Sorry I've been running off at the mouth like this," Tamra concludes. "I had no idea what a relief it would be to purge myself. No wonder you're in demand." She begins another story and is just leading up to the details of the night that she'd leaped on Charles's back when Wadine interrupts.

"How do you think your family history fits into all of this?"

Tamra considers this question a minute before responding. "You're right. It looked as if we were perfect for one another. When it comes to families, we have so much in common, the way our parents stressed edu——"

"I'm talking specifically about your father."

"Well, of course. He was an educator, but Mama cared just as much about——"

"Tamra, I'm referring to the alcoholism."

"Daddy has quit drinking, or at least he's determin——. By the way, will you not interrupt me anymore, please?" Tamra says. "I'm trying to make a point."

"Is this one of those subjects you don't like discussing?" Wadine asks.

"Not at all," Tamra says, trying to sound genial. "Mama and I discussed him for years. It used to be one of our favorite topics of conversation until my——"

"What was it like for you, all those years growing up with a drunk?"

At the mention of this word, she has to stop her head from jerking up. Before this day she has never heard anyone from outside her family refer to Seth as a drunk. But it's all right, she tells herself, and crosses her legs, wishing she'd insisted on getting some hamburgers before they'd started. She clears her throat. "Umm, would you please repeat the question?"

"What was it like for you, all those years, growing up with an alcoholic?"

"I don't know what you remember about my daddy, but he treated me like a little princess. He still does. I don't have any complaints about him."

"Somehow that doesn't surprise me."

"Now, what's that supposed to mean?"

"Tamra, what would you say if I told you that so much of the anger you feel toward Charles has to do with your father?"

She snickers quietly.

Wadine continues. "When someone's got their arms around a bottle it's hard to hug anybody else."

"Daddy was pretty affectionate. . . ."

"I'm talking emotional distance."

"You know how close we were."

"No, I suppose I don't. Tell me what Seth's response was the first time you told him his drinking really hurt you and made you so scared that your very life was shaped by fear."

"Okay, we weren't close that way."

"And when you chose a husband . . ."

"My husband chose me."

"Yes, and if I remember correctly, he began to pursue you just before you left the country. It's also kind of hard to develop real intimacy when someone is an ocean away."

Tamra sits with legs crossed, grasping her knees with clasped hands, and as she continues, she opens her two thumbs. "It's an interesting theory. If I'm reading you correctly, you're saying Charles is difficult because he didn't get what he'd planned on. He'd assumed I'd always be working, and what he got was a homemaker who wanted to spend real time with him."

Wadine looks around the room, as if she's talking to someone else. "Did ya'll hear me say any of that? . . . Oh, I didn't think so." She points a thumb toward a far wall. "They want me to get back to the subject of your father."

Tamra stands, pointing a finger at Wadine. "Let's just call this off, because I'm really feeling uncomfortable. I'll tell you one thing. This *is* one of my pet peeves . . . the idea of people always blaming their parents whenever they have the least problem."

Wadine remains calm as she says, "You and I both realize I'm onto something here. So at least humor me. You've spent two hours giving me a detailed rundown on everything Charles has done for the last decade except of course his bowel movements, and maybe that's next. I'll even listen to that, if you want, but sooner or later we're going to have to get down to business. We can do it now or later. But it will be done. I've opened a can of worms here, and if I don't know anything else about Tamra Lane it's that she has an insatiable curiosity. She won't just up and leave with so many questions unanswered."

Tamra sits down again and drums her fingers on top of Wadine's desk. "Okay, you want to talk about my daddy. Go ahead. What do you want to know?"

"You sound pretty angry."

"I wonder why. You're telling me that because of my father my marriage is coming apart."

"I'm not doing a very good job of this, am I?"

Tamra is quiet. But she agrees with Wadine.

Wadine sounds as if she has just been hit with a sudden revelation when she says, "The problem is that I've been trying to deal with my best friend in life the way I would any client who walks in here. And that's not going to work. But I have another idea." She fumbles in her drawer, then slides a sheet of paper across the desk with a chunky, black crayon.

"What are we going to do?"

"We'll pretend we're eight years old and it's raining outside, so we can't go out and play."

Tamra laughs. "And we're in that funky basement of yours."

"Uggh. Mildew, for days," Wadine says. "I can smell it." Her laughter slows. "We've just pricked our thumbs, our blood has mingled, but everyone knows that ritual. We like being different. So our sisterhood isn't official until we exchange important secrets."

"I don't have any."

"Let me finish."

Tamra nods.

"We've decided we can't use words. We want to communicate on the deepest level possible, so . . ."

She's stalling for time, Tamra can tell, making this up as she goes along.

"So we're going to draw pictures of our darkest secret, each of us, and when we show the other, we won't say a word. We'll know what the other is feeling, just from seeing the picture."

"It's not fair," Tamra says, "because you know what you're supposed to draw. I don't have a clue what you're looking for."

"Trust me on this," Wadine says. "Just stop talking and at the count of three, listen to the rain running in rivulets outside. Smell the mildew, and start. One . . ."

"Someone might . . ."

"Don't interrupt, just start . . . two, three."

Tamra begins. She has never fancied herself much of an artist and she looks up, saying, "This isn't going to——"

"Shut up!"

"That doesn't sound very clinical."

"How's this? Shut the hell up!"

Instead of retaliating, Tamra finds herself caught up in trying to make her picture look pleasant by drawing a house with a smoking chimney, birds, trees, and of course, the obligatory family out front. The stick figure of Virginia waits near the door, Seth beside her. Tamra hurriedly adds flowers, big clumsy daisies. Virginia could never do without those, and then pausing, she draws Virginia's hands around Seth's neck. His mouth is open, gasping for air.

She wants to be the first to finish, so she can say, "Okay, you first. Show me yours."

Wadine's head has been down, working busily at her chore. But Tamra can see she's crying. Wadine holds her drawing up. It is a cartoon of three panels. In the first, a woman stands with her hands on her hips, glowering at a small child. In the second, the woman reaches toward a tree and breaks off the trunk. In the third panel, the woman uses the trunk to beat the girl, who screams for help.

Tamra remembers the terrible beatings Wadine received as a child. One had been inflicted with an electrical cord; the welts had lasted for weeks. "Oh, Deenie," she says sympathetically, and attempts to rise from her seat. Wadine shakes her head and pantomimes for her to show hers. Tamra feels foolish. Wadine is a far better cartoonist.

Wadine studies Tamra's picture, giving it careful attention before she says, "You cheated."

"Did not," Tamra says.

"It was supposed to be one of your darkest secrets."

"That's Mama greeting Daddy at the door. He's come home drunk again, and she's choking the life out of him."

"Tamra, I hate to be the first one to break this to you, but that was no secret. Everyone knew your father drank."

"Thanks a lot."

"I was trying to make a point. This was supposed to be your secret, but you're not even in the picture."

"Oh." She turns the paper around for better viewing. "You're right. But you get the point anyway."

"No, I don't. Where are you?"

"From an existentialist standpoint?"

"You left yourself out of the picture."

"I was at your house, remember?"

"Show me where you were."

"I don't know." She feels teary without understanding why.

"You know just where you were."

"So you tell me."

Wadine lifts the fist with which Tamra clutches the crayon and moves it to the corner of the paper. "Were you over here, on the outside watching them?"

"Sometimes."

"Where was your place? You had one."

"Cut it out, Deenie."

"Come on. Help me out. Every player has a position."

"Stop!"

"Over here?" Their hands land between Seth and Virginia, and Tamra pulls away, as if she has been burned. Wadine slowly directs Tamra's hand back, between the two figures. Tamra draws, as if in a trance, a tiny, tiny figure, smack in the middle, hands raised, trying to keep the figures of Virginia and Seth apart. But she adds a smile.

"Thank you." Wadine says. "But would you mind completing it? The girl in this picture has no eyes."

She does, and just below them, she draws dozens of tiny droplets. They fall from the little insignificant face onto the grass, watering Virginia's lovely flowers, the crayon making tapping noises. Finishing, Tamra swipes at her own real tears. Her voice trembles. "Yeah, I was in the middle. So what?"

"So, turn that paper over and draw another family."

"Of?"

"Yours, today, with Charles."

This time she draws without argument. Charles walks into the bedroom, late, as usual. And there she is, hands outstretched, lunging at him, demanding he come home earlier.

Wadine turns the paper around, as if to get a better look.

"You left the children out."

"Come on, Wadine."

"My name is Dr. Drake."

She flings the crayon to the floor.

Wadine walks across the floor to retrieve the crayon, placing it on the desk. "Tell me what you're feeling, please, for the sake of those children you can't even bring yourself to draw."

Tamra opens her mouth, but for a while no sound emerges. When it does, they are strange animal-like cries, and then she says, "They're in the same place, in the middle, like I was." She places her head in her lap, sobbing. Wadine kneels and holds her.

When finally Tamra can speak again she asks Wadine how she'd known where her children would be.

"You'd be amazed at how many people would draw almost identical families on both sides of the paper. On one side, a girl could be getting raped by her father, with the mother's head turned, looking the other way. On the other side of the paper, it's her marriage, and she's recreated the same hell. All of us do that in some form or another, recreating the familiar. It's the root word for family."

She strokes Tamra's face. "I'm sorry that hurt so much. I had to get you to see it, so you could understand. I'm not taking Charles's side or going after your father. It's just that the only way to save a marriage is to turn the finger of blame around toward our own hearts, and use it as a guide for where we need to start. We get so hung up pointing at our lovers, we forget to look where we should."

Wadine returns to her desk as Tamra speaks. "But even if I work on myself forever, that's not going to change Charles. I'm not going to find a way to make him come home at night or to want to really be a husband."

"You can start with yourself, and I promise, Tamra, that will force him to change, one way or the other."

"How do I start?"

"It can take years, and you'll have to go back and look closely at how you were hurt without assigning blame. Your parents did the best they knew how to. But you've got to figure out what part of you is still hurting and needs to be healed."

"Can't I do that with you?"

"It's something that requires long-term therapy. It couldn't be done in a few visits."

Tamra looks at her hands. She can't remember feeling emptier. And she wonders how she'll find the strength to pick herself up and even walk out of the office.

Wadine seems to understand. "We have some time left. I have a four o'clock, but that gives us a couple of hours. Would you be willing to let me lead you through an exercise?"

"What kind?"

"You'll have to tell me."

"I don't think I understand."

"I use a process of self-hypnosis. Would that frighten you too awfully much?"

"Nothing frightens me more than the way I feel now."

"Then let me ask you to sit back and close your eyes, and when this is over, maybe you'll feel a bit more peaceful. But I can't promise that. And it won't be easy."

She takes a deep breath, ready to follow.

"Pretend you're looking into a pool of water and see many fish . . ."

"Like the pond at our——"

"Don't tell me. Just picture the fish, hundreds of them at first." She continues speaking, and Tamra is only aware of the sound of her voice and the tiny, gliding fish.

"But they all swim away, except for one. His gills are so bright, you're not surprised when he flips out of the water and showers your body with droplets of light."

Tamra feels stardust on her skin.

"The light falls in soft particles, dusting your forehead, warms your shoulders and on down . . ."

She feels almost as if she is levitating and she enjoys this, this letting go.

"That light," Wadine says, in what sounds like a faraway voice, "is the part of you that's always with you. It cares about your well-being, it showers you with intelligence and love. You felt it when you were young and open and trusting. . . ."

"Oh, I remember," Tamra mutters.

"Even now, it's there, shedding light on old secrets, where before there was only darkness."

"Yes."

"Ask that light what hurt you so terribly as a child."

She hears herself speaking in a childish voice. "What hurt me? I don't hear anything."

"That's your intellect talking. Let the light shine through that hurt part of you."

"I've asked again, but there is no answer."

"Feel the light, Tamra. Bathe in it. It's warm and protective. It will keep you safe. No one can hurt you. Now tell me where you feel the light?"

Tamra says she feels the light on top of her head. The shimmering glow warms her body. "It's on my face . . . *ahhhh*. My mouth . . ." She can feel the light traveling . . . over her arms, warming her breasts, her midriff. "*Ahhhhh*."

"Yes, Tamra, keep going."

"The light is on my stomach . . . and my hips . . . and my legs and my . . ."

"Tamra, why isn't the light everywhere? Why did it skip your pelvic area?"

"I don't know."

"Who touched you there, Tamra?"

"No one."

"Ask your light. Why is it so cold between your legs?"

Quickly she responds. "It won't say."

"Ask your light, Tamra. Trust it."

"No!"

"Just a few more minutes, Tamra. If you won't do it for yourself, be brave for Joyce, for H.P. To be the best mother, you need to know. Now repeat after me. . . . Who . . ."

"Who . . ."

". . . Touched me?"

"No!"

"No what?" Wadine asks.

"Stop, stop now. She'll hear you." She lowers the pitch of her voice. "You're my wife. I want you." The lighter voice again. "No. Please. Stop!" Tamra knows she holds her own hands to her mouth. She bites down hard. "Oh, please, oh, please, stop." Then huskily, "Shut up! She'll hear you."

"*Ahhh*, Tamra. It was Virginia. It wasn't you, and she fought him off, didn't she?"

"No."

"Then why, why didn't she fight him?"

"Stop, oh, please, please."

"Why didn't she fight him? Stay with this Tamra. Ask your light to help."

"I can't."

"Why?"

"It hurts."

"It hurts because you've taken her pain. She didn't fight him because of you, right? She didn't want to frighten you. She probably thought of it as one more secret. But you knew and you shared her guilt and pain. Where has it settled?"

"Down here . . . inside . . ." She hears herself groaning but doesn't know how to stop. It hurts."

"Yes. I know. But as much as I love you, I can't take this journey with you. You can either remain in that pain, or move through it. You're too much of a fighter to give up."

She doesn't want to talk but Wadine insists.

"What happened after the rape?"

"Me, with Big Mama."

"And where'd they go, Tamra?"

"My father, home. My mother, New York."

"New York! Here?"

"She came back to us. . . . Oh, I'm so tired. I have to stop."

"Tamra, you're so close."

"I can't go any further. I can't. I'm too weak."

"Then pray with me. Pray as if your life depended on it. We aren't asking much here, God. We know we're your children. You've made us capable of so many miracles. Give her the strength she needs. She's fighting to get her life back."

"Ohhh."

"Tamra, I feel your strength. You've always used it to fight for people you love. Use it to loosen that shroud you've buried yourself in. Fight for a real life, for a marriage. Now, tell me. Your mother went to New York, just as you have, after a rape. But think. Why did she come back?"

"She was angry. She didn't want to come back."

"Yes. She went back, and she was angry. Just the way you were going to return. You were both bound to go back. All of you have such a strong sense of family; so strong and loving, Seth and Virginia passed on strength even they didn't utilize. So you're going to work at it and find the answer. Once and for all, ask that light another question. Why did Virginia come back?"

"School was starting. I was in Nanticoke and had to go back to Salisbury. She knew my father couldn't raise me."

"Why? Why would she believe an intelligent, loving, and kind man couldn't raise you alone?"

"He was a good man but he couldn't be counted on."

"Yes, Tamra. That was the message she spoon-fed you. Just as her mother had fed her. They passed that message on like an Olympic torch: That any man you loved would disappoint you. And the message has been so powerful, even Charles couldn't prove differently."

"Oh, I have to stop."

"But was Virginia right? Did your father disappoint you?"

"It always seemed he would. We never knew when . . ."

"And so you spent your life in anticipation of disappointment. What a sad, frightened little girl you must have been. All dressed up in those fancy clothes, waiting to be disappointed."

Tamra remembers herself at the picture window. It is the day of the parade and she and Mama wait for Seth. He won't come, Virginia warns. The whole town will know. Her body is chilled.

"You're still waiting, aren't you Tamra? But who's the man you expect to disappoint you now? It's not Charles. Look again. It's Seth! Look at him. See who he is."

Tamra stands, sobs racking her shoulders. Wadine holds her. Her dear and only friend, telling her to cry, to feel the sadness. To praise herself. That she has worked hard. And she does cry, for a long time, sloppy and wet on Wadine's shoulder. And her friend, her sister, weeps with her. They stop, wipe one another's eyes, and then cry again.

Not until the sun has crossed the room does she stop crying. Wadine pats her hand. "You understand now why you must go back to Charles?"

"Because so much of it has been my fault?"

"Only halfway. He was Seth's understudy because he knew every line by heart. That's what attracts people. They sense that with this special person they can get the same kind of dynamics going, but this time, make it better."

Tamra's breathing has slowed. Although she is spent, she senses her body swelling with an unfamiliar sense of well-being. They sit together quietly until the doorbell rings. Tamra feels light-headed when she stands. Wadine answers the door and can be heard asking her clients to remain in the waiting room. Back in her office, she advises Tamra to rest for a while, says that people often feel woozy after sessions like these. "It's as if all these years you've just been feeling with your intellect, instead of your body, and suddenly that energy and sensation of being fully alive takes over." Tamra rubs her own arm, touching her face as if it's new to her.

"One of my clients said she felt a sudden sense of weightlessness," Wadine continues, "as if telling her secrets lifted a burden from her."

Tamra agrees. She feels so odd. But she doesn't want to sit in that outer office again. She can't. She wants to test this feeling of buoyancy on the street, away from the safety of this friendship. "I have to get back to Brooklyn and pack," she explains.

Wadine offers to send her home with Phillips.

This time Tamra won't be coerced. "Thanks, but he's not driving me anywhere. I'm going to take the subway."

"I don't think you have any idea of where you are," Wadine says. "Your trip yesterday was crazy enough, and that was only four stops on a Sunday morning."

Tamra reminds her of her clients waiting. She won't change her mind, she says. By now she's slipping her coat on. "And that was three stops . . . three stops to Wall Street. You don't know because you're so afraid of taking the subway. That's not meant to be a criticism, but that's your choice. I can't live that way anymore. Not in Nanticoke or New York."

Wadine follows behind her. "You simply can't go out there by yourself on the subway."

"Watch me," Tamra says. And she steps out into the cold sunlight. Phillips looks as if he has been sleeping. Jerking into position, he starts the engine. Tamra waves at him. "See you back in the hood."

"Tamra," Wadine calls, "this is crazy."

"No," Tamra says, "what's crazy is being in this city but not living in it." She spreads her arms. "This is all part of New York and I won't go home until I see at least a little of it."

She's certain Wadine is watching when she stops to genuflect before the Colonel.

$$\underline{50}$$

Tamra October 1990

SHE KNOWS SHE has been rude to Wadine and must seem terribly ungrateful but this time she avoids self-criticism. There's so much of her life she wants to examine and reconsider. And time may be running out. She doesn't trust this sense of rejuvenation and thinks maybe it will leave her any minute. She has no plans, doesn't even know where the devil she is. But she wants to test these new feelings.

Wadine surmised that Tamra had come to New York to work with her, but that was only half right. She knows now that she's also there to retrace Virginia's steps. She allows herself, for the first time, to consider her mother's desperation and fear, imagines her focusing only on the most dismal aspects of the city, just as Tamra had. And surely Virginia had resigned herself to returning home without hope for change.

Tamra feels that aspect can be different. But how without convincing Charles they need therapy? How, without replicating much of what just occurred in Wadine's office, can she persuade him that they have recreated the drama of their parents' marriages?

Though she needs time to think, she must, for the moment at least, concentrate on where she is. An elderly woman approaches, dressed from head to foot in black, her face covered by the veil of a small hat. In both hands she carries heavy shopping bags. Tamra calls to her but the woman does not respond. Perhaps she has difficulty hearing. Is it worth it to try to catch up with her? She has already passed. But she thinks of Big Mama, who is just the sort of person one turns to for direction in life, and she rushes up to the old woman, gently tapping her shoulder. The woman raises her head as if considering Tamra from head to foot. For the briefest of moments, their eyes meet. Tamra speaks slowly: "Can you direct me to the nearest subway?"

The woman does not respond. Tamra walks away certain there has been something eerie about the encounter but quickly dismisses her uneasiness when she sights a fruit stand up ahead. Latin music, from large, mounted speakers, filters out onto the wide boulevard.

The proprietor is a smooth-faced, balding man who wipes his hands on an apron and offers her clear and easy directions. The news is good. The subway's only a block away. Before starting out she looks around the store and notices the colorful arrangements of oranges and mangos, bananas and plantains, coconuts, tomatoes, and peanuts. Now this is a store Charles would enjoy. She would love to bring him here, she thinks, her body swaying as the tenor sings. The owner smiles and asks, "You like Tito Puente?"

"I like . . . ? I like . . . ?" she's giggling. "I'm not so sure what I like. But I want something . . . different. What can you suggest? It has to be something I've never tasted before."

He pinches two fingers together in delight. "I have a fruit that's been waiting for a beautiful woman."

"Well, she's here, isn't she?" she says, and she follows him around the store, her hips gyrating beneath her coat. He leads her to a stand of small, dark fruits, wrinkled and ugly, like hard prunes, and lifting one, places it carefully in her palm. She turns it over, searching the skin for magic, and he calls in Spanish to someone behind the beaded curtain.

A woman with two long braids and stick pins between her teeth walks out, half bowing, urging before her a bashful girl dressed in what appears to be a wedding gown. "My wife and daughter," he says proudly. "They are preparing for Maria's confirmation."

Tamra smiles at the daughter, thinking there are few times in our lives when we are this new of face, hopeful and lovely. She says to the girl in a confidential manner, *"Muy bonita."* The parents look on emanating a sense of pride and dignity.

The wife reaches behind a counter and gives her husband a small paring knife. Taking the fruit from Tamra, he cuts it open, revealing green, fleshy seeds. He then spoons the pulp out and holds it near her lips. Without pause she bites, and with great delight chews the sweetness. *"Ummm."* She'd forgotten how hungry she is. "What are those called?"

"Passion fruit."

"I wonder why that name."

He speaks with an accent. "Probably because they are ugly outside, and like the passion of a woman, not something you can judge until you taste." He smiles at his wife.

Tamra buys twenty, which makes for a weighty sack, and he tosses in three limes for free, telling her to squeeze them over the chilled fruit and serve it to her husband.

She looks to the man's wife, who stands beside him. "It works?" she asks.

The man translates for his wife, "Does this fruit light the fires of passion?" And the woman, looking somewhat embarrassed but amused, nods her head vigorously. *"Si, señora, si."*

Back on the streets Tamra carries the tune in her head. "Da da, da, da, da." From a distance she can see the subway stairs will be an obstacle. The bottom four steps leading to the elevated tracks are no longer there, creating the strange sight of a stairway dropping as if from the sky, then simply ending three feet from the ground. How do the people who run this city expect passengers to get up, she wonders?

Before she can devise an answer she sees a crowd of teen-agers in an empty lot, and she recalls Mrs. Twichell's warnings about how dangerous the city's teen-agers can be. But she's determined to start looking at life differently and believes that to do so, she must first see the real New York—the New York millions refuse to leave. Peering at the group again, she notices the clean, white high-tops they sport, even the girls, and those goose down jackets again. Like Shisheemay's guests, as if they've all shopped at the same store. She's not the only one staring. They seem to have realized she's a stranger. When she looks back evenly, they laugh.

They're children, she tells herself, and could be mine or Wadine's or the children of anyone I care about. And besides, who understands kids better than I do? Drawing closer to the crowd, she's disappointed that these girls smoke and curse, but agrees that if this were her playground, she'd curse, too. As she passes, their loud voices drop to a murmur. The only distinguishable noise is from a radio: *"We gonna kill that nigga, tonight. We gonna kill that nigga, tonight."*

She has been so captivated by the teen-agers that she is just now noticing that she's in front of the broken stairway and still has no clue about how she'll get up. Crawling is out of the question. Surely there has to be another entrance someplace nearby. But no, if New York is going to be some sort of Olympian challenge, then she must use this stairway. An idea flashes through her head, and without thinking it through, she backs up several yards, wraps the plastic of her grocery bag around a fist, and runs. One of the teen-agers asks loudly: "What's that fool doin'?"

She isn't sure herself. All she knows is that just before reaching the stairway, she leaps . . . up. And landing on a step, she comes down hard on her knees, and they hurt, but not so terribly. The bag of fruit, most of it now crushed, has cushioned her fall. She picks herself up with as much self-respect as she can muster. But what does it matter? She's never going to see these kids again. And at least she's on the stairs. "That bitch is crazy," one teenager comments as Tamra walks up.

And one girl, as brash and independent as her own daughter, shouts over the laughter of the others: "That's awright. I hope when I'm that old I can jump like that."

She continues up the stairway and uses her one token to pass through the turnstile. The next stairway leads to a long, deserted platform, with the name of the subway stop obscured by graffiti. It seems to be Gun Road. She paces. She has to keep moving. The cold bites into her face.

She's at the far end of the platform when she sees several boys, perhaps some of those who'd been below, advancing in her direction. They've given her no logical reason to be frightened, but she is. She doesn't have a pocketbook for them to snatch. But she does have a few bills left in her pockets. And maybe if they make demands, she'll offer these. But wait. What the hell is she thinking? If they do hassle her, will she really give up that easily? Not on her life.

The boys are probably waiting for the train, just as she is. But like Seth has taught her, nothing beats a plan, even a hastily concocted one. The three boys together are obviously a lot stronger than she, so she decides she has one real advantage. If they are from that group downstairs they already think she's crazy, too, and she is, but just a little.

Swinging the bag of fruit over her head, Tarzan style, she flings it against a graffitied wall, freeing her hands for movement. Then she walks toward them, menacingly, in a bopping style, the way Shaft had in a movie she'd seen years before.

And she mouths a word that distorts her face as she tries it for the first time and finds it so shapes her being that surely when the boys are only a few feet away, they can read her lips which stretch to enunciate: "Mother fucka, mother fucka." It's like fuel powering her engine. And the boys seem to know that if they have any intention of tangling with her, they'll have a crazy Black woman on their hands. They move aside, surprise spouting from their mouths in gusts of frozen air. She passes, delighted with herself, and she cackles, mouth open. It can only add to the image, she thinks. When the train pulls into the station, she climbs into it's belly and sits. This time she won't watch for floating faces. She knows just who she is.

Several other passengers are in the car. A Chinese woman eating a knish slides over to make room. Tamra can smell its fragrance. Across the aisle sits a young man who has a thin mustache and is wearing a too-small hat and sandals with heavy socks. She wonders if he's new to this country and if he's terrified the way she'd been only hours before. She longs to tell him that the only thing he cannot be in New York is afraid. When the man sneezes, Tamra looks up smiling. "God bless you," she says. He nods his head in thanks. Sitting beside him is a young African-American girl who reads a textbook and chews down hard, cracking her gum. Tamra's glad she's reading.

The ride is long and tedious and she wants to get out and run back to Brooklyn. When the car does finally clear out she notices there are mostly business people left, and they are just settling in when the sliding door to the adjoining car opens and a young man enters who has a voice like Eddie Murphy's. "Good afternoon, ladies and gentlemen," he says, and she can almost hear a collective "oh no" from the other riders. Some bury their faces behind newspapers and books, others feign sleep.

He introduces himself as the subterranean comedian. "Okay," he says, "I can see that look in your eyes and I know what you're thinking. I am homeless but I'm not here to beg. I work for my food. I know you're sick of the problems on these subways. They're dirty, crime-ridden, and don't run on time. But nobody talks about the biggest problem of all—the ugliness." He raises his voice dramatically. "That's right, two out of three people who ride the subways are ugly. If you don't believe me, look at the person sitting next to you. But let me warn you . . . don't look across the aisle, 'cause somebody's probably looking back at you."

People seem too embarrassed to laugh. Tamra holds her laughter in. "How do I know about the ugliness? I know because like you, I too used to be ugly. I was so ugly as a child, my parents beat me for it. I got so tired of being beat, I called the child abuse hotline. You know who answered? My mother. She said, 'Is that you, Junior? Boy, I'm goin' to kick your ass.' " His routine, which lasts at least another five minutes, may not be funny to everyone else, but Tamra has longed for a chance to laugh, and she does. By the time he concludes, she's letting it all out and it feels good.

At the end of his monologue she applauds, at first by herself, then a few others join in. The comedian seems so delighted with the response that he has almost forgotten the second part of his mission. But after more bows he whips off his hat and passes it before the others. Tamra puts in five dollars and he whistles. "Come on, don't anybody else have some bills? . . . No, lady, sorry, I don't take no food stamps."

Another Black woman, short, with a business suit peeking from beneath her fur coat, an attaché case in her lap, is in this section of the car. She turns away as the comedian approaches. "Umm hmmm," he says. "That's okay, I understand, sister. By the way, where'd you get that weave? Sure looks natural." The woman reaches involuntarily toward her hair as he adds under his breath, "Thing looks like it wants to be taken for a walk."

Tamra stands. The train has slowed for her stop. His hat quickly fills with money and he looks up for a minute, calling to her. "Hey, lady, you're not from around here, are you?"

She says no, she's not.

"Then where you from?"

She feels everyone watching. "From the Chesapeake," she says proudly.

"I heard of that before. Near an insane asylum, right? One of my uncles escaped from there."

People are laughing audibly when she calls out: "If he ran away from the Chesapeake, he is crazy." They smile at one another briefly, and as she exits she hears him continue his pitch. "You folks better learn to be as kind as she is, 'cause one day, there'll be more of me on the train than of you. . . ."

Out of the subway the winter air feels fresh and inviting, and she lets her coat swing open while waiting to cross the steet. A leering man slows his car, its trunk crumpled and held down with a chain and padlock.

"Hey, you, fine Mama you, want a ride?" he says.

She says, half-teasing: "You ought to be ashamed of yourself. You're old enough to be my grandfather."

He grins, a tooth missing. "You ain't no spring chick yourself. Besides, I wasn't even talkin' to you." He points at a young, attractive brunette who stands nearby. And she and the woman laugh at his brashness. Tamra hears herself sounding as loud and as uninhibited, she thinks, as the checkers at Sloan's.

She's still smiling as she walks into Wadine's building, and without pause, takes the steps at a trot. In the penthouse, Wadine looks as if she may have been crying, and Stephen, who has answered the door, comforts his wife. "You see, she's here, honey. I told you she'd be all right."

Tamra says: "Doggone right."

Wadine eyes Tamra suspiciously.

"Don't look so uptight, girlfriend," Tamra says, and she shakes Wadine's shoulder. "I'm more than fine, thanks to you and this wonderful city. Better than I've been for a long time."

She puts her arms around Stephen and Wadine's backs, smiling devilishly. "Where are the kids?" she asks.

"Mrs. Twichell took the little ones to the park," Wadine says, adding "Atunay is at a fencing lesson."

"So ask me," Tamra says.

Wadine's eyes dart to Stephen's, as if they're both concerned about her mental stability. They signal each other that they should play along with Tamra, and Wadine says, "Ask you what?"

"How many New Yorkers does it take to fix this city?"

"How many?"

Tamra practically shouts, "How the fuck should I know?" Then adds softly, "You should excuse the expression."

Wadine is wearing her concerned doctor's look again. "If I didn't know you better, I'd swear you were drunk."

"Being on the streets of New York is like shock therapy."

"Good," Wadine says, and Tamra watches her trade another guarded look with Stephen.

Tamra turns toward him. "Your wife has helped me a lot." She wonders how much Wadine has told him and decides it doesn't matter. "But I've got one more tiny request." And she looks at Wadine hoping she'll read the sense of urgency she feels. "I need her to come back to the Chesapeake with me, just for a few days, for something small, like saving my life."

Wadine shakes her head no vigorously. "You need to find a stranger. Someone who can work with you regularly. Charles will never go for it

. . . me coming down from the city, interfering with his——"

"Trust me, he'll do it." She isn't as certain as she sounds, but she keeps talking, finally begging.

When this fails to work, and Wadine retreats into stubborn silence, Tamra says to Stephen, "Have I ever told you about the time Wadine and I had a cooking class and she was so desperate for a date she——"

"Tam——"

"Better say yes, quickly. You see, Stephen, the captain of——"

"Tamra."

She likes the sound of her name being called by someone she loves, and she is enjoying the feel of being a mischievous spirit. Always before she has seen and admired this behavior in many of the people she loves. Today it emanates from her. The newness makes her giddy. "And so Deenie got up in the . . ."

Stephen looks puzzled until Wadine smiles. Tamra shares a secret communication with her old friend, thanking her.

$$51$$

Tamra and Charles *October 1990*

CHARLES IS WITH her as they cross the lobby of the Salisbury Holiday Inn, and she squeezes his hand. He's been so sweet since last week when, with children in tow, and lots of balloons and streamers, he'd greeted her at the airport. How can she convince Wadine that she has traveled to the Chesapeake needlessly? They won't require long-term therapy or even a session, Tamra had said on the phone. He'd been perfect, coming home early, even barbecued a couple of the dinners. Going away certainly had worked wonders. But Wadine had insisted on coming. She'd told her parents already, and the trip was planned. Charles had said it just wasn't right, having Wadine come down just for them and then pulling out. They owed it to her, he said. And so, she had given in. What the heck, Wadine would see them and rejoice for them.

Tamra smiles lovingly at him in the elevator. And he puts his finger to her chin, saying he's thinking about the cotillion, that it was held right here in this hotel. She wonders if he's nervous about seeing Wadine and she wants to assure him there's no reason to be. They couldn't possibly be happier.

He knocks at the door to Wadine's suite. Somehow that seems especially important, that he, not she, be in control of this day. What if they had had a session with Wadine? Would she have uncovered anything interesting in Charles's life? His parents had been so different from hers, seldom even raising their voices.

They each return Wadine's cheerful greeting, and as Charles throws his arms about Wadine's neck, Tamra reads the tension in his shoulders. She wants to get the subject out in the open, quickly, to relieve his anxieties. Wadine directs them to two armchairs but Tamra interrupts, saying with embarrassment: "I don't know how to begin. . . . I know you're happy to hear things have just righted themselves. That work you did with me was so helpful, and Charles . . ." She looks to Charles for support, but no help there. He appears mortified at the idea of her discussing their marriage with anyone. "We've been like newlyweds," Tamra continues.

"I am delighted," Wadine says. "But that doesn't mean you can't sit, does it?"

As they settle into chairs, Tamra looks about her. It's some sort of meeting room. She'll have to be sure to reimburse Wadine for the expense of all this. Such a waste. She'd made the request so impulsively. Wadine sits facing them, smiling. Tamra's puzzled. "What is it?"

"I was just thinking that I haven't heard Charles say a word. So everything has really worked out for you, eh, Charles?" He mumbles yes, and Tamra is annoyed with them both: Wadine for pursuing this despite their obvious discomfort, and Charles for not forcefully reassuring her friend that all is fine. Wadine asks him, "How should I interpret that kind of lackluster response?"

He clears his throat. "Yeah, everything's fine."

Tamra squeezes his hand like a tube of toothpaste, as if she can push some enthusiasm out of him.

Wadine coaxes, "I don't want to put words in your mouth . . ."

Tamra thinks, *Then don't. Leave it alone.*

Wadine continues ". . . But Charles, how come you don't sound like everything's fine?"

He talks with his hands. "You have to know that this . . . this isn't as easy for a fellow. We can't just start opening up and gushing. . . ."

"That wasn't at all what I expected," Wadine assures him. "Suppose you ran into your pa and he took you aside and asked if things were really better between you and Tamra. What would you say to him?"

Realizing that she is seated on the edge of her chair, Tamra pulls herself into a more comfortable position. Charles is saying, "I guess there's a part of me that says everything's going to remain all right———"

"Until?"

He mumbles something Tamra cannot understand.

Wadine says, "Until you slip up how?"

He shifts in his chair uncomfortably. Tamra has never seen him timid like this. He adds, "It could be anything. I never really know, until she blows up. Then she might take off again."

Tamra wonders how the conversation suddenly changed from a three-way conversation to one that excludes her. She interrupts, saying to Charles, "I'm not going anywhere without you."

Charles continues talking to Wadine: "It's another full-time job. I don't dare come home late again or spend too much time on the phone———"

Tamra interrupts, "Just a minute, now. I wish you'd stop talking about me like that. There aren't any hard and fast rules governing our relationship."

"You're right, honey," he says, "you kinda make 'em up as you go along."

Tamra crosses her arms and glares at Charles. Why did he have to start saying all this in front of Wadine? He'd had plenty of time to talk to her at home.

"Tell you what," Wadine says, maintaining her brisk tone, "why don't we try something simple. Both of you might want to share thoughts with me about what, if you could change something about the other, that might be?

He nods toward Tamra, challenging her to begin, but she doesn't want to. "I wouldn't change a thing about Charles."

"What about you, Charles? Would you change anything about Tamra or your marriage?"

"I'd want more than a temporary cessation of strife."

"So you think what you're experiencing at home is only provisional?"

He speaks softly. "Let's put it this way. Next week I'm going to address a group of businessmen united to restore the bay, and the man who's going to introduce me asked for a copy of my curriculum vitae. So I ran a list of my accomplishments through my head: graduated from college with honors, kept a family farm profitable through diversification . . . But as I thought about it, I realized my greatest accomplishment may be something I can't put on paper—that I've remained married for thirteen years to one of the most vexing women I've ever met."

How dare he! As close as they'd been in the last few days? Even making love in the shower this morning. And what about Wadine? It was as if she wanted to stir up trouble.

Wadine turns to Tamra and asks, "Would you like another chance to sound off about Charles? This may be one of your few safe opportunities."

She's surprised at the change in her voice as she begins unenthusiastically. She doesn't want to criticize him, and her self-confidence has dwindled. "He . . . er . . ."

Wadine interrupts, asking them to direct their comments to one another. Tamra continues speaking barely above a whisper. "*Ummm*, and he cares too much about his relatives, more than me and the kids." Wadine interrupts again.

"Tam, why don't you try talking to Charles at eye level? He's so much taller that it might make you feel more capable of really communicating if you can look him in the eye." She gets Charles to stand and helps a shoeless Tamra up, first on a chair, but that's too high; she towers over him. They try the footstool beside the stage. Now they are face-to-face, and Tamra likes the feel of it.

Once again, Tamra begins slowly, but soon the words come tumbling out. "You call me controlling, but do you know you've controlled our lives for the last decade, with your business needs? This sudden complaining in here is just a prelude to your going back to your old ways. This behavior will last a few more weeks and then, poof, you're outta here, back to the old schedule of 'see you when I can.' "

She has more to say and does, telling him she's dissatisfied with his decision to keep Cousin Johnny on the payroll. Telling him off feels intoxicatingly pleasurable because for once, he doesn't interrupt and she can just let it all out. He may be silent but he's not looking too mild-mannered anymore. She doesn't care. She's about to climb down when Wadine suggests she remain up there temporarily.

"Charles, why don't you explain to Tamra which of her character traits you find so vexing."

There's a long pause and Tamra doesn't mind helping him out. "Remember that alphabet game we used to play with the kids?"

He looks puzzled, and she says, "Come on, you know. I'll give you the letter, you supply the word." She figures there's not much he can say. She knows she has been a good wife, so she feels generous.

As if realizing that, he says, "Naw. This isn't a time for games." Wadine assures him it's all right with her. But still, he persists, they should try something else. No, Tamra says, just try it. He relents. He'll give it a try. He begins grudgingly when Tamra says with a smile "A."

He appears to work hard at coming up with a word, and finally offers, "arrogant."

She shrugs, as if to say, Okay I'll accept that. And she's off to "B."

He smiles wryly. "Out of respect for you ladies I'll leave that one out."

"C."

"Critical . . . hey, look, we can stop if you like."

"Don't worry about me," she says, "or are you worried you won't be able to come up with the words?"

"Disrespectful, but wait, also domineering," he says, and before she can get the next letter out, he is off, filling in the blanks, without her prompting, as if he's counting off a list in his head: "Envious . . . frustrating . . . grating . . ."

"You're groping."

"Humiliating, intolerant, judgmental . . ." He pauses here and grins before saying "Kakapoo-like."

"What the hell is that?"

"A large parrot in the jungles of New Zealand that screams when you walk in late."

She shouts: "L!"

He smiles devilishly. "Right now, you're livid."

She is, and getting angrier by the minute. "Why don't you just go on without me. I obviously have so many negative traits you . . ."

"Melodramatic . . . negative, opprobrious—that means abusive and insulting."

"You don't look like Merriam Webster. But I suppose next you'll turn into——"

"Pessimistic, quixotic, resentful . . ." (he's shouting now) ". . . self-righteous, tense, unreasonable, unrealistic, ungrateful . . ."

"One per letter, mister, and I have a list of my——"

"Vengeful, worrisome . . ." He turns to Wadine. "What do you do if she has lots more personality defects than letters?"

Tamra, still on the footstool, shouts, "I'd like to tell you what to do with them!" She has her hands on her hips, and although she's shouting she doesn't give a damn who hears her as she says: "You've been showing off at my expense since we were kids. I'm sick of it, sick to death. And I'm putting you on notice. Go ahead. Act like an animal." (And here, her head bobs with the words that grind through her teeth.) " 'Cause honey, you done met your match."

When he grins, she reaches to slap him, and suddenly Wadine is between them, hands up like a referee. "I'd say you two have a teensy bit of hostility to work on."

She directs Tamra to a chair against a far wall and sits before Charles, suggesting they begin what may be a long day.

52

Charles *October 1990*

HE'S BREATHING HARD as if he's just completed a winning race, and except for the temporary discomfort of the heat from Tamra's scowl, he loves the sense of being first at the finish line.

"That's a neat little trick of yours," Wadine says to him.

"I've always been good with letters," he says.

"No, not that game," Wadine says. "I meant the one in which you get Tamra to act out your anger so you can continue to be Mr. Nice Guy." They regard one another silently before Wadine says, "But you do seem genuinely angry with her now."

"You've got that right. I'm sick of her disrespect and her not appreciating a damn thing I do."

"Would it be correct to say that all you want from your wife is peace?"

"Right." He feels he must answer carefully, but he's too emotionally winded to think it through.

"What was the most peaceful time in your life?"

"When I was a kid, before I had any major responsibilities."

"I've always wondered what life would be like on a farm."

"Pretty idyllic," he says and for the next several minutes describes the childhood of his memory, the majesty of the land, the respect the family's property engendered, and the security of growing up in the warmth of his parents' watchful, loving gaze.

"Wow," Wadine says as he finishes. "Sounds pretty Norman Rockwell."

"It wasn't perfect. My sister and I didn't always get along."

"That's Norman Rockwell, too. But despite your lovely recreation of the highlights of your childhood, I'm sure much more occurred beneath the surface, just as it does in any family. So help me out . . ." Wadine stood, moving her hands through the air, brushstroking his memory. "Here we are on the Chesapeake, circa 1963. Let's picture an evening in the life of the Lanes. Let's see, Vicky's on the couch reading a fan magazine?"

"No, her diary," he says. "She was always writing in it."

"Good, so she's with her diary, and you're home after working in the fields, and you're on the couch . . ."

"Listening to the radio. Juan Marichal is up."

Wadine continues, "Pa comes in late, but that doesn't upset your mother. She hustles over to the stove and prepares a plate for him, knowing he's worked up an appetite."

"That sounds right," he says, leaning back a bit, enjoying the peacefulness of the memory, and he listens as Wadine continues.

"Let's shift our vision over to your mother. Dinner is over. She's just fed Pa. It's been a long day, but being a good farm wife, she's still not resting. Help me picture this, Charles. What did she look like back then?"

"Beautiful, like Tamra. But it's hard to describe someone you see every day. My ma was steady as a rock, predictable. You could set your watch by her. When you heard her stirring in the morning, you knew you had a half-hour 'til breakfast, and the same with every meal. She was always there . . . usually in the kitchen or somewhere in the house. But she never looked like a housewife. And to this day, she's dramatically elegant. She wore her hair combed back . . ." He brings his hands to the nape of his neck, ". . . in what I once heard described as a chignon; always attractively dressed, and yet there was something wholesome and thoughtful about her. Farm wives aren't as a rule, idle people. They take pride in their work, everything they do, from changing babies to scrubbing floors, all of it is of equal importance. Even when they finish their chores, they take up something else, canning or helping out at the church. And they're supportive of their husbands because they understand their very survival depends on working that land."

"*Ummm*, I hear you," Wadine is smiling. "What a tribute from a son. She sounds wonderful, Charles. In fact, when I close my eyes, I see her. So you close your eyes, too. Hear the sounds. Radio's turned down low, there's lots of static. Seems none of the rooms were well-lit in those days, so Vicky has to squint to write. Everything is peaceful. And then, there's your mom. Dinner's over, she's working quietly, only a few feet away. Look up at her, Charles. What's she doing?"

He pictures himself on the couch. There's the old Nash Kelvinator, new then. Ma's at the sink, the back of her well-ironed shirtdress moving as she works, charm bracelet jangling.

"What's she doing, Charles?"

He studies his mother again and says: "She's digging ditches . . ." He opens his eyes quickly. "I mean *doing dishes.*"

"Hmm, an interesting slip of the tongue, don't you think?"

He shrugs, feeling more guarded, as if Wadine has somehow tricked him.

"Why do you think you might have said that?"

"I have a feeling you've got a theory about it," he says.

"I do. Is it okay if I share it?"

"Go ahead."

"Digging ditches is pretty hard, miserable work, isn't it? Whether you're in the hot sunshine or blistering cold, whatever the weather or the surroundings, you wouldn't necessarily be happy digging ditches, even if you're in the bosom of your family. Maybe your mother was surrounded by the family just as you described, but you sense she wasn't happy."

He leans forward. "No one talked about being happy or unhappy in those days. You had kids and you didn't complain about how much work they were. You just did your job."

"Oh, so she enjoyed it?"

"I don't think she overflowed with joy. I think she might have been depressed, but that was what was great about her. She never complained." He hears Tamra shifting in her chair.

"What do you think she was unhappy about?"

"Oh, she didn't make a secret of that. She was the daughter of a college president. Her brother was a lawyer. Her sisters married professional big shots. When one of them married a clergyman, she called it marrying down, but he became a bishop in D.C. When Ma married my pa she expected he'd be a surgeon."

Wadine shakes her head understandingly. "Big difference between a surgeon's wife and settling for life on a farm."

He nods, yes, big difference.

"And yet despite this disappointment and her background, she treated your Pa's career choice with respect?"

He laughs bitterly. "She thought farmers were about as dumb as any other farm animal."

"Hmm. Then it was your dad who's even more remarkable. Although he knew she had a low opinion of his work, he accepted that?"

"Most of the time, I guess. He made little jokes about her family and their education now and then."

Tamra mutters from behind them: "More than now and then."

"Do you think those jokes may have hurt her?" Wadine asks.

"That was probably his intention."

"So despite her disappointment and resentment, and at the same time, your dad's awareness that his prize of a wife did not respect him, they maintained a peaceful marriage, eh?"

"I suppose looking at it that way, it doesn't sound very peaceful."

"I think not."

"But I'm still not making the connection," he says. "They weren't the perfect couple, but most people aren't. Tamra and I had a different start. She knew from day one that I was going to farm. And she was the one who decided to give up her work and stay home with the kids, after the baby di . . . Well, I supported the idea of her staying home, but I didn't ask for that. So our marriage was completely different."

"You're rolling right along with me, Charles. I'm enjoying this. We've never had a chance to talk before. You're right. Your circumstances were quite different. And yet, in so many ways, they were the same. But before we get into that, let's go back to that house and visit that room, looking again below the surface. Do I sense an undercurrent of disquiet?"

"Things could get tense."

"Was there a favorite child?"

"Without a doubt, me. My sister's never gotten over it."

"Was it because you were the son?"

"And I was the one who would inherit the land." But his mind lingers on Vicky and all her broken sadness, curled up on the couch, the less-favored child, and he wonders why he didn't stand up for his sister. It had been a terrible way to be treated. Tamra would never allow this for one of their kids.

"Tell me your thoughts. Don't hold back, please."

"I was a favorite to each of my parents for different reasons. When it came to Pa, he naturally preferred me because we worked together. And I always looked up to him. You couldn't find a wiser man. For my mother it was different." He searches through his memory. "It's hard to explain."

"And yet, it's important that you do. Try picturing your ma with you. You're alone now. What are you two doing?"

"Vicky's probably in her room. And the ball game is over, so Ma and I are listening to the news on the radio and the two of us are discussing world affairs. She always treated me like . . . someone older, I guess."

"Like a companion?"

"You could say that."

"How?"

"Some of my best memories are of being alone with her. A lot of times she'd take me over to the cedar chest she had in her room and it was filled with pictures, all of her family." He gestures, behind him, toward Tamra. "Tam has had them restored and they're all over our bedroom."

"I'm surprised you noticed," Tamra says.

"Maybe it's a good idea if we confine our comments to just the two of us," Wadine says. "Let's go back to that cedar chest and the photographs of your mother's family."

"Yeah, these were people who really made a name for themselves. She was so proud of them."

"And proud of you, too, I'm sure. Now tell me, did she take your sister to this trunk also?"

"Maybe she did but I never saw that. I don't think so."

"So this was a woman who didn't necessarily have a happy marriage but she did have a favorite child, her son. That's not in the least unusual. Everyone needs companionship. And you became her stand-in for much of what she didn't have in her marriage—someone who'd provide her with the intellectual calisthenics she craved. If your pa graduated from college he was certainly smart enough. But from what you tell me about him and his manner, he may have renounced all things intellectual. So your ma turned to you for solace. And I bet she thought pretty highly of you."

"There has never been anyone in my life who expected more."

"And you haven't disappointed her, have you? Just a few minutes with you and it's impossible not to notice your shining intelligence. Even when we were kids we heard about you. Your mother must have been pulled to you, also. I bet you were a great source of pride and comfort to this woman, this daughter of a college president. Who more than she could appreciate the virtues of your mind?"

He's flattered but he doesn't know how to answer this and so he waits for her to continue.

"So wouldn't it fit . . ." (she winds her hand around in a spinning motion) "help me out here, Charles . . . that if she expected a lot of you, she wouldn't want you to wind up the way your dad had, on a farm?"

"She never said that."

"What did she say?"

"What do you mean?"

"With her trips down memory lane of this uncle who was the first so-and-so and aunt blah-de-blah who ran the school of XYZ. What do you think her message was to you?"

"She never said a word against me becoming a farmer."

"Charley Chaplin didn't have to say a word either, and he could make ten million people laugh or cry."

He's never considered the possibility that his mother may have delivered some subtle message through the photographs and he still doesn't believe it. So he takes awhile, pretending he's giving it a lot of thought, before he says: "I suppose she was saying that like my ancestors, whatever the obstacles, I could do anything I wanted in life."

"*Umm hmmm.* Is there a possibility she might have been encouraging you not to become a farmer? She might have even considered it as a way of saving your life. And there's something far more important. What better way to get back at Pa than by using you as a model for what she wished he was?"

Wadine is quiet for a long while, and then she speaks again, but slowly. "What strikes me as essential is that you were right in the middle of your parents in this quiet war."

"They wouldn't have done that to me."

"It's usually not intentional, but parents set the stage. You didn't put yourself there. That's where they put you. One wanted you to move toward a life of the soil, the other inspired you to flee."

"It worked out all right."

"Yes, and look at all you've accomplished. How did you finally choose which dream you'd follow—your mother's or your father's?"

"The decision was made for me. Now, that's a day I remember. My father spoke to my coach and told him I wasn't playing in summer league. I've always thought that dead wrong."

"How did you feel about that?"

"I was upset."

"Upset. Is that some kind of code word for angry?"

"It was the worst day of my life, except for, you know. . . . I was a boy and I'd been hoping to lead the team to the state championships. We had a good chance."

"Why didn't you refuse to go along with his plans for farming? Maybe not as a boy, but later?"

Charles answers quickly. "There wasn't a choice."

"What was he holding over your head?"

"I was raised with a sense of honor."

"Ahh," Wadine pronounces, holding up a finger as if she has hit upon something important. "So the price of turning him down was a loss of honor."

"You could say that."

"Shame, not only for you, but for your entire family, as well as the generations that had come before you."

"Something like that."

"While on the other side, you faced the possibility of another loss— your mother's respect if you did take the land."

She has led him up a one-way road and there's no turning back. He wants to tell her she's wrong but he cannot. The facts seem irrefutable. He sits quietly digesting this information.

"So, tell me about your mother on that day."

"What do you mean?"

"It wasn't just your dreams that had been dashed, but hers as well. I bet she really let your dad have it."

"I don't remember her being there at all."

"You said she was always there; predictable, steady as a rock."

He's annoyed now. "She wasn't there, that's all."

"Maybe your father kept it from her."

"He didn't have to hide anything. In those days a man was the head of his house."

"Let me see if I've got this right. There you were on the worst day of your childhood, as you put it, and this woman who was as steady as a rock suddenly wasn't there."

"Correct."

"Don't you think it odd that she'd made the implicit promise of support-ing you if you wanted a better life, but on the most important day she wasn't there to back you up?"

He thinks she's making too much of this.

"Your mother seems to have left you twisting in the wind."

"I don't believe that."

"Believe what you like. But don't you find it somewhat odd that you were left alone like that?"

"Oh, I see what you mean. I wasn't alone. My godmother, my Aunt T.J. She's Pa's sister. When I got home that afternoon, she'd dropped by." There's a lengthy pause as he begins reassembling that long-ago day.

"What is it, Charles?"

"You're right in one respect."

"How so?"

"It was unusual for Ma to be gone. And my godmother never just happened down from Washington. She worked legendary hours. She wouldn't have dropped by. That conversation with her was the start of me giving in. She was the one who got me to participate in that debutante scene in Salisbury. Without a doubt, it absolutely went against the grain of what Pa wanted for me. It's as if Ma and Pa had struck a bargain. I'd be a farmer;" he laughs here, "but I'd be in the cotillion, as if to ensure I wouldn't be a complete savage."

He tries to feel something about any of this, but there is nothing. "It's funny. I've gone over that day so many times in my mind, but I always forgot the part about Ma not being there."

"It's precisely because you were going over it in your mind that you missed it."

He finds that he feels more kindly toward Wadine as she continues. "If you had looked to your heart for understanding, you might have discovered the painful message you learned, and make no mistake about it, it was an important one. You live by it and it has ruled your marriage."

The room seems now only to be filled with her words. "After all those years of being her little substitute husband sitting there, entertaining her, in the white shirts and ties, when you were younger, and then when you'd grown some, keeping her intellectually satisfied the way the real 'important' folks back home do, after all that, she didn't keep her side of the bargain.

"And there was a bargain," Wadine continues. "She and your father made it the day you were born and when they introduced you to the world as their child. All parents make the same bargain; it goes along with keeping you fed and safe. They aren't always easy obligations to fulfill, and that's why it takes two to make a child. It's a system of checks and balances. If one requires something of you that is unreasonable, the other must step in. That's the bargain. No matter what the cost to the defending parent. He or she must wait until that child is out of hearing, so he can confront, or talk it over, or bar the door, or grab the child and run, and defend to the death; shout if necessary. *'This is wrong, and I will not let you do this.'* You should have been given your life. Your mother knew that, but she didn't fight for you. So who could blame you for never letting a woman in close again? The message you learned is that women will let you down. And for fifteen years 'women' has meant only one person, Tamra."

The room is so quiet he can hear the wheels of a luggage cart in the carpeted hallway. For the last few minutes he has felt as if he were watching an old "Perry Mason" rerun in which his mother will jump from the witness chair and shout that yes, she is the guilty party. He'd like to smile at his little joke, but is unable to.

As if reading his thoughts, Wadine says, "Let's keep moving, Charles, because although you're not convinced, I think it's important to draw some comparisons." Wadine counts off on her fingers.

"Your father married an intelligent, beautiful woman who didn't respect him. And by the way, she probably wouldn't have, even if he had become a surgeon. She was unhappy long before she married him, but she blamed him for her lifetime of disappointments. And his way of communicating anger was by teasing. How does that compare with the way you and Tamra interact?"

He says nothing. This may be clever but he fails to understand how it provides practical implications for getting along with his wife. If Wadine senses that he's withdrawing, she shows no intention of quitting.

"One of the first statements you made to me this morning was that your beautiful, educated wife doesn't respect you or appreciate your achievements. It's no coincidence that the lack of respect you feel is almost identical to what you witnessed between your parents."

He looks away from the gold carpet, his head jerking up. "You aren't suggesting I deliberately married a woman who wouldn't respect me?"

"On the contrary. I'm saying you married a woman, and no matter who she was or what she did, even if she'd spoken to you in a language you didn't understand, you would have still heard the same message: that farmers are as dumb as cows, that they aren't worthy of respect." She continues in a quiet strain. Laying out her case, step by step. "It is also no coincidence that you fell in love with a woman raised in a home with the same degree of agitation and strife that you'd been raised in. Hers may have been a bit noisier, but your parents quietly acted it out."

"You may be right."

"I know I am. You looked for someone you felt comfortable with, you already knew the lines. How would you have known how not to fight? If you'd both been blind and had fallen in love, getting married wouldn't mean you could suddenly see."

He completes her thought. "Nor would it mean we could suddenly be peaceful."

"I think not."

"So we have to learn."

"Excellent idea, but I don't think that's possible for you."

"Explain that."

Wadine rubs her hands together as if rolling out the right words. "I don't think you can have peace with your wife if you're at war with yourself."

"Now you've lost me."

"When parents are at war, Charles, whether quietly seething or involved in all-out warfare, children are wounded noncombatants."

"I didn't know anything about my mother not respecting my father until I was much older."

"Trust me, Charles, you knew. Children always know on a subconscious level. You knew you weren't supposed to be sitting there, taking your daddy's place, and you were furious about it. You knew you deserved a life of your own. But you also knew you couldn't let your father or your mother down. And since they were pulling you in opposite directions, that must have literally torn you apart."

"I think I'm finally following you."

"You took over the land to please your pa. But there was still your mother, so you also became an agri-businessman in the suits, the handmade shirts, working, working, working like a hamster on a wheel, hoping to earn her respect by being something other than a farmer."

"I think you may have something there."

"I find it interesting that you can speak of this all so dispassionately."

"It was so long ago."

"Or maybe the sadness has simply been buried."

"That might be."

"How old were you when you realized your pa expected you to be a farmer?"

"Early as I can remember."

"How about when your mother began to send the messages about how wonderful the world is out there for sophisticates?"

"The same."

"Even younger than H.P. What if it had been your little boy? Would you want him to have such a painful choice?"

"Of course not."

"Well, know what, Charles? You didn't deserve it, either."

In his chair, he studies his hands. This was a time in his life he wouldn't mind forgetting. He feels the weight of it.

Wadine presses her fingers to her lips, as if in thought. "I think it's of the utmost importance that we do some emotional work and talk about these experiences without relying purely on your intellect. I want to get to little Charles, not the affable, corporate whiz he has become. I've got an idea."

She rolls newspaper into a cone and hands it to him, asking him to swing. It's obvious she doesn't know a thing about baseball. "This is a little too light," he says apologetically, adding more paper and twisting. Before he swings he removes his jacket. The Y of the suspenders presses into his back.

Wadine pushes back the chair as he spreads his feet, swinging. He's excited, explaining to Wadine techniques learned long ago. Leaning against a closet door, Wadine holds her chin in thought. "Keep swinging," she suggests. "And while you're at it, I'd like you to tell me about the death of your son."

He hears Tamra's quiet gasp.

Charles stops swinging. He hates feeling set up. Wadine, of all people, should realize that. And he grows angry as she continues to insist. She says, "I know it's difficult but stay with me. Keep swinging and talk about losing your son."

"Of course it was difficult," he says and resumes swinging.

"Hard work under the blazing sun is difficult. What was this like? Your son died, Charles." The only sensation he can feel now is the breeze from his swings. He will try to drown her out. Instead, he hears her all too well.

"But then, maybe, since you had another boy, little Seth's death didn't matter."

He swings furiously.

"You're not saying a word. I'd like you to swing and talk to me. You're strong and I know you have the courage to do this."

He must first unclench his teeth if he is to speak. When he does, his voice cracks, so he starts again. "I loved my boy."

He's swinging sporadically.

"Please, keep swinging and just talk."

The room is silent until he speaks again. "There needed to be two boys. . . . It was a miracle, two, the same age. It had been stipulated . . . the land goes to the oldest son. Twins could share the load. They wouldn't have to do it alone."

"And so when you lost little Seth, it was a double loss because it reminded you . . ."

"I wanted them to have a choice. . . ." He swings feverishly.

"So they wouldn't have to do it alone, the way you had to. So they could have the choice you were denied. You were a child once, and every bit as precious and vulnerable as your own babies. . . . Then you thought finally it could be made right, but you lost that dream, too. It died with your boy and you were probably just as unwilling to grieve for him as you were to grieve for your own life."

If he were to speak now, he knows his voice would be thick. Losing his boy, he wants to say, was far more than difficult. It was and still is agonizing. But he won't take that chance. He can't say that. He quits swinging. It's a mistake. He knows immediately, because he can't catch the tears. He hides his eyes, feeling ridiculous. Shoulders shaking, the sadness for his son floods over him. Crying before two women like this. He tries sucking it back in, but the feelings won't stay down.

Wadine's voice again. "Can your wife do anything to help?"

"No! It was talking about my boy that threw me."

"Maybe you're thinking: 'You bitch. You didn't come to help me when I was fighting for my life. . . .'"

"No, she didn't."

"You're right. Your mother didn't come. But look across the room. She's lovely and brilliant, sophisticated, but she's not your mother. Look, look for yourself."

He takes another blow into the hankie before looking across the room. "I know she's not my mother."

"I'm not so sure. When she asks you to come home, to be close to her, you hear your mother's words, that you aren't good enough. As Tamra's closest friend, I have to tell you, Charles, she doesn't say that. I have a desk full of letters. She brags about you. She adores you. She didn't desert you on that first day of practice, and she didn't desert you when she went to New York. She just needed to get strong again. She's prepared to stand by you and help you fight for your life. And if you open up and let her share that grief, you don't have to be alone another minute."

Tamra crosses the room and stands before him, holding her hand out. She too is crying, her mouth twisted, and she waits for him. He can't seem to stop looking at her.

"Tamra," Wadine says, "I'd like to introduce you to Charles. And Charles, allow me to acquaint you with Tamra. She's your wife."

"Oh, Charles," Tamra sobs. And they cross the space that seems to stretch like a wide, hard field between them. They cross it, and come together. He sits, pulling her into his lap. She strokes his hair, his cheeks, his chin, covering him with soft, soothing kisses. He can only remember later that he has heard the door open and shut. It is Wadine, leaving them alone, for what seems to be the first time.

53

Tamra and Charles October 1990

THERE IS A soft knock and Wadine enters with a key, a smile on her face. They are still together on the chair. Tamra speaks first. "I don't know what to say, Deenie."

"That you'll write me and tell me of your progress in therapy. I won't bug either of you about it. But I promise, if you don't, you'll fall back into the same old ruts, just the way you had when you walked in here this morning."

She smiled apologetically. "I always tell my clients that the little kid in the middle of parents, whether it's someone who's actually negotiating for peace, or sitting there trying to keep the angry parent appeased, grows up to be so focused on everyone else. He or she is like the witch who casts a spell over the enchanted forest, trying to control what others say and do. Instead of the wand, we use our rage or self-righteousness or depression or money or drinking or working or whatever, to exert the control. I don't think either of you wants to train another generation in these patterns."

They talk for a long while, Wadine leading them through practical issues, including how together, they will handle Cassie and Cousin Johnny, and Charles signs a hastily written contract stipulating the number of days he can comfortably be at home evenings, all night, no questions asked.

As they finish, Tamra notices that her friend looks a bit timid and she soon understands why. Wadine says, "I want you guys to do something for me. It's going to sound a bit crazy but . . ."

"Anything," Tamra and Charles say.

"Okay, stand up."

"I don't think I can take anymore baseball," Charles says.

"Or standing on a footstool," Tamra adds.

"Don't worry," Wadine calls from the next room, quickly returning with a broom. When Tamra and Charles stare in confusion, she says, "You can appreciate how difficult it was for me to come to Salisbury, rent their most expensive suite, and convince housekeeping I needed a broom."

"For what?" Tamra asks.

"I want you to jump it."

Charles says, "Like the slaves, when they married?"

Wadine says, "Slaves were able to love even in the most horrendous circumstances. I ask this of couples when I believe in them. And it's a tribute to the slaves. No relationship could survive a more trying test than a life sentence of sexual and physical servitude to a series of masters. They started their lives with absolutely nothing but love. It's also a reminder that given our history in this country, each time a Black man and woman commit to this union it's not simply a marriage, it's a miracle. And the physicality of this act can help you remember that from this day forward you're separating yourselves from the ghosts who've been between you. You can't have a real marriage if Seth and Dalhia and Virginia and Harlen are in the middle."

They agree to Wadine's unusual request. "Good," she says. "The first part of this little ceremony always cracks folks up, but I do it anyway. I want you both to turn around and wave. You're going to symbolically say good-bye to your parents." Tamra feels foolish as she raises her hand a few inches. Charles goes as far as to make a playful bye-bye movement.

Wadine's voice is more serious. "That's not the way you say good-bye to someone who has shaped your life. Don't get me wrong, you'll see them again, but not as their dramatic understudies, as independent adults who've moved on in their marriage. So really say good-bye." She lifts Tamra's and Charles's hands, waving them briskly. "Say good-bye to their disappointments, to their stifling anger and dissatisfaction. Come on now, you two."

Tamra waves on her own accord, but that is not enough for Wadine, who insists, "Say it!"

Tamra finds she's crying again, as she speaks the words. "Good-bye, Daddy. Good-bye, Mama. Good-bye."

Wadine says, "Okay, this is the fun part. Join hands, take a deep breath, and jump." She and Charles turn away and toward Wadine, who kneels and with solemnity holds the broom handle and waits. Tamra glances toward Charles, seeing him clearly and certain of him.

She has loved him from the time they shared a book together as children. Years later, she married him in a gown of shimmering pearls. They'd started their first life together riding off, of all things, on a horse into the sunset; created a family of their own; and now this, a broom. She bends her knees, prepared to leap, and somehow she knows with certainty that if she must, to reach the other side, she can fly.